Acclaim ... *Gone*

"[A] down and dirty immorality tale." —*The New York Times*

"The books of Andrew Vachss are much more than great entertainment. They are a fierce crusade for all victims who can't fight back, especially the imperiled children to whom Vachss has devoted his considerable talent, and his life."

—Carl Hiaasen

"If I were to compare Andrew Vachss to any other writer, it would be Charles Dickens—his larger-than-life characters, his deep commitment to the innocent victims of our society, his hopes for redemption." —Walter Mosley

"The Burke books make the noir-film genre look practically pastel. . . . The plot-driven stories churn with energy and a memorable gallery of the walking wounded."

—*The Philadelphia Inquirer*

"One of the best Burke novels in years, gritty and violent as ever but also philosophical and even moving."

—*The Capital Times* (Madison, WI)

"[Vachss] writes a hypnotically violent prose made up of equal parts of broken concrete block and razor wire."

—*Chicago Sun-Times*

"There's no way to put a [Vachss book] down once you've begun. . . . The plot hooks are engaging and the one-liners pierce like bullets." —*Detroit Free Press*

"Andrew Vachss's work is all about horror, outrage, moral indignation and the blood of commitment. Vachss is the voice of righteousness confronting a powerful and cowardly evil."

—James Ellroy

"Vachss is in the first rank of American crime writers."
—*The Plain Dealer*

"Andrew Vachss has become a cult favorite, and for good reason."
—*Cosmopolitan*

"Vachss has obviously seen just how unable the law is to protect children. And so, while Burke may be a vigilante, Vachss's stories don't feature pointless bloodshed. Instead, they burn with righteous rage and transfer a degree of that rage to the reader."
—*The Washington Post Book World*

"Vachss' writing is like a dark roller coaster ride of fear, love and hate."
—*The Times-Picayune*

"Andrew Vachss continues to write the most provocative novels around. . . . It is difficult to write about a burning social issue and still keep the story at white heat, but Andrew Vachss does it seamlessly."
—Martha Grimes

"When the history of crime fiction in the twentieth century comes to be written, if there is any justice, the name of Andrew Vachss will be up front, up-close and flagged up as very dangerous. . . . His writing is raw, jagged-edged and staccato and also spookily sexy."
—*The Telegraph*

"Many writers try to cover the same ground as Vachss. A handful are as good. None are better."
—*People*

"[Vachss] takes a genre that appeared dead and reinvigorates it."
—*The Fort Worth Star-Telegram*

"Andrew Vachss belongs to the proud but perhaps waning tradition of the socially-committed literary tough guy. His fine, unsparing novels are driven by outrage, and are as powerful as any being written in our day."
—Laurence Shames

"Andrew Vachss is one of my favorite writers and I never miss one of his books. He brings incredible passion and flair to the mystery genre."
—James Patterson

Andrew Vachss

DEAD
and GONE

Andrew Vachss has been a federal investigator in sexually transmitted diseases, a social caseworker, a labor organizer, and has directed a maximum-security prison for youthful offenders. Now a lawyer in private practice, he represents children and youths exclusively. He is the author of numerous novels, including the Burke series, two collections of short stories, and wide variety of other material including song lyrics, poetry, graphic novels, and a "children's book for adults." His books have been translated into twenty different languages and his work has appeared in *Parade*, *Antaeus*, *Esquire*, *The New York Times*, and numerous other forums. He lives and works in New York City and the Pacific Northwest.

The dedicated Web site for Vachss and his work is
www.vachss.com.

BOOKS BY ANDREW VACHSS

Andrew Vachss

DEAD and GONE

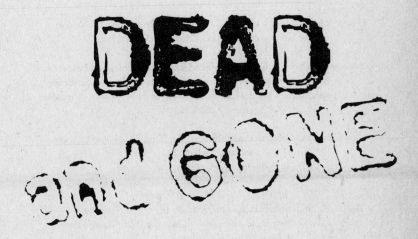

Vintage Crime / Black Lizard

VINTAGE BOOK

NEW YORK

FIRST VINTAGE CRIME/BLACK LIZARD EDITION,
SEPTEMBER 2001

The Library of Congress has cataloged the Knopf edition as follows:
Vachss, Andrew H.
Dead and gone / Andrew Vachss.—1st ed.
p. cm.
ISBN 0-375-41121-6 (alk. paper)
1. Burke (Fictitious character)—Fiction. 2. Private investigators—New
York (State)—New York—Fiction. 3. Missing children—Fiction.
4. New York (N.Y.) Fiction. I. Title.
PS3572.A33 D42 2000
813'.54—dc21 00-040565

Vintage ISBN: 0-375-72526-1

Book design by Virginia Tan

www.vintagebooks.com

Printed in the United States of America
10 9 8 7 6 5

for Alicia Jimenez:

jibara, abused child, migrant laborer, garment-district worker, defender of her family, protector of her neighborhood, savior of damaged creatures, nurturer of a revolution, mother to my brother . . . heroine.

all your days on this earth were without rest. always you waited for it to be your time. always waited in vain.

and now you wait for us.

en nuestros corazones nada ha cambiado. serás adorada y respetada para siempre. trabajaremos sin descanso para que te sientas orgullosa de nosotros.

espera pacientemente, Mamá. pronto será como antes fue, todos juntos.

pero sin dolor.

Technical assistance:

Lieutenant Paul Nolin Berthelotte, USN
Professor James Colbert, UNM, USMC (1970–1971)
Sergeant Mike McNamara, Licensed for Life

DEAD
and GONE

You know what it takes to sit across the table from a man, listen to him talk, look into his eyes . . . and then blow his brains all over the wallpaper?

Nothing.

And the more of that you have, the easier it is.

"**Y**ou pick a spot yet?" The voice on the cell phone was trying to come across as bored with the whole thing, but I could pick up little worms crawling around its edges. Impatience? Nervousness? No way to know for sure.

"No," I told him. "And if I can't find one in a few minutes, we'll have to do it next time."

"Hey, pal, *fuck* you, all right? There don't have to *be* a next time."

"Up to you."

"Hard guy, huh? I guess that's right—it's not *your* kid."

"Not yours, either," I said, my voice level and unthreatening, sending my calmness out to him. "We're both professionals—how about we just keep it like that? This is a trade. You know how trades work. Soon as I find a safe spot, I'll pull in, just like we agreed, okay? We'll hook up, do our business, and everybody gets paid."

"You don't find a spot soon, *nobody* gets paid."

"I'll get back to you," I said, and killed the connection.

It had taken weeks to get this close. A missing kid. Too young to be a runaway, but there'd been no ransom note. Just a . . . vanishing. That was almost ten years ago. It wasn't a media story anymore. The cops told the parents they were still looking. Maybe they were.

The parents were the kind of people the cops would put out for, that was for sure. She was a gynecologist; he did something in biochemistry. But they were also first-generation Americans; Russians. So, when they got a call from a man who spoke their language, a man who said he ran a "recovery service" on commission, they took their hopes and their fears to Odessa Beach. Not the one on the Black Sea, the one in Brooklyn.

In the Russian mob, even the grunts have a hierarchy. You can read their rank right on their bodies—the specialists mark themselves with prison tattoos. The symbols tell you who's the thief, who's the assassin, who uses fire, who does bodywork. But they didn't have anyone who does what I do. So Dmitri, the boss, reached out across the border. To a Chinatown restaurant run by a Mandarin matriarch who trafficked in anything except dope and flesh. She didn't sell food, either.

"Half a million dollars?" I asked her, seated in my booth in the back, the third bowl—of a mandatory three—of hot-and-sour soup in front of me.

"They say," Mama answered. Meaning: she wasn't endorsing it herself; she wouldn't vouch for anyone involved at the other end.

"*And* a hundred for me?"

"For whole trade," she said, reminding me that I hadn't found this job on my own—they'd called her. The whisper-stream knows a phone number for me. After it bounces around the circuits, it eventually rings at one of the pay phones in the back of Mama's restaurant.

"Six hundred," I added it up. "And Dmitri, he's going to taste, too, right?"

"He say, same country, he help for nothing."

"And *you* say . . . ?"

Mama just shrugged. We'd never meet the parents. What they wanted was a middleman. The hundred large was all there was as far as we were concerned, no matter who else was getting what.

"Why come to me, then?"

"Cossacks know I find you. Say you know . . . these people."

"You mean they think—?"

"Not *same* people. *Those* people."

"Ah." Sure. Who knew the freaks better? They raised me. Recaptured me every time I ran, aided and abetted by the only parent I ever had: the State. I learned from the freaks, did time with them. And, when I got the chance, I hurt some of them.

Never enough of them, though. Those scales would never balance.

Mama was silent, letting me decide. Work was money. This deal wasn't a retirement-size score, but it was strong cash.

Any other circumstances, she would have been all over me to take it. Instead, she looked a question at me.

I knew what she needed to hear. "I can do it," I told her. Meaning: I could trade cash for a stolen kid and just walk away. Keep it professional.

Mama gave me a sharp look, then nodded slowly.

Whoever they were, they knew their business. I was waiting at the corner they'd had the Russians send me to, standing next to a pay phone. It rang. I picked it up.

"You're going to hear me say a 917 number. I'm only going to say it once. You walk *away* from that pay phone. *Far* away. When you get far *enough* away, you call the 917 number. Don't bother writing it down—it's going to disappear after this one call. That's the way we're going to work this, until we get it all sketched out. A new number each time, understand?"

"Yes," I said, keeping it short. If he thought I was trying to prolong the conversation, he'd smell cop. And that would end it.

"You ready for the number?"

"Yes."

He gave it to me. I shook my head "No!" at the men from Dmitri's crew who'd been standing next to me and walked over to where my Plymouth was parked, keyed the ignition, and took off.

I drove all the way out of Brighton Beach, one hand on the cell phone the Mole had built from spare parts around a cloned chip. As soon as I got clear, I punched in the number he'd given me.

"Go ahead," is all I said.

"We're not going to play around," he told me. "The Russians, they're *already* satisfied, understand? So don't be asking any questions about the merchandise. All you and me have to do is figure out how to make the exchange."

"Safest place is right out in public."

"Safest for *who*, friend? I don't think so."

"Just tell me how you want to do it."

"That's the problem—I can't think of a way to do it and still be safe. And I *have* to be safe. Otherwise, I'm just going to keep the merchandise. I was told *you'd* know a way."

Who told him? The Russians? Someone else? Or was this just his way of saying he was putting all the weight on me? I spun it through my mind quickly, but nothing came up on my screen.

"You know East New York? The flatlands south of Atlantic?" I asked him.

"Sure. Not a chance."

"Maspeth, then? By where the water tanks used to be?"

"Nope. I'm not going anywhere near tunnels, chief."

"Hunts Point?" I offered, letting just a trace of annoyance show through.

"Where in Hunts Point?"

"You know what I'm driving?" I asked him, ignoring his question, trying to feel my way through to him. He talked like a pro, flat-voiced, detached. But what pro snatches a kid, keeps him ten years, and then turns him loose? The cash wouldn't be worth the risk. He kept saying "I," as if it were just him, as if I were dealing with the kidnapper himself. But that didn't ring true. He had to be a middleman, same as me.

"No," he answered.

"Listen close: 1970 Plymouth, four-door sedan. Painted a dull-gray primer with a bunch of rust blotches on the sides. Outside mirror's held on with duct tape."

"Sounds like an old yellow cab."

"That's exactly what it is. You won't see many like it still alive. But the *next* time you see it, it's going to have a broad stripe of Day-Glo reflecting tape, orange, front-to-back. No way to miss *that* in your headlights, right?"

"So?"

"So I drive to Hunts Point. Triborough to Bruckner Boulevard to the Avenue, make a right, okay? Then I go out into the prairie, moving nice and slow, make a few circuits. There's a thousand places for you to stash a car in there, and I don't know what *you'll* be driving, see? You watch me pass by, you check for tags and wait. Or you pull right out behind me; do it however you want. Soon as you're happy, you ring me on my cellular. . . . I'll give you a number for that night."

"How'll I know it's—?"

"Let me finish. You'll like it. I find a good spot. I park. You watch me from a safe distance. You sound like a man who knows where to get some night-vision optics. Make your own decision when to come in. Or not. Soon as you're ready, you tell me what you're driving so I don't spook when I see you pull up. We make the exchange, takes about fifteen seconds—me to check for a pulse, you to count the cash, okay?"

"I'll get back to you," he said.

He'd done that. And tonight, he was somewhere behind my rear bumper, watching and waiting.

I pulled into a strip of concrete that dead-ended at the river. Some kind of garbage dump or recycling plant to my right, wasteland to my left. I did a slow U-turn until I was facing out the way I'd come.

I saw a pair of headlights blink on and off once, about a hundred yards away. Had to be him. I thumbed the cellular into life.

"Yeah?"

"How's this?" I asked him.

"I don't like that abandoned car on your right."

"If you were closer, you could see it's wide open. Nothing left but a skeleton."

"You got a flash?"

"Yes."

"Get out. Shine it on the car. Light it the fuck *up*, understand?"

I didn't bother to answer him. Just pocketed the phone, climbed out of the Plymouth, walked carefully over to the stripped-to-the-bone car, and sprayed it with a megawatt halogen beam. In the ghost-white light, the car looked like an Oklahoma double-wide after a tornado.

"I still don't like it," the phone said. "Find another spot."

I didn't say a word. Got back in the Plymouth and pulled out . . . slowly.

He passed on my next choice, too. And the one after that. I went on autopilot, hardly speaking at all, mechanically searching for spots. I left the cellular on, the lifeline between us.

"Change of plan." His voice cut into my thoughts.

"What?"

"*I* found a spot. Just past the meat market. Drive back over there."

"Right."

It was only a couple of minutes away. But when I drove by, slowly, I couldn't see anything but a couple of burnt-out hookers waiting on a semi. Or a serial killer. Car-trick roulette, with all their blood-money on the double-zero.

"Keep going," the voice said.

He must have me on visual now, I remember thinking. I didn't answer him, just let the Plymouth motor along, a touch past idle.

"See the train?"

Train? I saw what was left of an abandoned railway car sitting on rust-clogged tracks. "Yeah," I told him.

"Kill your lights and pull in there."

The ground was all ruts. I drove real slow, like I was worried I'd snag an axle, but the Plymouth's independent rear suspension handled it fine. I'd told the trader the truth about what the car had started out as, but all it had in common with the original was the body.

I figured he was somewhere in the shadows, and in a four-by, too. He didn't know what the Plymouth could do, so he thought he'd given himself an edge.

But it was me who had the edge—my Neapolitan mastiff, Pansy. One hundred and fifty-five pounds of war dog, resting comfortably in the Plymouth's padded trunk. Pansy's about eighteen years old. I'd raised her from a tiny pup, weaned her myself. She's lost a step or two. But you couldn't have a better partner at your back. More than a partner . . . part of me. And, like everything that was part of me, we'd chosen each other.

When I got almost parallel to the boxcar, I could see I'd been right on both counts. His ride was a black Lincoln Navigator, crouched in the boxcar's shadow.

"Get out," his voice came over the cellular. "And keep your hands where I can see them."

I did that, moving like I had major arthritis, slitting my eyes against the expected blast of light.

He didn't disappoint me. It was so white I felt the heat. Then it blinked off. I kept my eyes on the ground, waiting for the ocular fireworks display to fade.

The driver's-side door to the Lincoln opened. A man got out. At least I thought it was a man. I'd never be able to pick him out of a lineup.

"Where's the money?" he called over to me.

"In the back seat."

"Get it . . . slow."

I walked stiffly back to the Plymouth, opened the back door, reached for the satchel on the floor. At the same time, I pushed the button to pop the trunk. Not all the way, just to the first detent. Maybe six inches of space. But Pansy was free now.

I stiff-walked back to where I'd stood before. Dropped the satchel to the ground at my feet.

"Step away," the man said.

"No. This is as far as I go without the kid."

"You'll get the fucking kid, friend. Just move off a few feet, that's all."

I did that.

"Get out here!" he snarled over at the Lincoln.

The passenger door opened and a kid got out. I couldn't see him real well . . . only knew he was a boy because that's what the Russians had told me. Real skinny. Wearing a dark jacket and jeans. His pale hair was shaved on the sides and spiked in front. The kid seemed to know what he was doing—walked to my left until he was out of the shadow and I could see him better.

"We trade steps now," the man said. "One for one. You get closer to him; I get closer to the money. Got it?"

"Yeah."

"Now."

We each started walking, me slower than him. I still had the edge—the kid could move on his own, but the money couldn't. As soon as I got close enough for the kid to hear me, I said: "Come over here to me. Everything's going to be all right now."

The kid started toward me. I stood my ground, turning my head slightly to watch the guy pick up the satchel. The kid made some kind of grunting sound. I looked back and saw him holding a pistol, aimed right at the center of my chest. I tried to dive and roll, but I was too slow—the first couple of shots hit me in the rib cage. I staggered back, groping the darkness like it was a handrail, felt another shot slam into me somewhere.

Then I heard Pansy's war cry as she launched over the rutted ground, heading for where I'd fallen. The kid saw her coming, the hellhound on his trail. He turned and ran but Pansy hit the back of his thigh and pulled him down like a lioness dropping an antelope.

The guy near the money started shooting at me. It felt like a sledgehammer to my kidneys. He ran past where I was lying in the dirt, yelling something. I was fading, going dim.

Two more men piled out of the Lincoln. They both shot at Pansy. She dropped. But she struggled back to her feet, still locked on to her enemy. Pansy reared up high, threw her head back, and shook it violently until a chunk of the kid's throat came loose in her jaws.

It all slowed down then. Pansy looked at me. I saw it in her eyes. She spat out what was left of the kid and started for the shooter nearest me. I couldn't speak. I tried to hold her eyes. To say goodbye. They cut her to pieces with bullets. The pieces of her tried to get up. They kept shooting.

Then more shots came from another direction. The bass-voiced boom of a shotgun and the *ccrraack!* of high-speed ammo.

"We're taking fire!" one of them screamed. Another voice, calmer and harder: "It's been 911'ed. Finish it!" A man rushed over to where I was on the ground. I saw him raise his hand. A sunburst went off inside my skull. I rode the sound of the gunshot all the way into the black.

felt it. Close now. That dull-gray, anonymous violence-shark that cruises every prison, slashing out at random, triggered by something too primitive to reason with. All you could ever hope for was to stay out of its way.

But I wasn't back in prison. I was underwater. And the shark wasn't some metaphor. The water wasn't deep—I could see the surface a few feet above me. I was crouched behind a girder of some kind, waiting. Doing the death math: I was going to run out of oxygen soon. But the shark was hovering, gliding back and forth, waiting for me to show myself.

It wasn't that far to go, but once I made my move, I was committed. My hands felt along the girder, looking for a weapon, knowing it was useless—this was a shark, not another convict. But I was helpless against my conditioning.

I found something . . . something sharp. I let myself float toward the surface, trying to keep my back against the girder. The shark whirled and came at me. I raised my hand to stab, but I was moving in slow motion and . . .

The shark was gone. I was in a tunnel. Like a subway tunnel, but clean. And no tracks. I wasn't walking, but I was moving. Like on a conveyor belt. It felt peaceful and safe.

Then I saw the light up ahead. A beautiful circle of soft, gentle, pure white light. It was very bright, but not blazing—it didn't hurt my eyes to look at it. The circle was surrounded by pink and gold ribbons, soft and gauzy, woven-together tendrils of light, framing the entrance. A sweet, safe place. No sharks there. I heard sounds. Not . . . music, I don't know what to call them. All I knew was that they were calling me.

I opened my arms to pull the sweet light toward me. Then the pink and gold ribbons turned into blinking red-and-blue neon tubing, and I knew what had been calling to me. I was raised on whore's promises—I'd know them anywhere.

The circle of white light was small now. I braced my legs on either side of it, my hands scrambling, looking for something to fight back with. I touched a thick cord of some kind. Metal, hard plastic. I ripped it free from whatever was holding it. A whip to drive back whatever wanted me. I couldn't see a face, but I lashed at where one should be, my legs rigid against the sides of the circle.

I hit whatever it was. Felt it connect.

The light went out.

A mask on my face. As tight as my skin. Huge flat disks over my eyes. My hands . . . strapped down. Some bad S&M dream? No. I knew what it was. A dream, sure. But from when I was a kid and they . . .

But I wasn't a kid anymore. I could hurt people now. I reached for them, clawing.

"Pavulon!" someone yelled.

I was in a bed. In a room filled with mist. Machines ticked and beeped and purred. I tried to move my hands. No good. Nothing worked. Captured.

I willed myself to stay calm. They'd have to get close sooner or later.

"You were almost gone." A woman's voice. A beautiful woman, I could tell from the sound. Her voice was a polished river stone, burnished by her life.

"I . . ."

"There are people who want to talk to you. Can you talk?"

"Uh . . ."

"Just to me. Try and talk. To me only. I will not ask you questions. You ask *me*, yes?"

"Hospital?"

"Yes. You're in the ICU. My name is Rose; I'm the supervisor here."

"What time is it?"

"About eleven. Eleven at night."

The next day? I thought. *Twenty-four hours?* I remembered the meeting, the . . . *Pansy! What happened to my . . . ?* But the nurse wasn't one of us. "What day?" I asked her.

"The twenty-first. Of September."

What? The meet had been the last day of August. "Who wants to talk to me?" is all I asked her. My voice sounded like someone else's.

"The police," she said, nothing in her voice.

"I'm . . . arrested? That's why I can't move?"

"No. You cannot move because you kept . . . fighting. There

was a tube in your throat. You tore it out. And the IVs, too. That is why we had to use the restraints."

"What's 'Pavulon'?"

"Ah. I *knew* you had some consciousness. Pavulon is a paralytic. You kept ripping loose of the restraints, attacking . . . something. It was a medical risk, but, if we had not done that, you would have died."

"What happened?" I asked her, making her the trial horse for the lie I would have to tell the cops.

"You have no recollection?"

I recollected everything that counted: who I was, and what I had to do.

"I was driving in my car," I said softly, testing the lie. "Then I . . . Was it an accident?"

"We don't know," she said. "You were dropped off in the ER by two men. They left before anyone could question them."

"Tired . . ."

"Yes. You sleep now."

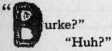urke?"

"Huh?"

Two white men in cheap suits.

"I'm Detective Baird, and this is my partner, Detective Wheelwright. We need to ask you some questions."

"Who?"

"Baird. And this is—"

"Burke. Who's Burke? Where is—?"

"You."

"What?"

"Burke. You. That's your name, right?"

"I . . . don't know."

"Shit!" one of them said.

"They warned us he might not remember," the other one responded. "Shot in the head, you got to expect some . . ."

"How are we supposed to—?"

"Tired . . ." I said, falling away.

"It's me, baby." A whisper. Close to my ear.

"Michelle." I knew her velvet-and-honey voice like I knew my own heartbeat.

"You're going to be all right," she promised.

"How did—?"

"Ssshhh, honey. You're in the Stepdown Unit now. But there's cops all over the place. Be careful what you say."

"But . . ."

"I always thought I'd look great in one of these nurse's uniforms," she said. "Too bad you can't see. I'm dazzling. Except for these tacky shoes."

"I can't . . ."

". . . remember. That's right. Yes, baby. Stay with that one until we can figure out how to get you discharged and disappeared. Just rest, okay?"

"You had a seizure," the guy in the white coat said. "It's not uncommon. Given enough shock to the overall system, the body goes on 'stun.' It just shuts down. It's almost like being underwater for a half-hour and still surviving."

I was *underwater*, I thought. But I kept it to myself; didn't say anything. Just let my eyes close and went back to waiting for one of my own to come for me.

"I know you must be frightened," he said, in a voice like he was hoping for it, just a little bit. "When you've been in a coma, the brain short-circuits. It's not unusual . . . to have a short-term-memory loss, I mean. It'll come back. Don't push it. Just relax and get better, okay?"

"Tired . . ." I mumbled, and fell away from him.

A nurse poked at me. It was dark everyplace but right by my bed. "Time for your pills," she said.

I just looked at her. She dropped one of the pills on the floor. Knelt quickly, picked it up, rubbed it on her smock, and dropped it back into the paper cup. "Here," she said. "Make sure you swallow them all for me, okay?"

I took the pills. Then I closed my eyes.

My name is Rich. I'll be caring for you." He was all in white, like a doctor—but no doctor would have said that, so I figured him for a nurse.

I didn't say anything.

"This is a morphine pump," he told me, pointing at a blue box on a long stalk. Tubes ran out of it. Into me. "With this, you don't have to ask anyone for a painkiller, you control it yourself. And it goes right into the bloodstream, so there's no delay in absorption. Much better than needles, I promise you. Here, can you hold this . . . ?" he asked, putting something that felt like a jumprope handle into my palm.

I nodded that I could.

"Good!" he said. "There's a little button on the end—feel it? You push that, and the pump sends you a jolt. It's limited to six an hour . . . about one every ten minutes. If it doesn't feel like you're getting enough, the dosage can be adjusted. Just let me know, understand?"

I held up the handle, so he could see it.

And pushed the button, so I could feel it.

What happened to me?"

"You were beat up real bad, pal," one of the cops said

to me. Baird or Wheelwright, I couldn't remember which one he was.

"Why? Who would—?"

"That's what we're trying to figure out. You got a few broken ribs, like someone worked you over with a piece of pipe. One of the ribs went into a lung. That's why they had to open you up."

"The nurse said I was . . . shot?"

"Right in the head," the cop said.

"Maybe that's why he can't—" the other cop said. I could see the one talking to me give him a hard "Shut the fuck up!" look.

"Ah, Mr. Burke, he's got a better memory than you think, partner. The bullet took out an eye, but it missed the brain. Just 'scored' it, whatever the hell *that* means. The docs say he'll get his memory back . . . just a matter of time."

"I'm . . . Burke?"

One of the cops laughed. The other just watched me. I could see his outline through the blur in my eye. My one eye. I moved my hand to find the other. It was all bandages there.

Rich told me my lungs had puddled with fluid from being on my back so long. He gave me a tube with a mouthpiece and some beads at the top. I had to blow . . . *hard* . . . until I could rattle the beads. A dozen times. Every couple of hours, he said.

I was in a room with three other beds. Curtains around the beds. The other patients got visitors. Nobody came for me except the cops.

I heard one of the cops arguing with a nurse. They wanted me in a private room. So they could talk to me. The nurse said there was nothing she could do about that—they'd have to talk to someone in Administration.

They came and got me the next day. Just rolled me onto a gurney and wheeled me down the hall, into an elevator, through another hall, into a room. It was a private room. A dingy private room built into a corner.

I still didn't get any visitors except the cops. But they came every day.

I knew what that meant. I worked the breathing tube until I got too exhausted to hold on to it. As soon as I got my hands to work again, I went back at it. Over and over. The pain burned my blood, it was so bad. But my lungs got emptier. I could see the results of that . . . all over my chest. When Rich was on duty, it got cleaned up fast. When he wasn't, they just left me like that.

The IVs fed me. But it was hate that gave me strength.

Days passed. They finally took out the catheter. Then the needle that was taped into a vein above my collarbone. The metal stand that held the morphine pump also held some bags of clear stuff running into two different IVs, one to my elbow, the other into my wrist. When they were all done unhooking me, I was bound only to the morphine pump.

As soon as I was sure no one was around, I tried to stand up. The first few times I fell. But the morphine pump stayed attached to me. The stand was on little wheels. I waited until Rich was off-duty, made my way out of the room. It took a long time, maybe fifteen minutes, to travel the few feet.

When I got into the hall, I saw a handrail running the length of the corridor.

I tried to pull the morphine pump along with my right hand, using my left on the railing. I took one step and a wave of black washed over me. I knew I couldn't fall. I held on. Nobody paid attention. When I felt stronger, I made my way back into the room. I sat on the bed. It took forever to get the lines adjusted. I rolled onto my back and went out.

Every day, I went a little farther down that hall.

It hurt to eat. The hospital food wasn't as good as the stuff they served the last time I was Inside. I chewed it very slow. One mouthful, one minute. Getting it down right, so I could keep it there.

Rich brought me some cans of Ensure, and I drank them all.

They took me for CAT scans. MRIs. Echocardiograms. They looked into my eye with lights.

Every day, sometimes twice a day, they drew tubes and tubes of blood. The veins on my arms finally collapsed and turned black, like I was a used-up junkie. They switched to tiny needles, took what they wanted from the webbing between my fingers. It went very slow when they did that. Hurt more, too.

A psychiatrist came. She didn't ask me much. Mostly tried to make me feel better about not remembering anything. She said it wasn't unusual. Not to worry. They wouldn't discharge me until I was all better.

A woman with a face that meanness made ugly asked me about health insurance. I told her I had a real good plan. Full coverage. From my job. I was an . . . I couldn't remember, but I knew I had coverage. Her lizard lips told me the police said I was a man with a long criminal record and no known employment. I told her that was silly. She said they took my fingerprints. I told her that was silly, too. She was angry at something. Later, she brought me a bunch of papers to sign. I signed them all. With an "X," like she said to.

It was a teaching hospital. That's why they were always study-ing me, this one resident said. He was working on his skills just by talking to me, perfecting that superior-snotty-scary tone they all need to armor themselves against the world's knowing that they don't know much.

Early one morning, Morales showed up. I'd known him a long time. A cop. He'd never liked me, but I didn't take it personally. Morales didn't like anyone except his old partner MacGowan. And MacGowan was long gone—pulled the pin on himself rather than talk to IAD after Morales smoked a bad guy and then flaked him with the throwdown piece he always carried. Morales was an old-style street roller, not a trace of slickness in him. A pit bull—once he locked on, he'd die holding the bite. And if he owed you, he'd pay it off or die trying.

He owed me, heavy.

"What happened?" he asked, no preamble.

"Who're you?"

"Gonna be like that, huh?"

"Like . . . what? Who *are* you?"

He pinned me with his black ball-bearing eyes, as commu-nicative as mirrored sunglasses. I looked back at him, blankness burning through haze.

"You really don't . . . ?"

"You . . . you're a cop, right?"

"How'd you guess, pal?"

"The only people who come to see me are cops. There's two others. Blade and Weber, or something."

"Baird and Wheelwright. They're out of the Four-Four in the South Bronx."

"Oh."

"Yeah. You don't know me?"

"Was I . . . Am I a cop?"

His laugh was metallic. He reached down, took my hand. He turned it over, looked at the palm, as if he was going to tell my fortune. "You didn't have a piece on you when they dumped you here," he said. "That don't mean nothing by itself. But the gauntlet came up clean. You passed the paraffin."

I made a noise. Less than a grunt, just enough to let him know I was listening.

"Deal is, the hospital's got to call us whenever there's a gunshot wound. It's the law, okay? There was no ID on you. Nothing. So they run your prints. That's when they tested your hands for powder residue."

I made another low noise.

Morales reached over and took my hand. "Give me your best," he told me, squeezing slightly.

I squeezed back. With all I had.

"Not yet," Morales said.

He dropped my hand, turned his back, and walked out of the room.

When you're in solitary, either you spend all your time getting ready, or you go somewhere else . . . inside your head. But the ticket to that other place costs too much. And there's no guarantee it'll be a round-trip.

So you do push-ups. Start wherever you can. Maybe just five, before you fall on your face. Doesn't matter. Nobody's watching. Do more the next time. *Every* time.

Isometrics are good, too. Walls are perfect for that.

Then you work on your mind. Remembering. Trying for every tiny detail. Every ridge, warp, taste, and texture. You do replays. In slow motion. Paying attention to the women you've been with the way you never did when you were right next to them. No fantasies allowed. They're dangerous . . . part of that ticket to somewhere else. Got to be real. Memories. Truth. Whatever happened. Whatever *really* happened—nothing else allowed.

You can't force memories. What color were those striped pants Belle used to wear? Vertical stripes. Michelle told the big girl they were slimming. Remember those stripes. They climbed up her long legs nice and parallel, but when they got to her butt, they ran in opposite directions like they were scared of each other. Remember her grunting and tugging at them, trying to get them on. What *color* were they? *Concentrate.*

But don't press. It's there. It's in there. It's all in there.

And I was going to need every bit of it soon.

In solitary, you don't tell time by the sun, or by a clock. You tell it by meals. No matter what they are, no matter how bad they taste, they mark the time. Sometimes you can get a trusty to talk to you. Sometimes even a guard. If you're connected good enough, your people can get stuff to you, too. But you can't count on any of that. Just the meals. And the getting ready.

I worked and I rested and I ate. That's all I did. But I did it all as hard as I could, gave it everything I had. So I'd have more to give it the next time.

"The optic nerve was impacted," one of the endless doctors told me. "The bullet also tore some of the muscles that keep the eyes operating binocularly."

"What does that mean?" I asked, speaking slowly. Carefully, like I wasn't used to it yet.

"There won't be any need for a . . . prosthesis. The right eye won't process images, and there may be some slight pigmentation shift, but it's organically sound. It doesn't have to be removed. It may, however . . . wander a bit."

"Wander?"

"The two eyes will no longer work as one. You'll still be able to read, drive a car, do everything you did before. Your depth perception will be affected, but that's just a matter of acclimation— you won't even notice it after a while."

"Oh."

"I'm sorry," he said. "But you're one lucky man; I can tell you that. If the bullet had been a fraction of a millimeter off its path, you'd be dead. Or severely brain-damaged, without question."

"I can't remember . . ."

"That's really not my department," he brushed me off. "My specialty is ophthalmological surgery. This consultation is about your vision. We wanted you to have a sense of the various . . . sensations you'll be experiencing when we remove the bandaging."

"When will you—?"

"In a week or two, perhaps," he said dismissively. The three young residents didn't say anything, watching him deal with the stupid bum who'd gotten himself beat up and shot in the head.

When he was done, they followed him out of the room, a small flock of white-coated sheep.

"The reason it hurts so much to swallow is that your sternum is cracked," Rich said.

"Sternum?"

"The central bone in your chest. In fact, it's the central bone in your entire body. All the other bones grow from that point."

"Oh."

"And, of course, your throat is significantly abraded. From when you ripped the tubes out."

"I don't . . ."

"Of course not. You were unconscious then. Or, at least, in some subconscious state. Anyway, there's no permanent damage. Everything will heal. You'll be the same as you were before."

"What was I . . . before?"

"That will come, too," Rich promised.

I would *not* think of Pansy. I would not do it. I knew what it would cost. I had to wait until I could make the payments.

"How's your memory coming?" one of the cops asked me.

"I remember *you*," I told him, trying for a proud tone in my voice, like a good kid who'd done all his chores. "You're Detective Bond, right?"

"Baird."

"Sorry."

"That's okay," he said, shooting a look over at his partner. "Any of it coming back to you?"

"The accident . . ."

"Accident? No. You were shot. In the head. Didn't they tell you?"

"Said . . . something. My eye. But I thought it was . . . in the car, maybe? Then it crashed? I don't . . ."

"Come on," Baird said to his partner. They both stood up and walked out.

Cops play suspects like they're fish.

"Fish"—that's what the cons call new prisoners.

"Incoming." In war, that word's always bad news. Inside, it means fresh meat . . . but some of that news can be just as bad, if you read it wrong.

Inside, they test you right away. But even the wolves walk soft and patient. The ones that don't, sooner or later they make a mistake. They think some skinny, baby-faced kid will give it up the first time he gets threatened with a beating. Or a shank. But some of those little kids, prison is the nicest place they've ever been. And they know just what to do to make it even nicer.

In prison, the wolf population is stable. They're always around. But not always the same ones.

The first thing you do when you hit the yard is— *Stop!* I shouted inside myself, nothing showing on my face. My mind was . . . drifting. I needed to focus. I had started with something. Where had I . . . ?

Yeah, okay, the cops. Playing me. Like they had all the time in the world. I knew what a crock that was. Sure, they knew who I was. Knew somebody had tried to take me out, too. But I wasn't dead. This was no homicide investigation, just another "assault, perp(s) unknown." And they had enough of those on the books to build another World Trade Center just from the paperwork.

Their ace was the hospital, keeping me locked down the way no judge would. It's not a crime to be a victim in New York. Even if you're a career criminal on the Permanent Suspect List for a dozen different Unsolveds.

If they knew who I was, they knew I had people. "KAs"— Known Associates—is what they'd call my family in their records. For cops, family is something you're born into. Pure biology.

Didn't use to be that way with them, but now they don't even trust their own kind. The Blue Wall had cracked too many times; too many cops had rolled on their "brother" officers. They didn't think of themselves the way they used to when a cop had to be Irish to get above a certain ceiling in the Department. Didn't matter what you called it—integration, immigration, affirmative action—it all played the same in the end. Once NYPD stopped being all-white, it stopped being all right with a lot of them.

And the rest of them all knew it.

Screenwriters who spend a few nights in the back of a squad car for "background" always make hatred of Internal Affairs part of the "character" of any cop they want you to like. Of course, screenwriters are the same twits who believe *omertà* is rat-proof.

So the rules may have changed, but cops still play the same old games. There was a phone right next to my bed. I never got any calls—that wasn't why it was there. I wondered what part of the City's budget was paying for my private line. And what tame judge had signed the wiretap order.

One night, real late, I reached for the phone. Punched seven different buttons at random, making sure I didn't hit the 1 or the 0 to start. A man answered, his voice blurry with sleep.

"Hello?"

"Is Antonia there?"

"*Antonia?* What're you, fucking insane, Mack? There ain't no Antonia here!"

He slammed down the phone.

I did it a few more times: seven buttons, punched blind. Mostly, I got a recording saying the number was not in service; twice I got answering machines; the last time a black woman, middle-aged, her voice tired. Just coming home from work, or just getting ready to leave.

"There's no Antonia here, mister. What number you trying to reach?"

"I . . . don't know," I told her, sadness in my voice. Then I hung up.

"Play with *that*, motherfuckers," I remember saying to myself, just before I fell asleep.

A few more days passed. Then the cops tried something even weaker. This time the phone didn't just sit there—tempting me, they thought—it rang. I answered it on automatic, like a guy who had no specific memories of who he was, but knew he had to be *someone*:

"Hello?"

"Burke? It's me, Condo."

I knew him. A collector for Maurice, a bookie I used to place my action with. People thought he was called Condo because he was the size of a damn condominium. People who didn't know him, that is. The rest of us knew where his handle came from: he was for sale or rent. That was one of the reasons the rollers picked him; the other was because I'd know his voice on the phone.

"Huh?" is all I said.

"I heard about what happened to you," Condo said, his voice low and confidential, just between me and him. And the whirling reels of tape. "I got the lowdown on who tried to get you done. What's it worth to you?"

"What? Who *is* this?"

"I *told* you, man: Condo. You know me. Now, you want this dope or not?"

"You know who . . . did this?"

"What?"

"You know who . . . hurt me?"

"That's what I'm trying to tell you, man. How much is it worth—?"

"The police . . ." I said, my voice getting weaker.

"They don't know nothing, man. I got this from—"

"The police said it was on purpose. I . . . don't remember. A car . . . something about a car. Tell the police. They're trying to help me. Call the police. Tell them who did this. They need to know."

"Are you fucking insane?"

"I know you?"

"Of *course* you know me, man. I *told* you . . ."

"Then you know me? You know who I am?"

"The fuck's wrong with you?"

"I . . . don't know. I don't know . . . who I am. I can't . . . Can you come here? You're my friend, aren't you? Maybe if I see your face I'll—"

"You crazy cocksucker!" Condo said, and slammed down the phone.

T he cops had to be getting desperate. Eventually, I'd get better. At least enough to be released. All they could do was wait for that, and watch. But Rich said they never discharged people

who were amnesiac, just transferred them to "another facility."
He looked sad when he said that.

I couldn't figure out why the cops were on this so hard. Had
they found that kid's body? So what? It wouldn't link to me.

Unless they found Pansy and . . . I felt my heart stop for a few
seconds. It just . . . stopped. Pansy. She'd be all they'd need to
know I'd been there.

I made myself calm, worked with what I had. The "two men"
who brought me to the hospital, they had to be family. And they
must have unwrapped the Kevlar from my body first—that's why
the doctors thought the broken ribs and stuff were from blunt
objects, not bullets. So my people must have Pansy's . . . body.

The cops, they had nothing.

Endurance. Outlast them. Sooner or later, they all get tired. I
had no strength anyplace but in my mind. So I worked there.
Stayed there. I knew my job. And Morales had made it clear that
I wasn't ready to do it yet.

E ven in prison, I'd never worked out, except when I was in the
bing—solitary. But there was that one crazy time when the
Prof was convinced I could make it as a boxer when I got back to
the World. So he'd started training me. And, even then, we
weren't working on building muscle; it was flexibility the Prof
said he wanted. But in solitary, working out was something you
did. Had to do.

So I did it in the hospital. On the sly, careful. Testing each
area, seeing where the give was, what held—getting ready for
them to open that door.

Every day. Every night. There was a TV in the room, but I
couldn't figure out how to turn it on. No radio. I never asked for
one. Just kept working.

But after a while, I realized this was a mistake. So I asked
Rich, and he got the TV turned on. "From Central," he told me.

"Huh?"

"Everything's on computer," he said. "In fact, every time you hit that morphine pump, the computer records it."

"How come?"

"For billing," he said, a thin smile on his face.

I worked the needle out . . . slow and careful; it would have to go back in the same place. I hit the morphine pump. A tiny bit of liquid came out of the needle's tip. All right.

Nothing on TV. Nothing about me. Nothing about a shootout. Nothing about a kidnapping, a killing, nothing. Plenty of news about crime. *Most* of the news was about crime, like always. But no picture of me; no "Do You Know This Man?" stuff.

I hit the morphine pump again, watching the liquid spray its lie into the computer's bank ledger.

The cops were down to nothing. I was brain-damaged and didn't know who I was . . . or I did, and was waiting to make a break for it. If they thought I still needed the morphine six times an hour, they'd think I was much further away from making a move.

I could walk by then. Even with the pump attached, I could move pretty good. And I could lift the whole thing off the ground with one hand, too. No way to test my legs, not really.

At some point, I realized I didn't want a cigarette. I wondered if this was a chemical change, or just me getting used to being in solitary again.

Every time the cops came back, I'd let them see I was a little stronger—it would have made them suspicious if I wasn't—

but I acted even more anxious about who I was. When was I going to find out? How come my picture wasn't on the news? Wasn't anybody looking for me?

"We already know who you are, pal," one of them told me. "So we're not looking for you. I was you, though, I'd be worried about who *is*."

"That's enough," his partner said, a thread of disgust in his voice.

"Hey! I was just telling my man Burke here—"

"Yeah. You told him. Come on. We got other things to do."

I couldn't tell if this was another variation of the good-cop/bad-cop routine. Either way, they were wasting their time. Where I come from, "bad cop" is the same word, said twice.

And if they thought they could keep me here with their little games, they were crazier than the people who had padded cells for return addresses on the postcards they wrote in crayon to the radio shows they picked up from the fillings in their teeth.

As if calling me by some stranger's name was supposed to ring my bell. "Baby Boy Burke" is what they put on my birth certificate, after the teenage whore who dropped me out of her womb disappeared. I guess Burke was the name she gave the hospital, so they passed it along to me. Probably wrapped my low-birth-weight body in yellow crime-scene tape instead of a baby blanket.

Born bad.

I know how it works. They could follow me around, put a guard outside my room, crap like that. But that was a major commitment of manpower. So all I needed was the one card that's never out of my deck: Patience.

I know all about waiting. It's my greatest skill. Sooner or later, they'd pull off the guards. Sooner or later, there's always an opening.

Besides, I was safe where I was. Like the nasty-voiced cop said, *they* knew who I was, so they didn't need to ask the public. I was logged in as a John Doe. And whoever had tried to take me off the count probably thought they'd gotten the job done.

I wasn't worried about my place going to hell while I was in the hospital, either. I live in an abandoned building. Off the books, under the radar. The only reason I ever had to go there was to make sure Pansy was . . .

No! I couldn't let that part in—it was more pain than the morphine could ever hope to touch. But I had something I *could* let in, welcome back home. Hate. It filled my veins, building with every circulation my heart pumped, giving me all I needed.

They killed my dog. Killed Pansy.

I don't know how that would sound to a citizen. But since I'll never be one, why would I care? I'd never needed a jury to tell me I'd been judged at birth. I was back to where I was as a young man, that "don't mind dying" train I rode until I got lucky and landed in prison instead of Potter's Field.

But I wanted to die like my partner had . . . with the blood of my enemies in my mouth.

So, every day, every way, I got stronger.

And waited.

A guy came up to my room. He said there was a Rehabilitation Institute attached to the hospital. If I kept improving like they expected, I'd be transferred down there soon.

He gave me a few tests to see how my strength was coming along. I deliberately held back, but he told me I was doing great. Another week or so, I'd be transferred.

I asked him a lot of questions, all wrapped around the only ones I cared about. When he told me that there were no private rooms in the Institute, that they had one of the highest staff-patient ratios in the country, and that the entire day was "activity-scheduled," I knew I couldn't make a break from there as easy as I could from where I was.

Time was tightening. But still nobody came for me.

A few days later, Rich told me my lungs were perfectly clear. "You did a great job," he said, smiling approval. "You must have worked very hard."

"I've been working just as hard in my head," I told him. "Trying to bring it back . . ."

His face turned sad. "Don't worry about it. That part, it has to come on its own. And it will, as soon as it's ready."

"You're sure?"

"No question about it. I've seen it a hundred times."

"Thank you," I said. Meaning it.

He said "Sure," and walked out, waving his hand to hide his face. But I'd already seen the tears. He had a good heart, that kid. But he was a lousy liar.

The floor outside my room was a rectangle, with a nurses' station near each end and a bank of elevators in the middle. A full lap around the perimeter took me almost an hour the first time I tried it. Now I could do a couple of dozen without stopping to get my breath. I'd been off the morphine for ten days, but I'd kept the billing computer happy. And anybody watching wouldn't see I was disconnected. I moved slow, taking my laps. Just like on the Yard—eyes down, but always watching.

If cops were watching the door to my room, I couldn't see them. Or any of those little dots that tip you to a minicam.

But I couldn't see what was at the bottom of the elevator's ride, either. And I couldn't leave the floor to find out.

There had to be a reason why none of my people had come. The cops had all their faces, but Michelle had gotten through once. Why . . . ? Sure! That was *before* the cops made their move on me, before the whole private-room game. That had to be it.

Maybe the cops had some patience of their own, figuring they could outwait my people.

No matter how I played it out, it came up NFG all the way. No Fucking Good. If my people came for me, the vise would close. And if they didn't . . . Ah, no use in thinking about that. They *would*. They were waiting, but they wouldn't wait forever.

Well, fuck that: the State had made me into a lot of things during my life, but it wasn't going to turn me into a goddamn Judas goat.

"**W**here are my clothes?" I asked Rich when he came on duty.

"Your clothes?"

"I must have clothes. I mean, I was driving in the car before it . . . happened. I must have been dressed, right?"

"Oh. I see what you mean. They're probably right over here in the closet. . . ."

The "closet" was a free-standing wardrobe. Rich opened the door. Turned to me with a puzzled expression. "There's nothing here," he said. "Give me a few minutes, I'll see if I can find out where they put your stuff."

I already knew where it was—in a forensics lab being vacuumed for evidence to help them put me back where they knew I belonged. Or in an NYPD evidence locker, waiting to nail the coffin they were building for me. But I kept my face blank and confused, watching him leave.

It took him about an hour to return. "Apparently, there's some sort of rules for a person who was . . . assaulted. The police—"

"But what do I *do*?" I asked him, depression leadening my voice. "I have to get dressed *sometime*, don't I? I mean, if I'm ever going to get better? So I can find my—"

"Of course you do," he said. He was trying to be soothing, but I could feel the anger beneath the surface. He was in the right profession, caring for other people. I wondered how long he'd last, working next to people who didn't.

"This . . . thing," I said, plucking at the hospital gown. "It's embarrassing to walk around in. Even if I just had a pair of pants, I could maybe . . ."

"I'll find you something," he said.

The next night, Rich gave me two pairs of light-green, bleached-out pants with a drawstring instead of belt loops. I knew where they must have come from. When I told him I didn't know how to thank him, I was telling the truth.

About one in the morning, the hospital floor was nearly as dead as some of its patients. I started my walk. A janitor with a huge square bucket on wheels stuffed with spray bottles of cleanser shuffled past, not looking up. The nurses' station nearest my end was quiet—only two of them, absorbed in conversation. One glanced my way for a second. Curiosity, not concern.

After all those weeks of shuffling by, I had every room in the corridor catalogued. I knew what I needed, but it was still a crap-shoot. I was completely unconnected from the machines by then, but I still pulled the morphine pump along with me. You'd have to be real close to see the tubes were loose and dangling under my hospital gown.

I told myself, if it didn't work tonight, then tomorrow night. No panic. Breathed slow, through my nose, shallow and steady.

The first room I wanted was a four-patient unit. I slipped inside. Machines made their noises. Somebody was asleep, breathing through an oxygen mask. I parted the curtain, found the call button for the nurses' station, and hit it a couple of times. Then I stepped to the door, looked back. All clear.

I moved again, quick now, all the way around to the other side of the corridor, shielded by the bank of elevators. Found the other room I wanted. A private room. Young man inside. Life-support systems kept him from crossing over. The room was empty, but his closet wasn't. I grabbed a red pullover, a denim jacket, and a pair of fancy basketball sneakers. Stepped over to his door. Peeked out. It was as empty as before. Maybe one of the nurses had responded to the call button, maybe not. I was betting they'd take their time, the way they always had with me.

I walked to the staff elevator, still dragging the morphine pump, the stolen stuff bundled under my other arm. Hit the switch. Heard the motors engage. Waited.

The car was empty. I stepped inside, hit the button for the first floor, shoved the morphine machine into the far corner and draped the hospital gown over it. Then I stepped into the sneakers, slipped on the pullover, and put my arms into the denim jacket.

When the doors opened on the first floor, there were a lot of people moving around. A pair of interns brushed past me, impatient to get somewhere. But no cops—if they were on watch, they'd be on the other side, at the visitors' entrance.

I stepped into the crowd, followed the signs to the ER. Nobody paid the slightest attention to me as I walked through that frantic, noisy, bloody mess and continued right on through to the exit.

A couple of bluecoats were standing outside, smoking. They gave me cops' glances. I didn't look at them, just limped away, the bandages around my head all the evidence they'd need that I'd just been "treated and released."

As soon as I turned the first corner, I realized I wasn't in the Bronx. I could see the FDR in the distance, so I was in Manhattan, on the East Side. A wave of panic welled up inside me. A setup? Would they be waiting? I breathed deep through my nose, steadied myself. If it *was* a trap, they'd be watching—I had to keep playing my role.

My hands were shaking. My fingers wouldn't work right. I couldn't tie the damn sneakers, and I was afraid of tripping. I sat on the curb and pulled the laces out. The sneakers were too big— they flopped when I walked, and I had to move slow, arching my feet deeply to keep from losing them.

But I *had* to move. I could make a collect call, but the cops might know about the pay phones at Mama's. I could call the

Mole—his number was off their radar—but the cops would be checking every pay phone around the hospital once they found out I was gone. It wouldn't take a computer long to run all the numbers within a certain time frame, and that could open doors the Man never knew even existed.

All right. No calls. And going to Mama's was out. The Mole's junkyard was in the Bronx. The Prof and Clarence cribbed in Brooklyn. Michelle changed hotels like she changed hairstyles. All too far to go unless I could bum some change for the subway. And at way past midnight, I didn't like my chances.

I kept moving east, toward the river. Under the FDR, there'd be all kinds of places to hide. From the cops, anyway.

But I was weaker than I'd thought. Every step was slow. I passed a homeless man, asleep in a doorway. Maybe I could just find a spot like that, become part of the landscape. . . .

I knew what that meant, those kinds of thoughts coming. Just another way of going to sleep in a snowbank. After a while, you're not cold anymore.

I stopped walking. Leaned against a building, my hands auto-groping for a pack of cigarettes that wasn't there. Okay, the street signs were coming into focus. I knew where I was. And that I wouldn't survive the night outdoors. Only one way to go, then. I about-faced and headed west, toward Park Avenue.

The Thirty-third Street subway was deserted. No clerk in the token booth. I slipped under the turnstile, grunting with the pain. Made my way down to the platform, found a bench. A young couple were on the next bench over, still party-blissed, not in a hurry.

Time passed. I was alive in every nerve ending, but I didn't have much left in my tank. If a roving wolfpack of teenagers decided to have some fun with the bum, I wouldn't be able to stop them. And if the cops were close by, if they had an alert out to Transit, I'd have to keep faking it. Tell them some story about "going home" to . . . I don't remember.

The downtown No. 6 finally pulled in. I shuffled aboard. The car was about half full. I wanted to keep away from people, but I needed to sit down, too. I was still making up my mind when a woman who looked like she worked till midnight cleaning offices got up. I took her seat. I wanted to thank her, but her face told me why she got up—she figured I must come with a smell to match my looks, and she didn't want any part of that.

The train let me out at Canal and Lafayette. Plenty of people; plenty of traffic, too. I couldn't tell if anyone was paying attention. I started my walk.

Chinatown runs twenty-four/seven, but most of the activity isn't on the streets once the tourists clear out. And I was close enough to a batch of different homeless camps so that I didn't get a second glance as I shuffled along, watching as close as I could to see if I had company.

The way you signal Max's dojo is to push the bell for the warehouse loading bay three times, fast. A light flashes in Max's place, on the top floors. He's deaf. If he's around, the side door will click open. You step into murk, even in daylight, but Max can see you from the landing.

I prayed for that click. When it came, I slipped inside and pulled the door closed behind me. There was a blur in the blackness as Max vaulted down. I felt him land next to me. Opened my hands to tell him I was . . .

woke up inside Max's temple. I recognized it right away. No disorientation. Just . . . weak. Sunlight slanted in through a window above me. I was under a sheet, naked. And safe, for the first time since I wrapped myself in Kevlar and went out to trade some money for a kid. I felt myself drifting off. Didn't fight it.

ax was there when I opened my eye. I shaded that eye with my left hand, turned my head from side to side, signing "looking." Then I pointed at myself. Max shook his head "No." I used both hands, made the sign for opening a newspaper, moved my head to show I was scanning it. He shook his head "No" again. Then he put his fists in front of his eyes, opened them to make the sign for glasses. Thick glasses. The Mole. On his way.

I made a gesture of thanks. Max ignored it, stepping over to me, running his fingers all over my body, checking. When he pushed against any part of me, I pushed back, letting him test.

Then he moved away from me. Held his hands far apart, pointed two fingers at each other, and brought them together so they touched. I sat up. Tried the same thing. Missed by a few inches. Shook my head, concentrated. I couldn't make the connection. I tried it again, slower. No go. One finger was closer to my body than the other. Instead of touching, they kept overlapping.

Max closed one eye. Used the other to make sure I was watching him. Then he brought his two fingers together so quickly it was like watching a vapor trail. They hit as precisely as if they'd been on rails. He pointed at me. Then at his wrist, where a watch would be if he wore one. Sure.

It would take time, but I could do it.

Max bowed slightly, disappeared.

I started to practice.

The Mole was cutting through the bandages on my head, using scissors with the lower blade in the shape of a spoon. As soon as he finished, Michelle unwrapped them, slowly.

I looked around the room. Nobody said anything.

"Do you want a mirror, honey?" Michelle asked.

"I . . . guess so. It's that bad, huh?"

"It just . . . doesn't look like you anymore, baby. They had to . . . you know, to . . ."

"I know."

The mirror they handed me was a 2× magnifier. The man looking back at me had a shaven skull, crisscrossed with stitches. I knew there was a metal plate under there. Titanium, the doctors had bragged to their lab rat. The man's left eye was hazel, with flecks of black. The right eyebrow had been shaved off.

Underneath it was a weird bronze iris, marbled with yellow. The man was hollow-cheeked, pale. The top of his right ear was gone, neatly cut away. His right cheekbone was slightly indented around a small depression crosshatched with surgical staples.

My own mother wouldn't recognize me, leaped into my thoughts. I cracked a joke to myself about how that was okay—I wouldn't recognize her, either. A tear ran down my face. I guess the bullet had done something to the ducts. I wiped it away. Took in a deep breath, turned around.

"What happened?" I asked the Prof.

He didn't move from the far corner, but his voice carried, a legacy from his preaching days. "The trap snapped, brother. It was a hit from the git."

"Yeah. The kid . . . the one I was supposed to be buying back . . . he came out shooting. If it wasn't for the wrapping, I was gone. He put a couple into me quick, knew what he was doing."

"We couldn't name the game until they was almost done, son. We had you on the Mole's tracker-thing, but we had to hang back until they got into position. By the time they did that, you was already pulling in, so we got way back in the weeds. Figured we could block 'em out if they tried to get bogus and split. We heard the first shots before we could see anything. Then we started pumping back at where their truck was stashed. They scrambled. We moved in, scooped you up. One look, we knew we couldn't handle it ourselves. So we got you over to the ER and split."

"You didn't drive all the way back into Manhattan?" I asked, avoiding what I needed to know.

"No way. We went straight to Lincoln. I don't know why they transferred you over to the other place. Maybe they had some special stuff over there. . . ."

"But you found out where I was?"

"Sure. Wasn't that hard. My boy Clarence knows half the damn nurses in the city."

"When it was going down . . . could you tell how many there were?"

"The one guy who went over to get the money, he was the boss. There was at least two more in the truck they had, besides that kid."

"They were good, too. I got hit a few times, even in the dark."

"They came to kill, not to fight," Clarence said, his island-voice blue with contempt. "When my father cut loose with his scattergun, they did not even return fire. If it was not for that one boss, they wouldn't have even come over and—"

"—tried to finish me."

"Yes, mahn. My father didn't hit any of them—too far away for his weapon. But one I took, for sure."

"Did they—?"

"Motherfuckers picked up their dead," the Prof cut in, knowing what I wanted. "Pros. When we got there, their truck was *flying* out. We only had the one car, and we needed to get yours out of there, too. Plus, we had to get you to the hospital."

"But you took . . . ?"

"We took your dog, honeyboy. We wouldn't leave her there. You know that," he said gently.

"Where is she?"

"She is with us," the Mole said. Meaning: buried in his junkyard.

"We got your car stashed," the Prof cut in quickly. "And Clarence and I got into your crib, pulled out a bunch of your stuff. I don't think the cops know about it, but . . ."

"You did the right thing. How much longer were you going to wait?"

"Before what?"

"Before you came and busted me out of that place."

"Bro, we had no way to go. We knew where you was, but the place was crawling with cops. Nothing on the news. We didn't know how to play it. I mean . . . maybe you wasn't in no shape to be getting out; maybe you needed some more . . . work, whatever. And they couldn't hold you forever, we figured."

"I played it like I lost my memory," I told them all.

"Yes, honey, we know," Michelle said. "That ugly brute of a cop, Morales? He came into Mama's one night. Told her: 'I went to visit this guy in the hospital. Thought I knew him. Guy named Burke. But he didn't know me. Didn't know himself. Got some memory problem. From being shot in the head and all. I don't know when he's going to get better. But he's real weak now . . . no condition to travel.' So we knew what the score was. All we could do was wait."

"They were waiting, too," I told her. "For you. For any of you. Now we have to see what they do."

"What *can* they do, bro?"

"They can play it straight, like I'm a patient with amnesia who walked away from the hospital. It won't make America's Most Wanted or anything, but it'd be good enough for the local news."

"It's been—"

"I know," I said. "Max told me. Blank. So they're playing it like they know the amnesia thing was just shining them on. But so what? There's no bodies up there in the Bronx—nothing to want me for. And nobody followed me here. . . ."

That last was a question, and they all knew it. I'd done my best to check for tags, but I wasn't sharp when I made my break. And part of me knew I'd done wrong—if I brought the law to where Max kept his family, it was something that couldn't be fixed with a moving van.

Nobody said anything. I took their quiet the wrong way. "I couldn't have made it to my place," I told them. "Not without a car. The buses don't run enough at that hour . . . and people watch too close on them, anyway. I had to stay underground. This was the closest place I could . . ."

"You came alone, homes," the Prof assured me. "They knew you was here, they'd have made their move. Been three days. No way."

"I've been here three days?"

"Four, counting today, bro."

"I don't . . ." I cut myself off before I could say the word "remember." *It was all an act, goddamn it. You fucking "remember" that, don't you?* I kept my bitter sarcasm inside my thoughts, wondering if my face was flat to match.

Max came close to me. Tapped his heart. Used his finger to draw a circle around it. Then he spun his hands into that same circle, the fingertips touching, an impregnable barrier. He closed his two hands into fists, watching my eyes.

I nodded. Got it. Nobody had come *close* since I'd shown up. Max's temple was never unwatched. Even Mama never understood the Mongol warrior's relationship with the mixed-Asian street gang that poached off the more established shock troops of the Tongs. But everybody knew about the vacant-eyed boys in their fingertip-length black leather jackets and silk shirts buttoned to the throat. And that they would kill for Max as casually as a suburban kid would click the mouse on his computer.

"I have to—"

"You don't have to do *anything* for a while, baby," Michelle said, patting my forearm. "You're going to need some serious rehab. And some medication."

"What medication? I don't remember which—"

"Oh, *pul-leeze*," she mock-pouted. "How long do you think it took my man to get into their little computer?"

"You mean the Mole—?"

"What *other* man would I be calling mine?"

"Michelle, give me a break, okay? You're saying the Mole hacked into the hospital computer, right?"

"Right. And we know every single medication you've been taking, every single little report they logged."

"What's my name on their machines?"

"Well, they don't have a name. You're a John Doe to them. But we still put it together in two minutes. We had the physical description, time of admission, nature of . . . injuries. You know."

"Sure," is all I said, wondering why the cops hadn't put something into the computer themselves. Maybe the insurance companies wouldn't let them. This is New York. Money doesn't just talk here, it's Dictator-for-Life.

"Do you need . . . ?"

"What?" I asked her, too sharply, put off by something in her voice.

"The . . . drugs, honey."

"If you mean antibiotics or whatever other kind of crap they were giving me in those pills . . . I guess so. But if you're dancing around the morphine, don't. I haven't had any for weeks."

I told them how I'd done that. The Mole nodded like it made sense. The Prof chuckled. Michelle just watched me.

"I'll be fine," I told my family. "But there's something I've got to know first. And only Mama will know the answer."

"I'll roll on by and say hi," the Prof volunteered.

"Thanks, brother," I said, closing my eyes.

"**N**o, bro," is all the Prof came back with.

"No what?"

"No show, no go. Man hasn't said word one."

"Dmitri thinks I'm . . . what, then?"

"No way to tell. Depends on where he stood at the beginning."

"These Russians—the parents—they didn't get their kid back."

"Right."

"And they didn't get their money back, either."

"True."

"And it was *real* money, Prof. Remember, I went through it myself. Told Dmitri I wasn't handing over some Chicago bankroll for the kid, take a chance on the wheels coming off."

"Sure. All true, I'm with you."

"So they *took* the money. Must have—the one guy had his hands on it when the kid came up blasting."

"Okay . . ."

"What about *our* end?"

"Huh?"

"We . . . I was supposed to get a hundred large, for the whole deal. We were going to whack it up, like always. Dmitri paid half up front. To Mama. You ask her if he ever paid the other half?"

"No, son, I didn't. She was supposed to be the go-between, that's all. They don't know nothing about our . . ."

He let the sentence drift away. None of us said the word "family" out loud if we could help it. Not because stupidass Godfather movies had perverted the term, but because we'd all known the truth of its perversion way before we were old enough to be watching movies.

Mama was in business. Dmitri wanted to do business. He fronted half; that was the usual deal. Why would he pay off the other half for a job that never got done?

"All right, so he hasn't come around with the other half. But no way he can blame anyone but himself for what happened. We didn't set it up. He put us in contact and we took it from there."

"I don't see where you're going, Schoolboy."

"Let's say Dmitri got all that cash from the parents of the missing kid, okay? Now he shows them . . . what? Nothing. They lost their money, and they don't have their kid. So I guess it's on them for trusting whoever made contact. Unless they just turned it over to Dmitri and asked him to handle it. Then they'd be pushing him. And he'd be pushing, too. . . ."

"So you think . . . ?"

"I don't know what to think," I told him. "But I know how to find out." I looked over at the Mole. "How much longer before I can get up, move around, do some work?"

The Mole opened his mouth to spout a bunch of biomedical stuff. Then he thought better of it and pointed at Max.

I nodded. Sure, that was the only way to find out.

We started the next morning. Max doesn't have any weights in his dojo, but it's full of all kinds of things that take muscle to move. Before we went near any of that, Max took a stance opposite me and gestured that I should do whatever he did. He kept it simple at first, just basic stretches, probing for my range of motion. I could see him marking the limits in his mind, matching them up against whatever he'd be satisfied with at the end.

I looked longingly at the heavy bag. Max shook his head. Spread his hand wide, inviting me to do the same, then adjusted until his fingertips met mine. And pushed, slightly. I pushed back. Nothing. I pressed harder, felt a tap on my shoulder, caught Max's eye. He breathed through his nose, filled his lungs, then exhaled as he pressed his fingertips against mine. My hand crumbled. Yeah, I'd forgotten everything.

It was about three weeks before Max let me try some light sparring, his hands heavily gloved so that he wouldn't hurt mine when he caught the punches. And he did, every one. But he could have done that no matter what shape I was in, so I wasn't discouraged.

The depth-perception thing *did* discourage me. I couldn't judge distances, kept going way short with my jab. And anything that came from my right side—well, now it was my *blind* side.

The Prof came by to watch once in a while, keeping up a running fire of commentary the way he had when he was training me, years ago. But this time, none of it added up to what I had. Max finally shook his head at the Prof. Then he stepped forward with his left foot, sliding his right behind it, closing the gap between us. Showed the move to me.

"Max got the facts, Schoolboy," the Prof conceded. "You ain't gonna keep nobody at the end of your jab no more. Got to get close. No need to guess when you inside his vest."

Another thing gone. I'd never been much of a power puncher, even when I boxed all the time. Finesse was what I'd finally learned. And now it was useless.

That was the day Max started showing me places to touch a man that would paralyze—nerve clusters, pressure points, arterial junctions. It was tricky—you had to hit at least two of the points at the same time, and I'd probably never be able to do it in hand-to-hand fighting. But if I could get someone into a grapple . . .

"I want to help, too, mahn," Clarence said one day.

"I *need* your help," I assured him. "You still tight with Jacques?"

Jacques was a Jamaican gunrunner Clarence worked for a long time ago. Before the Prof became his father, as he had once become mine.

"I get you whatever you need, brother," he said, his blue-black face calm as still water.

I needed something that matched what was left of my body. The nine-millimeter Clarence carried was a precision instrument, its bullets like wasps, fast and sure. But if you missed a vital spot, a man could take a hit from a nine and keep coming. I needed something for close-ups. And I needed whatever I hit to go *down*.

"Three fifty-seven," I said.

"Colt Python is best, mahn. Four-inch barrel?"

"Unless you can get one shorter."

"Jacques can fix your trick," the Prof put in. "The factory don't make it, he'll fake it. But you know the score—custom costs more."

"A nice wide hammer-spur," I told Clarence, holding my hands about three feet apart so there'd be no mistake. "And no front sight."

"It's going to buck, mahn," Clarence warned me.

I looked over at Max, caught his eye, pointed to my wrist. I made the gesture for firing a gun, showing the pistol kicking, my hand flying up. I opened my hands in a question.

The Mongol nodded. Grasped my wrist with his hand. I flexed the wrist. It was like trying to lift a TV set with the back of my hand. Max shrugged—not sure.

"Okay," I told Clarence. "I guess I'll have to try it out. You got a place where—?"

"After dark," the West Indian said.

Clarence piloted the colorless, shapeless blob of a Toyota through the devastated blocks south of Atlantic Avenue. "I did not want to use my ride, mahn. We still don't know what they may be watching for."

"Good," I said from the back seat, knowing what he really meant. Clarence never brought his beloved British Racing Green

'67 Rover 2000 TC along when he thought there might be shooting. He could live with damage to it—after all, he'd restored
it from scrap—but the prospect of police forfeiture made him
psychotic.

With a dark-blue watch cap covering my head and an old
Army field jacket providing bulk that I didn't have, I looked
like . . . nobody. But I still looked white. And in that neighborhood, white meant cop, junkie, or victim, so we were playing
it safe.

The basement was lined with bags of cement mix, stacked so
deep you couldn't see an inch of the walls, much less a window.
The ceiling was thick foam acoustical tile. Even the floor had
some kind of rubberized mat over the concrete. Clarence handed
me a pair of ear-protectors. "Outside, nobody hears nothing,
mahn. But in *here*, you blow an eardrum for sure, you don't
cover up."

I slipped the protectors on. Clarence did the same. Then he
walked into the darkest corner of the basement and came back
with the pistol. I tilted the protector to listen.

"A Python, like I said, mahn. This is standard, all the way
around. Nobody's touched the piece or the ammo."

"I can just . . . ?"

"Sure. Blast away. We test much heavier stuff down here, no
problem."

I aimed the pistol at the far wall of sandbags, squeezed the
trigger slowly. *Too* slowly. I realized I was even testing the
strength of my damn finger, said *Fuck it!* to myself, and cranked
one off.

The gun bucked hard, but I was anticipating the ride and
brought it back down into firing position off the momentum. I
looked over at Clarence. He nodded approval, flicked his index
finger a few times, quickly.

Okay. I snapped out the remaining five rounds, resisting the
temptation to use my left hand to steady my right wrist. Felt all
right. I gave it a few seconds for the echoes to be absorbed, then I
pulled off the ear-protectors.

"How'd it look to you?" I asked Clarence.

"Looked pretty steady, to tell the truth, mahn. Your wrist is strong, I think."

"Any way to check on a grouping?"

"Sure, mahn. But the longest distance we got here is—"

"—more than I need," I said.

Clarence found an old newspaper, carefully tucked it in between some of the sandbags. In the dim light, I could only see a faint white rectangle. I stepped closer, looking for a six-to-eight-foot range. Raised the pistol.

Then I stopped. Turned to Clarence. "How far away am I?" I asked him.

"You about, I would say, fifteen feet, mahn. You want me to measure?"

"Yeah."

Clarence paced it off. "Fifteen and a piece," he confirmed.

Christ! Just like the damn boxing—I'll have to be closer than my eyes tell me. I stepped forward, cutting the distance in half. "I want six feet. How'm I doing?"

"You about ten, brother."

I took another two strides. Looked over at Clarence. He nodded. We both put our protectors back on. I popped the cylinder, turned the gun up, extracted the empty cartridges, put them in my pocket, and reloaded. Then I put the pistol in my belt, made myself relax. When I was calm inside, I took the gun out, aimed it slightly below the center of the white blob even as I was cranking off the first round. I pulled until it was empty.

We went over to look. Clarence took out a pocket flash, inspected the newspaper. It was shredded in the center. He studied the results, professionally objective, a physician seeking a diagnosis. "Looks like four of them within about, maybe, eight inches. One I cannot see, mahn. Perhaps it went . . . off—that can happen with the first round. The other, it is right here," he said, pointing to the extreme upper left corner of the paper.

My wrist didn't throb at all.

I did a half-dozen more full cylinders, then switched to my left hand. Nothing changed much. Maybe I was a touch more accurate with my right hand, but, at that distance, it wouldn't matter much.

"What do you think?" I asked Clarence.

"I think," he said, "that you could handle a shorter barrel. Colt makes a two-and-a-half-inch. And Jacques can Mag-na-port it for you."

"What's that mean?"

"Revolvers, they blow out a *lot* of gas, mahn. What Jacques does, he cuts these little slits right along the top of the barrel," Clarence explained, illustrating with his fingernail. "Some of the gas comes out *there*, too. So what happens is, it helps bring your hand *down*, counteracts the buck, see?"

"That sounds perfect."

"But you have to be *very* close, now. Especially for that first shot. With this piece, you put one into a man, he will go down."

"Die?"

"Anywhere in the body or the head, yes, mahn. An arm or a leg, it would . . . maybe. A solid hit, he would go into shock. But if the paramedics got there quick . . ."

"Okay. Fair enough."

"You want hollowpoints? Hot loads on the powder, too?"

"Mercury tips."

"Mercury tips, I do not like them, mahn. For small slugs, sure. They tear right on through, and the mercury is a good poison to leave behind. But the .357, nobody knows why, exactly, but it has the highest one-shot kill ratio of any of the handguns. There are bigger ones, but this one hits the hardest."

"Just a little drop," I told him. "For luck."

"All right, mahn. So that would be one Python with—"

"Two," I cut him off.

"Ah," is all he said, getting it.

I spent every day working. For breaks, I stayed inside my head, trying to connect the dots.

I found out one thing I needed to know. The way I usually learn things—by making someone sad. Only this time it wasn't me doing it to myself.

If Max or his wife, Immaculata, had any problems with me staying there, or even with the crew coming by all the time, they never let it slip.

I guess they never even said anything about me being there to their daughter, Flower. I've known her since the day she was born. The child spoke Vietnamese and French, thanks to her mother, and could sign back and forth with Max even faster than I could. Mama, who insisted the child, being *her* grandchild, was pure line-of-descent Mandarin back to before they put up the Wall, was teaching her one of the Chinese dialects. English she picked up from the rest of the world. Her impeccably polite manners were those of a warrior: Respect, not subservience. Understanding, not awe.

Sometimes Flower called me "uncle," but that was only in the presence of strangers. She knew her parents and I were part of a family. A family of choice, the only kind us Children of the Secret ever trust. Only Mama insisted on a formal title. *Very* formal. It was "grandmother" in English, and whatever it was in the other languages seemed to satisfy her.

Max can read lips, but I never know how much he's getting, so I always sign along when I talk. I was standing with my back to the beaded curtains that close off the dojo from the rest of the floor, pacing a little. Max stood across from me on the mat, watching, immobile as stone. I was telling him about where I was stuck.

I was just getting to the part about how I had been dealing with Dmitri long before it happened, middlemanning shipments of weapons he was selling. His clients were a crew of Albanians up in the Bronx who wanted to make a contribution to the Kosovo relief effort. Dmitri had the ordnance; I had the contacts. We did business, and business was good.

Suddenly, I heard, "Burke! Burke! You're back!" and the sound of running footsteps. Flower burst through the curtains, ran a little bit past me, whirled, and went "*Oh!*" She froze, her eyes locked on my face. My new face. "I thought . . ." she said, her voice trailing off.

"It's me, Flower," I told her, keeping my voice soft and gentle.

"What happened? Oh, Burke, your face, what . . . ?"

She started to cry then. I tried to take her to me, but she ran to Max. The Mongol scooped her up like she was cotton candy, held her close to him, communicating with tender touch. He must have seen it coming. Max maybe can't hear, but he can feel vibrations as if his whole body was a tuning fork—I've seen him listen to music by putting his hands on the speakers. So he had to have known Flower's footsteps.

And he must have known that her mother wouldn't be far behind. When Immaculata swept into the room, one long red-lacquered fingernail leveled at his chest, Max quickly kissed Flower, then gently lowered her to the ground.

"What is *wrong* with you?" Immaculata said to him, voice quivering, her gesturing hands eloquent with anger.

Before Max could answer, she knelt and spoke directly to Flower. "It is Burke, child. *Your* Burke. Don't be frightened. There was an accident. Burke was hurt. But he's getting better now, all right?"

The little girl looked up at me. "It's true," I told her. "There's nothing to be frightened of."

"I'm not scared," she said solemnly. "It looks like it . . . hurts you."

"Nah. Let's face it, I wasn't all that good-looking to start with, right?"

But I was aiming at the wrong spot. That might have gotten a giggle from a teenager, but Flower was too young and too old to respond that way. "No man is as handsome as my father," she said. "But you always looked . . . like . . . I don't know . . . not like this."

"I won't always look like this, Flower. Promise."

"I don't care how you *look*," she said, stamping her little foot. "I just don't want you to *hurt*."

Immaculata shot a glance at Max over the child's shoulder. It was short of fatal, but not by a whole lot.

Max made a gesture for "true," tapped his ear, pointed to Flower. Then he made the sign of pouring one test tube into another, holding up the receiving vessel to the light, checking the results.

Immaculata nodded, slowly. Getting it, but not liking it much. I'd been asking everyone if my voice sounded the same to them—it sure as hell didn't to me. They'd all assured me that I sounded the same, but Flower, innocent Flower, she was the perfect test. She hadn't seen me since I'd been there. But when she'd heard my voice . . .

"I'm sorry," I told Immaculata, trying to take the weight for Max.

"It's all right," she said. "I understand. And so does Flower." The little girl nodded, solemn but not distressed anymore.

"Thank you," I said, bowing. Max understood the thanks were for Immaculata, and the bow for him. I knew what it had cost him to use his precious child in any kind of experiment. But he was right—it was the only way to tell.

I didn't need my voice to say goodbye to Pansy. The Mole showed me where she was buried, her grave nestled in a triangle of rusting steel girders, long lengths of rebar wound through it to make a wreath. It was strangely beautiful, like the charred ground beneath a launched rocket.

Mama had given me a box of brilliantly colored little papier-mâché constructions. "Burn when you say goodbye to puppy. Be waiting for her in new place." Each was a perfectly rendered miniature. Everything Pansy could ever want, even an exact replica of her treasured giant rawhide bone. And a sheepskin mat that looked as if it had been cut from the original.

I'd seen those symbolic representations for use at funerals in Chinatown shops, but never ones like these. Mama had to have custom-commissioned them. And brought them over to Max's place herself. It was the first time I'd ever seen her outside her restaurant.

"What about the play money?" I asked, expecting her to tell me a dog wouldn't need money.

"Real puppy. Send real money," she said. And handed me a thousand in crisp new centuries.

We all have our beliefs. Mama lived hers.

Standing there, I realized I couldn't say anything. I'd said it all while Pansy was with me. Said it the only way that ever counts . . . with my behavior. Nothing to say, but I stood there for a long time. First trying not to cry. Then letting it go.

Belle was there, too. In that same graveyard. Belle, who loved me and died for me. I didn't miss her any the less after I'd settled her score. Didn't hate myself any the less for having put her in harm's way, either. But I gave her the respect she'd earned, honoring that she'd gone out the way she'd wanted to.

Belle had drawn a pack of squad cars off me, out-driving the best NYPD had and making it back to where we were supposed to meet. But they'd poured enough lead into her that all she had left was the strength to say goodbye.

You can never really balance the scales. Taking a life doesn't return the one the killer took. But any death of a loved one is a test of faith. And my religion is revenge.

With Belle, he'd been easy to find. I knew who he was. Her father. I knew *what* he was, too. So killing him was even easier.

With Pansy, I didn't know who. Not yet. But when I did, it would play out like this: they were gone, or I was.

"I'll see you soon, girl," is all I could make myself say to her.

The Mole set up the meet. He'd done it before. It was always the same—I wanted something from them or they wanted something from me. Money never changed hands. What we traded was information. Or work.

"Dmitri is ex-Spetsnaz," the unremarkable man said. He was a little shorter than me, slim, with dark wiry hair and leathery skin that made him look older than he was . . . I guessed. He wasn't one I'd ever seen before, but his eyes had the same look they all have.

"What's that?" I asked him.

"The elite of the Russian military. Like the Special Forces or the SEALs. But now, in today's Russia, they are not heroes; they are throwaways. They are paid nothing, they live in squalor, they have no prospects."

"So they hire out?"

"Some do. Not all. Some are loyalists to the core, waiting for the return of Communist Russia. But most of them could not survive without some other employment."

"Dmitri?"

"Dmitri is a criminal. He was a criminal in Russia; he is a criminal here. But his group is small. Operatives for hire, not what you Americans like to call 'organized crime.' His group has no foothold that would interest the Mafia, so he has no basis for a partnership."

"What kind of foothold *would* interest them?"

"Gas stations are one example. The Mafia arranges for all the stations to buy bootleg and avoid the gas tax, which is enormous. Then the profits are divided. Money laundering is another. There are many small businesses in the Russian neighborhoods. All-cash businesses. But Dmitri is no businessman, despite his opinion of himself."

"So he could have just been hired to do the job?"

"An assassination? Certainly. But it is not likely."

"Why?"

"It was too elaborate. You have been alone with this man, more than once, yes?"

"Yes."

"So he had many opportunities. Dmitri has military training, but he is no master tactician. If he had been paid—paid *enough*—to risk a homicide, he would have acted on it when he had the chance, not given you so much time to ascertain his intent."

"Is he an enemy of your people?"

"Perhaps once." The man shrugged. "If he was paid to be so, perhaps again. But all Dmitri wants now is money. A pogrom would not bother him morally, but he would not participate unless he was paid. And now in Russia there is no one to pay him. Afghanistan was their Vietnam. But, unlike America, they never recovered.

"The IMF had to bail the Kremlin out after it defaulted on its own bonds, and devalued the ruble. There *is* no 'Russia' anymore. And what shreds are left would not, *could* not spend the time or the resources to keep our people imprisoned. A little corruption, a little bribery, yes. After all, Russia was once the ultimate bureaucracy. But there is no government policy preventing our people from coming home."

"Still, you know a lot about him. . . ."

"We know a lot about many people. They are not *our* people, but they could be of use, someday. In our trade, today's enemy is tomorrow's asset."

"Would you know who his second-in-command is?"

"They are no longer military, Mr. Burke. No more chain of command. He has fellow thugs, that is all. He is the boss, not the general."

"So if he were to step down . . . ?"

"Hah! Dmitri would never *step* down. Ever. And should he be . . . removed, there would be the usual scramble for power. An orderly succession is highly unlikely."

"But, eventually, no matter who took over, you would know, right?"

"Yes. They have no secrets from us. Some we buy, some we . . . acquire. But all we get, eventually."

"Thank you. For all this. I know the value of information. If I can ever be of service to you . . ."

"You are with our brother," the man said quietly, for the first time including the Mole in his glance. "This is for him, not for you."

had to play it as if the Israeli's info was gospel. And I had to play my lone ace very carefully. You only get one chance to take advantage of someone believing you're dead.

t took another ten days to set up a meet with Dmitri. The prelims were handled over pay phones. I was a guy who knew a guy who knew a guy, voice-filtered. The "buyer" was a crazy old man with maybe six months to live—advanced aplastic anemia. He wanted some surface-to-air missiles so he could bring down one of the camouflaged helicopters ZOG kept sending over his compound. That way, he could show the whole world the kind of covert surveillance the Jewocracy was conducting against patriotic Americans.

Not only that, the old man was psycho enough to pay retail. A sweet score for Dmitri. Ten points to me for the steering, talked down from twenty-five.

But Dmitri wasn't moving from his restaurant. Dealing with strangers, that was the only place he'd do business, no exceptions. The guy was in a wheelchair, too fucking bad—they could just wheel him in. And no problem about an interpreter—Dmitri was proud of his English.

"No," I said, flatly.

"They'd never—"

"No," I told Michelle again. "If this doesn't work out, it's going to be messy."

"And you think I can't—?"

"It's not for you," I said. "That's the end of it."

"*Because* . . . ?" she insisted.

"Because they won't recognize *me*. I won't look like this forever, but, for now, I'll get right past their screens," I said, wondering even then if I was being honest with myself. "But *anyone* would know *you* again, honey."

Michelle loved to shop, but she wasn't buying any of my lame flattery that night. "Who, then? You think *Max* is going to be able to disguise himself. As *what?* The Mole? Sure! And don't even *think* about the Prof or Clarence; the last time a black man was in that neighborhood was before the Russians took over. They'd get more eyeballing than a porno movie. But a woman in a nurse's outfit . . . Just *think* about it for a minute."

"I . . ."

"Oh, wait here. I'll be back," she snapped.

We had almost three more hours to keep planning before Michelle returned. Only now she was a blonde, with skin tanned so deeply she looked like a Puerto Rican in a wig. Her heart-shaped face was roundish now, her full lips were much thinner. And her eyes were a bright, fake blue. "Who's going to recognize me *now?*" she demanded.

The Prof looked her over appreciatively. "You don't loosen up on that skirt, they gonna follow you home anyway," he said.

"Fine!" Michelle snapped back, in no mood to play. "I'll be in a nurse's uniform, remember?"

"I know a better way," I said.

"You are sure of this?" the Israeli asked me.

"Are you asking if I'm guessing, or if I'm lying?"

"If you are guessing, you are a fool. And we will not work with fools. If you are lying . . ."

"He is not lying," the Mole said quietly.

The Mossad man turned to face me, his dark eyes trying to hold mine. But his eyes were a normal person's, working as one. So he had to settle for only one of mine at a time, and it threw him off. "Dmitri is going to sell SAMs to Nazis, that is what you are telling us?"

"Not *German* Nazis. Not some remnants from World War II. *American* Nazis. A few assorted freaks with Master Race fantasies."

"So? Such people are no threat to us."

"That's right," I told him truthfully. "But Dmitri's a merchant. If he'll sell to Nazis, he'll sell to Arabs."

"All Arabs are not our enemy. That is what you Americans believe, perhaps, but it is wrong. Only a tiny minority thwart the possibility of peace between us."

"A tiny minority's enough, today. Arab extremists in America aren't any different from our home-grown Nazis. They both like to blow things up. The World Trade Center, Oklahoma City . . . what difference? You know how it works. They may hate each other, but when it comes to Jews, they're all of one mind."

"You are saying . . . what?"

"It's what *you* said. Dmitri was in Spetsnaz, so he was military. *Elite* military. And there's no doubt that *tons* of heavy weapons were left over when the U.S.S.R. came apart. It's out there, and it's for sale. Hell, I've even heard talk about plutonium. . . ."

I let my voice trail away, watching his eyes. He was good, but I caught the spark, used it to jump-start the rest of my pitch: "But what Dmitri's outfit's running here isn't military supply," I told him. "It's just straight crime product: drugs, whores, gambling, loan-sharking, extortion. When I wanted to work that shipment of guns to the Albanians, I dealt with Dmitri personally, not his crew. The ordnance part is all his . . . his own separate piece. You understand what I'm saying?"

"That is why you wanted to know who Dmitri's successor would be, yes?"

"Yes," I lied.

"It would be nobody from Spetsnaz. He was a rogue even within his own unit, in Russia. Whoever replaces him will be a gangster, not a soldier."

"Without access to the military stuff, then? Without the contacts?"

"Yes. Of course. Dmitri would never share such . . ."

As his voice faded, he finally found my good eye. And held it this time.

I shaved carefully—no picnic with my distorted depth perception. Spent some time looking at my face in the mirror. My new face. A nerve jumped in my right cheek, the bullet scar at the center of the tic. I pressed against the spot and the tic died.

The ambulette was a converted Chrysler minivan, painted a dull beige, with red crosses on both sides and the back. It cruised the Brooklyn block slowly, searching for an opening. Finding none, it double-parked right in front of Dmitri's joint. The light-bar on its roof went into action, indicating pickup or delivery. The driver dismounted, came around to the curb side of the van, opened the sliding door. A hydraulic device noiselessly lowered a wheelchair to the street. Inside was a man wrapped against the fall cold in a heavy quilted robe. The driver became an attendant, wheeling the man onto the sidewalk. He returned to the van, pulled the sliding door closed. Then he pushed the wheelchair inside the restaurant.

A short, squat man with dense black hair covering the backs of his hands came from behind a small counter to the right. He stared expectantly, but said nothing.

The driver, who looked like Central Casting for Aryan—tall, well built, blond-and-blue—said, "Dmitri?"

"Over there," the squat man said, pointing at a table to the left, where a thick-bodied man in a dark suit sat alone, his back to the wall.

The driver pushed the cripple over to Dmitri. The Russian didn't offer his hand. Just watched, taking a long, deep drag of his cigarette. The red Dunhills package was on the table to his left.

The cripple waved his hand vaguely at the attendant, who immediately turned smartly and walked out of the restaurant.

The attendant paused on the sidewalk for maybe five seconds. Then he re-entered the ambulette, climbing behind the wheel.

I was alone with Dmitri.

"So?" is all he said.

"You don't recognize me, old friend?" I asked him.

"No. How would I—?"

"Listen to my voice, Dmitri. Listen close. You've heard it before. On the phone. In person. When we were packing that satchel together a few months ago. Remember?"

"You're . . ."

"In my hand, under the tablecloth, there's a .357 Magnum. Six heavy hollowpoints in the chamber. Listen. . . ."

The sound of the hammer clicking back was a thunderclap in the silence between us, as distinctive to Dmitri as a cancerous cell to an oncologist.

"We are not alone here," he said, calmly.

"Every one of your men's behind me. They couldn't get between you and the bullets."

"Perhaps not. But you would never—"

"I don't care," I said softly. Giving him time to read my face, see that I meant it.

He nodded slowly. "What do you want?"

"Good," I said, acknowledging his understanding. "You thought I was dead, right?"

"Everybody thought you were dead," he said, shrugging.

"Sure. There's only two ways it could have gone down. Either you set me up, or someone set you up."

"There is another way."

"And what's that?"

"Burke, this was business. You understand? Just business. These people come to me. They say their child is kidnapped. And the man who has him will return him for money. They want me to deliver the money. And they will pay for that service. I tell them, of course we will do that. I would have sent one of my people. But then they say there is a condition. It must be *you* who delivers the money."

"Me by name, right? So they knew . . . ?"

"That we had done business together? Yes, I think. Otherwise, why would they think I could . . . ?"

"All right. So you knew it was me they wanted. And that it was no kidnapping."

"That I did *not* know. It is all over the street, how you feel about kids. And about those who . . . use them. I thought perhaps they wanted someone who might do more than just pick up the child."

Dmitri was good. That last bit was a slick stroke. "But they didn't approach me themselves," I pointed out, nice and calm.

"If they had, would you have done it?"

"Not without references." I took a slow breath. "So you're saying *that's* what they paid you for, huh?"

"It is all how you look at it. I did not think it was a plan to murder you. Otherwise, why put all that money into your hands?"

"Because if we hadn't counted it—together, remember?—I wouldn't have gone out that night."

"I did not know, I tell you."

"Which means the hit squad wasn't yours."

"If it had been mine, you would not be here."

"They were pros, Dmitri. They just got a little unlucky. And a couple of them got dead."

"Ah. This I have not heard."

"Okay, who was it who hired you?"

"That I could not say."

"You mean, *won't* say, right?"

"It would be bad business. They were clients. They paid for a service. I delivered that service. I have a reputation."

"Me, too."

"Yes. You are a professional, as I am. I don't believe you would attempt to kill me in my own place. And, anyway, what would you kill me *for*? I am not going to tell you their names. And you're alive. . . ."

"They killed my dog."

"Your . . . *dog*?"

"My dog," I said, willing the trembling out of my voice. I wouldn't say her name in front of this . . . professional. "So that's enough. For me, anyway. Enough for me to blast you right here. Either you give up the names, or I pull the trigger."

"That is a child's bluff," Dmitri said gently, spreading his hands wide. "I am sorry, Burke. But you—"

The explosion sucked all the sound out of the room in its wake. Dmitri slammed back into the wall, gut-shot. I stepped out of the wheelchair, hit the switch on the armrest, took a deep breath, and walked around to where Dmitri lay on the floor. He looked dead. I put three rounds into his face. His head bounced on the floor. When it came to rest, his brains were outside his skull.

The compartment under the wheelchair was spewing thick yellow smoke. I stepped through it and saw two men with Uzis standing in the entranceway to the restaurant. As soon as I emerged, they started blasting away—shooting high, the spray keeping everyone on the ground. I walked toward them, then between them, and jumped into the passenger seat of the van. The engine was running, the van was already in gear, the driver holding his foot on the brake . . . and a semi-auto in his hand. The spray-team piled in behind me, and the van took off.

We never even heard a siren.

I carefully removed the clear plastic shrouding from my finger-nails, one by one. Then I started soaking my right hand in a jar of kerosene—revolvers really spread their powder residue around. The dismembered pistol was already on its way to an acid bath.

I felt like a man who'd just worked a long shift at a lousy job. The same job that would be waiting on me tomorrow.

I went back to being dead. Stayed deep underground. Spent every day working out, harder and harder. It was nearing Christmas by the time I heard from the Mossad man.

"His name is Anton."

"The new boss?"

"Yes. But not easily, not without bloodshed. Some of Dmitri's old crew have moved on. The new organization is smaller."

"And this Anton, he's not ex-military?"

"No," the Mossad man replied. "He's an ex-convict. A career criminal."

Like me, flickered in my thoughts before it blinked out. "Thank you," is all I said.

"Who is this?" The voice on the phone was hard and weaselish at the same time.

"My name doesn't matter," I told him. "I'm the one who sent you that present . . . the one wrapped in green paper with a red ribbon."

"Ah!" he grunted. "What is it that you want?"

"You got the present. The ten grand was in exchange for a piece of information."

"What information?" he asked, suspicion dominating.

"Nothing about you. Or your crew. Dmitri dealt with some people a few months ago. I know he kept records. I know you have those records. All I want is their name and address."

"How would I know which—?"

"They were a married couple. Russians. Not in the business. She was a doctor, he was a scientist. Their child had been kidnapped."

"How much is this information worth to you?"

"Ten thousand dollars, Anton. And I already paid you."

"I think it is maybe worth more."

So he already knew. "Maybe it is worth twice that," I came back, surprising him.

He paused, then responded, "Agreed."

"Okay. You already have half in front from me. A good-faith payment. To show my respect. I will get the other half to you when you give me the information."

"How could I be sure of this?"

"Remember the rest of the present I sent you?"

"The piece of chalk?"

"Yes."

"What is the purpose of that?"

"For your people to draw the outline around your body. You know, like the cops did around Dmitri. When he was on the floor, dead. I gave him the same choice I'm giving you. He picked wrong. So now I deal with you. If you pick wrong, I deal with whoever follows *you*, understand?"

"You threaten me?"

"Threaten? I am making you the same offer I made Dmitri, that's all."

"Dmitri was a fool. He thought that the most important thing was to be some . . . soldier," he said, spitting on the last word.

"You and me, we're alike," I told him. "We're not soldiers, we're businessmen. A soldier's mistake is different from a businessman's mistake. Greed, that is a businessman's mistake. Not one you want to make. Twenty thousand dollars for the information, that's enough."

"Call back here in twenty-four hours," he said. And hung up.

I pushed the "off" button on the cell phone. Then I used a hammer and a blowtorch to turn it into a puddle of untraceable plastic.

"A soldier is nothing but an armed bureaucrat," he said the next night. "And Dmitri proves it. Everything, he wrote down. Everything. An idiot."

"Government is government," I agreed.

He grunted in self-satisfaction. Then he slowly gave me a name, address, and phone number as if he was reading the info off an index card.

"Chicago?"

"Everything that is here, I just tell you."

"All right. I believe you."

"The rest of the money . . . ?"

"Is yours as soon as I check out the information."

"You said that you—"

"I said I believed *you*. Dmitri, that remains to be seen."

"What are you saying?"

"I offered you two choices. If the information is true, then you have earned the money."

"If it is not? If Dmitri . . . ?"

"Then that's it," I lied. "You keep what you have, and we'll be square."

I hung up on whatever he was in the middle of saying.

"Chi-Town?" the Prof asked me, puzzled.

"That part is legit," I told him. "Dmitri *said* the snatch took place in Chicago. What happened was, it made the Chicago *papers*, but they lived in Winnetka—it's like a suburb. A rich suburb. Anyway, that's where they lived *then*. And I figured they'd moved here after it happened. But maybe not . . ."

"Never change phone," Mama said.

I looked across the table at her. The first time I'd been in the restaurant since before . . . since before it happened. Mama hadn't reacted to my new face, just snapped her fingers for the tureen of hot-and-sour soup as if nothing had changed.

"Right," is all I said, acknowledging the truth. Your child gets kidnapped, the one thing you never change is your phone number. Just in case. Even after years and years. But phone calls could be forwarded. Maybe they carried a cellular everywhere they went, never used it for anything else, waiting—an amulet against the unthinkable.

"That chance can't dance," the Prof snapped. "Remember what that Dmitri motherfucker said, Schoolboy—they said it *had* to be you. You got the street-brand here, no question. *Too* much of it, you ask me. But Chicago? Son, your star don't shine that far."

"So they were living here, then? And the Chicago address is a dud?"

"Maybe Cossacks all lie," Mama said darkly, the memory of some obscure Sino-Soviet conflict igniting behind the emotionless mask of her face.

"Let's just go with what we know," the Prof said. "Click it off."

"All right," I told them. "It was a hit. I was the target. There were at least four of them. It was a good plan. I'd done that kind of work before—middlemanned a handover—so it made sense they'd pick me. And they knew I'd go for it, the kind of money they were paying. They picked a spot that should have been perfect. Even the kid—that was a sweet touch. I was *expecting* a kid. Gave them an extra split-second to get off first, before I snapped wise. They might have figured I'd have backup, but they didn't think anyone could get close enough without tipping them off. They didn't figure on the Kevlar, though. Or on . . ."

My throat stopped up. I couldn't say any more.

"She went out the way I want to, son," the Prof said, reading me like I was forty-point type.

"Yeah." I ignored the pain-flash, got back to my summary. "They were cool under fire. At least their leader was. Took the extra time to make sure I was gone, picked up their dead, didn't leave a trace."

"They thought they left *you*, mahn," Clarence said.

"Wouldn't have mattered," I told him. "That wasn't unprofessional of them; it was smart. With my track record, being found dead in Hunts Point—what would it tell the cops? Nothing. Nothing to connect to them, and a ton of possible suspects out there, too."

"That's where *we* got to look," the Prof said.

"I don't get it."

"Listen up, then. *We* got to be the detectives now. Whoever tried to ice you, it cost *someone* serious money. Took a lot of time, involved a lot of people. That's got to be personal. The people who tried to do the job, I figure them for mercs. Hired hands. But the rest, that was about blood. Someone who hates you enough to do all that planning and spending. And someone who knows you enough to figure you'd go for that kid-exchange thing, too."

"That's not a short list," I said.

"Might be a *real* short list, we can get alone with those Russians for a few minutes."

"I don't think Anton—the guy who took over from Dmitri—I don't think he was lying."

"These people must be registered," Clarence said, suddenly.

"What?"

"Immigration, mahn. I know about this. I do not know how much truth there is in what you were told, but, if they were from another country, they would not be citizens so easily. They could move, but they would have to notify . . ."

I exchanged a look with Mama. She nodded.

I thought about it later, watching alone as the gray dawn drove off the black night. I knew the best info-trafficker in the City. And what I had to do.

A public place is the safest," Wolfe said over the phone, unaware she was echoing me from . . . before it happened.

"Safer for who?" I asked her, trying to reach across the barrier I'd built between us.

"Me," she said, flat.

"You think that . . . ? You think *I'd* ever . . . ?"

"What're you saying to me?" she challenged. "That I *know* better, right? That I know *you*?"

"I thought you did."

"So did I," she told me.

After so many years of wanting to be with her, I'd finally . . . had a chance, is the best way I could put it.

When you come to a fork in the road, you're supposed to stop and consider your choices. Me, I never even checked for oncoming traffic.

I'd had a chance. A real one, not some convict's fantasy. Whenever there's a choice, there's a chance. You know how men are always fearing they're getting past it, that they won't be able to do the things they once did? Not me. I wish I *had* been past it. Wish I'd changed.

But I'd gone right back to my old ways with that Albanian arms deal. Then blood came up. Pansy's blood. And it filled my eyes until I went blind.

I might have gotten Wolfe to listen about the guns. Maybe. Plenty of citizens here thought we should have been arming the Kosovars. But it was just a matter of time before her wires dipped deep enough into the whisper-stream to pick up on who did Dmitri right in his own joint.

When I'd killed Dmitri, I'd done the same thing to my chance with Wolfe.

It's harder to spot tags in bad weather. You see a guy behind you wearing a ski mask in July, you don't have to be a CIA agent to know something's off. But with the sleet coming down New York–style—cold, dirty, and crooked—everybody was bundled up.

I docked the yellow cab, watchfully. The cab stand was empty—weather like this, every hackster in the city was out there scoring. I rent a cab whenever I need to move around invisibly. For years, I had a deal with a dispatcher for a fleet. He'd pull a cab out of service, let me use it for a shift. I'd pay him for the use of the cab, and give him whatever I put on the meter, too. It would go on the books like he was driving himself that day, and we were both happy.

But the fleets are just about gone now. What you have is individual owners or mini-fleets—two cabs and up. TLC medallions are limited, and they go for a fortune when they're auctioned off. The only way to buy one is to finance it through a broker, and the new owners have to keep their cabs in motion around the clock to make the payments. So what they usually do is drive one shift themselves, then rent their cab out for the others. It's called a horse-hire. The renter pays a flat fee, keeps whatever he pulls in.

It's a gamble, especially since the renter pays for his own gas, too. Some of them cut the odds with removable meter chips— reprogrammed to click off extra mileage—but most of them work seven days, never stopping, urinating into plastic soda-bottles, eating while driving, saving every dime . . . so they can buy one of those precious medallions for themselves. Midtown Manhattan is cab-clogged all the time. But try to find one in Brooklyn, or get one to take you to Queens. Even if you're white.

But I never have a problem getting one of the horse-hire guys to take two fifty cash for a shift. He wouldn't book that much profit on his own, and he can have a day off with pay. I've got a valid hack license—the only thing fake about the plastic dash-placard is the name. And Clarence had picked up cabs for me before, so the guy I was renting from wouldn't have to get all nervous at my new face.

It was four blocks to where I had to meet Wolfe. I had a half-hour to cover the ground. If anyone was following me, they were better than I was.

esley taught me there's no such thing as a dead man. Only bodies go into the ground. If you leave footprints deep enough, you're still around.

Long after Wesley died, a kidnapper-killer came on the scene. A creature so rational from emotion-stripping that he went lunar from it. He knew the secret. He had Wesley's ice in him. So deep he thought he could take over. *Be* Wesley.

I was in the middle of that. And, at the end, the only one left standing.

That was when Wolfe told me I had the choice. I could . . . maybe . . . be with her. All I had to do was find out. Was it me I had to change, or just my ways?

It turned out to be me. And I couldn't do it.

She was sitting in the back corner, at a table by herself. It was one of those places where you order your meal at a counter, then carry it over to any empty spot. I saw she had a mug of something in front of her, so I stopped and got myself a hot chocolate. Then I walked over to her. Slow. Making sure she picked up on my approach.

"It's me," I said. Same way I'd introduced myself during our last phone call, relying on her knowing my voice.

"I know," she replied, motioning with her head for me to sit down.

She looked the same. Long lustrous hair flowing like a mane, red-tinged brunette except for two white wings flaring back from the temples. Pale gunfighter's eyes. A soft sweet mouth, now drawn flat.

"I know I must look—"

"You look the same to me," she said. I knew it was the truth. Real women, they don't see with their eyes, the way men do. Good damn thing, or I'd still be a virgin.

"It didn't happen the way you heard," I told her, keeping my voice soft, watching her eyes.

She didn't look away. "How do you know what I heard?"

"I don't . . . exactly. But I know you think I . . ."

"And you didn't?"

"That part is true. But it wasn't like you think."

"You keep telling me what I heard, what I think. . . . Why don't you just say whatever you have to say?"

"I had a job. A kid had been snatched, and the people who had him wanted to return him. For cash. I was supposed to be the transfer-man."

"What does that have to do with—?"

"Let me finish, all right? You wanted me to say it, I will. This isn't bullshit; it's background."

She nodded slowly. Didn't say anything more.

"The guy who set the whole thing up was . . . the guy who got himself killed."

"And you didn't—?"

I cut her off with a stare. She held it just long enough to show me she wasn't intimidated, then nodded again. That's when I saw Pepper out of the corner of my eye, reading *Variety* at a table off to the side. Pepper works with Wolfe. Her citizen job is being an actress, but she's part of the network, has been for a long time. And if Pepper was around, her man, Mick, wouldn't be far away. Wolfe met me without backup plenty of times. I could see those days were over.

"This . . . guy, he was the only one I dealt with. I went to the meet wrapped so heavy I could barely walk. It was out in Hunts Point. I had cover, but they had to hang back. The kid—well, *a* kid, anyway—he stepped out of the car and blasted me. No warning, no conversation. He came out shooting. It wasn't a swap; it was a hit. And I was the target."

"How could they know it would be you?" Wolfe asked, her years as a prosecutor overriding anything she was feeling. Or not feeling.

"Not what you're thinking," I said. "The . . . dead guy . . . he didn't pick me. The people whose kid got kidnapped, *they* picked me. That was one of their conditions, I found out later: it had to be me to deliver the money."

"You checked the—?"

"There *was* a kidnapping. It was in the papers. And the transfer-money was all there. Every dime."

"How many were on the set?"

"At least four, counting the kid. If he was a kid. I *think* he was. But it was dark, and I wasn't that close."

"Just you. And four of them. And still you . . . ?"

"When the kid popped me, I took the rounds in the Kevlar . . . and whatever that stuff was that the Mole wove over it. I dropped. Pansy charged out of the car. She went for the kid. The guy behind me, the one picking up the money, he shot at her, but he missed. Pansy got the kid. Brought him down. Two others came out of their truck. My people opened up. The leader—the guy with the money in his hand—he told them to clear out. But to finish me first. That's when I got . . . this," I said, touching the right side of my face.

"So they John Doe'ed you at the hospital?"

"Yeah. Only this happened in Hunts Point, right? But I was transferred. When I came to, I was in Manhattan."

"Why?"

"I don't know."

"Did your people drop any of them?"

"Pansy got one," I said, my voice strangling on pride and pain. "She got the kid. They . . . killed her. Right there. Right in front of me. They killed her and there was nothing I could . . ."

My face was leaking. Just on the right side. I wiped it away with my palm, hard.

"Another one of them got it, too. But they took their dead with them. And my people took Pansy. There's nothing left there but blood in the ground."

"So you went back to . . . the person . . . to find out . . . what?"

"A lot of stuff. But once I found out that the people whose kid was taken made it part of the deal that I be the transfer-man, all I wanted was how to find them."

"And he wouldn't—?"

"He killed my dog," I cut her off. "He killed Pansy."

Wolfe took a sip of her coffee, her pale eyes steady on me. "People say things like that all the time. 'If anyone ever hurt my dog, I'd kill them.' But they don't mean it. It's just their way of saying how much they love their pet."

"Pansy wasn't my—"

"I know," she said, gently. "But what do you have now?"

"You mean, without that . . . person, right? Here's what I have: The names and last known address of the people who hired him. And the knowledge that somebody wants me dead bad enough to pay a whole ton of money to get it done."

"You're well away," she said. "It's been months. Whoever wanted you, they don't know how to find you. If they could, they would have made their move already."

"I'm not going to spend the rest of my life as a target."

"What's the difference, if you're a target they can't hit?"

"Because there's other things I'd rather be."

"For instance?"

"At the other end of the sniper-scope," I said.

She looked into me. I wanted to reach across the table and just . . . touch her hand, maybe. But I froze. It was her call.

"I need a few days," she said. "And your passport."

I handed it over. Wolfe got up and walked away. Pepper flashed me her trademark grin, telling me to stay where I was. I could feel someone standing just behind me. I sipped my cold hot chocolate, alone.

When I was a kid, I thought there was a way not to hurt. I wanted to be like Wesley. Ice. So cold inside that I wouldn't feel a thing. Wesley was the only one I ever knew who actually got past it all. He had no hate in him. Nothing made him angry. All he wanted was to get paid.

But he got tired. So tired that he checked out.

Wesley taught me the difference between sad and depressed. People never get that one. I was born sad. I probably knew my mother didn't want me even before she climbed out of that bed in the charity ward and strolled back to wherever I'd been sperm-donored. I'm what happens when the trick tricks the hooker.

My birth certificate may not have had a full name on it, but it did have a number—and I've had one or another of those ever since. I've been a file, a case, a subject, a foster kid, a mental case, a JD, a convict. None of the endless agencies ever knew me. They always got it wrong. But that didn't matter to them—they always had my number.

When you're depressed, it all slips away. You stop caring, about anything. A depressed person, he can't feel anything for anyone else. Empathy dies first.

That's the way they labeled Wesley. Killer sociopath. He wasn't a man; he was a machine. You gave Wesley a name, you got a body. And Wesley got paid. A never-miss, platinum-proof perfect assassin. No friends, no family, no lover, no pets. No apartment, no house, no home.

And what it finally came down to was . . . no reason to be here anymore.

He went out with a bang. A *big* bang, taking a couple hundred along for the ride. Those kids at Columbine? They weren't the first. Wesley was. He walked into an exclusive high school in the suburbs, carrying enough munitions to smoke every living human in the joint. And the truck he drove up in was full of some kind of poison gas, too. He went in there to die. And, like every other murder he planned, it worked.

Crazy. Maybe that's what you'd think. Depressed, suicidal. It wasn't any of that. He was tired, that's all.

He left me something. A note. A suicide note, the way the cops saw it. For me, it was an escape hatch. In that note, Wesley took the weight for a lot of stuff I did. Signed it with his own fingerprint . . . the only part of him that the world ever recognized.

If he'd been depressed, instead of just DNA-deep sad, he wouldn't have looked out for me that one last time. We were brothers. Came up together.

Wesley was ice, even then. I wanted to be just like him, once.

It was Wesley himself who told me the truth. He had no fear in him. And it wasn't worth it.

So I knew. I wasn't depressed; I was sad. I don't know what other people who are sad do to fight back. I know *some* of what they do. Drugs, booze, sex—risks. I don't know if it works for them, or for how long. But, for me, I could BASE-jump on cocaine and it wouldn't change a fucking thing.

The only thing I ever can do is let both the monsters in. Fear and Rage. One keeps me alive and the other makes people dead. If you took them from me, I'd just be sad. Nothing else. Empty and sad. That's when the Zero calls. That's when I want to go and be with Wesley.

Maybe it would be like when we were kids. Leaning up against an alley wall, sharing a cigarette, eyes scanning, on full alert. Waiting.

Depending on who showed, we'd run, fight, or rob them.

But I don't really believe that. I know where Wesley is. I know why they call it the Zero.

But it pulls me, still.

Max got back from Mama's, came upstairs to my room, signed "telephone." Then tapped his heart, pointed at me.

I shrugged a "Huh?" back at him.

He made the gesture for "Wolfe."

I called at eleven, like she'd left word to.

"It's me."

"Immigration has them still at that address."

"Illinois?"

"Yes."

"Could it just be lag-time in getting the records updated?"

"It could be," Wolfe said softly, "if I were relying on their records."

I got the message. "Last contact?" I asked.

"Almost a year ago. They made an application to sponsor a relative."

"I'm missing a piece. More than one."

"We've got someone out there."

"INS?"

"Chicago PD."

"You said . . . Never mind. He's *with* you? Or just someone who can be worked with?"

"The former. And you and he have mutual interests, anyway."

"How could that be?"

"He wants the missing kid," Wolfe said.

Even if the DEA wasn't lurking around every big-city airport, fitting passengers into their lame "profiles," everyone on my side of the line knows better than to buy a ticket with cash. That one's a guaranteed red flag. They want photo ID now, too, so slipping through the cracks isn't as easy as it used to be.

I didn't know how far my new face would take me. Didn't know if they had an alert out. My old mug shots wouldn't match up. I knew they'd photographed me in the hospital more than once, but never without the bandages. Still, the two Bronx detectives had seen the new face enough times so a police sketch artist could probably get pretty close.

It had been a long time. Happened in late August; now it was the tail end of January. Wolfe said there were no wants-and-warrants out on me. But that didn't mean they weren't looking—you don't need a warrant to bring someone in for "questioning," especially a two-time felony loser with no known address.

I wasn't worried that anyone loyal to Dmitri was looking. I didn't think there was anyone loyal to Dmitri still alive. If they were, they were holed up somewhere, waiting for their chance to get out of town. Or for a clear shot at Anton.

But whoever set the whole thing up, *they* were waiting. Or thought I was dead. And I had no way to tell which.

I shook my head, as if the movement would clear my thoughts. There were too many possibilities. And not enough data. Maybe whoever set it up *did* think I was dead. The shooters would have reported that I'd been hit. And that they'd put a round into my skull to make sure. An unidentified guy found dead in the Hunts Point wasteland wouldn't have been enough to make the papers.

There *would* be a record, though. Homicides get investigated, even if not all equally. There'd be an attempt to identify any dead body. And if whoever tried to cap me knew anything about me, they'd know my prints would fall in five minutes.

So they had a tight time-frame, a location, and plenty of resources. And with Dmitri getting blown away, more than enough to add it up. I had to play it like a hand of five-card stud, now down to the final bet. I couldn't see their hole card, but there were enough other gamblers at the table so that I had a pretty good count of the deck. I was betting they knew they hadn't finished the job.

Wolfe had returned my passport. Some guy nobody recognized dropped it off at Mama's. It was the same one I'd given her in the restaurant: the beautiful forgery she'd had made for me a while back. The new one had the same phony name. Only now the photo matched my new face.

But that didn't mean I should be quick to use it. No matter how big the organization that had tried to kill me was, they couldn't have been watching all the ways out of town—especially *this* town—for the past few months. So they couldn't trap me at the border. But they could follow my trail . . . if I was dumb enough to leave paper footprints.

Clarence drove me to Philly. Only took a couple of hours, even with the sporadic snow. I shouldered my duffel bag and stepped into the terminal at Thirtieth and Market, where I grabbed an Amtrak for D.C. It was about ten minutes by cab from Union Station to the bus depot. I was on a Greyhound to Chicago by a little past midnight.

We hit Pittsburgh by morning, changed buses in Cleveland, made a rest stop somewhere in Indiana, and rolled into Chicago around three-thirty in the afternoon. Going by bus, it takes quite a while. And you have to do without a lot of features the airlines provide. Like metal detectors.

"You know this town?" The voice on the phone was cop-hard, but with an unmistakable Irish lilt.

"Been here a few times is all."

"You're not far from Wells Street. Just walk south—away from the lake—a couple of blocks. There's a bookstore in the twelve-hundred block. Big one. Called Barbara's. They're used to all kinds of people in there. I'll meet you outside at nine tonight. Just stand outside, to the left of the door as you come out. You smoke, right?"

"No."

"Well, just *carry* a cigarette, then. Explains why you're standing outside in this weather."

"Okay."

The bookstore was much bigger than a first glance would tell you. When I walked in, I saw a long narrow corridor with a counter to the right. But it spread out to my left, and just kept going. I wandered through the stacks, passing time until the meet. Walls of books. I thought about how much reading I'd done since . . . it happened. When I realized how close I'd come to losing my sight, I turned as indiscriminately greedy as a just-paroled prisoner in a whorehouse. I read everything I could get my hands on. Once I settled down, I kept up the reading but got more selective.

The last few months had been a lot like being back Inside. Reading, lifting weights . . . getting ready. And most of the time spent scheming about what I was getting ready for.

I spotted a new Joe Lansdale novel, one I hadn't read. I almost grabbed it, but I checked myself in time. Maybe they wouldn't remember every customer, but they were much more likely to remember someone who'd actually made a purchase. Independent bookstores aren't like the chains. The people who work for the indies, most of them really love books. They'll use any purchase to engage you in a conversation, find out what you like, try to hand-sell you something *they* like.

My cheap plastic electronic watch said it was five minutes to the meet. I knew it kept better time than the Rolex I had stashed in my duffel. I stepped outside and stood with my back to the building, cupping my hands around the flame from the butane lighter as I got a cigarette going. As soon as I did that, a flashlight blinked on and off from inside a white Nissan sedan parked at the curb. The passenger window moved down in sync with my approach. I leaned in.

"How's Wolfe these days?" the driver said.

I got in.

"Clancy," he said as he pulled away, holding out his right hand.

Askew," I told him, shaking his hand. "Wayne Askew."

"Wolfe's?" he asked. Meaning: he knew my true name, and was the new ID one of Wolfe's creations?

"Yeah."

He nodded, satisfied. Wolfe's papers were the best in the business. If I got popped in his jurisdiction, odds were I'd get past the screens—as long as they stopped short of printing me.

The Nissan was overflowing. One cell phone was recharging from the cigarette-lighter outlet in the console, another sat on top of the dash, next to a small tape recorder, two pagers, and a notebook. There were a half-dozen pens clipped to the dash, and a sheaf of papers bulged from behind the sun visor. The windshield featured a series of hairline cracks. The ones in the dash were well past hairline, deep scars that showed the foam padding underneath. The back seat was covered with cartons, their tops cut off to make a filing system. Books were stacked haphazardly throughout the car, like pebbles from a carelessly tossed *I Ching* reading.

"You got a place?" he asked.

"No. I figured I'd wait until—"

"Okay. Where's your stuff stashed?"

"Bus station. Twenty-four-hour locker."

He nodded, not saying anything, letting the fact that we were heading for the depot speak for itself. He stopped outside. I went in, opened the locker, grabbed my duffel. When I got outside, I saw his trunk was open. I tossed the bag inside and climbed back into the passenger seat.

"You got a change of clothes with you?"

"Sure."

"I mean a *change*, not fresh clothes. If you want to work the area I think you do, you have to dress the part. Can you go upscale with what you're carrying around?"

"I can if I can get into a decent place for a few hours, take out the creases, clean up, and all; no problem."

"All right. What about cash?"

"How much do you—?"

I interrupted myself when I saw the look on his face. Mumbled, "Sorry."

"You think we're all a pack of bribe-taking slobs?" he said, chuckling.

"No," I said truthfully. "A lot of cops aren't slobs."

"Hah! All right, look, the thing about money is this: you're going to *need* money if you want to poke around in the ritzy suburbs. That homeless-guy look you're wearing, the only thing it'll get you in the places you need to visit is rousted."

"Fair enough."

"And you'll need transport, too."

"I can pay whatever it costs. But I don't want to book this ID if I don't have to."

"I can get you a car. But not Hertz rates."

"I'm fine with that."

The hotel was right off the lake. We walked straight over to the elevators. The security man at the entrance to the elevator bank opened his mouth, then shut it without a sound when Clancy grabbed his eyes.

The room was on the twenty-first floor, with a view of a driving range below.

"It's three hundred a night," Clancy said. "That includes the room showing as vacant on the computer."

I handed him twelve C-notes, saying, "For the car, too," as I did.

"Be downstairs tomorrow morning," he said. "Six a.m., okay?"

"I'll be there," I told him.

I unzipped the duffel, started laying out my stuff carefully. Especially that shark-gray alpaca suit Michelle had insisted I spend a fortune on.

"This will never show a *hint* of a wrinkle, honey," she'd said. "Just hang it in the bathroom and run the shower full-blast hot for an hour or so—it'll be new every time you put it on."

Remembering her muttered threats about never allowing a wire coat-hanger to invade the sacred alpaca, I located a wooden one in the closet and got the steam working.

Everything I had with me was new. Michelle had measured me herself, done all the shopping. That way, she got to do all the selecting.

"You need a *look*, sweetheart," she said, talking quick and nervous, the way she does when a topic upsets her. "With that face . . . until it heals, I mean—then you can have plastic surgery and it'll all be . . . Anyway, in an Army jacket, you look like a serial killer. But in *these* clothes, baby, you'll look exotic, I swear it."

So I'd kept quiet while she spent my money on all this new stuff. Didn't bother to bring up that I already had a place full of new clothes, an abandoned factory building near the Eastern District High School in Bushwick. That had been about Pansy, too. I'd watched her being carried out of my old place on a stretcher, the whole place surrounded by NYPD. I thought they'd killed her, but they'd only tranq'ed her out. We managed to spring her from the shelter, but I'd had to find a new place. And leave everything I had in the old one.

When that happened, Michelle had said what a great opportunity it was—I'd needed a whole new wardrobe, anyway. Now that was gone, too.

NYPD had come calling because my old landlord had 911'ed me, saying the crawl space in his building where I lived was being used by a bunch of Arabs as a bomb factory. I'd had a sweet deal with him for a lot of years. His son was a rat who loved his work. I'd run across the little weasel hiding in the Witness Protection Program when I was looking for someone else, and I traded my silence for the free rent. It was unused space up there anyway; didn't cost the owner a penny.

But when his kid got smoked in Vegas, the landlord decided I was the one who'd given him up, and dropped a ten-ton dime on me. Pansy might have been killed then, but the cops had heard her threats when they'd started battering the door down. So they'd called for Animal Control instead of going in—no way to tell a dog you've got a warrant.

I tracked the landlord's unlisted phone and rang him one night. Told him I'd had nothing to do with what happened to his kid—the punk was addicted to informing, and Vegas was the wrong town for that hobby. I also told him that my dog could've been killed by his little trick.

He said he was sorry. He'd just assumed it was me who fingered his son. He said he'd make it right.

I told him he'd never see it coming.

Lying on the hotel bed in the Chicago night, I told myself the truth. The people who'd tried to hit me, they were pros. No question about it. Just a job. The ones I wanted were the string-pullers, not the puppets.

But the puppets had killed Pansy.

I thought about the setup I'd had for her, back at my place. The huge stainless-steel bowl anchored in a chunk of cement so it could withstand her onslaughts, the inverted water-cooler bottle, the dry dog food she could get for herself if I wasn't around, the tarpapered roof where I'd take her so she could dump her loads without my having to walk her on the street. The giant rawhide bone that she adored so much she'd never annihilated it the way she had every other toy I'd gotten her, the heavy velour bathrobe she used as a blanket, the sheepskin she slept on . . .

Training her with reverse commands, so that "Sit!" meant attack. Poison-proofing her so she wouldn't take food unless she heard the key word. Working with a long pole and a series of hired agitators until she'd learned to hit thigh-high, not leave her feet and make herself vulnerable.

Playing with her in the park. Coming home to her and never being alone when I did.

Looking out at the dark, my hand on her neck, together against whatever might be out there.

The vet telling me her arthritis just meant she was getting old. Telling me she didn't have forever; at seventeen, Pansy was way past the limit for her breed.

Knowing that I might prolong her life with a special diet, but that she'd rather go out earlier and keep getting the treats she loved so much. The only change I'd made was that I never let her near chocolate anymore. The vet told me chocolate was toxic to dogs, could even be fatal. So I'd switched her to honey-vanilla ice cream.

Glad I had made that decision now.

But so fucking sad that, some nights, I was afraid to sleep.

I was getting used to my reflection in the mirror. Michelle had made all the cosmetology decisions. "Your hair changed color, baby. I was going to touch it back to black for you. But you know what? I think steel's your color. And keep it very short—that's so very severe." I never got it together enough to ask her what the hell that meant.

I was going to grow a beard, just to let it cover the bullet-scar. But it was a failure. The damn thing grew in black, streaked with red and white—called a lot more attention to my face than the scar would.

Michelle fixed that, too. She gave me some stuff that came in a tube like lipstick, but once on, it blended with my complexion. "One girl's scar is another's beauty mark," she had explained. I never asked her what that meant, either. I'd heard enough when she said that I was lucky to have lost an eyebrow to the surgeon's pre-op razor because it would grow back in neat and clean and men never pay attention to their eyebrows and they're what set off the eyes and . . .

The outside sky was dark. Couldn't get a clue about the weather. Checked my watch, the white-gold Rolex now. "It's not ultra-ultra, like Patek Philippe or Piquet," Michelle had counseled, "but it goes with the look. Yellow gold would be tacky, and stainless would be too down-market. This is perfect."

I didn't feel perfect, but it was time to go.

Clancy was in the lobby when I came down, chatting with the girl at the front desk. He took out a small notebook, wrote something down. I didn't think it was a license number.

He strolled over to where I was standing, said, "You got a coat with you?"

"Just what you saw yesterday. It wouldn't go with this."

"Traveling light, huh?"

"Yep," I said. Thinking of the twin to the Python that had totaled Dmitri, now taped inside the toilet tank in its waterproof wrap.

"Well, it's no big deal. We'll be indoors."

I followed him outside, where he handed something to a guy in a hotel uniform. Whatever he handed him was wrapped in green.

The Lexus SUV that rolled up to where we were standing was green, too. At least, I'd call it green—Lexus probably calls it something like Rainforest Morning Mist Emerald. Clancy walked around to the driver's side. I climbed into the front bucket seat.

"You've got a valid driver's license?" he asked, as he pulled onto an eight-lane divided highway and hit the gas.

"New York," I told him. Thinking how the photo wouldn't exactly be a perfect match now.

"Good enough. This is the car you're borrowing. I have to teach a class today. Turns out it's right in Winnetka. You come along, get a chance to scope out the area, right?"

"Sure. What's the tariff on the car?"

"There isn't any. It's a police impound, seized in a drug bust. It's already been vacuumed and tagged. The plan is to use it as an undercover vehicle in a few weeks. The plates will trace right back to my department, so, if you get in a jackpot, tell the arresting officer to call up and ask for me. They'll make you for a CI."

"Okay. Thanks."

"Well, you can't cruise around the neighborhood you want in a Chevy. This one, nobody'll notice."

I made a sound to indicate I understood. He drove in silence for a bit, then said: "We're on Lake Shore Drive. That's Lake Michigan out there. When it's on your right, you're heading north."

"I thought you were a Chicago cop," I said.

"I am."

"But you're teaching a class in Winnetka?"

"Believe it or not, Winnetka's still part of Cook County. We wouldn't patrol there, of course, but it's inside our jurisdiction for the classes."

"What kind of classes?"

"It's called Licensed for Life," he said, a deep, rich vein of pride in his voice. "The idea is to give kids interactive information about drunk driving, try to save a few lives."

"Does it work?"

"Well, I can tell you this, we taught thirteen hundred classes last year, all by request. And from the feedback we get from the kids, we believe they're really taking it in. There's no way to give you statistics, not yet. The program is too new. But there's no question that tons of kids have contacted us *after* the classes, telling us about situations where they took action to avoid *becoming* a statistic. We don't give grades, we're not part of the faculty, so there's no point in brown-nosing us. And, besides, all these years in the business, I can tell when somebody's hosing me. They're not."

The highway narrowed a lane or two. Still heading north, near as I could tell, but I couldn't see the lake anymore to orient myself.

"We're on Sheridan now," Clancy said. "Ahead of schedule."

I restrained myself from saying that, the way he drove, we'd be ahead of *any* damn schedule.

"First class isn't till eight," he said, glancing at his watch. "I know a place where we can get some coffee."

"Who pays for the classes?" I asked him, sipping my hot chocolate.

"That's a good question," he said, chuckling ruefully. "We live on small grants. Sometimes they come in, sometimes they don't. It takes a long time to train an officer to give the classes. They get paid for every one they teach, but it doesn't even cover their travel expenses—sometimes you have to drive a three-hour round trip to teach a one-hour class. Everyone who's observed the program, everybody who's checked it out, they all love it. If we had a way to turn promises into dollars, we'd have the endowment we need. But, for now, we just scramble and hope."

"How come the insurance companies don't fund you? It sounds like a great investment for them. One drunk driver alone can cost them millions."

"We get a little from them. Not enough. Not near enough. We can't take tax money to do it—no way to get that past the city council. What we need is a commitment," he said, his tone saying he had already made one himself. "Some foundation to promise they're going to give us support for maybe ten years. Long enough for them to do their double-blind studies, prove on paper what we already know from actually *doing* it."

"You fancy your chances?"

"I'm Irish." He grinned.

The guard at the school entrance smiled and waved us in . . . once he made sure I was with Clancy. The teacher greeted us outside the classroom. He was a middle-aged, middle-sized man who looked tired. "Detective Clancy," he said, "thanks for coming."

"My pleasure," Clancy replied. "Let me introduce Mr. Askew. He's going to be working with us for a few days."

"Are you a police officer, too?" the teacher asked.

"I'm a filmmaker," I said quickly, before Clancy could respond. "We're interested in the possibilities of making a docu-drama about Licensed for Life."

"Well, that's a wonderful idea!" the teacher said, enthusiastically. "I've heard nothing but good things about it."

"I'm sure," I said, my tone implying that I'd need to make that decision for myself.

"You think I'm standing up here as a *joke*?" Clancy barked at the class, reacting to some giggling over in one corner. "You think all cops care about is taking bribes and eating donuts? You need to pay attention to this. *Close* attention, understand? This is serious business."

He reached in his breast pocket, took out a large white napkin that said DUNKIN' DONUTS in big red and orange letters. He began to clean his glasses with it as he glared at the students. The first student to spot it cracked up. In a minute, the whole class was laughing.

Somehow, Clancy took them from there through a series of anecdotes about drunk drivers that started out funny and ended ugly. By the time he got to a story about a "two-car, five-body" crash he was called out to investigate . . . and found his fifteen-year-old daughter in the back of a squad car, not badly injured herself, but assaulted by the image of her best friend's face splattered against the windshield . . . they were rapt, totally focused.

He backed off then, playing them expertly, like a professional angler giving a fish some line. He asked them questions they should have known the answers to—the penalties for driving under the influence, for instance—then provided the answers when they dropped the ball.

The finale was a pair of goggles he called "Fatal Vision." He told the class the glasses would show them what the world looked like through a drunk's eyes. One kid volunteered to try them out. Clancy walked him through the whole routine—fingertips to nose, walking a straight line—and the kid flopped like a fish on a pier. Then he asked the kid some simple problems—counting backwards, naming the last four presidents—and you could see the kid struggling before he came up with the responses. "Easier with your eyes *closed*, right?" Clancy asked him.

"Right!" the kid agreed.

"Some drunks try to *drive* that way," he said, harshly, offering the kid a high-five. The kid missed by three feet and would have fallen on his face if Clancy hadn't caught him. The class roared.

Clancy finished strong, telling them one truth after another. Some of them *were* going to drink. This wasn't about preaching abstinence—this was about survival. When he stopped talking, the class was dead silent. "Scared Sober," I thought, sarcastically. But then they broke out into spontaneous applause, their faces serious, some teary.

The teacher's face was a study in surprise—these kids were way too cool to clap, especially for a cop.

The bell rang for the next class. Clancy was surrounded by students, all trying to tell him something. Or ask him something.

The teacher just watched, his mouth gaping.

"Does it always go like that?" I asked Clancy, watching as we drove through a neighborhood so lush it seemed to bloom in the dead of winter.

"Pretty much," he said, smiling. "It's more art than science, and there's horses for courses. Some of the guys, they can work anywhere. Others, you have to pick their spots. But I've never done a class where I didn't get *some* response. Some . . . engagement."

"You really believe in this, don't you?"

"It's the most important thing I've ever done in my life," he said, conviction braided through his words. "I took out a second on my house to keep the program going while we wait on the foundations."

Wolfe had set this whole thing up like a blind date. I didn't know what she'd told Clancy about me, but she'd told me a lot about him. A karate expert, he'd once taken down two armed robbers without drawing his gun. He was *the* man when it came to coaxing confessions, practicing a different martial art there, combining his Irish charm with a cobra's interior coldness. He'd broken dozens of major cases, earned enough commendations to fill a file cabinet, graduated from the FBI National Academy. Gold medalist at the World Law Enforcement Olympics four straight times. Three kids, all top students.

"I get it," I told him. Telling him the truth.

He gave me a look. Held it. Then nodded as if he was agreeing with a diagnosis. "What do you feel comfortable telling me?" he asked.

I knew we were done talking about his dreams. "I'm looking for a couple, man and wife. I've got an address."

"You came all the way here to see if they'd be home?"

"No. They know something I need to know."

"You carrying?" he asked abruptly.

"No," I said, limiting my truth to handguns, not mentioning the Scottish sgian dubh—Gaelic for "black knife," a weapon of last resort—in my boot. The knife was a thing of special beauty; a gift from a brother of mine, a nonviolent aikidoist who knows there are situations where a man needs an edge.

"What's your cover?"

"I'm going to tell them I'm the law," I said. "Federal. You know their kid was—"

"Yeah. It's cold-cased now. But it's not closed."

"Right. *Supposedly*, the kidnapper made contact with them, told them he'd sell the kid back. They went to this guy in New York—"

"Why New York, if they live here?" he interrupted.

"*Supposedly*," I said, emphasizing the word again, making it clear that I wasn't buying any of the story—not anymore, "it was because they're Russians, and the guy they contacted, he's a big player in the Russian mob. They wanted a transfer-man."

"We've got no shortage of Russian gangsters here."

"I know. And it gets worse. What I found out—*after* the wheels came off—is that they came to the guy in New York insisting on me. That was part of the deal—I had to be the transfer-man."

"And the guy in New York, he told you . . . ?"

"Nothing. Made it seem like a regular handover situation, me getting paid to be in the middle. I've done it before."

"I know," he said, surprising me a little. I hadn't put any restrictions on what Wolfe could tell him, but she's usually real clingy about information.

"I didn't know they were from Chicago. The way it was rolled out to me, I figured they were local."

"So why not ask the local guy?"

"He's dead," I told him.

"Natural causes?"

"Considering his business, I'd say yeah."

He didn't blink. "Why is it so important? I mean, something was fishy, sure. But you're out of it, whatever it was."

"The transfer-money was half a million dollars. Plus another hundred for me to handle it. And whatever else they had to spread around."

"And . . . ?"

"And there *was* no kid. It wasn't a handover. I met them where they wanted, and they came out shooting."

"Is that where . . . ?" he asked, touching a spot on his own cheek.

"Yeah. Just a fluke they didn't total me."

"So it was all about you."

"Only about me. Whoever wanted me spent heavy cash, took some risks."

"But they missed."

"So?"

"Yeah. You figure they'll just try again, right?"

"I don't know how deep their connect runs. They can't be sure I'm *not* dead. I was down when the hit men took off. And they'd put one in my head before they left. I was on the hospital computer as a John Doe, but the cops knew who I was—they visited me a few times."

"What did you tell them?"

"That I lost my memory. From the head trauma. I had no idea who I was, much less what happened."

"They must have loved that."

"No. But the hospital backed me up—the story was plausible. They had nothing to hold me on, anyway. One night, I just walked away."

"So there's no way of knowing what *they* know."

"I guess that's right. This is a new face for me. And I've been underground, even deeper than usual, for months. This happened back in August."

"Tell me again why you need to talk to these people out here."

"They wanted me done. Or they work for someone who does. Whoever that is, they may not know if I'm dead or alive, but sooner or later, they'll find out. I want to find them first."

"You're not here to take them out?" he asked, the warning clear in his tone.

"No. No way. Whoever went to all that trouble, it *couldn't* be people I don't know. I figure the ones out here for branches, not roots. Anything happened to them, my last door would be closed. You want to go back, get your own car? I can find the address myself, no problem."

"We're already here," Clancy said, pulling into a long driveway between stone columns.

"How much would a house like this go for around here?" I asked Clancy.

"Somewhere between three-quarters of a million and one-point-five, depending on the grounds, what they got inside, like that. It's high-end, but not cream-of-the-crop. Not for this area."

"It doesn't look deserted."

"Let's see," he said, opening his door.

The driveway had been shoveled. Professionally, it looked like, the edges squared. The double doors set into the front of the house were massive, bracketed by tall, narrow panels of stained glass. A faint light glowed behind the glass.

"No bell," I said.

"There's got to be a tradesman's entrance around the side. This one, it'd only be for guests. And they'd use this," he replied, lifting a heavy brass knocker and rapping three times against the strike plate.

We waited a couple of minutes. If the cold bothered Clancy, he gave no sign. Me, I wasn't so sure.

"Come on," he finally said.

He strolled around to the side of the house as if he belonged there. I followed, keeping my mouth shut. Sure enough, there was a sort of outcropping off the house, with a single door set into it. And there was a bell. Clancy pushed it. We could hear its two-tone chimes from where we stood. Clancy moved so that he was taking up all the optic room the peephole offered. A metallic voice asked, "Who is there?" and I spotted the tiny speaker set into the door frame.

"Police," Clancy said.

"What is wrong?" the voice asked. A woman's voice, strongly accented. Sounded nervous. But maybe it was a tinny speaker.

"Nothing at all, ma'am. We're conducting an investigation and we thought you might perhaps be of assistance."

"Who are you investigating?"

"Could you please open the door, ma'am?" Clancy said, a trace of impatience in his voice.

I could sense decisions being made inside. Suddenly, the door opened. The woman was short, with dark hair cropped just past her nape. She was wearing a denim skirt and a man's white button-down shirt. Looked around late thirties, maybe younger.

"You are the police?" she asked, hovering between obsequiousness and challenge.

Clancy didn't flash his badge like most of them did. He took it out slowly, flicked the leather case open, held it out to her, palm up. "You can write down the number," he said gently. "Close the door, call the station, ask if I am actually a police officer. My name is Clancy. This is Rogers."

I didn't react to the instant name-change he'd conferred, just waited to see what would happen.

Clancy smiled. The woman's mouth twisted as if she couldn't make up her mind. "Please come in," she finally said.

We entered a kitchen big enough to be a New York studio apartment. "Do you want coffee?" she asked, gesturing toward a breakfast nook built into a bay window.

"That would be lovely," Clancy replied. "It's cold out there."

"That is not cold," the woman said, taking a ceramic pot from a fancy coffeemaker and pouring two mugs, apparently accepting that Clancy would be doing all the talking. "Where I come from, this would be springtime."

"Would that be Russia, then?" Clancy asked her, a brogue creeping into his voice.

"Siberia," the woman said, with the kind of pride you see in earthquake survivors.

"Ah. Well, here, when the wind comes off the lake, the temperature gets all the way down to—"

"It is not temperature that makes cold."

"You're right," Clancy said, gesturing with his coffee cup to make a salute, dropping the argument.

The woman made a sound of satisfaction. "You said you are investigating . . . ?"

"I did, indeed. But you are not the . . ."

"Owner? No. I live here. To work, I live here. My name is Marja."

"And the people who own the house?"

"They are traveling. In Europe."

"How long have they been away?"

"Oh, maybe couple of months. I don't keep track."

"They travel a lot, then?"

"Oh yes. Always they travel."

"Hmmm . . . How long have you worked for them?"

"I work for them since I come to America. It will be six years on February third."

"It must be hard on their work, to travel so much. A doctor has patients. . . ."

"No. Not anymore. They are retired. No more work."

"There's no such thing, is there? No more work," Clancy asked softly, closing the space around himself and the woman, moving me out to the margins. It was seamlessly beautiful technique, like the six-inch punch you never see.

"No," she said, sadness somewhere in her voice. "For some people there is always work."

"It must be difficult for you," he said, moving me even farther away from the two of them. "So much responsibility."

"What do you mean?"

"Well, even if they don't work anymore, they still have to have money. To pay bills. The electric, the phone. The cars. Food. Credit cards. Even to pay you, yes?"

"Sure, they need money. But they *have* money. And I take care of all the bills," she said, a different sort of pride in her voice.

"I see," he said, impressed. "Well, what we really need to do is talk to the people who own the house, you understand. So if we could have the address of wherever they're staying, we'll just . . ."

"I do not have the address," she said. "When they travel, they go with the wind. They have no plan. I never know where they stay, or when they are coming back. My job is to care for the house."

"But, surely, if there was an emergency . . . ?"

"There are no emergencies. If something happens to the house, I have numbers to call. The plumber, the electric people, the insurance company. And I know 911," she said, her mouth twisting again in what I guessed was a smile.

"I was thinking of children. You know how they can . . ."

"Ah. They have no children."

A fat cat the color of marmalade pranced into the kitchen. It ignored us disdainfully. The woman got up, opened a tiny can of something, and delicately forked it onto a white china plate. The cat approached, sniffed gingerly, then deigned to take a few queenly bites.

"Katrina is mine," the woman said, stroking the cat's lustrous fur. Answering a question nobody had asked.

"You scope the system?" Clancy asked me.

"Windows are wired. Probably to a central-station system. I'm guessing no motion sensors—that cat's got the run of the joint, I'd bet anything on it."

"She has to have separate quarters."

"Yeah. Hard to tell from that kitchen, but I think the space to the left from where we sat, that's the owners' area. To the right, that would be off toward the back. Hers . . . ?"

"Let me check a few things. I should have what I need by tonight. You got any in-between outfits?"

"I'm not sure what you—"

"This place where we're going, you don't want to look homeless. But you don't want to look like a lawyer, either, understand?"

"Tell me what kind of place it is, I'll buy some stuff."

"Good enough. It's a blues bar, off Rush Street. Not far at all."

He gave me the address, said he'd be there by ten.

The side door was rusted out, or else some fool had painted it the color of dried blood. Overhead, a little blue light winked from inside a steel-mesh cage.

I stepped inside, found myself in a two-man bracket: one average-looking, the other sumo-sized. The average-looking guy held out his hand, said "Ten." I forked it over.

The joint was long and narrow, with a small raised stage at the far end. And crammed so full of people the owner must have bribed the Fire Department. More black than white, but more mixed than most blues clubs. Places I'd been, the high-end spots had mostly all-white audiences, and the juke joints were almost all black. Maybe Chicago was different.

Clancy appeared out of the mob. "Come on," was all he said.

I followed him to a table right near the front but so far to the right that it was almost against the wall. A woman with corn-rowed hair surrounding a hard face was sitting there. When she saw Clancy, she flashed a killer smile, showing off a gold tooth. She stood up, gave Clancy a kiss. He introduced us, calling me Rogers. Her name was Zeffa.

"Son'll be on in a minute," she said to us both. "Should have been on already, but the first set ran long."

We took seats. I was thinking . . . *Son?* . . . but didn't get my hopes up.

I looked around for the woman in the red dress. There's always a woman in a red dress in joints like this. I wanted to be sure I wasn't sitting too close to her.

The drummer suddenly cracked out a back-beat, hammering the talk-buzz into silence. The guy working a stand-up electric bass added a line, the harp man cranked off a few sharp notes, and the rhythm guitarist carried the lead for a minute, building.

An unmanned black guitar rested against the front-most microphone stand.

A slim man strode out on the little stage. He was all in black, including a cowboy hat with a heavy silver medallion just over the brim. His coat was so long it was almost a duster. He reached down, picked up the black guitar . . . and the crowd went berserk.

He smiled gently, a handsome man with strong cheekbones and a beard, bowed his head a few inches in acknowledgment. Most bluesmen open with an up-tempo number, get the crowd into the action. But he started with "Bad Blood," a true-tale ballad that pile-drivered its way down to where you lived, if you'd ever lived at all. His long fingers were flint against the steel strings, drawing fire . . . and painting pictures with it.

I don't know how he did it. I can't imagine he'd be able to put it into words if anyone asked.

The crowd was insane . . . and under control. His control. He was dealing for real, and the crowd was in his hands—spontaneous reaction to spontaneous combustion. As he teased an impossible run of unreal notes out of the steel slide, a thick-bodied man in a yellow silk shirt stood up and yelled out, "That's the real thing, brother!" as if he were waiting on a challenge.

You could almost *see* the notes flow out of that black guitar—a liquid ribbon of honey and cream, draped over concrete and barbed wire. For a slice of time, I was transported. Lost in the truth. Feeling . . . connected to something more than me and mine. I reached for a cigarette. Came up empty. Zeffa was next to me, on my left. Her hand dropped to her purse. She flicked it open one-handed, pointed to a pack of Carltons. The pack was right next to what else she was packing—a dull-black Glock.

I thanked her with a nod. Lit the smoke. Took a deep drag. It tasted like crap, no hit at all. I put it in the ashtray and let it burn down.

The man with the black guitar finished his set . . . barely. The crowd kept demanding "One more!" and he kept going with it. Finally, he just bowed slightly, touched the brim of his hat, and stepped off the stage and out the back.

"Son Seals!" the announcer shouted, as the man walked off with his black guitar.

"Come on," Zeffa said.

We followed her to a basement where ratty old couches were stacked against one wall. Son was seated, alone, smoking a slim black cigar. Zeffa introduced us. I didn't know what to say, so I just said the truth.

"You're the ace," I told him.

"Thank you," was all he said. Not grabbing the title, but not disclaiming it, either.

Clancy made a motion with his head. I came over to where he was sitting. The basement was filling up, people clotted, waiting for a chance to spend a minute with the legend. Zeffa watched them warily, making the access decisions one by one.

"They're gone," Clancy said, no inflection.

"How do you—?"

"They slipped up. Or they couldn't stand paying taxes under two IDs. INS still has them in Chicago, but that's no big deal, they're both green-carded, both waiting on citizenship. Once applicants get to that level, INS figures it's *their* job to keep in touch, see?"

"Sure. If they miss an appointment, it's their problem. Might even delay their application. But it's not a problem for the government, so long as they pay their taxes."

"Right. And they're okay with the IRS. But we've got a *state* income tax here. And they haven't filed in almost three years."

"Maybe they didn't have any income."

"That's possible. Here's what's not: neither of them has visited a doctor or a dentist for all that time."

"How could you know that?"

"They have medical insurance. A very good plan, not one of those HMO deals. And they haven't filed a claim. Not one."

"Maybe they gave up the plan, and they're paying cash. Or maybe they switched plans."

"Sure. But if that's so, why would they keep paying the premiums?"

"Oh."

"Yeah. And why would they keep paying big numbers to insure their cars, but not maintain them?"

"How can you be—?"

"One," he said, tapping his index finger, "they each have a Mercedes. Two, both of the cars are still under warranty. Three, neither car has been serviced at the local dealer in all this time. And four, both cars are insured to the max, including zero-deductible collision. And they haven't missed a payment."

"You think . . . ?"

"What?"

"There's a garage, right? Around the back, maybe?"

"Around the back, yeah," Clancy said. "Behind the house, set off to the right. The driveway—you know, that horseshoe shape?—it spins off to the side to connect there."

"Would you happen to know if—?"

"There's no alarm. The garage is the same material as the house. Stone. Three-car size. Automatic doors. Free-standing. And there's a little window on the side."

"Okay."

He shook his head.

"What's the problem?" I asked.

"You are. This isn't your territory. You're working alone. You get popped, it'd be bad."

"I won't get—"

"That's right. Because there's a better way."

I wasn't going to drive the way Clancy did, so I left plenty of slack, arrived forty-five minutes to the good. Clancy was ten minutes early. He took the wheel of the Lexus and meandered through the streets until he found a spot he liked, then pulled over in a copse of trees. I stepped over the console into the back of the SUV. The rear seat had been folded down—there was a lot of room. I lay down in the back, pulling three khaki blankets over me until I looked like a puddle of wool. Clancy drove away.

"If she's home, you'll have thirty minutes safe," he said. The Lexus was so quiet I could hear him perfectly. "If she's not, we'll have to come back. Give me five minutes. If I don't come back by then, go for it."

I felt the Lexus pull into the driveway. I checked my watch. My nice cheap watch with a little button that lit up the face: 7:16.

It was 7:23 when I slipped out the back door, closing it behind me, but blocking the lock with a strip of duct tape. I moved around to the side of the house, saw the light in the kitchen window. I crouched to stay below it. The garage was exactly where Clancy had said it would be. The little window was nothing. I didn't even have to touch the glass; just slipped a pry bar under the soft wood and worked it back and forth until the seal broke. I climbed inside, let myself down to the floor gingerly.

I took out my mini–Mag Solitaire, a tiny black flashlight with a controllable beam. A burglar's best friend—you turn it on by rotating the front bezel, no click.

Three cars. The two Mercedes weren't exactly a matched set—a tiny little SLK, bright yellow, and a big black 480E sedan with AMG badges. The other car was an Audi A4, blue. None of the cars was covered—it looked as if they were used all the time. I looked inside the big black sedan. Couldn't see any little red lights blinking. No burglar-alarm decals on the windows. No lock on the steering wheel. And . . . yeah, key in the ignition. What the hell was that all about? I quick-checked the other two cars. Exactly the same, right down to the ignition keys.

I could be out the window and into the bushes at the side of the house in a few seconds if an alarm went off. And if that happened, Clancy would naturally run out here to investigate, telling the woman to stay where she was. More than enough of an edge for the little bit of risk I'd be taking.

The big sedan gave off a whiff of stale air when I opened the door. I felt the muscles at the back of my neck loosen when my brain sent the message to my body: *No alarm!*

I carefully turned the ignition key just far enough to light up the electronic instrument panel, noted what I needed. Did the same thing to the little yellow two-seater. Neither glove compartment held anything but the owner's manual.

The Audi was a different story. The glove compartment was crammed full of junk. I checked my watch: 7:46. Not enough time left. I rifled through the paper as quickly as I could, the mini-Mag in my teeth, gloved hands on the papers. Nothing. I was putting it all back when a roll of pre-printed mailing labels fell out. I looked closer. They were all addressed to the same person, and the return address was a PO box in Winnetka. The person they were addressed to wasn't either of the names I had for the Russians, but why else would . . . ? The street address was in Vancouver, Washington, complete with bar-coding at the top. I peeled the last label off, then stuck it lightly to the inside of my coat.

Back outside, I checked the window's appearance. It would pass, unless someone was paying a lot more attention than it looked like they ever had.

I let myself back into the Lexus, got under the blankets, and closed my eyes.

It was at least another half-hour before I heard the driver's door open.

Clancy drove to where he'd left his Nissan, but said to leave the Lexus where it was—he'd drive me back himself.

It was a quick run—we were going against the traffic. Besides, Clancy drove about 50 percent past the limit, returning pages on his cell phone, concentrating all over the place. He pulled into the drive for the hotel, cut the engine.

"What'd you get?" he asked.

"Pair of Mercedes, just like you said. I couldn't make out the years—I haven't been able to do that since the sixties—but they looked pretty new."

"Colors?" he asked, consulting his notebook.

"Black for the sedan, yellow for the little roadster."

"Checks out," he said. "Sedan purchased March of '98; SLK, purchased May, same year. What did you get for mileage?"

"The sedan has thirty-five hundred and change, the roadster less than three."

"Sure. Haven't been driven for years."

"The keys were in the ignition."

"Yeah. Marushka probably goes out there, turns them over every once in a while, keeps them from going stale."

Marushka, huh? I thought to myself. I'm no linguist, but I know the "ka" at the end of a Russian name means "little one." I thought about the girl at the front desk of the hotel. Recalled something else Wolfe had told me about Clancy. He was divorced. And a major cock-hound. But all I said was, "I found something else, too."

He looked a question at me. I unpeeled the label carefully, handed it over.

"Vancouver. I was there once for a tournament. It's . . . Wait a minute, this isn't Vancouver in Canada, it's in Washington State."

"Yeah."

"And she had a whole roll of these labels?"

"Uh-huh. Probably printed them up herself, on a home computer. Pretty handy things to have if you're remailing everything that comes in. They probably send everything back to her, too. That way, there's a local postmark on everything."

"You put it all back the way you—?" He caught my expression, cut himself off in mid-sentence. "Can you hang around another couple of days?"

"I'm in no hurry," I told him.

The bar was in a part of Chicago called Uptown. Clancy was at a table with two other guys, one built like a bull, with "COP!" written all over his face, the other a young blond guy with Slavic cheekbones and the flat expression of a working thug. They both spent about a minute memorizing my face, not making any secret about what they were doing.

"See you later," the big one said, as he got up to leave. He might have been talking to anyone at the table.

The younger one got up, too. He didn't say a word.

"Friends of yours?" I asked Clancy.

"Good friends."

"They both on the job?"

"Mike is. Zeffa was," he said, explaining the pistol I'd seen in her purse. "Zak isn't."

"The kid? What's he, between jobs?"

"He's a writer," Clancy said, pride strong in his voice. "In fact, both of them are."

"They're here gathering local color?"

"No," cutting it off.

"It's your car," I told him. "And you're driving."

"Here's what I got," Clancy said, getting down to it. "The little boy's mother reported him missing on June 29, 1990. His DOB's April 4, 1986, so he'd just turned four. No signs of a ransom kidnap—and no note ever turned up. The parents were together, so it wasn't one of those custody grabs. Whoever took him came right into the back of the house. Like with Polly Klaas, only nobody actually saw this one go down."

"Or found a body."

"Yeah," he said. "Or the dirtbag who did it, either. None of the kid's possessions were missing. You know how it works after that: they checked the kid's friends, used the search-and-rescue dogs working off his scent, combed the maximum area a kid his age could travel by himself . . . everything. Finally, he went from missing to missing-and-presumed."

"Presumed dead?"

"Not necessarily. But with no ransom note, no contact from anyone, and no body, we figured it for a sex-snatch. And that maybe the kid was still alive. Some of them turn up, even a lot of years later, like the Stayner kid out in California. If we haven't found a body, the BOLOs stay out there for every confirmed abduction, no-clues disappearance. *All* of them. Doesn't matter if they'd be adults by the time we find them, people're still looking. We're looking for *this* boy, too."

I took a sip of my ginger ale, thinking Wolfe was right—this was a personal thing with Clancy. "When does school let out around here?" I asked him.

He gave me a sharp look. "End of May," he said.

I gave him a neutral look back.

"Yeah," he said, quietly. "And it was broad daylight, that time of year." He put two fingers to his forehead. "It wasn't my case."

"I know. When did the Gee come in?"

"Maybe a week later. The record's not clear."

"I saw that story in the newspaper. . . ."

"That was a while afterwards. They kept it quiet, didn't want to spook the kidnappers, in case it *was* about money."

"Maybe it wasn't about money *or* sex," I probed.

"What, then?"

"They, the parents, they knew how to find the . . . guy who got shot in New York. If they were players in the Russian mob, maybe washing money, the snatch could have been a message."

"It's possible, I suppose. But nothing like that came up when they were being investigated. Look, that kind of case, you have to eliminate all the possibilities. You know how many kids are killed every year by their parents, or the boyfriend of the mother, or . . . ? Dumped in some vacant lot, reported missing. And the perps go on TV crying crocodile tears and ask everyone to help them search for their precious baby. Something like this, you *have* to check the parents, see if maybe *they* weren't the perps."

"Like they did in Boulder? With JonBenét Ramsey?"

"This isn't Boulder," Clancy said, his voice as stony as his eyes.

"Sorry. The parents, they came up clean?"

"They did. And it wasn't because the job was sluffed. Everybody got talked to. Teachers, their pediatrician, their housekeeper, neighbors; you name it. Not one person had the slightest suspicion of the parents. No history of child abuse. Not even a hint of booze, or drugs. Or domestic violence. The parents themselves were asked about enemies, and they said they hardly even *knew* anybody over here."

"What about an old grudge? From the old country?"

"It's possible," he said again, the "*anything's* possible" unspoken, but clear on his face.

"The reason I ask . . . I'm guessing that nobody on your side could have known about any connection to the Russian mob back then. No way they could have."

"You're right. *If* there was a connection back then, it didn't show up anywhere in the investigation."

"Okay."

"I got a friend in the Bureau," he said, dropping his voice. "We've got photos of the kid from just before he disappeared. There's a computer program, factors in everything known about the subject, right down to his genetic makeup. Anyway, this program 'ages' the subject. He'd be, what, fourteen or so now? The kid you saw when the thing went down—would you recognize him?"

"Not a chance. It was dark. I never really got a look at his face. He started shooting right away."

"Wolfe's good people," he said, out of the blue.

"I know."

"Is she in this?"

"You spoke to her. What did *she* say?"

"She said she's known you a long time. Sent along your sheet, but said it didn't tell the whole story, so she filled in a lot of the blanks. Asked me if I'd do her this little favor."

"So . . . ?"

"So Wolfe doesn't ask for favors. She trades. Unless it's personal. She didn't say anything about herself, just about you. So it comes out like you and her . . . ."

"No."

"Right," he agreed. Too quickly. "She said as much. Said you and her . . . you weren't going to be together. That you were a criminal in your heart."

"But . . . ?"

"But somebody has a bull's-eye painted on you, and you needed to get off first."

"It's not that simple."

"Never is. Look, I'll see you later. Midnight, one o'clock, how's that?"

"Fine with me. I'll be at the hotel . . . ?"

"Sure. That works. Me, I got a date."

I slipped the blue lens on the mini-Mag, played the light over the keypad to the in-room safe all good hotels provide nowadays. I didn't want to open the safe—I wanted to see if anyone else did. The safe is programmed by the hotel guest. You pick whatever combination of numbers you want. But a pro knows what to do. Clean the keypad thoroughly, apply a thin coat of wax. When the mark opens "his" safe, he *leaves* marks. Most people pick a three-digit combo. They do that, it takes just a minute to box the trifecta, cover all six possible combinations. Of course, you do this *after* you've tried the mark's birthday, if he's left that info lying around.

It's hard to tell if a hotel room's been tossed. Some maids pick up every scrap, straighten every edge, put things away for you. Some don't. The usual tricks—a hair pasted across an opening, a paper match wedged between two abutting layers of clothing—are a waste of time in hotels. But the safe . . . that will usually tell you if someone with access has been poking around. I carry what I need every time I go out—cash, passport, ID, tools—so if things go bad I never have to return to the room. Losing the gun would be no tragedy. It doesn't trace to me, my prints aren't on it. And the cash would always get me another.

The safe's keypad was untouched.

I was kicking back in the room's easy chair when the tap came at the door.

Clancy.

He walked in, pulled a chair away from the desk, carried it over to where I'd been sitting.

"How old do you think she is?" he asked me, as soon as I sat back down.

"She?"

"Marushka."

"Thirty-five, forty?"

"She's twenty-seven."

"Okay."

"Twenty-seven and frightened. Fear'll age you quicker than booze."

"But not overnight."

"No. Not overnight."

"So she was just a kid when she first came here. . . ."

"Yeah. She sends money home. There's no jobs, she says. So she's supporting her whole family."

"Not so bad. She lives in a beautiful house, has a nice car all her own, plenty of time on her hands. . . ."

"Plenty of time to think, too. She gets deported, her whole family goes down."

"Why should she get deported?"

"She's sponsored. The people who own that house, all they need to do is withdraw."

"She'd still have options."

"What options? She's got no special skills. No way she'd get an exemption."

"You think the people who brought her here are threatening her?"

"No. I don't think she has any contact with them."

"She forwards their mail. . . ."

"I think that's right. Almost has to be. But there's no communication coming the other way. Her phone records—no long-distance calls, in or out. She's got a cellular, too. Those are the best. For us, I mean. So long as the target uses his phone, you can find out where he's using it *from*. I don't mean the *exact* location, like Lojack or anything, but which city for sure. And sometimes right down to a tight grid. Anyway, her cellular, every call's been made from the local area."

"Did the people who own the place have cellulars?"

"They did. But they terminated service more than two years ago."

"So that thread has snapped."

"Yeah . . ." he said, dragging the word out. "Burke?"

"What?"

"She's not in this."

"Who?"

"Marushka."

"I understand."

He stood up. I packed my stuff while he waited. If he noticed the plastic-wrapped package I stowed in my duffel, he gave no sign.

Clancy dropped me off at the bus terminal on Harrison. I reached over to shake his hand.

"Thanks. For everything."

"It was for Wolfe," he said, keeping everything clear. "Besides, I figure, you get lucky, we may find the kid yet."

"I know," I told him, pulling a thick manila envelope from my coat pocket. I handed it to him.

His face flushed and his eyes went alligator on me. "I told you—"

"It's for Licensed for Life," I said.

He took a deep breath. Let it out his nose, slowly.

"I need a receipt," I told him. "You're a 501(c)(3), right? This is a charitable contribution."

"*You* file with IRS?"

"Wayne Askew does."

He reached into the back seat of his Nissan, found the right box, extracted a pad of receipts.

"Make it out for twenty-five hundred," I said.

"That's too—"

"There's twenty large in that envelope," I cut him off. "But Wayne Askew doesn't earn the kind of money that he could donate that big to charity, so . . ."

"Christ!"

"It's good to have something to believe in," I said.

I took my receipt and got out. Clancy hauled my duffel out of the trunk. Stuck out his hand again. This time, his grip transmitted.

I bought a ticket to L.A. Round-trip, in case anyone was watching—in person or at an anonymous computer somewhere. A real bargain for two hundred bucks. The woman behind the barred window didn't even look up as she slid it through the slot.

I had almost an hour before the bus left. Plenty of time. I finally found what I wanted—a tall, rawboned man with a lined Appalachian face. He told the guy on the bench next to him that he was going home. To West Virginia. Chicago was just another bitch who hadn't kept her promises.

I slipped my cell phone into one of the big plastic bags he was carrying. The working class may be able to afford decent luggage now, but the out-of-work class has to improvise. I figured he might use the phone once he discovered it, but more likely he'd sell it. Either way, if anyone was wired in, good fucking luck to them if they thought they'd located me.

We chugged away around two in the morning, set to arrive L.A. just before nine the night after the next one coming—a few hours under two full days.

The bus was more than half empty. I settled in, grateful for the privacy.

Although it was a much longer run than Philly to Chicago had been, we made only one stop. Las Vegas, on day two, a half-hour layover. Just enough time to pick up all the high rollers who'd left their return plane ticket in the same pawnshops where they'd left their jewelry.

You could see it stamped on their faces—if they'd had just one more shot, they would have flown from Tap City to Fat City, non-stop. That wheel was about to turn, the slot they fancied was warming up, the dice couldn't *keep* breaking against them. . . .

It was a crowded, morose trip into East L.A. And, from there, maybe a dozen miles and half an hour to another planet. Beverly Hills.

"Nice to see you again, sir," the bellman at the Four Seasons said. Faking it, figuring he couldn't lose even if he was wrong.

I carried my own bag.

The smartly dressed young man behind the front desk didn't blink at my field jacket and two-day growth—people in the movie industry are special, right? He found the reservation in a minute.

"You'll be with us three nights, is that right, Mr. Jones?"

"That's right."

"Great! Now, if we could just have your credit card for an imprint . . ."

"It should all be direct-billed."

"Let me see. . . . So it is! We have a lovely large room for you, sir. On the sixth floor, overlooking the back gardens. Will you be needing any help with your luggage?"

"I can manage," I said, taking the white paper folder with the key, patiently waiting while he explained about the honor bar, the gym, my choice of newspaper in the morning. . . .

The room was fresh and clean. I was tired. And down in minutes.

When the phone rang in the morning, I picked it up without saying anything.

"Everything all right, honey?"

"Perfect," I told Michelle. "That corporate-credit-card thing worked like a charm."

"I charm everything I touch, baby."

"That's the truth."

"Are you okay?"

"Didn't you already ask me that?"

"What if I did? A real answer would be nice."

"I don't know anything yet. I'm going up to Vancouver tomorrow, if I can hook up with . . ."

"I spoke with him. He says anytime you want. Any*thing* you want."

"He's got a good memory."

"So do I, sweet boy. Be careful."

"Don't worry. I know I'm working blind."

"**I**s it really you?" the tall, slender man with the cream-in-coffee complexion asked. I knew he was a few years past my age, but he looked twenty years younger.

"It's me, Byron."

"Sounds like . . . you. Mind talking some more, just so I can be sure?"

"When's the last time you flew a four-engine Connie?"

His face didn't twitch, but his eyes flashed. Flashed *back*. To the tiny airstrip on the Portuguese island of São Tomé. To a big plane loaded to the brim with stockfish from Iceland—the maximum amount of nourishment for its space and weight. Then the frantic run over black water and even darker jungle, hoping the Nigerian jets with their hired-killer pilots wouldn't get lucky. No parachutes on board. Everybody riding had their own reason for risking death, but none of them was willing to risk being taken alive.

It was the tail end of 1969, just before the breakaway country of Biafra fell to Nigeria's overwhelming military superiority. Already at least a million dead. Mostly kids. Mostly from starvation.

Biafra was nothing more than a dream for whoever was left then, a tiny jagged piece of jungle, as vulnerable as a crippled cat in a dog pound. By that time, it was fully landlocked. Their leader had fled to the Ivory Coast. A Red Cross plane had been shot down. Even the media was gone.

Tribalism on full amok. If the Biafrans kept fighting, actual genocide was a real possibility. No point running guns in there anymore, but without food nobody would live long enough to surrender. For a landing field, there was only a dirt track cut into the jungle. We came in, guided by a radio until we got close. Then they fired the string of flares on the ground. A thirty-second window.

Byron set the big plane down softly. Before he could shut off the engine, people charged out of the jungle, desperate the way only starvation can make you. One man ran right into one of the still-whirling propellers. At least his terror died, too.

In a short while, the plane took off. I stayed on the ground.

It was maybe ten days later—I think I already had malaria by then, and things were fuzzy—when it happened. Byron was standing off to the side of the plane, watching the unloading, anxious to get back into the sky. But there were enemy planes in that sky. Huge chunks of ground blew up all around us from whatever they were sending down. No point in running—the blasts were completely random. And nobody ever used that foul tunnel they called a bomb shelter twice.

Suddenly, Byron went down, a piece of shrapnel in his thigh, blood flowing, not spurting. The rest of the crew ran for the plane. "We'll pick you up on the return!" one of them shouted.

Byron knew what that meant. He started crawling to the plane, pulling himself forward with his arms, the useless leg dragging behind him, holding him back. I ran ahead of him to the cargo door of the plane, pulling the .45 out of my field jacket.

"Hold it!" I yelled at the two men in the bay.

"We got to go!" one of them shouted back over the roar of the engine. "The sky's filling up!"

"Go get him!" I yelled, pointing with my empty hand at where Byron was still crawling.

"No way, man. He'll leave us!"

I knew who they meant. The copilot. The pilot now. I gestured them to step back, boarded the plane. "No, he won't," I told them. "The faster you get back, the faster you can leave."

They jumped out to get Byron while I went forward to explain things to the guy at the helm. I stood there explaining things until I heard them come back into the plane. Then I put up the pistol, ran right past Byron and his "rescuers," jumped down, and headed for the deeper jungle. The plane took off.

I wasn't sure Byron had made it until a few years later. A group of hijackers I knew were trying to put together a team for a job at a private airport, and his name came up as a candidate. The guy who recommended him said he'd worked with Byron a couple of times and he was solid.

We never did that job, but Byron had come to one of the meetings. It was . . . awkward. He didn't know what to say, and neither did I.

And now we had another chance.

"You know," he said, "I never asked you . . ."

"What?"

"Why you did it."

"I don't know," I told him, truthfully. I was nineteen years old when it happened. I couldn't have told you why I was in that jungle, in that war, much less why I . . .

"I think that's a problem with people," he said softly. "Who cares about the 'why'? I don't. Sorry I asked."

"Sure."

"Okay, what's on the agenda?"

"I need to check something out. In Vancouver, that's just—"

"—over the border from Portland," he finished for me.

"Yeah. Look, I won't bore you with all the details, but I'm supposed to be dead. So I need a way to go in under the radar."

"Who better than me?" He smiled. "I live there."

Byron's ride was a restored-to-new oxblood Jaguar XKE coupe. He drove it like it was a real car, though.

"You're doing well for yourself," I said.

"Wait till you see the plane."

It turned out to be one of those baby jets, with a custom cabin designed for luxury, not space utilization.

"Yours?" I asked, as I settled in next to him.

"Right!" He laughed. "It belongs to the studio. That's my job, flying very important people around to very important places."

"And you can just . . . ?"

"Borrow it? Sure. They bought this sucker in the glory days, back in the late eighties, when money was gushing. Today, the smart boys rent—like time-shares: use it when they need it, pay by the hour. But this one's all theirs. Nobody pays attention. They wouldn't know what a flight log was. And they never check on fuel and maintenance. Only risk is if one of the big shots gets a sudden whim, decides he needs to go to Vegas or something."

"That'd cost you your job."

"I don't think so," he said, unconcerned.

"Recognize it?" Byron asked, banking low over a string-of-jewels city.

"No."

"Seattle."

"Not Portland?"

"You come *up* from L.A., you come *down* from Seattle, see?"

"But how far is . . . ?"

"Couple of hours. Don't worry, I got you covered."

"These things hard to drive?" I asked Byron.

"Not really, so long as you know the limitations. A stretch limo's just a regular sedan with a reinforced section let into the chassis. You're adding a ton—no exaggeration—to the unsprung weight, so you've got a major inertia problem. A car like this, it won't pull a lot of g's on a skidpad, and the stopping distances are much longer than normal. But you stay within its envelope, it's no problem."

"This belong to the studio, too?"

"Yep. Seattle was the closest place to Portland where the studio has a presence."

"You're fobbing it off, but I know you've got to be risking your job, Byron."

"For borrowing their toys? I've been with the studio a long time. Piloted the planes, drove the cars. I've seen a lot, and never said a word. No, I wouldn't guess they'd try to move me out."

"You ever borrow their stuff before?"

"All the time. I was deeply involved with a man in Denver for a long while. Flew up to see him a lot."

"It still has to be a risk. I appreciate it."

"Burke, listen to me, okay? I've got a good memory. I'm a man. I pay my debts."

"Fair enough."

"You think they hired a black queer just because he could fly a plane?"

"Yeah, I did. The way I figured, it's just like it was over there: anyone who didn't want to fly with a certain pilot, they didn't like his color or his . . . anything, they could stay on the fucking ground."

"They were going to *leave* me on that fucking ground, Burke."

"Not because of anything about you. They were in a panic, trying to be hard guys, cut their losses."

"Maybe you're right. But it doesn't matter. Dead is dead. If I hadn't gotten on that plane, it would have been a slow death on the ground."

"Yeah, well . . ."

"Anyway," he said, expertly sliding the huge limo around a slow-moving pickup truck, "you never answered my question, so I'll answer it for you. They hired me for what is euphemistically called 'executive protection.' You understand what I'm telling you?"

"You're a bodyguard, too?"

"Licensed to carry," he said, pulling the lapel away from his jacket with his left hand to show me the shoulder holster. "And to clean up the messes they make."

"So they're not going to fire you."

"They're not going to fire me," he confirmed, voice soft. "I know where the bodies are buried." Meaning: he'd buried some of them himself.

"I got it," I told him.

"And I figure," he went on as if I hadn't spoken, "whatever it is you're doing, you can tell me as much about it as you want. Or nothing, if that's what you want. But if what you want is cover, I can't think of a better one than this. Anyone runs these plates, they come right back to the studio. You look . . . I don't have the words for it, exactly. Not exactly cool or hip or anything like that, but edgy enough so it'd work, no problem. Truth is, all you have to say is that you're in the business, with a studio connect, and doors will open. Legs, too. Anything you want. This whole country is psycho for the movies. What do you say?"

"I was going to low-profile it."

"Look, Burke, just stop me if I'm over the line here, okay? Michelle didn't tell me much. If you're here to do some work on someone, I'm your man."

"It's not that. The people I'm looking for, they have information I need."

"Information about whoever tried to make you dead?"

"Yes."

"Okay. Let's see how it plays."

"**D**idn't we just pass the exit for Vancouver?" I asked.

"We did. But unless you're planning to make your move at three in the morning, *our* move is to keep going, take the bridge to Portland, hole up for a few hours."

"You have a place there?"

"Not me. But—"

"—the studio?"

"Right. The Governor. Best hotel in town. And they got suites built on the roof now; every one's got a patio."

"With an awning?"

"Don't believe that stuff about it raining all the time up here. I mean, it *does* rain, but it's not a steady downpour or anything."

"What about the check-in?"

"This is the *studio*, partner. They don't even have to see you, you don't want. And I can sign you in as Mr. X, they won't even blink. I assume you've got a change of clothes in that bag."

"Yep."

"Carrying anything else?"

"In my bag," I said.

"Works for me," he said, guiding the limo over the bridge to Portland.

An hour past sunup, we went back the way we'd come. It only took us a few minutes to get across the bridge and back into Vancouver. Byron had a street map. It was easy to locate the address. But as soon as I saw the block, I knew I'd used up my luck for the day. The address was for one of those commercial mailbox joints. The "suite" number I'd taken from the labels was just a rental box.

"Fuck!" I said, softly.

"Let me scope out the place," Byron said. He didn't wait for my response.

I watched him cross the street and open the door to the mail-box place. Then I shifted position so I could scan the area, and settled down to wait.

It wasn't long. "It's a real small operation," he said, getting back behind the wheel. "Maybe four hundred boxes, all against the left-hand wall as you walk in. No windows in the boxes. Everyone has their own key. I figure the way they make their money is taking FedEx, UPS, stuff like that. Tack a couple of bucks onto the regular price, save the customer a lot of running around."

"No way to lurk, right?"

"No way at all. I asked the woman behind the counter about prices and stuff, like I wanted to rent a box. There was only one guy in there, getting his mail. It's empty—no chairs, just a flat table like they have in the post office. You don't have business in there, they'd spot you in a second."

"Damn."

Byron didn't need a translator. "You want to try some cash?" he asked.

"No. It'd be like putting all your money on a real long shot. If whoever we try to juice dimes us, the targets might spook and run."

"You got pictures?"

"No. Just names."

"Hmmm . . . We need something like the bang-dye the banks put in money bags when they're being robbed."

I didn't say anything, accepting that Byron had dealt himself in, letting my mind drift over the problem. A dozen different people went in and out in the next fifteen minutes. A lot of traffic, but no surprise. The Post Office will rent you a box, but they won't sign for FedEx, and you can't give them a call and ask if a certain letter came in for you. A lot of small businesses use these places as their regular address.

"Let's go," I finally told him. "This limo might be just the thing at a nightclub, but it sticks out here big-time."

"Okay. What's our next move?"

"I think I've got a way to put that bang-dye in their bag."

"You know someone who speaks Russian, Mama?"

"Sure. Plenty people speak."

"You know somebody out here?"

"West Coast?"

"Yeah. Portland area would be best."

"Find out, okay? I call tomorrow, same time, okay?"

"Okay."

I stayed in the hotel all day, curtains drawn over the windows, "Privacy Please" sign on the door. Trying to think it through. Byron said he had someone he wanted to hook up with, gave me his pager number, and told me to beep him if anything jumped off.

Options. The Post Office used to have a form for tracing people who left a forwarding order with them. A stalker used this public service to find a woman once. And killed her. The Post Office doesn't use that form anymore, except for businesses. Besides, those forwarding orders expire after a year or so. No good.

I could send them an oversized envelope and tag it in some way—a giant red sticker would do the job—and then try and spot it in the hand of someone leaving the drop. But it was February. People wore coats. And carried bags. No good.

I could probably get a photo of the Russians—INS would have them on file. Or maybe Clancy could sweet-talk a snapshot out of Marushka. But that could dead-end easily enough. They could be paying someone to fetch the mail for them. Or even be using the mail drop as a way station, forwarding it from there to somewhere else. *Anywhere* else. No good, squared.

I had to go with the bang-dye idea. And play it for a delayed explosion.

The phone rang at ten that night.

"What?" I answered.

"You have car?" Mama asked. I could tell she was talking on a cellular, guessing the outgoing lines on the bank of pay phones in the back of the restaurant were tapped. Everyone in my family is a player in different things, but one thing we all play is safe.

"I can get one."

"Okay. You go tomorrow. Wear ring."

The directions she gave me weren't that specific, but all I really needed was the town. And the name of the boat.

We looking at a hot LZ?" Byron asked later that night.

"No. It's just a meet."

"With a stranger, right?"

"Right."

He gave me a look. I nodded agreement. Then I asked him, "Can you fix me up with a car? I don't want to rent—"

"Sure. I got a special one I've been dying to try out, anyway."

"Byron . . ."

"Like you said, it's not hot, right? I heard the Oregon coast's beautiful. And it's two-lane blacktop all the way down. Can't wait."

What the hell is *this*?" I asked him the next morning as I climbed into an electric-blue coupe bristling with scoops, spoilers, and fender flares, riding on tires that bulged like steroided biceps.

"This, partner, is a Subaru."

"Not like one I ever saw."

"Not like one *anyone* in America's ever seen. Vancouver is the

Subaru port—it's where they ship their cars from Japan. This one's an Impreza 22B-STi, a homologated rally car. They only sell them over there—they don't meet emissions requirements, and, anyway, they only build a few hundred every year, and those are snapped up immediately. This one's destined for a gray-market conversion."

He slid the car through the light downtown traffic. It snarled like a pit bull on a too-short leash.

"What you've got here is a two-point-two-liter boxed four, with a mega-boost turbo and aluminum intercooler. Makes well over three hundred horses. See this?" he asked, touching a heavy knurled knob on the center console. "It controls a locking-center differential. This is full-time four, but you can dial the split your-self. It locks at fifty-fifty."

"It's not exactly subtle," I said.

"Where've you been, man? This is the West Coast. They don't drag-race Mustangs and Camaros out here—it's all rice-burners."

"Front-wheel drive?" I asked, skeptically.

"Yep. With micro-motors, boosted to the max."

"And on the bottle."

"Now you're getting the picture. This beast, trust me, we're hiding in plain sight."

"Fair enough."

A light, misty rain started to fall. Byron grinned, and gunned it out of a long left-hand sweeper, kicking the tail out just a notch, his hands delicate on the small padded steering wheel. "It's an easy spot to find, don't worry. Besides, it's daylight."

I thought of the landing lights on that dirt track in Biafra a mil-lion years ago. Byron nodded silently, as if he was right in sync with me.

"See any whales yet?" he asked, tilting his head toward the ocean on my right.

"Whales?"

"Whales for sure, partner. This coast is like the whale-watching capital of the world. That's why the tourists come."

"Can't imagine a whole lot of tourists this time of year. Won't be summer for a while yet."

"Maybe not, brother. But the whales don't come for the tourists, right? The tourists come for the whales."

"Sure."

"You're not even curious, huh? You ever see a whale?"

"No."

"If you ever did—up close, I mean—you'd never understand why anyone could kill one."

"All you mean is *you* couldn't kill one. The people who do it, they probably get as close as any whale-watching tourist. Closer, even. And they still pull the trigger."

"Evil motherfuckers."

"I don't think so," I told him. "If they did it for fun, maybe. Or if they made the things suffer before they killed them. Tortured them, I mean. But it's just food to some people, right?"

"Food? Those things, I swear to God, they're practically human."

"And those kids in Biafra—what were they?"

He was silent for a few miles, concentrating on his driving. Then he said, "And what was I, Burke? A nigger queer. In a jungle a million miles away from civilization, in a place where there's no laws. No affirmative action. No hate-crimes legislation. A free-fire zone. You remember some of the mercs . . . not the guys who thought they were fighting Communism or liberating a country. You know the ones I mean—the ones who thought being a mercenary meant having a license to kill niggers, and getting paid for it. You don't want to say why you saved me over there; you want to say you got no idea, you were just a kid yourself; that's okay. But you had to have asked yourself why you went in the first place."

I looked over at Byron. He downshifted just before a series of serpentine curves, his face set, mouth a straight line.

"I haven't asked myself questions about why people do things since I was a little kid."

"What happened then?" he asked.

"Nobody answered," I told him.

The *Ly Mang* looked like a Hudson River scow with a shack growing out of it. I left Byron in the car, made the approach myself. A short, muscular man with the face of an Inca was doing something to a net on the deck, working at a slow, deliberate pace. He raised his head as I came closer; watching, not moving.

"Is Gem around?" I asked him.

"Who are you?" he responded, his accent more in the rhythm than in the sound.

"She's expecting me."

"Today?"

"Yes."

"Stay there," he said, flicking the knife he had been using closed with one hand.

I slouched against one of the massive posts holding up the pier, patting my pockets for the pack of smokes that wasn't there. A mistake. Habits are patterns, and patterns are paths. Trails for trackers. I was somebody else now, and I had to stay there.

A girl in a pink T-shirt and blue-jean shorts came out of the cabin. She said something I couldn't hear to the Mexican, then vaulted over the railing to the pier, landing as lightly as a ballerina.

Her hair was jet black, framing a delicate Oriental face. A slim, leggy woman with a tiny waist, she could have been sixteen or thirty-five. But when she got close enough for me to see her eyes, there was no chance of mistaking her for a teenager.

"I am Gem," is all she said. If standing out in the cool weather dressed like that bothered her, it didn't show on her face.

"I don't know who you spoke to, but I'm the man who—"

"The man from New York?" she asked, her eyes deliberately glancing down to my right hand, where the fat emerald on my pinky finger sparkled in the sun. Mama's ID.

"Yes."

"You need someone who speaks Russian?"

"And writes it. Like a native."

"Yes. For how long?"

"I don't . . . Oh, right—you mean, how long will I need your services?"

"Yes."

"I can't say, exactly. I want you to write a letter. Then I want you to meet the people you are writing the letter to. And talk with them."

"Where would this be?"

"Vancouver. Near—"

"I know where it is. You came from there?"

"Yes."

"I would go back with you, is that correct?" Her voice was precise, unaccented. Soft.

"You don't have to. The letter you write, it will say you will meet them in Portland . . . so there would be at least a week between the letter and the time you go into action. You could write the letter here—I brought everything you would need with me—and come up to Portland on whatever date we pick."

"A week would be all right. I have business in Portland. You will cover my lodging and meals while I'm there, is that fair enough?"

"Sure."

"You must have a car . . . ?"

"Right over there," I told her, pointing to the Subaru.

She took a long, slow look at the car, making it clear she saw Byron in the driver's seat.

"Perhaps you should tell me a little more, first."

"Like what?"

"Who told you where to find me?"

"Look, the only person I dealt with is Mama. I don't know who she—"

"Mrs. Wong is your mother?"

"Not my biological mother. It's a term of respect. Everyone . . . close to her calls her that."

"Ah. I do not know her, not personally. But the people I

deal with, the people who I get my jobs from, they know her."

"Since *they* know her, why don't you—?"

"Yes. All right. Give me twenty minutes, please."

"**S**he's a pro," Byron said to me as the woman approached the Subaru, pulling one of those airline-size suitcases on wheels behind her.

"Why do you say?"

"No way a girl like her packs in fifteen minutes. She had the suitcase stashed somewhere, ready to roll."

I got out of the car, opened the little trunk. She retracted the pulling handle, picked up the suitcase with one hand and gave it to me. It was twice the weight I expected.

I closed the trunk, opened the passenger door, and started to climb in the back seat.

"May I ride back there, please?" she said. "I will fit much better than you would."

"That's okay."

"I insist," she said, not smiling.

I found the ratchet on the side of the seat, slid the backrest forward, and stood aside for her to climb in. She studied the back seat for a few seconds, then spun around gracefully and dropped down without a glance or a handhold.

"This is Byron," I told her. "Byron, this is Gem."

They each made polite noises. Byron started the engine, shoved the gearshift forward, and we were off.

The Subaru was loud—the combination of a high-stress engine and soundproofing sacrificed for lighter weight. After a while, it felt like being inside a small plane.

"You can stay at the—" I began, turning as I spoke so I could engage her, start a little connect between us.

She was curled up in the back, asleep.

"Do you live in Portland now?" she asked, startling me out of wherever I'd gone in my mind.

She was sitting up in the back seat, hands in her lap, leaning forward so her face was close to mine. She smelled of jade and ocean.

"No," I said, rotating my head on my neck, hearing the sharp little cracks as the adhesions blew out. "We're just in town for this . . . assignment."

"You have hotel rooms, then?"

"Yes."

"Together?"

"No."

"I would prefer not to be registered anywhere," she said, shifting her focus to Byron. "May I stay in your room?"

"I'm going to have company tonight," Byron told her. "At least, I sure hope I will. Burke's got a whole suite. Two bedrooms."

"Would that be all right with you?" she asked.

"It would be fine," I said, wondering why she'd asked Byron first. Keeping the question to myself.

Byron dropped us off at the back entrance on Eleventh Street. We took an elevator to the top floor without having to go anywhere near the front desk.

"This is it," I said, opening the door to the suite. I gave her one of the plastic slot-cards most hotels use instead of keys now. "This will get you in and out whenever you want."

"Thank you."

"That one's empty," I said, pointing toward the second bedroom. "Do you want me to—?"

"I will be fine," she said, taking the suitcase from me and walking into the bedroom.

I went into my own bedroom, closed the door, undressed, and

took a long, hot shower. After putting on fresh clothes, I went out to the living room. Gem was seated delicately on the couch, a laptop computer open at her side.

"If you want to tell me about it, I can tailor my work more properly," she said.

"I'm not sure what you mean."

"You want a note written in Russian, is that not correct?"

"Yes."

"There are several translation programs," she said, tilting her head in the direction of the laptop. "They are technically adequate, but they have no feel for the idiom. Anyone with high language skills or native fluency could detect the use of software. So, if you need authenticity, especially if you require a certain persona—an elderly lady, a young man, a business person, a . . ." She looked directly into my face, her eyes so dark I couldn't see a separate pupil. ". . . a soldier—the programs would be inadequate. Certain kinds of . . . messages would never be in a person's handwriting. In such cases, a mechanical device of some kind would always be used."

"I understand," I said, wondering how many ransom notes she'd typed in her young life.

"Yes? Then you must decide how much you wish to tell me."

"I have to make a call first."

"Of course," she said, curling her sleek legs under her and pulling the computer into her lap.

t took a few hours for the cell-phone relay to connect. Finally, I got Mama on the line.

"Mama, I need to know: how far can I trust this woman? You said you didn't know her."

"Not know her. She know me."

Meaning: Gem knew her by more than mere reputation—she knew people who knew Mama personally. And what Mama was capable of.

"Is that enough?"

"She make call, earlier. Ask about you, why you call me 'Mama.'"

"She called you?"

"No. Call friend. Pao."

"She's Cambodian, then?"

"Yes, Cambodian. All same with Pao. This girl, Gem, Pao call her 'Angkat.' Girl easy to find. Anytime. No problem. What you tell girl, *she* not tell anyone, okay?"

"Okay, Mama. Thanks."

"Watch everyone," she said. And hung up.

Pao was a Cambodian woman who ran a network like Mama's. I'd only met her once, at the restaurant. I couldn't begin to guess her age, any more than I could Mama's, but I knew they went way back. Mama had told me "easy to find." Meaning, if Gem double-crossed me, there'd be no place for her to hide . . . and she'd know it.

When I went back into the living room, she was still on the couch, as if I'd been gone minutes instead of hours. I sat down in the armchair and said, "Do you want to hear the story?"

She got up without using her hands, like smoke rising from a cigarette. She took a couple of steps toward me, then dropped to her knees, clasped her hands, looked up at me expectantly.

"There is a Russian couple," I said, not looking directly at her. "Man and wife. From Chicago. They had a child. A son. He was abducted when he was around four years old. Disappeared without a trace. There never was a ransom note. No body was ever found. They never heard a thing. A lot of years passed.

"Then, one day, they were contacted by a man who said he had their boy. The man wanted to exchange him for money. A lot of money. The Russians, they were immigrants. Nervous. Didn't trust the police. So they went to a gangster. A Russian, like them, in New York. He hired me to handle the transfer. I was there, with the money. A kid got out of the ransom truck. At least it looked like a kid—it was dark. But it was a trap. The kid shot me. So did some others. They ran away, thinking I was dead.

"It took a long time for me to heal. Then I went to see the man who set it up for me to make the transfer. He told me that the Russians had insisted on me for the job. So whoever was lying in wait, they knew I'd be the one coming. I'm who they wanted to kill. It was never about a ransom payment—it was a murder setup.

"The Russians don't live in Chicago anymore. They have someone there who keeps up a front for them, but all their mail is forwarded here. To Vancouver, I mean.

"I need to talk to them. I don't know what they look like. Or where they live—the Vancouver address is a mail drop. I figure, if I . . . if *you* . . . write them a letter, in Russian, I might be able to get them to come out in the open."

She knelt there quietly, deep dark eyes on me, waiting. When she saw I was done, she blew out a long stream of breath, a cleansing act like yogis do. Then she asked, "You wish to find out who wanted to have you killed?"

"That's not past tense. If they knew I was alive, they'd *still* want me dead. I have no way of knowing what they know. It cost major money to set this whole thing up. So they may have resources I don't know about. Access to information."

"Why were the arrangements so complicated?"

"I thought about that, too. And maybe they weren't. Not all that much. I don't live aboveground. I don't have a home. Or an office. Or a hangout," I said, dismissing Mama's from that category—she wasn't exactly open to the public, and I couldn't think of a worse place to try and take me out. "If they wanted to hit me, they couldn't just go out and look for me; they'd have to bring me to them."

"Do you believe this gangster person was involved?"

"I don't think so. For two reasons: One, I'd had to meet with him to get the money to deliver. So, if he was going to hit me, why not just do it right then? Two, there *was* a kidnapping. There *was* a missing kid. The Russians *did* run. . . ."

"How long?"

"I don't . . . Oh, you mean, how long have they been running?"

"Yes."

"About a year, as near as we can tell."

"And the attempt on your life was . . . when?"

"Sure. I know. They were in the wind before it all went down. There's pieces missing. Big pieces."

"Would it not be better to ask this gangster person more questions?"

"He's no longer available," I told her.

"I see."

She went quiet then. So did I. Finally, she looked up at me from under her eyelashes, said, "Do you feel comfortable with me . . . like this?"

"You mean . . . talking about this stuff?"

"I mean with me on my knees," she said softly.

I closed my eyes, reaching for the answer.

"Yes," I finally told her.

"Because . . . ?"

"It's . . . I don't know . . ."

"Safer?"

"Yes."

"I understand," she said, barely above a whisper.

We ate in the restaurant attached to the hotel. A nice place—clean and pretty quiet, considering the bar was right in the center of everything. Gem ate . . . carefully, I guess would be the word for it. Slowly, chewing every bite a great number of times. But steadily, too, never varying her pace. She finished a whole roasted chicken, right down to cleaning the bones with her small, very white teeth. And a large tossed salad. Four helpings of rolls. Three large glasses of apple juice. A plate of fried onion rings. A side of roasted potatoes.

I did most of the talking, and there wasn't much of that. A thin rain slanted down against the plate glass of the window next to our table. All around us, activity. Between us, peaceful quiet.

The waiter came and went, raising his eyebrows a couple of times, silently comparing the diminishing pile of food in front of Gem with her slim frame. He opened his mouth to ask her where she put it, but I caught his eye and he closed right down.

Gem ordered a slab of double-fudge cake for dessert. I had the same, mine with twin scoops of vanilla ice cream on top. "Oh!" she said, when she saw my addition. Then she helped herself to one of the scoops.

When she was completely finished, Gem wet her napkin in a glass of water, then patted her mouth and lips. "You didn't say anything," she said.

"About what?"

"About me being such a pig."

"A pig? You eat as neatly as a . . . I don't know."

"Neatly, yes. But a lot."

"I understand."

"You . . . understand? *I* do not understand."

"I'm sorry. It's none of my business."

"It is I who should apologize. I invite your comment, then I make you feel bad for it. Please tell me . . . what you meant."

She returned my gaze. Serene, not confronting. But not backing away.

"There was a time when food was very precious to you," I said.

"Yes. Do you know when that was?"

"Twenty, twenty-five years ago?"

"Yes. But you . . . guess, do you not? I mean, you do not know this for a fact; it is a surmise?"

"That's right. The beast got loose in Cambodia in 1975, I think."

"I was five years old," she said, her voice soft and dreamy, but her eyes stayed on mine, unblinking. "My father was a lawyer. You know what happened to anyone with an education? To anyone with any knowledge of the world outside the fields?"

"Pol Pot."

"He was only one of them. A symbol. A horrible butcher, yes. But he did not kill three million people by himself. The Khmer

Rouge were swollen with lust for blood. If the Vietnamese had not come, the killing would have gone on until there was no one left to die."

"How did you—?"

"My parents knew they were coming. They knew there was no escape. My mother was a peasant born. She had friends in the fields. My parents handed me over. My new people tried to provide for me. It was . . . impossible.

"I . . . eventually lived with a guerrilla group near the Thai border. They purchased me from the people who had me. They were not freedom fighters; they were drug lords. When the leader discovered I could do sums very quickly, he got me books. About money. He was very interested in money.

"The books were mostly in English. Some were in Russian. There were Russian soldiers in the jungle. Independent outfits. It was as if they all knew governments would fall, but heroin would always have value. Like gold or diamonds. So they traded together. Made alliances. I became the translator for the leader. He could trust me, because I was a child, so I had no power. Even if I could have escaped, the jungle would have devoured me.

"I was very patient. One night I was able to leave. In Thailand, money is god. I had to be very careful. Anyone would hurt you. Anyone would take your money. But I did speak English. I found some students. American students. In the Peace Corps. One of them helped me buy papers. I came here. First to California. I had names of people. I found some of them. And then I found myself."

"Why would you tell me this?" I asked her.

"To be fair. I know about you."

"What could you know?"

"My . . . people, in New York, they say you are a man for hire."

"Even if that were so—"

"But here, you are hunting for yourself. This is personal, not professional."

"Why do you say?"

"Because of what you do *not* say. About money."

"I don't understand."

"You hired me. I am a woman for hire, and you hired me. But you never discussed the price of my services. As if it did not matter to you. So either you are concerned only with your target, or you plan to cheat me. Or dispose of me."

"You're pretty relaxed for someone who'd even consider that last . . . thing."

"All my life, I have had only minutes—minutes at the most—to make decisions about people. One day I will be wrong. That day I will die."

"Is that . . . I don't know, Buddhism or something?"

"It is the Zen of violence. It has no logic, only essence. There are no computations, no calculations. No facts. Therefore, no theories."

"It sounds dangerous."

"No. It is a total thing. Do you know the fear of not knowing? Do you understand the terror of being utterly without power, in the hands of those who might use you, might hurt you, might kill you . . . might do . . . anything?"

I looked at her, saw trace lightning the color of iodine flash in her black eyes. "Yeah, I do know," is all I said.

"Yes," she said, accepting my answer as truth. "So you do not wait for decisions to be made by others. You *act*. If you succeed, you hold the power of your decision. If you fail, you die. It is the only way."

"The Tao?"

"If you like. The Way is not *one* way. We are born into this world differently, one from the other. There is no fate. No destiny. There is only random chance. When you act, you alter that randomness. It may be for your good; it may be for your death. But it is better to make the decisions for yourself. No matter the outcome, the fear is gone."

"Fear is the key," I told Gem later that night as she sat lotus-positioned on the carpet, a plain white tablet on her thighs.

"Controlled fear. We have to spook them enough to get them out in the open, but not so much that they take off."

"What they do *not* know, then?"

"Yeah, that's the way I figure it, too. If we address it right to the drop box, they'll know we have at least that much."

"Do you know what you want to say?"

It was another hour before it was done. Gem worked silently, setting up her gear with the practiced, careful movements of a bomb-maker. First she sprayed some cleanser on the surface of the desk and wiped it vigorously with a silk scarf. "Formica," she said, in a satisfied tone. "No fiber transfer." She coated her hands with a trace of talcum powder and slipped on a pair of surgeon's gloves. Next she took out a factory-sealed box of typing paper, opened it along one seam with a single-edged razor blade, and took out a sheet. She wrote quickly and precisely, using a cheap roller-ball pen, the kind they sell a few million of every year. "Purchased in Corpus Christi, Texas, about two years ago," she said when she saw me looking at the English version she had copied from.

Gem's handwriting was more like printing, only the slight serif on some letters and the right-hand slant hinting at individualism.

Sergei & Sophia—

Dmitri is dead. You are connected to this through the boy. There is danger for you. Dmitri kept records. For your own safety, we must meet. I will be in O'Bryant Square at the corner of Park and Washington on Monday afternoon, at 2:00 p.m. I will be wearing a bright-red jacket.

It was signed "Your Friend."

Gem picked up a small can of compressed air. She sprayed the single sheet of paper thoroughly, using the gentle sweeping motion of a graffiti tagger, then folded it precisely in thirds.

Next she opened a new packet of manila-colored Monarch-size envelopes—I could see they were the self-sealing type—and addressed one carefully. Then she inserted the letter, peeled off the strip to expose the adhesive, and rubbed her gloved thumb along the seam to make sure the seal was tight. The stamp came from a roll; a stick-on.

Gem slid the stamped, addressed envelope into a Ziploc bag and sealed it.

"If we mail it today—Tuesday—they will get it on Friday at the latest. That still gives us Saturday as a fail-safe."

"If they check their box every day," I reminded her.

She shrugged. I knew what that meant: they would or they wouldn't—it was out of her hands. And there was always another Monday.

Later that day, I stood very close to Gem, holding the mailbox slot open and shielding her as she made the Ziploc spit out its contents.

"Do you know this town?" I asked her.

"Why? What is it that you need?"

"Unless you brought a red coat with you, it's what *you* need."

A smile played across her face. "I love shopping," she said.

We found her a brilliant red coat—a hunter's jacket, the guy in the store told her. She also found a pair of lace-up boots she fancied. And some other stuff.

We had a late lunch with Byron at a little restaurant he knew about. He held his lips in a whistling position as he watched Gem eat, but no sound came out.

"So you figure on me coming back no later than Sunday morning, okay?" he said.

"Perfect. Thanks."

"Sure. Tell you what—drive me out to where I've got the limo stashed. I'll take it back to Seattle; you keep the hot rod until I get back. The suite's covered, no worries there."

"You want me to meet you at the airport Sunday?"

"No need. There's always plenty of cabs around at PDX. And that way, there won't be any phone calls."

"Speaking of . . ."

"How many you want?"

I spent the next couple of days prowling Portland. Knowing I didn't have enough time to really learn the streets, but wanting to get a sense of the terrain. I'd checked the plaza where we'd set the meet—it was only a few blocks from the hotel—and I knew it couldn't be boxed without a damn regiment standing by. The hotel was my trump—a place to duck into where I could just disappear.

Anyone interested might check the lobby, but no way the hotel was going to stand for a room-to-room unless it was the police asking. Whoever they might be considering for backup, I was sure the Russians weren't bringing the law.

Gem always passed on coming along with me. Said she had some things to do. Sometimes she was there when I got back, sometimes she wasn't. She must have found a greengrocer nearby—the living room smelled like a fruit stand from all the produce she had stacked in various spots. Refrigeration wasn't a problem; Gem ate everything she scored the same day she brought it back. She asked me once if I wanted some pomegranates. I played along and told her no thanks. She ate them all, neatly and completely.

My first day of prowling turned up a bakery a few blocks away. A good one, from the smells. Picked out a half-dozen pastries. Plump ones, oozing with custard and cream. Gem gave me a sly smile and a wink, as if I'd just bribed her. And a tiny trace of a wiggle as she pranced over to the desk to arrange the pastries in a neat, precise row.

She washed them all down with hits from a huge bottle of water, talking between bites.

"You are in danger?" she asked.

"Yeah. I just don't know from who."

"But the people I am to meet—they will know?"

"They'll know something. Maybe the solution to the puzzle, maybe just another piece of it."

"If there was no danger to you, you would not be seeking them?"

"No."

She regarded me soberly, despite a mouth surrounded by powdered sugar. I felt like I was cocaine on her scale: telling her I weighed a kilo while her readout said two pounds.

"It cannot be as you say. Not *only* as you say."

"Why?"

"You are in a rage. A cold, black rage. When we talked . . . before . . . you told me you understood the fear. I believe that is true. But you are being hunted, yes? You were almost killed, and by people you do not know. Where is your fear now, Mr. Burke?"

"It's there, I promise you."

"Is it? Whoever your enemies are, you could hide from them. But what you want is their blood."

"Why would you say—?"

"Revenge is only for small things," she said, her voice a thin strand of white-hot wire. "For my country, for my people, there can be no revenge."

"So you forgive the Khmer Rouge?"

"So *you* mock me? What do you know of our . . . suffering?" she said, something deeper than anger in her tone. I figured she never finished the first time she talked about it, so I just shut up and listened. "What revenge could you imagine for such a scale of evil?" she went on. "Could there be revenge for what Hitler did to the Jews? Or Stalin to his people? For Idi Amin? In Cambodia, it was not one tribe against another. It was not Rwanda. Or Bosnia. Or Northern Ireland. It was not even the 'class struggle' so beloved of Marxists, although Pol Pot claimed to be one. What happened was that the monster was set free.

The monster in men that kills, and tortures, and rapes for . . . for the pure evil joy of it. Revenge? For true revenge, we would have to kill the Devil."

"There is no Devil. There is no 'evil' that gets loose. It's all inside humans. Some humans. And it's those humans who have to pay."

"*Which* humans? The ten-year-old boy who bashed in babies' skulls with a shovel because his leaders told him the babies were the seeds of the privileged class? The people who made moral decisions *not* to kill died for their choice. Would you *cleanse* all Cambodia to be certain none of the guilty escaped?"

"No. But they can be found if only—"

"Found? Perhaps. Some of them. Some few of them. But even South Africa has a Truth and Reconciliation Commission. They are trying to heal their country, not exterminate all those who committed atrocities. Rwanda is going to have trials. They will take *decades*, and only a handful of people will be punished. Only zealots want revenge. Most people, what they want is food. They want safety. And they want a future. Revenge will provide none of that."

"That's their choice."

"But not yours."

"Not mine."

"People have hurt you. In your life, yes?"

"Yes."

"Were you always able to have your revenge?"

"No. Some of them . . . I could never find them. Others died before I could."

"But you still hate?"

"I don't think I do. I don't hate the dead—I hate what they did."

"So . . . now? Why do you hate now?"

"Could you come here?" I asked her.

She walked slowly over to where I was sitting, turned her back, cocked one hip, and perched on the arm of the chair.

"I want to tell you something," I said.

I t took a long time to tell her. I didn't start out to do that—just wanted to explain how Pansy had died, loyal past death. But I kept going backwards, all the way to when Pansy was a pup. How you were supposed to wrap an old alarm clock in a towel and let the puppy sleep next to it—it would sound like a heartbeat from her mother, and comfort her. I let her sleep on my own heart instead.

When I stopped talking, she stayed quiet. I could barely see her in the darkness that had dropped like a lazy curtain.

"Who pays?" she whispered.

"Whoever was there. Whoever sent them."

"And then you are finished?"

"Yes."

"I do not believe you," is all she replied.

T he next morning, she was gone, the door to her room standing open. I was up by five-thirty, so she must have taken off when it was pitch-dark outside. I flicked on the light in the hall. It threw off enough to show me that her suitcase was still there. The living room held no note. Her laptop was missing.

I showered and shaved, aimless, taking my time. Went out and ate a slow breakfast: a toasted bagel with cream cheese and pineapple juice. The cream cheese had little bits of chive, sharp and clean. The juice tasted like they'd just taken a machete to a fresh batch of pineapples that morning. But the bagel was a flop—mealy, flabby, and with no real crust. I guess what they say is true.

I found an OTB a few blocks from the hotel. But even though it took plays on out-of-town tracks, all the action was on thoroughbreds or the dogs. I only bet the trotters. And I fucking *hate* greyhound racing—I know what happens to the dogs as soon as they lose a step or two.

Back to learning the streets. I spotted a poolroom, but shrugged off the temptation—the fewer people who got a close-up of me before the meet, the better. Traffic was often clogged, especially where they were building a trolley line through town, but the drivers seemed either resigned to it or more polite than I believed people in cities could get.

By midday, I'd found a giant Borders on Southwest Third. Turned out the place took up the whole corner. I saw more gorgeous women in their coffee shop than you'd see in an L.A. restaurant. But these girls were all reading books, not waiting on tables, so I never talked to any of them.

I just strolled, looking around. I kept seeing signs that said Portland was the "Rose City," but I didn't see any roses.

After a whole day, I decided that the Northwest sector looked most like places I was used to operating in. And that the Horse was loose in Portland's streets, riding a lot of young kids, its weight too much for them to carry. I knew the end of that script.

Gem didn't come back that night. I watched television until narcolepsy set in. Didn't take long.

On waiting-day number three, it rained. I continued my learning on foot, London-cabdriver-style, getting the nuances I'd miss behind the wheel. Couldn't cover a lot of ground, but whatever I covered, I covered tight, working my way around and behind O'Bryant Square.

It was one block square: ground-level at one end, full-width terraced at the other, the steps perfect for sitting. No fences or gates, so it had easy access to all four of the streets that made up its borders.

I never found it empty, no matter what time I went past. Homeless nomads with clear plastic sacks of recyclables they'd rescued from the trash, students with their backpacks and attitudes, burnt-out runaways. A guy in a business suit was meeting a woman who couldn't have been his wife from the way he kept eye-sweeping for anybody he might know, a young girl was drawing something in a large tablet, two men in their thirties openly shared a joint. And pigeons. Plenty of pigeons.

When I got back, Gem was there, perched on the arm of the easy chair like she'd been when I told her about Pansy. She didn't turn around when I came in.

"Why don't you sit in the chair?" I asked her.

"I was saving it for you," she said, almost formally.

"Thank you," I replied, in the same tone.

I sat down.

"Do you want something to eat?" I asked her.

She flashed a smile, nodded her head.

"Anything in particular?"

"No. Just—"

"—a lot, right?"

"Yes."

t was the first time I'd tried room service since I'd been at the hotel. No risk, as I saw it. A hotshot studio exec like me, who'd look twice at an exotic dinner companion in his room? I ordered as if there were three people eating, and came up only a little short . . . which I cured when I told Gem I didn't want my dessert.

She took three chunky white pills with her meal, not making any big deal about it. I didn't ask, so I was surprised when she said, "Monocal. It's the only way to get fluoride bonded with calcium."

"Why would you need that?"

"Osteoporosis," she said, unsmiling.

"But you're not old enough to—"

"Malnutrition can induce it very early, especially if there's any bone-marrow exposure."

I didn't say anything. Thinking about Biafra again. All that marrow exposed.

"It's not a difficult regimen," Gem said. "Heavy on the calcium, fluoride to bond it home, no brown sodas . . ."

"Brown sodas?"

"Coke, Pepsi, root beer. . . ."

"That's bad for you? If you have . . . ?"

"Osteoporosis? Yes."

"I didn't know."

"It is of no consequence," she said. "A man like you will never die of osteoporosis."

We watched the late news together. They replayed part of an interview with the human who'd watched his friend snatch a little girl inside a two-bit casino. Watched him drag the child into a bathroom and start to work on her. When he was done watching, he walked out. Maybe played with the slot machines. His friend came out about twenty minutes later, his work done. The human never said a word. They found the little girl's body in that bathroom, raped and murdered.

The casino's videocams had most of it—right up to where the killer chased her into the bathroom. He got nabbed a few days later. His friend was telling the interviewer *he* hadn't done anything wrong; he just did what he thought was best for himself. That human's at a fancy college now, studying engineering.

"Fucking maggot," I said, half to myself.

"Most people do what he did," Gem said.

"What do you mean?"

"Most people, when they observe the worst things that are done, they only watch. Or turn away. Because they fear if they were to do something the evil would turn on them, too."

She got to her feet and walked into her own room.

I took a shower. Washed my hair. Brushed my teeth. Shaved. Killing time. I knew I wasn't going to sleep. It happens sometimes, no point in arguing with it.

The living room was all shadows except for a small, dark-shaded lamp on an end table by the couch. I didn't want to turn on the TV or the radio, and there was nothing to read but yesterday's newspaper. I started making charts in my head, putting the players on it like chess pieces.

The shadows shifted. Gem stepped into the faint light. Her hair was free and loose, face calm. She was nude, her slim body catching the shadowy light in her own shadows.

"Yes?" she said, just above a whisper.

I stood up. She turned and walked down the hall, a willow in a gentle breeze.

S he sat with her back against the bedboard, hands clasped around her knees, watching me take my clothes off. When I came closer, she made a *click-click* sound with her tongue.

The only light was spillover from the living room, but it didn't matter—I was too close to her for my eye to focus anyway.

Her hands were exploratory. Unpracticed. I took a handful of her lustrous hair, pulled her face toward mine. She moved so that her face was in my neck, made some sound I'd never heard before.

Her skin was velvety, faintly coated with moisturizer. I slowly traced the inside curve of her thigh toward its apex. Halfway up, my hand snagged on a spot of raised, gnarled flesh. I moved past it. As soon as I did, Gem made another noise. I moved my hand back down to the scarred patch of flesh, put my thumb on it lightly, and rubbed it in little circles. She twisted her hips, slid one leg over me.

"Yes?" she said again.

I put my hands on her waist, moved her more upright, so she was straddling me. I could feel her wet heat, and I slipped inside like a fox into a thicket. A fox with the hounds close and coming.

She grunted, thrust her hips against me, opening, taking me in so deep that our pelvic bones hit.

I fell into a gentle rhythm, no urgency. She threw back her head, the cords on her neck standing out.

I reached back to her small, tight bottom and pulled her even closer. It was as smooth and languid as underwater swimming. She . . .

. . . was on her knees next to me, bending all the way forward, her lips against my face. "What did you see in your window?" she whispered.

I shook my head. Hard. To clear it. The last thing I remembered, I was inside her. What had—?

"I don't . . ."

"A window opened, yes?"

I didn't say anything, trying to go back—what? A minute? Ten minutes? To when I'd lost . . . I was underwater with . . . with the shark. The shark coming for me again.

"What's a window?" I asked her.

"An intrusive image. Unbidden. Sometimes, when a person concentrates very hard on something, the brain's safeguards slip. And . . . other things come in."

"But . . ."

"It happens to me, too," she said. "My mind is like a computer screen—I see whatever is happening before me, in real time. But, sometimes, a little window opens inside that screen. A window of memory. It widens and widens until it *is* the whole screen."

"What do you do, then?"

"I used to scream. Now I just let it come. Because I know it will go if I . . . let it. The window's power comes from resistance. I do not resist."

"But I wasn't seeing . . . anything. Just you."

"And then it opened up, yes? Tell me."

I closed my eyes. The window was gone. I reached for her. She came close, cheek against my chest. I held her there while I told her about the shark. And how I still keep seeing Pansy cut down. Again and again.

It was a long time before we fell asleep. My cock stayed small and soft. But it didn't feel useless, nestled in her cupped hand. I drifted away to an unbroken black screen.

Gem was gone when I woke on Friday. I heard the shower running. Then it stopped. She opened the door to her bathroom, looked at me in her bed, and said, "Did your room come with a bathrobe?"

"It did. But I . . . It's not clean—I used it last night."

"Good," she said, walking past me, dripping, her hair wrapped in a turban of towel.

I ordered a pair of three-egg omelettes—ham, cheese, mushrooms, and onions—with sides of sausage links, home fries, and three large glasses of apple juice.

Ordered something for myself, too.

"Is Gem the way your name is pronounced?"

She smiled. "You mean, *not* how it is spelled, yes?"

"Yes."

"Why do you ask?"

"If I had to write your name . . ."

"Oh. Do you not use e-mail?"

"No. I don't even have a computer."

"Oh," she said. And went back to her food.

She never did get dressed, shucking my bathrobe when the place got warm enough for her. All she had on her body was a thick black PVC band on her wrist, one of those ultra-chic new watches, I guessed.

Nude, she was about as self-conscious as a politician stealing. I just watched her, the sunlight coming through the windows playing against her gentle curves.

Gem took out a small, flat leather case and unzipped it. I could see the gleam of highly polished metal inside. She removed an assortment of what looked like dental picks, a vial of murky fluid, tiny circles of white gauze. Then she unsnapped something from the underside of that thick rubber watchband. It was a beautifully machined piece of blued steel tubing. As soon as she flicked what looked like a mechanical pencil and a long rod came out the front, I knew what she was holding.

"What caliber?" I asked her.

"This one is chambered for twenty-fives."

"More than one?"

"Two, yes."

"Not much of an impact with—"

"But very, very small," she said, tapping the underside of her wrist. "And subsonic ammunition. Very quiet."

"You have to be—"

"Close. Yes."

She cleaned the mini-Derringer with practiced movements, her square-cut nails clicking on the metal every so often. When she was done, she came to where I was sitting. Bent down and kissed the side of my neck, her dark-nippled bleached-earth breasts against my face, fresh-harvest hair all around us both.

"Yes?" is all she said.

It didn't work any better than it had the last time.

Gem took a very long time to put on her makeup. She was sitting lotus-positioned, working by sunlight before a large portable mirror she'd set up in the living room. Looking over her shoulder, I could see her face in the mirror. But I couldn't see where all the makeup went.

She took a long time in her room, too. When she came out, she was wearing a green plaid pleated skirt and a green wool blazer with a school crest on the left breast pocket. Plain black loafers and white knee-highs. She slipped on her backpack, bowed her head slightly to me. She looked about sixteen.

"I will be back in a few hours," is all she said.

Most people would have a hard time with all the waiting I had to do. Most people weren't raised in places where patience was one of the few ways you could resist what they were doing to you. But, sitting there, thinking it through, I got some of the windowing again. As if, when I pushed hard enough with my mind, I cracked some membrane and the memories flowed like lava, unstoppable.

It was dark by the time Gem came back. She slipped her backpack off her shoulders, let it fall to the floor, then walked over to me, an expression on her face I couldn't read.

She sat delicately in my lap. Unfastened the top two buttons of the white oxford-cloth shirt she had on under the blazer.

"Would you like me to leave this on?" she asked, shyly, her face buried against me—I could feel the heat.

"No."

She shivered.

"What's wrong?" I asked her.

"You're ice now."

"Sorry."

"No, I am sorry. What I said . . . it was wrong."

I tugged on her thin shoulder so that she was facing me. "It wasn't wrong," I said quietly. "It was sweet. You were trying to . . . help me . . . with what's wrong."

"I insulted you."

"No."

"Yes. Yes, I did. I did not mean it as you believe."

"How do you know what I believe?"

"The ice. It does not lie. But I am a grown woman, not a child. For today, for what I had to do, it was a disguise. But an outfit, when you know the truth, is not the same as—"

"No. You're right. But it's too . . . close."

"Close?"

"To the line. A grown woman wants to dress up as a schoolgirl, it can be cute and sexy. But only if it's real obvious she's grown, understand? The way you're made up, you look *too* real."

"Ah."

"I don't need a window for that," I told her.

"I understand."

"Do you, girl? There's . . . lines, okay? All kinds of things turn people on. As long as there's two—hell, two or more—players and they're grown, it's nobody's business. Some people get excited by feet. That's fine. But there's freaks who get excited by *kids'* feet. That's . . . not."

"Why is that . . . not?"

"Because kids don't agree to play. They *can't* agree. It's not in them, to make those decisions. Like the maggots who spank their kids for entertainment."

"To spank a child is wrong?" she asked, gravely.

"A smack on the rear end if a little kid runs out into the street or something? I'm not going to say that. What do I know? I don't have kids. Never will. But . . . you go on-line, dial up any newsgroup that's into spanking. You understand what I'm saying, right? Spanking as erotic. You'll see adults looking for other adults, fair enough. But you'll also see people who talk about 'disciplining' kids. How come they go to a sex board if it's about parenting? Think about it for a second. They're nothing but child molesters. And they get a pass from the law—it's not illegal to spank your own kid, even if you're doing it only to get your rocks off."

"You have so much hate."

"You think so? You don't have any idea."

"Did someone . . . when you were a . . . ?"

"Lots of people," I said. "Lot of places. Lots of times."

The tears running down her face ate through the heavy makeup, the girl-child vanishing, a woman taking her place.

"It will take a long time," she said that evening, looking at me through the mirror before her to where I was lying on the bed.

"What will?"

"For me to get dressed."

"Sure. What difference does it—?"

"Do you want to watch me?"

"Watch you get dressed?"

"Yes."

"I—"

"That is where the secrets are," she said. "When a woman undresses, men think she is revealed. But it is as a woman dresses herself that the truth of her is shown."

"And you don't want me to—"

"I *do* want you to. I have been . . . unfair."

"Gem, I told you, it isn't your—"

"Not about the . . . outfit. I mean . . . when you . . . retained me, you knew . . . what about me?"

"That you were fluent in Russian. That people who my people trusted vouched for you."

"And . . . ?" she asked, covering her face and neck with cold cream.

"That's all," I told her, truthfully.

"The woman you call Mother—"

"Mama."

"Is that not the same—"

"No," I said, crimping that wire before it sparked.

"She is well known. To the people from whom I get my . . . assignments. Very respected."

"Uh-huh."

"Yes. And . . . I made some inquiries. You understand, it is good to know the people with whom you work," she said. I didn't say anything, not sure if she was insulting my own professional-ism for not getting more info on her, or rolling out the carpet to a door she was about to open. I shifted my posture to tell her I heard what she said . . . and was waiting for the rest of it.

She started to remove the cream. Gently, patting it off with a washcloth. "There are many . . . rumors about you, Burke."

"Sure."

"They cannot all be false."

"Is that some mathematical certainty? Some law of nature?"

"In a way, it is," she said, seriously. "Some rumors must have a factual basis, if they are to stay alive long enough."

"Or they have enough people continuing to come forward and say, 'Yeah, I was abducted by aliens, too.'"

"You may have your jokes," she said, calmly, doing something around her eyes with a makeup pencil.

"I'm not making fun of you. Just of people who take rumors to the bank."

"You have been in prison."

"That's no secret."

"Some say you have killed," she said, no emotion in her voice, all her focus on the dark-red lipstick she was carefully applying.

"See? There's the difference between facts and rumors."

"And some say you are insane."

"I'm sure."

"A very selective insanity," she said, eyes very wide in the mirror, working on her lashes. "It is said that when children are hurt you go blind with rage."

"Is that right? Who says that?"

"Some of the same people who say you have killed."

"Naturally."

"No," she said. "*Many* say you have killed. Some say you kill for money, a professional. *Different* people speak of your rage. A professional has no rage."

"You'd know that," I said, flat-voiced.

"Yes," glancing at me in the mirror. Her eyes were heavily shadowed by then, a bluish-green color.

"Is this another disguise?" I asked. Meaning all the makeup she was piling on.

"Not yet. Be patient," she said, now painting her fingernails the same shade as her lips.

"All right."

"I want to go out later. Is that okay?"

"You don't have to ask me if—"

"No. I don't mean I am going alone. I want you to take me."

"To eat, right?"

"No." She giggled. "I am aware that you consider me a sow. Where I . . . live now, there is a little bar. It has a pool table. I always watch, never play. I would like to play. I understand it takes practice to play well. But I need to know the rudiments of the game before I can practice. And I hoped you would teach me."

"What makes you think I—?"

"Am I incorrect?" she asked, gravely.

"No."

"Ah." She smiled, waiting.

"I don't know a poolroom around here," I lied, smoothly.

"There is one very close by. And there is another, perhaps ten or fifteen minutes away by car. Probably that would be best . . ." she said, thoughtfully.

"Because . . . ?"

"Be patient," she said, again, combing out her midnight-thick hair.

I lay back on the bed, slitted my eyes, watched as she climbed into a micro-pair of near-transparent panties, then sheathed her legs in sheer stockings with seams down the back. She turned to face me, looked over her shoulder at the mirror, snapped the elastic tops of her stockings experimentally, checked the seams. Then she put on a pair of gleaming black spike heels with ankle straps. Checked herself again. A piece of red jersey the same shade as her lipstick expanded from its tube shape to cover her bottom . . . and not much else. She slipped a black silk tank top over her shoulders. It fell short of the skirt's waistband. A necklace of tiny beads the same shade as the lipstick and the skirt went over her head, then around her neck.

She leaned against the wall, extended one perfect leg just a little, shot her hip. "What do I look like now?" she asked.

"I'm not a fashion consultant," I told her, seeing the trap surrounding the cheese.

"But not a little girl?"

"Not hardly."

"Well, will you teach me to play?"

"I . . . Looks to me like you already know how."

"You know what I mean, Burke."

"I'm not sure I do," I said. "The way you climbed into all that . . . stuff, it can't be for the first time. If your point is that you're not a little girl, I got it. I wasn't confused about that before, Gem."

"Yes. But . . . you said . . . lines. There are always lines. Some people are drawn to them. As if there was a mystical place near the border, where the lines are drawn. But you . . . you don't want to go near such places."

"No."

"Because you once did and . . . ?"

"There's a difference between venturing close to the rim and being thrown there."

"The . . . choices, again, you mean?"

"When you're a kid, there *are* no choices. That's the biggest fucking lie they ever tell. Like sticking a pistol in your face, cocking it, and asking for a loan."

"Yes. It was that way for us, too. The choice—to be a soldier in the Khmer Rouge—it was no choice at all."

"Adults have—"

"Stop it! I respect your pain. But it is not all the pain that the world knows, Burke. There could be no 'resistance' in my country. The people outside the cities, they never had weapons. They never had communications. The Khmer Rouge came with weapons. And with orders. If you did not join the killing, you were one of 'them': those who *should* be killed. You could try to flee. Many did. But how could you fight? Moral choices are for those with power. You can judge the monsters, not the victims. We were *all* children, then. Without power, without recourse. With no one listening for so long. So we did whatever we could to survive."

"I'm sorry. I didn't mean to—"

"We were all children," she said again.

Then the schoolgirl who had cried for what had hurt me a million years ago came over to me. I held her against me while the woman in the hooker's outfit cried for her lost and ravaged people.

I couldn't comfort Gem. Couldn't make it stop. So I did the only thing I could—stayed the course. She cried herself to sleep. Silently, the way she must have learned in the jungle.

She was so taut, she vibrated. I pulled the bedspread up so it covered her shoulders, kept my arm around her, waited. Her body didn't so much relax as unstiffen. Slowly, in sections. She was breathing regularly, in measured little gulps, but so shallow that her rib cage hardly flickered. Gradually, her right knee came up, rested on my thigh. Her hand explored my chest. Finally, she tucked the tips of her fingers into my armpit and shuddered slightly, and her body went soft with deeper sleep.

I must have drifted off with her after a while. Her butterfly kiss on my cheek woke me. I looked over her shoulder at the digital clock on the side table: 11:44. We'd been out for hours.

"It's not too late," she said against my face.

"For what?"

"To learn to play pool!" she said, a sweet stubbornness in her voice.

"You mean tonight?"

"Yes!"

"Gem, look. I—"

"You said you would."

"And I will. But let's . . . compromise, okay?"

"How?" she asked, propping herself on one elbow, watching me.

"I'll take you, okay? But not in that outfit."

"Why not?"

"Come on, little girl. You walk into a poolroom dressed like that, I'll be in a half-dozen brawls before we get near a table."

"Huh!" she snorted. But ruined the effect with a giggle.

"Come on. All you need to do is—"

"I will change my clothes," she said, almost formally. "But it took a very long time to apply all this makeup. I will not remove it."

"All right," I said quietly, wondering if she knew what her crying had done to the paint job . . . if she'd glance at herself in a mirror before we left.

I grabbed a quick shower. Changed into chinos and a pullover. I was just about finished when Gem came into my room, wearing a pair of jeans and a hot pink sweatshirt. All that was left from her streetwalker's outfit was the spike heels.

And all the makeup was gone.

She saw me looking at her fresh-scrubbed face. "You won't forget, will you?"

"Forget what?"

"What I looked like . . . before?"

"I doubt I'll *ever* forget it, girl."

"You will remember, while we're out together, yes?"

"I promise."

The poolroom was nothing like the joints where I'd learned to play as a kid. The tables looked ultra-modern, with the short ends canted at a spaceship angle. The pockets were some kind of hard plastic, not mesh. The lighting was ceiling-recessed, without individual drop-down lamps for each table. No beads strung overhead—each table had little dials you could turn to mark the scoring. The felt covering each of the tabletops was all different colors—every one except green.

And not a single NO GAMBLING sign in sight.

Even the music was pitiful pop and sappy soul. I was thinking maybe Gem could have worn her outfit without any trouble, but I kept that thought to myself.

We got a plastic tray of balls, took an empty table against the wall. I showed Gem how to check a cue for straightness, how to examine the tip to make sure it was properly shaped. She was gravely attentive, not interrupting.

I demonstrated how to make a bridge, how to cradle the butt end of the cue lightly in her right hand, how to stroke.

Then I went through the fundamentals, concentrating on the relationship between the cue ball, the object ball, and the pocket.

Not once did she demonstrate any impatience.

I lined up a bunch of balls in a fan around the corner pocket and put the cue ball a couple of feet back, at the midpoint of the fan, and Gem started to practice.

Her first shot went in, but the cue ball followed right behind. I showed her how placing the tip of the cue slightly below center would stop the white ball at the point of contact. The first time she tried it herself, the ball hopped. I caught it on the fly, not surprised.

"Was that a good trick?" she asked, smiling.

"It's a good trick if you can control it," I told her.

"I think I can . . ." she said, and, before I could say anything, hopped the white ball right off the table again.

"Uh, that's a pretty advanced move," I said. "Maybe we should wait until you've had a few more games under your belt, okay?"

"Yes," she said, narrowing her eyes in concentration.

It took maybe half an hour for Gem to get the concept of angles. She had a delicate touch with the cue stick, chalking up after each shot as I'd shown her, forming the bridge with her left hand carefully each time. Except for two guys on a nearby table who didn't even pretend to play whenever Gem bent over and took a long time to line up a shot, we might as well have been alone.

Never once did Gem ask to play an actual game. She just went through each exercise I showed her, focusing hard.

"You are very patient," she said, echoing my own thoughts.

"How do you mean?"

"Well, it cannot be much fun for you, to watch me and not play yourself."

"It's a great pleasure to watch you."

Her creamy beige cheeks took on a sprinkling of cinnamon. "You know what I meant," she said.

"Sure. But I wasn't kidding. You're really learning. And it *is* a pleasure to watch."

After a while, we played an actual game. I started her with straight pool. It's the hardest version to play, because you have to call each shot, but it's the best one for learning how things work on a table. I missed most of the shots I took, not pretending it wasn't on purpose, setting up various opportunities so Gem could have a look at them.

I'd expected the lack of depth perception to affect my game, but it didn't seem to—the balls went where I wanted them to go.

We didn't keep score.

One of the men on the next table strolled over, said to me, "You interested in playing for a little something?"

"No thanks."

"Come on. Your girlfriend can watch you in action, what do you say?"

"No thanks."

"My buddy and I, we've been watching you. Looks like you really know the game. I figured, maybe I could learn something, you know?"

"No thanks."

"Hey, man. Is that all you know how to say?"

I let the prison yard come into my eyes, told him, "I can say, 'Step the fuck *off*,' pal. You like that better?"

But he'd been raised so far away from prison yards that he didn't get it. His hand whitened around the pool cue he was holding. "You got a problem?" he challenged.

His buddy rolled up, stood behind the first guy's right shoulder.

I guessed the fancy tables and the middle-class music didn't mean so much after all.

"No problem," I assured the guy with the pool cue. "In fact, we were just leaving."

When I said "we," I glanced over at where Gem was to make sure she understood. She was gone. I had a flame-tongue flicker of fear, but then I spotted her—standing off to the side of the two men, feet spread, knees slightly bent. And a clenched fist at her hip.

"You want to take this outside?" the guy with the cue asked, his voice more confident than his hands.

I stepped in close to him, the red three-ball I'd snatched from the table when they'd first closed in cupped in my fist. "No," I said softly. "And neither do you."

It took him a couple of heartbeats, but he finally matched the music to the lyrics. "Punk!" he sneered . . . as he was turning his back to walk away.

"What style?" I asked Gem in the car on the way back to the hotel.

"I do not understand."

"Martial arts. What style do you study?"

"Me? I am no martial artist. Why would you think so?"

"Back there. When you made a fist. You put your thumb on top of your clenched fingers, not bent over the side, the way people usually do."

"It is better that way?" she asked, innocently.

"The way you do it? Sure. You can feel the difference in the muscles of your forearm. And you won't break your thumb when you strike that way, too."

"So!"

"Are you trying to tell me you make a fist that way naturally?"

"No. It is true, someone showed me how to do that. But that is all they showed me. It was a long time ago. I was just a small child. I always did as my elders instructed me."

"Didn't . . . whoever showed you, didn't they show you any more?"

"It was only that one night," Gem said, nothing in her voice. "The next day, she was gone."

I let it go. Some locks shouldn't be picked.

"You can never slam the window closed," she said later, in bed. "When you try, it only opens wider."

I lay there, wondering if it would ever be any different.

"It only opened a little this time, isn't that true?" she asked.

"Yes," I said, wondering how she knew.

"And then you tried to concentrate so hard on what you . . . what *we* were doing?"

"Yeah."

"And that opened the window more, do you see?"

"Then how can I—?"

"This is something you cannot fight by fighting. By fighting, you invoke it."

"Invoke it? It just popped—"

"No," she whispered, as if telling me a deep secret. "You *expect* it. And your desire to battle it brings it forth."

"What do I do, then? Surrender?"

"Not surrender. Accept. Sometimes the window will open. And sometimes it will not. You feel as if you cannot . . . lose yourself in . . . this," she said, her hand cupping my testicles, thumbnail gently scraping under the root. "But you can. Not by trying. By *not* trying. Go to sleep, Burke. There are no windows in your sleep. It will only be your body then."

"But if I'm asleep . . . ?"

"I will not be," Gem said, thumbnail resting against my root, sending a tiny tremor to where I thought was dead.

I was . . . maybe . . . afraid to ask Gem anything the next morning. Her eyes were shining, but I figured that was from the waffles with maple syrup, double-side of bacon and home fries, and the two chocolate malts she called breakfast.

She went out for a while. Came back with the Sunday paper. *The Oregonian*. Must be statewide, with a name like that, I figured.

We sat on the couch and read the paper quietly. By the time we finished, Gem was hungry again.

"You mind going over it one more time?" I asked her. "Tomorrow's the meet, and . . ."

"Of course," she said.

"I'll page Byron. No point doing it in pieces."

It took Byron less than an hour to show up. He greeted Gem almost formally, taking his cue from her. I wished I had his manners. Or maybe just his natural grace.

I drew a sketch of the plaza and the surrounding streets. Explained I'd be there first, and Gem should take whatever spot looked best to her. We couldn't script it any closer than that—no telling what other actors would be on the stage.

"You've got the tricky part," I told Byron.

"And I've got help," he said.

"We can't—"

"Not 'we,' partner. Me. I have a . . . friend. A very close friend. One that *I* can trust. All he knows is we're going to do a box tail."

"Does he know how to—?"

"Better than me," Byron said, pride in his voice. "He's a spook."

CIA? Did they have a "don't ask, don't tell" like the Army? And did anyone actually believe that bullshit? I let it go. A man who could hide from his own employers could certainly handle his end of a box tail.

"They're going to be edgy," I warned them both.

"Then we shall be calm," Gem replied.

"You're going to have to improv," I said to her. "It really doesn't matter so much what you say. You're only there to give information. Sent by a friend. A friend you never met—a friend of *theirs*, see? You're just the messenger."

"Yes."

"Whatever you do, no matter what kind of opening they give you, don't ask any questions. They'll be looking for that."

"I understand."

"Something else is happening. Something besides me. These people disappeared a while ago. Put some very complicated systems in place, must have been planning it for a while. And they can't be earning money legit; not in their professions, anyway. I saw their setup in Chicago. Expensive. *Real* expensive to maintain, the way they're doing it. Heavy front, heavy cost. It's a tightrope. We have to make them nervous enough to contact whoever set me up. But not panic them into running."

"What good will that do?" Byron asked. "There's a million ways for them to contact their principal, if that's what this is. Phone, fax, e-mail, telegram, FedEx, UPS, carrier pigeon . . . you name it. No way we can put a trap on all that."

"All this money, all this planning . . . Whoever wanted me dead isn't someone they can just call on the phone. They've got other things going. So they'll have cutouts in place."

"So you figure . . . the Russians reach out, it takes a while for whoever it is to get back to them."

"Yep."

"And we'll be waiting, right?"

"Watching."

"For what?" Byron asked.

"Fear is a communicable disease," I told them both. "Whatever makes them afraid, they're going to run to the people who put them in the jackpot, looking for answers. But, see, whoever put them there, *they'll* have to wonder, too. The wheels come off, you know the car's going to crash . . . but you don't know where it's going to hit."

"So you believe these . . . people, whoever they are, they will come to reassure the Russians?" Gem asked.

"Or to reassure them*selves*."

"You think . . . ?" Byron lifted an eyebrow.

"This was about murder, going in," I reminded him.

"So if they come to cut their losses . . ."

I nodded. Saw Gem out of the corner of my eye, doing the same.

t was raining when we got up the next morning, but the sun made its move before noon, and pressed its advantage once it got the upper hand. By one o'clock, it was almost seventy degrees on the street.

I'd been in the plaza for a couple of hours, making sure I had the bench I wanted. Byron was in position somewhere on the side opposite where I was, aimed the right way to exit quickly. I couldn't see the car he'd gotten for the job, but I knew it would be something bland. Maybe not as anonymous as his friend—the one whose name he hadn't yet mentioned—but close.

Gem would be walking toward the meet from somewhere within a half-mile radius, taking her time, the red coat neatly folded into her backpack.

I wasn't wearing a watch—it wouldn't have worked with my ensemble: Basic American Homeless. Stretched out on one of the benches, newspapers for a mattress, all my belongings in a rusty shopping cart, a big garbage bag full of recyclable plastic bottles next to me—the sorry harvest I'd turn into cash when the twisted wiring inside my mush brain told me to.

The clock on a nearby building read 1:54. If the Russians had come early, they were masters of disguise.

Gem strolled into the plaza, found herself an empty bench at an angle to where I was stretched out. She took out her red coat and shrugged into it before she sat down. Then she pulled out a thick paperback with a white cover and purple lettering. I'd seen it in her room: *The Thief*, some heavy Russian novel. She put a notebook to her left and cracked the novel open on her lap. She looked like a college girl, settling down for a long haul on her assignment.

I watched her through slitted eyes under the brim of a once-green John Deere gimme cap. She never looked up from the book. Three skinheads entered the plaza and draped themselves on the sitting-steps, clearing out the section they occupied as if their very presence was a natural repellent. Jeans, stomping boots, white sweatshirts with the sleeves cut off. Too far for me to read the tattoos, but I figured it was the usual Nazi mulch. They looked everyplace but at Gem.

Not good.

A man approached Gem. He was medium-height, with pepper-and-salt hair. Impossible to tell his build under the black topcoat he wore. They exchanged some words, and he sat down on her right. I was so focused in on them that I didn't pick up the woman until she was only a few feet away. She plucked Gem's notebook from the bench, handed it to her, and sat down in its place. Good technique—whenever Gem had to speak or listen to one of them, her back would be to the other.

I shifted my gaze to the skinheads. They were quiet, content to glare at anyone passing by, not talking among themselves.

The male Russian was talking and gesturing at the same time, intense. The female was still.

I couldn't see Byron. Couldn't tell if he'd scoped the skinheads.

Gem spread her hands in an "It beats me!" gesture. The Russian male pointed a finger at her face. She spread her hands again.

Suddenly, both Russians got up and walked away. Gem didn't look in their direction, just opened her book again, eyes down.

The skinheads slowly got to their feet, spread out, and started for Gem, their boots scraping on the concrete.

She stood up quickly, dropping the book.

I yelled "Hey!" and staggered off the bench, cutting them off.

They whirled toward me. Kids. Seeing another homeless man, probably wishing they had their squeeze bottles of gasoline with them. Veterans of a hundred street-stompings of color-coded victims. They were lazy and confident—a pack of garbage-dump bears, their predatory skills lost to Welfare. The leader swept a brass-knuckled backhand at my face. I slipped it, snapped my wrist. The heavy bicycle chain I had up my sleeve popped out. I went with its momentum, whipping the links across his knees. He went down, screaming something. The guy next to him spun to face me, thumbing the blade on his knife open, shouting, "Get the lemon nigger!" to the one still standing.

I backed off, engaging, pulling him to me, away from Gem. He made a couple of underhanded swipes with the blade, but never got within three feet, nervous about the chain.

"Fuck!" I heard the third one shout, but I didn't look over there. The guy with the knife did, turning his head just enough for me to get in with the chain. The knife clattered on the ground. The first one got to his feet, favoring one leg. I turned quickly. The guy who'd run over to Gem was sitting on the ground, holding his shoulder. The red coat was gone.

I took off, flying. Ran three blocks, dodging traffic. When I felt my breath get short, I stopped, turned to face them while I still had something left.

But they were nowhere in sight.

I shed the heavy overcoat in an alley Dumpster, along with the John Deere cap. And the chain. Then I wandered through two bookstores, a coffee shop, and a Native American crafts store, pumping some time into the mixture in case they had phone contact with others in the area.

Nothing.

I waited for rush hour, made my way back to the hotel along the sidewalks, circled the block twice on foot. Then I went up to the room.

Gem was seated by the window, wearing the fluffy white hotel bathrobe, her hair wet and glistening.

I let my breath out.

"You want something to eat?" I asked, by way of telling her that we needed to wait for Byron so she didn't have to go over everything twice.

She grinned.

Gem had honeydew melon and a pair of rare-roast-beef sandwiches on rye, slathered with Thousand Island dressing. And a glass of red wine. I watched her eat, not hungry myself, just chewing mechanically on my tuna, bacon, and lettuce club sandwich.

"What happened to the one who got close to you?" I finally asked her.

"I shot him."

"I didn't hear a—"

"With what I showed you. I told you it was very quiet."

"So there's a slug in him?"

"In his shoulder, yes."

"Damn."

"What is wrong?"

"Ballistics. I doubt they'd go to the cops, but your Derringer is marked now—you'll have to ditch it."

"I don't think so. The barrels are smooth-bores. No rifling."

"What kind of weird way is that to set up a piece? You probably couldn't hit a Buick with that thing."

"I could if I were sitting in it."

"How close were you?"

"I pressed the end of the barrel into his shoulder while he was grabbing me. That is another reason why it was so quiet."

"Was he—?"

"I cannot be sure. It seemed as if he wanted to . . . make me come with them. He acted as if he thought the others were right behind him. He did not consider that I might be armed. It is a great advantage."

"Just his bad luck you had the piece."

"It was his good luck," she said quietly. "If I did not have my pistol, it would have been this." She opened her hand. Inside was a long sliver of bamboo: wide at the butt end, as narrow as a hypodermic needle at the other. "For his eye. Then he would not have been so quiet."

"Where'd you—?" I said, stupidly, before I caught myself.

"You know," is all she said.

It was almost ten that night before we heard Byron's tap on the door. I let him in. He walked past me, pulling off a fog-colored silk raincoat, tossing it in the general direction of the closet.

"You want a drink?" I asked him. "Something to eat?"

"That minibar looks like it'll do me," he said. True to his prediction, he found a small bottle of cognac. "Just right," he said approvingly, settling back on the couch. "Want me to go first?"

"Sure," I told him.

"We've got their home base, brother. They diddled around for an hour or so. You know, double-backing, last-minute lane switches . . . even went the wrong way on a one-way one time. Très lame. They must have picked up those moves from TV. Then they got a little slicker. Parked their car, took a cab all the way over to the Northwest. They had another car waiting for them in Nob Hill—a Porsche. It was parked by that fancy cigar restaurant, the Brazen Bean. Looked right at home.

"I figure the first one for borrowed, a walkaway deal, have some stooge pick it up. No point spreading our manpower to keep it under observation.

"They must have decided there was no tail. Or that they shook it, whatever. From Pearl, they motored down to Lake Oswego. It's like a suburb. A very ritzy suburb, I can tell you. They got lakefront property, garage connected to the house. So we saw them drive in, but not enter the house. Didn't matter anyway. In a few minutes, they start turning on lights, moving around. They're still there."

"How do you know?"

"And they haven't had any visitors," Byron went on, holding up his pager to indicate his partner was still on the job. "At least not yet."

"How long is your guy good for?"

"Till I come and relieve him. It's not exactly the right surveillance spot for me, anyway. You know what the locals call Lake Oswego?"

"What?"

"Lake No-Negro," he said, sourly. "It's heavily patrolled, too."

"Got it," I told him. Then I turned to Gem. "Your turn," I said.

She got to her feet like a schoolgirl called upon to recite, hands behind her back, holding Byron and me in her gaze.

"You must remember that the conversation was in Russian. Some of it does not translate perfectly. Or it may sound stilted.

"The man approached first. He asked, 'Are you a friend?' I told him I was *from* 'a friend,' and asked him if he would like to sit down. He seemed undecided, but then the woman just . . . loomed up on my other side.

"'How did you find us?' the man asked. I ignored the question, and began to tell him the story we had prepared. But he was not interested in your Dmitri—he acted like he did not know him at all. It was as you expected. So I said what we had decided on: Dmitri had been murdered, and the killers were friends of the original target of the assassination attempt which occurred when there was an attempt to ransom back their son.

"The woman was very brusque. She demanded to know whom I represented. What I was really doing there. I told her I was only a person with a message for them. Only those who hired me could answer her questions. I asked her if she wanted to meet those people.

"But before she could answer, the man asked me about Petya. He wanted to know what had happened to Petya. I had never heard that name from you. The woman hissed at him to be quiet, called him . . . It is hard to translate, but it means a man who is no man. A . . . gelding, perhaps?

"Then she asked me, why did whoever sent me think she and her husband were in danger? They had done nothing wrong.

"I told her what we had decided on—that the person who had almost been killed was brain-damaged, a vegetable in a coma.

But his friends believed he had been set up, and the only lead was Dmitri. They went to see him, but Dmitri turned to violence, and he was killed. That left only them—the man and the woman. The people who employ me believed they would be the next targets. And that the information should be worth a great deal of money to them.

"But that did not work as you expected. Instead of trying to bargain, the woman asked me again who my employers are. Again, I told her I did not know them but I could arrange a meeting. When I said that, the woman made some kind of signal with her hand and they both got up. I could not see where they went, because the skinheads were already charging at me."

"Skinheads?" Byron asked.

"It looks like they wanted to snatch Gem," I told him. "Maybe take her someplace where she'd do a better job of answering their questions."

"Well, you're both here, so . . ."

"Yeah. And whoever hired the skinheads is the same one who hired the Russians. Maybe."

"Why only maybe?" Gem asked.

"First of all, they were kids. Not little kids, but teenagers. *Not* professionals. I can't see someone who'd spend a few hundred grand to hit me saving a couple of bucks now by hiring amateurs. And, from the way you tell it, they weren't there to watch the Russians. They were there to do whatever the Russians told them to—no orders going in. If it was a snatch from jump, they would have vamped on you from behind, while you were seated. It looks like they reacted to the woman's signal."

"So you figure, maybe the Russians aren't straw men after all?" Byron asked.

"You add up what went down earlier to the fact that they got in the wind before the hit on me went down—the answer's got to be no. They have to be players; we just don't know how, yet."

"I—" Byron started. The sound of his pager cut him off.

While Byron was dialing out, I picked up his pager from where he had tossed it on the couch. The only number showing was 411. So his man had information—it wasn't an emergency.

I couldn't make out what Byron was saying on the phone—he was probably keeping his voice down in case the guy at the other end had to keep things quiet.

Byron hung up, turned to me and Gem. "One of them went out. In a car. From the garage. Stayed out maybe a half-hour. My man figures they wanted a pay phone, playing it safe. Going to be daylight soon enough—we'll have to pull out. That neighborhood's not going for unexplained cars sitting around."

"All right," I said. "We've got the edge. They don't know what we know. No reason for them to fly."

Byron nodded. "When things open up tomorrow, we can do some checking. But that place—it sure doesn't look like any temporary rental. And there's one more thing. . . ."

"What?"

"My friend says he can code-grab the remote they use to open and close the garage. The driveway's nice and straight. And there's no gate."

"Let's see what happens," I told him. "That one's a last resort."

The ringing of the bedside phone woke me the next morning. I was lying facedown on the bed, Gem draped over me like a warm, soft blanket, her face nestled between my shoulder blades. She didn't stir as I reached for the phone.

"Yes?"

"We got a budget for this one, bro?" Byron's voice, as fresh as if he'd grabbed eight hours.

"Sure."

"On hand?"

"Yep."

"Can you meet me? On the waterfront? Just take Alder—that's the block the hotel's on—east. You'll know you're on track if the street numbers keep getting lower, okay? Make a right on Fourth, and a left on Taylor. Follow it down; you'll see the river. Find a place to park anywhere near Front Street, then just walk across and stroll north along the waterfront. I'll pick you out easy enough. Give it . . . thirty minutes, okay?"

"You got it."

"May I come with you?" Gem asked, her voice formal.

"Sure. But . . ."

"Yes?"

"We have to be there in less than a half-hour."

"Pooh! You think it takes me so long just to get dressed?"

"No. I mean, I was just—"

"I will wager with you. The last one ready to go pays for lunch."

"Can we just make it a hundred or so?" I asked her. "I don't know how much I need for Byron."

She punched me in the chest. Lightly, with the side of her fist, not the knuckles.

Gem practically dove into a lilac sweatshirt, then pulled a pair of jeans on as far as her thighs. She held the waistband of the jeans in both hands as she hopped over to the door, dragging them up over her hips. "I win!" she announced, breathlessly.

When I conceded that she had, she said "Hah!" And celebrated by immediately stripping and prancing into the shower. Still, we were on the waterfront, strolling hand in hand like . . . I don't know what . . . with a good five minutes to spare. We must have been walking in the right direction, because we found Byron lounging on one of the wooden benches, taking in the scenery. We sat down on either side of him. Gem turned sideways so she could see behind us. "That's okay, girl. It's covered," Byron told her.

"It's only eleven," I said to him. "You got something already?"

"A lot. I fronted it, but I need a couple of grand to get square. You said—"

"I got seven and change with me."

"Perfect. We got a deuce, deuce and a half, committed already, but I figure that could double if the stream keeps flowing."

"Hundreds okay?" I asked, reaching into the side pocket of my coat.

"Long as they're not private stock, bro. Computers and laser printers have changed the game. Any geek can make funny money in his house now."

"This is all clean," I said, handing over a bundle. "Used and random, too. I know you've got a man out there and—"

"That's *my* man, Burke. This cash is to grease some wheels. My *partner* is here for me, not for pay, understand?"

"I apologize," I told him, meaning it.

He nodded, closing the subject. Took a breath. "All right, here's what we got so far: the house cost the better part of eight fifty large. They put down three and a piece, financed the rest at seven and three-eighths, thirty-year, fixed. Income stream is all 'investments,' and it looks fine on paper—two mil and change in five mutual funds, three index, one value, and one Euro. Their TRW is squeaky clean—only thing they have going is a revolving credit line from American Express, and they pay *that* every month, no balance. Two phone lines. Long-distance bills run less than a hundred a month. They use U S West for a carrier, the chumps. State taxes paid right to the penny."

"Which means they—?"

"Yeah. Not just new names, bro. New Social Security numbers. And the names on the paper are as Anglo-Saxon as King James."

"So they're *deep* under."

"They are. But they're not visible enough locally for anyone to notice. That American Express account? The one they pay righteously? Some months it's damn near ten grand." He paused, made sure my eyes were on his. "For travel."

"Luxury cruises?"

"Sure. If you think Estonia's a playground for the rich and lazy."

"Estonia?"

"And Romania."

"What about the Philippines?" Gem asked, softly.

"Nope. Europe. All *over* Europe, but that's all."

I filed it. Filed Gem's question, too. "What else have you—?"

Byron held up his hand, reached in his jacket, came out with his pager, checked the screen, said, "More than I thought I would, Burke. See for yourself."

He held the pager so I could reach the window. This time the window read 411+++.

I raised my eyebrows, asking what the string of plus signs meant.

"Pictures," Byron said. "Let's ride."

Byron's ride turned out to be a nondescript dark-green Chrysler four-door. "Tradecraft," he said, apologetically. He suavely opened the back door for Gem.

She sat way forward, resting her chin on my shoulder, listening to Byron's travelogue as he crisscrossed streets.

"This is Southeast," he said. "Kind of a mixed bag. See for yourself."

What I saw was a string of antiques shops and used-book stores, and a vegetarian restaurant called Old Wives' Tales. A couple of blocks farther along, a pair of topless joints that looked right at home.

Byron turned off the main drag, his eyes scanning the block. I didn't know what he was looking for, and he didn't ask for my help, so I stayed inside myself, waiting.

He slowed at a small stone building—looked like an eight-family unit—then pulled into the driveway and continued until we were in a little alley. Byron reversed the car smoothly, and expertly backed it toward a big garage. The door opened and we rolled in. The door came down again, as silently as silk on silicon.

It was dark inside. No windows. A tiny red light came on in a far corner, no bigger than an LED. I flicked my eyes to my chest, thinking, *Laser sight!* But I couldn't see anything.

Byron turned off the engine. A tall man came out of the shadows. When he got closer, I could see he was white, somewhere in his forties, maybe, with a neat haircut, wearing a dark boxy-cut suit.

He bent down so his face was close to Byron's. I couldn't hear what passed between them. The tall man opened the back door and climbed in next to Gem. I half-turned so I was facing Byron, my good eye on the back seat.

"This is Brick," Byron said to us.

"My name is Gem," she said, holding out her hand.

He shook it.

"Burke," I told him. And he did the same. His grip was soft and dry. Contact, not pressure—no transmissions. I couldn't make out all his features, but he had a high forehead and a squarish jaw.

He took some photographs out of a manila envelope I hadn't noticed in his hand. "These two surfaced at oh-six-twenty-two," he said. "Just before first light. They came in a pickup, a Ford F150 with California tags." He read the license number to Byron.

"There goes the budget," Byron said.

"Shouldn't take as long as you might think," Brick replied. "Their truck was one of those 'Lightning' jobs—couldn't miss it, even from a distance. They were real limited production. Can't be that many of them running around."

He handed the photos to me, together with a pocket flash. "These are from a digital camera, downloaded and printed. The detail is very good, but you'll need to blow them up anyway."

"Try this," Byron said, taking the flash from me and handing over a rectangular magnifying glass. He trained the light where I was looking. Skinheads. In jackets—one leather, the other denim—and T-shirts. The photos showed them standing next to their truck; walking toward the Russians' house; returning. The last two shots were close-ups. Even under the low-light conditions, the clarity was better than the average mug shot—I'd know either of them again. And they weren't from the same crew as the plaza. These two were a decade, if not a generation, older.

I handed the photographs to Gem. Brick took the flash from Byron and held it for her while she checked for herself.

"These men were not the ones who—"

"They're not," I agreed with her. Then I asked Brick, "Are they known to—?"

"Have to wait on positive IDs for that."

"Can you do it from these photos?"

"Possibly. It's all on digital, and we've got programs that can work miracles with the pixels. But there's a better option. I creeped their truck while they were inside the house. Got some really excellent lifts. Too many, in fact. So it will take a while, run all the elims. But if they're in the computer banks, we should be able to pull them up."

"That was slick," I complimented him.

"Brick is James-fucking-Bond," Byron said proudly. "They'll never know anyone was there, either."

"Why would skinheads—?" Gem asked.

"There's all kinds of skinheads," I told her. "We won't know until . . ."

". . . some of the lines tighten," Byron finished for me.

When the Chrysler pulled out of the garage on Brick's signal, I was at the wheel, Gem sitting next to me. Byron stayed with Brick, saying they both had work to do.

"Makes me feel . . . useless," I told Gem.

"Because you cannot go with them?"

"Not go with them, go *somewhere*. Do *something*, you know?"

"Yes."

"What's wrong?" I asked her, turning left onto Burnside, thinking how Portland's street grid was pretty easy to navigate.

"*I* have work to do."

"Oh. You mean you have to go back to—"

"No. Work to do here. As I told you from the beginning. But I have . . . neglected it, somewhat. And I must devote myself to it for . . . a while now."

"No problem."

"You are not . . . concerned?"

"I don't know how you mean the word, little girl. Worried about you, what you're into? Or nosy about stuff that's none of my business?"

"The first."

"You speak, what, a half-dozen damn languages? You know at least that many ways to kill a man. Your IQ's off the charts. You survived what a couple of million people didn't . . . and that was when you were a little kid. It would be . . . I don't know . . . disrespectful to worry about you."

"But you call me 'little girl.' How does that square with what you just said?"

"It's just a . . . Did I insult you? If I did, I'm sorry. For me, it's a term of affection. Like . . . 'honey' or something."

"My language skills are not as complete as you appear to believe, Burke. But it does not seem the same."

"The same as . . . what?"

"'Honey' might be what you call a waitress."

"I wouldn't."

"I do not believe you would. I expressed it incorrectly. Let me try it from the other end. 'Little girl.' If it was in my language, and I had to translate it into English, it would come out as . . . 'cherished.' Does that make sense?"

"Yes."

"So you . . . ?"

"I don't know. It's just an expression."

"It is not just an expression," she said, gravely. "And you *do* know."

When we got back to the hotel, Gem ate one of her mega-meals, then announced she needed a nap.

The message light was flashing on the phone. The voice-mail system told me I had one message. When I retrieved it, all I got was the sound of fingers snapping, once.

From Max. Call Mama.

I switched fresh batteries into the cellular, put the old ones on recharge, then used the hotel phone to start the relay.

Nothing to do but wait, so I lay back on the couch and watched CNN with the sound off, reading the pop-up screens and practicing my lip-reading when one of the anchors came on.

The buzzing of the cellular brought me around—must have drifted off.

"Cop come," Mama said.

"One cop?"

"Yes. You know him. Come here, many times."

That wasn't as clear as it sounded. A whole lot of professions fit "cop" in Mama's vocabulary.

"Spanish guy? Cheap suit? Small eyes? Hard man?" I asked, not wanting to say a name on the phone.

"Yes."

"What did he want?"

"Thumbprint."

"I don't—"

"Want *your* thumbprint. Come back tonight."

"But the cops've got all the—"

"From . . . surface. Say want to 'lift' . . ."

"He say why?"

"No."

"Mama, you have . . . ?"

"Sure. Have your old—"

"Okay. Do it."

"You want Max?"

"Not yet. I don't know anything yet."

"But soon, maybe?"

"Maybe."

It was dark by the time Gem came out of her room. She was wearing a black silk sheath with a mandarin collar, the black spikes with ankle straps over sheer stockings, hair flowing loose, carrying a small black patent-leather clutch bag. Not a trace of color besides black, except her skin.

"I cannot be certain when I will return," she said, bending at the waist to kiss me softly on my neck.

"You have the cell number . . . ?"

"Yes."

"Look, I'm not doing anything now. Just waiting around. I could come along—"

"No, thank you," she said, formally.

"I wouldn't cramp your style or anything. Couldn't I just be the . . . driver, or something?"

"It would be a mistake. Fear is a mistake."

"I'm not—"

"You do not understand. Either the . . . people I must meet might think I was afraid of them. Or worse."

"Worse?"

"Or they would be afraid of you," she said.

I watched daylight break the next morning. I used to do that a lot, before. Different now. No Hudson River off in the distance. No cigarette in my hand. No . . . Pansy next to me. The window in my head opened. And the sky behind it was splattered with red.

I closed my eyes so hard the corners hurt. Impaled on my own truth. Wishing I'd bought some of the religion one of the foster homes had tried so viciously to beat into me. I tried to see my Pansy in some dog heaven. Lying on her sheepskin rug, gnawing on a rawhide bone, watching a boxing match on TV with me. Safe and happy. Doing her job. Loved.

But all I could see was Pansy snarling her last war cry as the bullets took her off this earth.

I breathed deep through my nose, expanding my stomach, taking the air down past my belly into my groin, holding it until it gathered the poison inside me into a little ball. Then I expelled it in a long, harsh stream, toxic yellow-green as it left. Lose the poison, keep the pain. I needed the pain the way a man who survives a bad car crash needs to feel his legs—to know they still work.

"They never killed you, sweetheart," I promised Pansy. "You're always with me."

My eyes flooded. I bit my lip. But my last promise gave me the grip I needed. "And you'll be there when we take them out, honeygirl."

For us, from where we come from, that's all the heaven we ever get.

You think it's sentimental stupidity, that's your business. But when we're keeping our promises, don't ever get in our way.

"What?" I answered the cellular.

"We're breaking it off for now." Byron's voice. "No action last night. Can't be in two places at once. Some of the stuff that has to be checked, it's going to take the personal touch."

"How're you fixed for—?"

"Plenty left, don't worry. My . . . partner doesn't work domestic, but he thinks there may be some interest in the visitors by his people, you with me?"

"All the way. You want me to—?"

"Hang, bro. I checked with the studio. It's a blank slate for the next week, easy."

"All right."

"Later."

"**M**ay I have your clothes, please?" Gem asked me the next morning.

"What?"

"We have been here a while; it is time to do our laundry."

"The hotel has—"

"Maids gossip," she said, with the air of one who knew from personal experience.

"There's no labels in my . . . All right, let's go do it."

"Do you know *how* to do it?"

"Laundry? Hell, yes. You think I don't know how to take care of myself?"

"Do you cook?"

"Well . . . no."

"And you 'take care of' your laundry by . . . what? Taking *it* somewhere, yes?"

"Yeah. Fine, I get your point. But—"

"Just put it all in the pillowcases," she said. "I will return later."

"**W**hy are all your tops the same?" she asked me, later that afternoon. She was refolding all the freshly done laundry on the bed in my room.

"The same? They're not—"

"They all have raglan sleeves. Is that a fashion preference?"

"Oh, now I see what you mean. No, miss, it's not about fashion. If there's no shoulder seam, your arms can move faster. Probably gets you an extra tenth of a second or so."

"And that is important?"

"Almost never. But for when it is . . ."

"I understand," she said, thoughtfully. "I must go out for a while. I will return when I can."

Hours later, I heard the door handle click, and I stepped quickly outside to the terrace. I'd already checked—if it came down to it, I could go across the roof to one of the other suites, smash my way into the glass patio door if they'd left it locked. Tear through the suite and out its front door into the hallway. If the suite I picked was occupied, it wouldn't slow me down much.

I stood with my back against the outer wall, twisting my neck to peer through the glass into my suite. When I saw it was Gem, alone, I pocketed my pistol and stepped back inside. She looked as fresh as when she'd left, regarding me solemnly with her hands on her hips.

"You prefer it outside?" she asked.

"Just cautious."

"Why not put the chain on the door, then?"

"I didn't want to slow you down. If you needed to get back inside in a hurry . . ."

"Oh."

I didn't say anything. I wanted to strip off her dress, check her for bruises. But I settled for watching her eyes.

"That was very considerate," she finally said.

I didn't like everything I could see in her eyes, but I didn't want to ask about it. So I tried another question: "You want something to eat?"

"Yes!" she said, smile flashing. "I have to take a bath, first. Can you order . . . ?"

"Sure," I promised. And reached for the phone.

It took about half an hour for the food to arrive. Another few minutes for the sharply dressed room-service waiter to set everything up. I scrawled something on the bill for the signature, added 20 percent for the tip. Took the guy another couple of minutes to say thanks.

Soon as he was gone, I tapped lightly on the door to Gem's room. Nothing. It was closed, but not shut, so my next taps opened it.

The door to her bathroom was ajar. "Gem?" I called out, softly. No answer. Something skipped in my chest. I stepped over to the bathroom door, pushed it all the way open. Gem was lying in the tub, her head on a couple of rolled-up towels, eyes closed. I touched the water. Still warm. Realized I was deliberately avoiding looking at her wrists. I put my hand behind her neck, pulled her toward me. Her eyes blinked open. "Burke. . . ."

"Yeah. You okay?"

"Yes. I am fine. I was just so . . . tired, I guess."

She reached up, slipped both hands behind my neck. I stood up slowly, pulling her along with me.

"I got you all wet," she said, her face buried.

"Ssshh," I said, slapping her bottom lightly.

She made a noise I didn't understand.

I walked her over to where the towels were racked. Found a big white fluffy one and wrapped it around her. Then I scooped her up and carried her over to the bed.

"You can eat when you wake up."

"Little girl."

"Huh?"

"'You can eat when you wake up, little girl,' that was the entire sentence, yes?"

"I—"

"I know what it means now. All right?"

"Yes," I said, patting her dry.

She was asleep before I finished.

It was a little past nine when Gem came into the living room. And started in on the food like it had been served a minute ago.

She was still chewing away when the phone rang.

"What?" I answered.

"Cop come. Same one. Say, find bone hand."

"Whose hand?"

"Not hand, bone of hand. Chop off at wrist. With ax, maybe."

"The hand was chopped off with an ax?"

"Maybe. Look like, he say."

"Whose hand, Mama?" I asked again.

"Cop say *your* hand. No flesh on hand. Just bones. But same place, find pistol, too. With thumbprint. Yours. Cop say, you leave hospital, people find you, kill you, cut off head, cut off hands, nobody trace. But cops find hand and pistol in big garbage can in Brooklyn. Way at bottom. Cop say, probably, they miss it when come to collect, stay there long time."

"Big garbage can" was Mama's term for a Dumpster. "Is it going to be official?" I asked her.

"Cop say you dead now. On record."

"Thanks," I said. Meaning: Tell *him* thanks. If she ever saw him again. Morales had owed me—big-time *and* long-time. And he'd just squared the debt.

went to my bedroom a little after midnight. Gem said "Good night, Burke," absently, absorbed in some footage of Russia's pitiful invasion of Chechnya.

I took a long shower. Used some of the fancy shampoo the hotel supplied. Shaved slowly. Nothing worked. I stayed tired, but not sleepy. I had to let it come when it would.

The sound of a wooden match cracking into fire woke me. I was on my back—must have finally drifted off. The room was dark except for the candle Gem had just lit, a stubby thing in a little glass holder. It smelled like citrus and blood.

"You must own the images, or the images will own you," she said softly, standing next to the bed, looking down at me.

I didn't say anything.

She walked out of the room. Came back in a minute with the wooden straight chair that had been next to the writing desk in the living room. She placed it ceremoniously between the bed and the candle, so it was backlit. Then she stepped to the side and gestured, as if parting a curtain to a display.

"Do you see this?"

"Sure."

"What do you see?"

"A chair. What are you—?"

"Watch!" she whispered. Then she sat down on the chair, facing me, knees together, hands in her lap. That's when I saw she was wearing the schoolgirl outfit. "When you think of the chair, you will see me, yes?"

"I . . . guess so."

"Hmmm . . . but *what* will you see, Burke? A girl, or . . ." She stood up, hiked up her skirt, turned, and sat, her legs straddling the chair this time, body facing away from me, looking back over her shoulder. ". . . a woman?" she asked, silk-voiced.

"A woman," I told her.

"Ah. A woman with too many clothes on, yes?"

"Yes."

She stripped right there on the chair, never taking her eyes off me, wiggling and squirming to slip her underpants down to her thighs.

Then she stood up, still facing away from me, pulled the panties all the way off, spun around, and sat back down in the same pose she'd used at first.

"It is not the same chair anymore, is it?" she said. Shifting her hips slightly to underline every word.

"No."

She came over to the bed. Bent at the waist and untied the drawstring of my pajama pants. Then she nipped at my thigh until I reached up and grabbed a fistful of her night-gleaming hair and pulled her closer to where I wanted her.

"A little bit now," she whispered against me. "Next time some more. And, some sweet night, Burke, the window that opens will be the one you wish."

I was afraid she'd want to talk about it the next morning, but the only thing that came out of her mouth was a demand for breakfast.

Fair enough. I left her still half asleep, face buried in a pillow, and went into the living room to order from room service. When I saw the wooden chair standing by itself against the back window, I realized Gem had gotten up during the night.

And when I looked at the chair, I could see . . . that she was right.

Gem wanted to return to the poolroom and practice some more. I wasn't crazy about the idea, thinking the same two clowns might be there, but she quickly pointed out that there were lots of places to choose from . . . and we weren't in a hurry, anyway.

That last was true. I couldn't make a move until I heard from Byron. And we had the cell phone, so . . .

We took a ride, just meandering, looking to stumble across the right place. South of Portland, I saw a sign that said we were entering Milwaukie. Wondered if it was a misspelling. A candy-apple-red Honda Accord coupe with mirrored checkerboard graphics angling across its flanks rolled up next to us at a light. It squatted on huge chrome wheels, with tires that looked like rubber bands, the sidewalls were so thin. It was major-league slammed, lowered so radically that I couldn't see an inch of ground clearance. The driver had a knife-edged buzz cut, set off by wraparound orange-lensed sunglasses. He blipped the throttle, letting me hear his turbo kick in, cocked his head in an invitation.

I was going to ignore him, but Gem pounded both little fists on the dash. "Yes, yes, yes!" she yelped.

The road was clear ahead as far as I could see . . . but that wasn't very far. I didn't know how the Subaru would do off the

line, but the Honda looked more like a canyon-racer than a drag-
ster anyway. I returned the guy's nod, switched my attention to
the light, and gave the knurled knob next to the gearshift a quick
twist to the right.

We both launched an eyeblink before the green, but it was
no contest—the Subaru's tractor heritage showed as it out-
torqued the Honda with a two-length leave. By the time the
Honda got up on its cams and its turbo started to whine, I was
already backing off in third gear, letting the engine brake me for
the next light.

The Honda driver pointed ahead through his windshield, then
gestured for me to follow him. So he *was* a canyon-racer after all.
No way I was going to try the twistees with that guy, especially in
daylight. I tapped my wristwatch to tell him I didn't have the
time. He aimed a finger at me, cocked his thumb, mimed cranking off a round. Meaning: next time, he'd make sure we played
on his field.

"Aren't we going to—?" Gem protested.

"I don't know where he wants to go, but this isn't the time," I
told her. "The last thing we need is some law-enforcement attention."

"All right," she pouted.

"Hey, come on. We raced him like you wanted."

"I thought it would be longer."

"Maybe sometime."

"Do you promise?"

"I promise to try, okay?"

"I . . . Oh, look! There's one."

I guessed Gem was one of those folks who think the food's better in a roadhouse.

The joint had a long bar, bunch of square wooden tables scattered around, a couple of red vinyl booths, sawdust on the
floor. But it was no honky-tonk—that was Garth Brooks coming
out of the jukebox, not Delbert McClinton.

It did have a pool table; one of those bar-size little ones with a slot for the quarters, designed for playing eight-ball and not much else. But that was fine with Gem—she said it looked just like the one in the bar near her home. Once I explained how eight-ball was played, she happily slammed balls all over—and occasionally off—the table, attracting some admiring glances, but no audio.

She finally pocketed the eight ball while I still had three stripes on the table, and rewarded herself with a brief "Hah!" of triumph. I was still congratulating her when a fat blond guy with a bad haircut and worse acne stepped up with a quarter in his hand, saying, "I got the winner."

Before I could say anything, Gem swung her hip into me to shut me up, said "Okay!" to the blond guy.

He slotted his quarter, waited for the balls to drop, took them out, and racked them. "Your break," he said to Gem.

"Oh, you go ahead," she replied, nestling against me.

I didn't move. Gem reached across her body with her right hand, grabbed my wrist, and pulled my arm around her neck. She turned her head until she found my hand, nibbled at it until she got my thumb in her mouth. Then she sucked on it, hard, her innocent eyes watching the blond guy.

He miscued, missing the entire rack. Somebody laughed. His face mottled red. Without waiting for a response from Gem, he snatched the cue ball, set it up again, and, this time, slammed it deep into the rack, scattering the balls. Two solids and one stripe dropped. He pocketed two more balls before he missed. Gem slowly disengaged her mouth from my thumb, walked over to the table with three times her normal wiggle, and bent over the table a long time, studying her shot. Which she finally dropped in. But that was it—she was done, not another shot was open. Grinning, she whacked away at the cue ball, turning away to walk back over to me while the balls were still flying.

"You made one!" one of the watchers advised her, pointing to the thirteen ball, which had slopped in off two cushions and a kiss.

"Thank you," Gem said politely. Then she sashayed back over to the table, where she tried the same trick. Only this time, no such luck.

The blond guy shot carefully. He was strictly a barroom eight-ball player—good enough to win a few rounds of beers, but any decent pool hall with full-size tables would have picked him clean in an hour. He finished by dropping the eight ball in the corner, to a round of sarcastic applause from the people watching.

"You want to try?" he asked me, face flushing, averting his eyes from Gem's lipstick-smeared mouth, gone back to working on my thumb.

"No thanks."

Gem wiggled against me, making "Go ahead!" noises even though her mouth was full.

"Shut up," I told her, smacking her bottom to underline the words.

Which only got a giggle added to the wiggle.

I raised my unencumbered hand in surrender. Gem let go of my thumb, giving it a last lick for luck. I put in a quarter, racked the balls for the blond guy the same way he had for Gem, stepped back to let him break.

He did a good job, pocketing one of each and leaving himself a nice open table. He only had two striped balls left when he finally missed.

"You gonna run out now?" he asked me.

"Sure."

"I don't think so."

"Okay."

"You wanna—?"

"Yes!" Gem interrupted, before he could finish his offer to bet.

He turned toward her. "How much?"

Gem's face was a mask of concentration. Finally, she said, "Five?"

"You sure you want to go that deep?" he sneered at her.

"You are correct," she answered. "Let us make it for two, all right?"

A couple of the men watching laughed.

The blond's flush turned angry. "Hey, you think it's such a lock, maybe you—"

"Oh, lighten up, Wally," one of the watchers said.

He slapped two singles on the table. Looked over at me. Gem reached in my jacket pocket like it was her own, pulled out my roll, extracted a pair of hundreds, put them next to the blond's money. As she did, she looked down, said "Oh! You meant two *dollars*."

That threw the watchers into convulsions. I moved quick to head things off. "Stop playing around," I told Gem, snatching the two centuries off the table, replacing them with a pair of singles of my own.

"Hey, pal," the blond snarled at me. "If you want to—"

I ignored him. Stepped to the table. The balls looked as big as grapefruits, the pockets as wide as bowling alleys. I made all the solid balls disappear in a couple of minutes, then closed with a tap-in on the eight.

I spotted two of the watchers high-fiving each other out of the corner of my eye. Gem slipped all four singles off the table and tried in vain to stuff them in the back pocket of her shorts.

"Ah, Christ. You're a pro," the blond guy said, not mad anymore.

"What was that all about?" I asked Gem, as soon I had the Subaru out of the lot and aimed back toward Portland.

"What do you mean?"

"Were you *trying* to start a fire?"

"I only wanted to race. I thought it would be fun."

"Uh-huh. So, when I cut that short, you . . ."

"Oh, don't be so foolish. I would never do anything to endanger you."

"No? Well, you've got a pretty bratty way of playing, then."

"Oh, you *liked* it," she said, bending her face forward and nipping at my hand on the gearshift knob.

We were in the middle of keeping my windows closed when the cellular trilled next to the bed.

"Damn!" Gem hissed over my shoulder. "I should have—"

I thumbed the phone open, said: "What?"

"We got the gen," Byron said.

"And . . . ?"

"And it wants analysis. Doesn't speak for itself. At least not clearly."

"When do you want to—?"

"We're way south of you. How's breakfast tomorrow work?"

"Perfect."

Somewhere in space, a satellite synapse snapped, leaving the phone dead in my hand.

"Do you remember where we were?" Gem whispered.

"My . . . mind does. But—"

"I can fix that," she said, pivoting on her knees and sliding toward me across the sheets.

"**T**he one on the left is Robert Alton Timmons," Brick told us, tapping the photograph on the table. It was one of the surveillance shots, now hyper-digitized, as sharp as a studio portrait. "His partner's Louis B. Ruhr."

"You had them on record?" I asked him.

"Half the agencies in the country probably have these two on record. Timmons served two terms for arson."

"A pro torch? Or a pyro?"

"Neither. He was a cross-burner. Graduated to synagogues and individual dwellings back in the days before we called stuff like that 'hate crimes.' He was AB on the inside, but that doesn't mean much—white guy locked down anywhere in California *better* link up, he wants to serve out his whole bit.

"Timmons is a floater, a maggot looking for fat corpses. He's been with the abortion-clinic bombers—still a suspect in a major

arson of one in Buffalo—but he's also put in time with
survivalists, the common-law courts people, couple of
zarro true-white religions. Even claimed to be a Phine.. ..iest
for a while—"

"What is that?" Gem interrupted.

"Phineas was a Biblical character who killed a race-mixing
couple," Brick said, his eyes on Byron, "so it doesn't take a genius
to see what their program is. The thing about them is that they
operate as individuals, not in groups, so infiltration has been next
to impossible. The 'priest' thing is a self-awarded title. Like the
spiderweb tattoos for skinheads that're supposed to signify you
killed one of the 'mud people.' Or a Jew. Or anyone gay." He took
a breath. Let it out. "The original Nazis tattooed their targets so
they could always find them later. The new ones tattoo themselves. So we can find *them*. Hitler'd be ashamed of the morons."

"You make Timmons for a hustler?" I asked Brick.

"Could be. When it comes to extremists on either side, it's
always hard to separate the true believers from the profiteers.
He's never stuck anywhere, but he's *been* everywhere. Held
rank in one of the Identity religions, worked security inside a
couple of compounds. You'd think they would have made him for
an agent, as many groups as he's joined and left. But I guess his
torch work's been the credential—no undercover's going to burn
down a building with people in it, and they know it. Besides, he's
a fanatical polygamist."

"What's that got to do with—?" Byron asked.

"I know what you're saying," Brick cut him off. "You can be
into polygamy without being a white supremacist. Sure, there's
all this 'Breed an Aryan baby for the race' stuff, but they're not
the only ones practicing.

"The thing about Timmons is, he's supposed to have shot one
of them over the guy's daughter. Timmons claimed the girl had
been 'promised' to him, so he wanted her handed over. The
father said she wasn't old enough yet—she was around twelve—
and Timmons blasted him and tried to snatch the girl."

"He wasn't prosecuted for that?" I asked. Not suspicious, just
trying to add it up.

"The guy he shot wouldn't testify. Said it was an accident. And Timmons never got away with the girl, so there really wasn't any pressure. Or any publicity. But it sure convinced them all that he wasn't working for ZOG, you know?

"Anyway, he's not the boss of that two-man team. That'd be Ruhr. Straight-up pure; hardcore, not some poser or wannabe. Timmons sports the typical '88' tattoo, but Ruhr, the only number on his skin is '14.' You following me?"

I nodded. The "Fourteen Words" of David Lane, a former leader in The Order. Right now he's serving life-plus for murder and racketeering in pursuit of an Aryans-only America: "We must secure the existence of our people, and a future for White children." Words so sacred to some White Night soldiers that they added "14" to their own signatures.

"Ruhr proved in with a prison homicide almost twenty years ago. It was a face-to-face shank job, one on one, so he only pulled time in the hole for it—that's the way it was then."

You think it's different now? I thought to myself, but kept quiet as Brick continued:

"He's a hit man. But not freelance. Only kills for the cause. We have it confirmed that he's worked overseas. Trips to the U.K.—he's a suspect in the assassination of an IRA official—and France, and Germany, for sure. Maybe others."

"So no way they're connected to the skinhead kids who tried to grab Gem?" I asked.

"We can't say that," he cautioned. "They're not on the same level, no question. But every contract hitter has to make his bones sometime. Ruhr wasn't any older than the kids you described when he started whacking people."

"Sure," I said. "Looks like he grew up Inside." I pointed to the swastika tattooed on the side of his neck. "That's a jailhouse job. And an old one—see how blobby the ink is?"

Brick just nodded agreement.

"And the connection to the Russians?" I asked him.

"Well, they're not Russian *Jews*, so they wouldn't be excluded, necessarily. You know, for years we've been hearing about a Stalinist organization, but nothing specific ever shows up."

"You mean inside Russia?" Gem asked him.

"No. I mean, sure, there probably is something like that going on there; who knows? But I was talking about outside the country. Didn't you ever wonder? Stalin was a bigger murderer than Hitler ever was. A greater fascist. Plus, he *won*. He survived it all, while Adolf snuffed himself in a bunker, sniveling to the end. How come Stalin never gets the kind of freak-worship Hitler does?"

"He wasn't about race," Byron said. "He was about power."

"So?"

"So what appeals to lowlife, beady-eyed, chinless, inbred, failure-flunky trash is the idea that they're *genetically* superior to the rest of us."

"And the cream will rise to the top?"

"Sure. Once they scrape off that crust of mud."

"This isn't about politics," Brick reminded us. "It's about what a pair like Ruhr and Timmons are doing in the picture."

"You're going to ask around your—"

"Sure," he told me. "But our agency's not supposed to be working Stateside, remember? Our intel on home-grown Nazis isn't as good as . . . Well, you understand what I'm saying."

"I do," I told him. "Thanks."

"What're you going to do now?" Byron asked me.

"I got places I can look, too," I said. "But I have to go home to start."

"How safe would that be?" Brick asked. Telling me that Byron hadn't kept anything back from him.

"I'm dead," I answered. Then I told them both about Morales' message.

"That I *can* check," Brick told me. "If you're *not* listed as dead on the law-enforcement computers by the time I get back, I'll get word to Byron, and . . ."

"I'll reach out for you, brother," Byron finished.

Our last night in the Governor, the window opened again. Gem was sweet and smooth about it, sliding off my limpness as if she'd finished herself, anyway.

"It happens to most people when they're . . . under great stress," she said, gently. "With you, it is the opposite, yes?"

"I . . . think so."

"It's not dissociation, is it? I mean, you know where you are and—"

"Yes. It's just the way you described it. I can see everything I'm doing, but I can also see myself *seeing* it. Like I'm watching. Then a little box opens. And the more it gets filled, the bigger it gets. Until that's all I *can* see."

"That's not like . . . not like the way I heard about it. From others."

"What's so different?"

"The trigger. As I said, some events cause so *much* fear that you—that people, I mean—cannot tolerate them. So they go somewhere else within themselves."

"Sure. That's dis—"

"Not . . . always. Some people can control it. So no matter what is happening to them, they are . . . outside it, do you understand?"

"Yeah. I do. But when I get afraid, it's not like that."

"Afraid? When have you been afraid?"

"My whole life."

"I don't mean as . . . a child. Recently?"

"All the time. Some times more than others, that's all."

"When the skinheads—?"

"Yes."

"Even in the poolroom?"

"Even then."

"And there was no window?"

"No. When I'm . . . in danger, or when I feel I might be, that's all there is. The danger. I focus on it so tight nothing else could ever have a chance to get in."

"But with me . . . ?"

"It's the . . . opposite of danger, I guess."

"Those are the best words anyone has ever spoken to me," Gem said. She kissed my neck, snuggled in against me.

She was deep into dreamless sleep in a few minutes. But I could feel her tears against my skin.

"Do you really have any leads?" Gem asked me the next morning, managing to talk with her mouth crammed full of food and sound ladylike at the same time.

"Not a lead, a person. Someone who just might be able to get me the answers. Make the connections, anyway."

"Are you going to see this person now?"

"No. It's not that easy. I don't know where he is. He moves around a lot. I have to send out feelers, wait for the lines to form."

"That is why you are going back to your home?"

"I'm not going back to New York," I told her, watching her ocean eyes for any flicker of surprise.

"Oh?" is all she said.

"I'm not sure it's as safe as I made it out to be, even if Morales got it done and NYPD has me down as dead. And I couldn't look for this person I need any more efficiently from there. It all has to be done over the phone."

"Then why did you tell—?"

"Brick? I don't know him. It's Byron I know. And Byron I trust."

"But Brick did a lot to—"

"He did. And I'm grateful. I owe him, no argument. But that's not the same as trusting him."

"You trust Byron. And Byron trusts—"

"*Byron* trusts him, that's right. And he took some real risks—"

"Lovers do incredible things for each other," Gem said, solemnly.

"But lovers fall out," I reminded her. "And when they do, things change."

"Sometimes."

"Sometimes," I agreed. "But there's other reasons, too."

"What are those?"

"Brick is a pro. But even pros make mistakes. If he *thinks* I'm back in New York, that's all the information anyone can get out of him. He's an agency man. My name may trip some wires inside his shop. He has to be loyal to them. And loyal to Byron, too. I don't want to put him in a cross. This way, it gets tight, he can tell them what he knows, and it *still* won't be a problem for me."

"So where will you go, then?"

"I'm not going anywhere."

"But this room—"

"Sure. I have to leave the hotel. But that's all. I'm going to stick around."

"And do what?"

"Lurk."

"I don't understand."

"Here's the deal, little girl. I can look for . . . this person I need over the phone. And I can work that from anywhere. But I can't be sure of finding him at all."

"Oh."

She went back to packing, fussing over the task long after she should have been finished. I'd been ready to go for an hour, but I didn't say anything.

"If you cannot find this person you seek . . . ?" she finally asked.

"Then I'm going to go back and visit those Russians."

"Oh," she said again, still not closing her little suitcase.

I went back to waiting.

Minutes passed before she said, "You don't have to . . . lurk close by, do you?"

"Not necessarily. But travel is a risk. Exposure. I need to go to ground. And I need to be close to the Russians."

"But you don't know anybody in Portland?"

"No. But I can always—"

"I have a better plan," she said, zipping up her suitcase with authority. "Now I must make a call myself."

The Metalflake maroon '63 Impala SS coupe glided to the curb where Gem and I were waiting, in front of the Melody Ballroom on Southeast Alder. The same Mexican I'd seen on the dock when I first met Gem got out, wearing a black wool baseball jacket with white leather sleeves. The trunk popped open. I wasn't surprised to see the battery nestled back there, or the monster stereo system. The trunk was huge, but with all the electronics, there was barely room for our bags.

Inside the car, another Mexican occupied the passenger seat. Gem and I climbed in the back. Gem threw one bare leg over my thigh, said, "This is Burke," to the two men. Then, nodding her head toward the driver: "Burke, this is Flacco. And this is Gordo." Both of them were solidly built, but neither remotely qualified as skinny or fat. They didn't offer to shake hands.

Gem pulled my arm around her like she'd done in the poolroom, nibbled at my thumb until it was in her mouth, then went to work like a little girl with a lollipop.

Neither of the Mexicans spoke. When the driver kicked over the engine, you couldn't mistake the sound.

"A 409?" I asked him.

"*Sí!* You like it?"

"I love it," I told him, truthfully, running my eyes over the white Naugahyde tuck-and-roll interior. "This is a thing of beauty."

"My heart is in this ride, *hombre*. My heart, and all my damn money." He laughed.

"Looks like you spent it well. Taking a piece from each, that's the only way to go."

"What do you mean, a piece from each?"

"You could have cherried it out, pure resto, all numbers matching, that kind of trip. And you *do* have some of that—looks stock from the outside, except for the paint. But this interior, that's custom. And that sound system . . . that's extreme. You didn't go lowrider, but it's dropped. And it's sure not back-halved, either; but I checked the big meats and the three-inch cans out back."

"It's all new underneath," the passenger put in. "Konis, air bags, and Borla out the back." He was wearing the same kind of jacket as the driver.

"You keep the dual quads?" I asked.

"That's right. And the rock-crusher's original, too."

He meant the M-22 four-speed tranny he was gently stirring with a Hurst pistolgrip. The 409 made torquy sounds even at idle. Once we got on the highway, it settled down into a throaty purr—geared for cruising, not quarter-horsing.

About an hour and a half later, Gem took my thumb out of her mouth long enough to remind the guys in the front seats that she knew a very fine diner just down the road a piece.

We pulled into an area of dense darkness near the dock; a light rain falling, just a touch past mist. Gem and I climbed out of the back, and Flacco popped the trunk from inside again. We hauled our bags out. Gem pointed to her right and started walking, leaving all the luggage to me. The Chevy moved off— the 409's growl sounding even meaner from the outside.

When I saw Gem step on the gangplank I must have hesitated, because she turned around, asked, "What is it?"

"You live on a . . . boat?"

"Yes. It is very nice. Come on."

"I . . ."

"Burke, what's wrong?"

"The boat . . . It's not going to . . . I mean, you're not going to, like, sail it, right? It's going to stay tied up?"

"For now, yes," is all the assurance I could get out of her.

I followed her onto the deck. I could feel it shift slightly, but I couldn't tell if it was our weight or the damn water under it making that happen. Neither prospect cheered me much.

Gem ducked slightly and stepped into the cabin. I followed her, expecting . . . I didn't know what. It looked like a little efficiency apartment with a Murphy bed. At least, I figured there must be a Murphy bed, because I couldn't see anyplace to sleep.

"The bedroom and the head—the bath—are downstairs," Gem said, as if reading my thoughts.

"Below this?"

"Yes," she said, suppressing a giggle. "Below this. We will actually be *under* the water there. Does that frighten you?"

"Yeah."

"Oh," she said, caught up short by my answer. "I was only teasing. I didn't mean to make light of . . ."

"It's okay. Water scares me, no big deal."

"Why?"

"Why does it scare me?"

"No. Why is it no big deal?"

"Because it's just a fear. They only count if you let them get in the way."

"Ah. So you will stay here, with me?"

"Does the boat rock at night?" I asked her, hedging.

"Of course. But there are no real waves in this cove. It is a very gentle motion. . . ."

"I guess we'll see," I told her.

It wasn't so bad down there. At least that's what I kept telling myself. Gem's bed was a single, but she fitted herself over me like a sweet-smelling sheet.

I woke up the next morning ready to go fishing. But I had to wait until past New York's nightfall to reach out to Mama.

"Gardens," she answered the pay phone in the back of the restaurant. One in the morning in New York, right in the middle of Mama's workday.

"It's me," I said.

"Very quiet here."

"Dead quiet?"

"Yes. Many people . . . hear news."

"Cop come back?"

"Not him. Others."

"What'd they want?"

"Not come inside. Just watch."

"Ah. They still there?"

"No. But maybe come back. Looking for—"

"Well, they won't see it."

"You not coming—?"

"Not for a while, Mama. Can you grab Michelle for me?"

"Sure. Where call—?"

"No call. Tell her to ask the Mole to send me some phones, okay?" And I gave her an address Gem told me was safe—a tackle shop a few miles down the road from where she was docked—and a name to use.

"Sure," she said, like it was a take-out order of roast-pork fried rice. "You need Max?"

"Not where I am now, Mama. We'll see, all right?"

"You see, you tell me, Max come, okay?"

"Okay, Mama. See you soon."

"Sure," she said. And hung up.

 fitted the cellular I'd been using in Portland into two halves of a Styrofoam block, wrapped it tight with duct tape.

"Why are you sending that phone away?" Gem asked me.

"Byron had this number."

"Yes?"

"So it's going back to New York. Like I'm supposed to be doing. A pal of mine'll make some calls on it over the next few days. Then he's going to trash it. Anyone checking, they'll know the calls were made from there," I told her.

"So if Brick . . . ?"

"Yeah."

"It is hard for you to trust, isn't it?"

"No. Not like you think, girl. If I don't *have* to make the decision, I don't, understand?"

"I don't think so."

"Sometimes, you don't have a choice. You're in a situation, you have to either trust someone or not. That's it. Black and white—yes or no, live or die. But most of the time, you don't have to go there. I don't have to go there with Brick. I don't *distrust* him, okay? But why should I go out of my way to trust him, either? Better to play it safe."

"And me?"

"I didn't tell *you* I was going back to New York, miss."

Gem's expression didn't change. But when she took the finished package from my hands and brought it over to the counter, there was an extra twitch to her hips.

I spent the next couple of days making charts. In my head. I knew where some of the wires ran. And I knew they intersected . . . somewhere. What I needed was the junction box.

The man I was searching for lived in the whisper-stream, but he was no myth. I'd known Lune since we were kids. And I knew what he'd be doing, guaranteed. I just didn't know where.

I kept drawing possibilities on my charts, waiting.

One morning, Gem was gone by the time I got up. And she stayed gone until it was dark again.

"For you," she said a couple of days later, handing me a box wrapped in brown paper. I knew what was inside. And that there wouldn't be fingerprints on any of it.

Three cell phones. Different brands, one not a lot bigger than a pack of cigarettes.

The last time I'd seen Lune face to face, he was operating out of a waterfront warehouse in Cleveland, in a section called the Flats. Over the years, that neighborhood had gone from hardcore to downright trendoid. Lune had pulled up stakes and moved on a while ago. But maybe he left a few roots in the ground.

The first few numbers I tried were disconnected. Even some area codes had changed. All I wanted was to leave a message. Lune had told me how to do that: say that my name was Winston, that my father was sick, then give whatever phone number I had for him to reach me—after I converted it by adding one to the first digit, nine to the last, and so on, working toward the middle of the ten-digit number, which was to be left unchanged.

When I'd gone through all the numbers I had, it was time to start seeding the clouds, hoping for rain. I reached out to organizations, groups, clubs, crews, gangs, associations . . . especially the ones with only one member. UFO documenters, alien abductees, Elvis-spotters, Illuminati true believers, anyone monitoring Scientologists, investigating the Monarch Program investigators, tracking werewolves, alerting the world to Remote Telemetric Surveillance, searching for D. B. Cooper, hiding from black helicopters, waiting for the Ascension . . .

Anytime anyone asked me who I wanted to leave the message *for*, I knew I was in the wrong place.

Four . . . maybe it was five . . . long days went by. I kept working the phones into the night, too—time zones don't mean much to the people I was contacting. Some of the conversations felt like an icepick to the eardrum.

"Drink this," Gem said, startling me out of wherever my mind had been, handing me a small white china cup.

"What is it?"

"It is tea. A special blend. Very good for headaches."

"I didn't say I had a headache."

"If you saw someone limping, would they have to tell you their foot was bothering them?"

"What's your problem?"

"My problem? My problem is your problem. But you don't see it as I do, yes?"

"Huh?"

"I can help you."

"You *are* helping me. And you helped me plenty already."

"So we are done?"

"Gem, this isn't the time to—"

"Please don't be a stupid man."

"I thought that was a redundancy."

She refused to giggle, but I did get a tiny smile at the corner of her mouth. "Maybe it is."

"Little girl, just explain to me whatever you want me to know, okay? I've been doing nothing but talking to *very* strange people for days. Maybe some of it rubbed off."

"You are looking for someone, yes?"

"Looking for him to get in contact with me, that's right."

"But you do not know where he is?"

"Right."

"So you are leaving messages in random places, hoping one of the people you leave a message with actually knows this person. Or how to reach him, anyway."

"That's the plan."

"Why is it that you do not ask me to help, then?"

"Honey . . ." I hesitated, trying to come up with a capsule description of a man who didn't fit *any* description. "It would take me a long time to explain the guy I'm trying to get in touch with. He's one of the smartest people I ever met in my life. But he's not . . . like other people. I don't think he'd recognize me—this isn't the face I had when we last saw each other—but he'd know my voice. And we have a communication code, for just between us. For all I know, one out of all the maniacs I've been speaking with *is* connected. If that's so, whatever I say is probably recorded. Maybe even voice-printed. It wouldn't make sense for a woman to be leaving messages *for* me, understand?"

"Of course," she said, biting at her lower lip impatiently. "But there are other ways to . . . leave a message, are there not?"

"Sure. I was going to try the personals columns of a few of the 'alternative' papers. One of the Capgras people might—"

"Capgras?"

"Capgras Syndrome. When a person believes someone has stolen his identity and become his 'double.' They're always serving 'Public Notices' in the personals, warning the world about the impostor. They usually provide a lot of 'authentication' info about themselves. Like their Social Security number, or some place they're *going* to appear in the future."

"My goodness!"

"There's also the 'lost passport' game. Where the relay-man puts a notice in the papers saying he lost his passport, offering a reward, you know. But the trick is, he gives the *number* of the passport he supposedly lost. And the country it was issued from. That's more than enough to send a pretty lengthy message in cryptography."

"But why would you expect such people—?"

"I'm just playing the odds, Gem. Most of them, sure, they're lost inside their own heads, or running their own games. But, for a few of them, Lune is the oracle. I just don't know which ones, so I'm just spraying and praying, see?"

"Loon?"

"L-U-N-E," I spelled it for her.

"Ah! French, yes? It means 'moon.'"

"I'm sure that's the root: 'luna.' But, in my man's case, it's short for 'lunatic.'"

"But if he's so intelligent—"

"Oh, he's a genius, all right. *Past* a genius. But he's . . . I don't know the word for it. *If* there's a word for it. I'll tell you one thing, though. When it comes to making sense out of a whole bunch of what looks like random human-behavior data, Lune is the man."

"I could still help," she said, hands on her hips.

"I'm not saying you couldn't. It's just that—"

"I could help *now*. Listen to me, please. Couldn't you try the Internet? Contact the websites of the same sort of people you've been reaching out to over the phone?"

"I wouldn't know how to—"

"Then be grateful you have a woman, you stupid man."

Hours later. Gem at her laptop: hair gathered into a thick ponytail, her back as straight as a West Point plebe's, fingertips playing the keyboard like a pianist. If she knew I was watching her, she gave no sign.

"Those sites you're sending e-mail to, won't they be able to trace back to you?"

She glanced up just long enough to give me a look so full of sweet indulgence it made me feel . . . geriatric.

It was dark when she came up on deck. I'd been there for a while, sitting in a castoff easy chair, thinking. She perched on the arm of the chair, apparently not bothered enough by the weather to put on anything over her T-shirt and shorts.

"Did you think I was bratty before?"

"When?"

"When you asked me that question about being traced through an e-mail."

"No. Ask a stupid question and—"

"You didn't think I was saying you were stupid!"

"Not stupid. Ignorant. And you were right."

"It was very bad manners on my part."

"You were busy. Absorbed in what you were doing. And you were doing it for *me*, to boot."

She swiveled her hips and draped her legs across my lap.

"You are a very forgiving man," she said softly.

"And you're a very sarcastic little bitch."

"I *meant* it!"

"Yeah? Okay. Sorry. I just . . . overreact to that whole 'forgiveness' crap."

"I don't understand."

I reached up, grabbed a fistful of her thick, glossy hair, pulled her face down so it was close to my mouth. "Is it important?" I asked her.

"To me, yes. It is very important."

I leaned back. Gem dropped into my lap. I took my hand from her hair and put it around her shoulders. She made a little noise. Then she settled in against me, waiting.

"When I was a kid, people . . . did things to me," I told her. "Ugly, vicious, evil things. But I didn't die from any of them. When I was older, I spent some time in a war. I didn't die from that, either. You know what they call me?"

"A man who—"

"No," I said, cutting her off. "A 'survivor.' For both. And that's wrong."

"Why is it wrong? You *did* survive. . . ."

"No. In war, they're *supposed* to try and kill you. Not in families. It's not the same. And that stupid label, it *makes* us all the same."

"Children of war and . . ."

"Children of the Secret. All of us who were raised by fucking beasts. Like it's a brand we can't shed. But we don't all go the same way. Some of us, we . . . copy whatever was done to us. Some of us just hurt . . . ourselves. And some of us, we hunt . . . them."

"So. You are one of those . . . hunters. And you do not forgive."

"In therapy—the kind they give you when you're a kid and they know you've been . . . hurt—they tell you, if you want to heal, *first* you have to forgive. You have to 'let go' of your rage.

"But you know what, little girl? When you're a kid, when they hurt you and hurt you and fucking *laugh* when you cry about it, rage is your friend. It stands by you. Stays close. Carries you when you can't walk on your own. It's cold and clear and . . . *clean*. When everyone else is lying, it gives you the truth. And the truth is, any fucking 'therapist' who tells you to forgive the people who hurt you—they're working for the enemy."

"I have no enemy to forgive. Or to hate."

"You're a child of war, like you said. But your parents did *their* job, honey. They did their best to keep you safe. You can't hate a whole national insanity. But tell me you wouldn't kill Pol Pot if he was standing in front of us right this minute."

"I . . . don't know."

"I would."

"You? Why? You had no—"

"I'd kill them *all*, sweet girl. I swear I would. Every one of them."

"Who?"

"I don't know what to call them. Torturers, maybe. The freaks who like to play with electricity in dungeons. The gang rapists. The death-camp guards. The secret police. The mutilators. It doesn't matter what you call them. I'd know them. Every single one. And if I could ever get them all in one place, I'd be the biggest mass murderer in the history of this planet."

She shuddered against me. "Wouldn't that make you as bad as—?"

"To some people. Not to anybody who counts with me."

"Is that why you are looking for . . . ?"

"What did you think, Gem? Somebody tried to cap me. I don't know why, but I've got to figure they'll try again."

"They could not find you now," she said, urgently. "You said so yourself."

"There's two ways to be safe, child. One is to hide. The other is to hunt. When I was a kid, I only had one way. I figure, whoever they are, they had their chance. Now I want mine."

She pressed herself against me so hard it felt as if our clothes had melted from the heat. I didn't say anything. It wasn't my turn.

"I told you," she whispered, finally. "I told you, before. Ever since I was a small child, I made decisions very quickly. I don't wait. I am your woman now. So even though I know what you want . . . I will help you do it."

After she went back downstairs—she called it "going below," but even the *sound* of that made me nervous—I tried to make some decisions of my own. In my world, people deal themselves in—or out—all the time. But there'd be no pot of gold at the end of the rainbow I was chasing. What I wanted was more of what Pansy had taken with her last breaths.

I didn't know what Gem did for money, but I figured her for an outlaw—no way she'd be connected to Pao's network otherwise. And my best guess was that the Mexicans were about as legal as angel dust. So it all came down to her backing my play because she was my woman.

I couldn't work that part out. I guess, when Gem made decisions, she didn't just make them quick, she made them alone.

Gem got *The Oregonian* on Sundays, and always picked up *Willamette Week*, too, an alternative paper that covered a different beat. I spent a lot of time reading them, trying to feel my way into the territory.

One day, I came across a piece about a con who stabbed another inmate. Turns out, in Oregon, you shank another guy Inside, you have to attend mandatory "anger management" classes.

I almost fell off my chair laughing. Prison stabbings have about as much to do with anger as rape does with sex. Knifings are always about a debt, or revenge, or self-defense against a rape. Or territory. Or a new guy blooding into a gang. Thing is, unless the joint is race-war tense, *nobody* carries all the time—it's a sure ticket to the hole. You want to stick somebody Inside, you plan it carefully. Even though the favorite target is the back—that spot between the bottom of the ribs and the pelvis, so bone doesn't turn the blade—you still need cover if you're going to get away with it. And a place to toss the blade as soon as you're done.

I've known prison assassins with a dozen kills and no busts. Wesley was the master. Nobody ever saw him mad. Nobody ever saw him coming, either.

The Oregonian handled straight news real well. Good combination of local and wire-service copy, although most of the coverage was about Portland, and the weather got a lot more attention than it would in New York. The *Willamette Week* was more about culture, and it told me one thing I filed away—Portland was a blues town, for serious.

But nothing in the personals of either one looked even remotely promising.

I went back to working the phones.

I was on the line with a guy in Detroit who said he knew a guy who knew a guy and—if I had the money—he might be able to bridge a connect for me . . . when one of the other cellulars buzzed. I hung up on the hustler, said:

"What?"

"Call for you, okay? Say you go Al-blue-quirk-key."

"Albuquerque?"

"Yes. What I say. You go Thursday. Go to airport. Two o'clock afternoon, walk outside to parking lot. See big car with stripes like tiger. You wait there. Okay?"

"*This* Thursday, the next one coming?"

"Say, 'You go Thursday.'"

"The person who called, what did he—?"

"Not man, woman. I say, 'Who calling?' She say: 'Give message to Winston.' Then say what I just say now, okay?"

"Okay, Mama. Thanks."

I leaned back in the chair and closed my eyes for a minute. Maybe it was longer. When I opened them, Gem was standing in front of me. "Can that computer of yours do airline schedules?" I asked . . . before she could ask *me* anything.

Less than half an hour later, she was kneeling on the floor next to my chair, scraps of paper spread out before her.

"There are many choices," she said. "Several different carriers, all going at different times of the day."

"Any of them get in with plenty of margin before two in the afternoon?"

"Oh yes. All leaving from Portland. Let me see. . . ." She crawled around on all fours from scrap to scrap, oblivious to the sweet show she was putting on. Or not—I know less about women than I do about stamp collecting. "Ah! You have . . . one, two, three . . . at least four separate choices. It just depends on how you want to be routed."

"Routed?"

"Yes. None of the airlines have direct flights. You can change planes in Phoenix, Oakland, Denver, or Salt Lake City."

"I don't care which airline. It's not like I've got frequent-flyer mileage to worry about. All I need is something that gets me in there around noon or earlier."

Gem took a *very* close look at one of the scraps on the carpet. A long look. I guess I do know a little more than I do about stamp collecting. "All right, then," she finally said. "Let us make it Phoenix."

"Great. Do you have a safe credit card you can use to make the reservation? I'll pay you in cash."

"Yes, of course. But you will need a—"

"I've got all the documents I'll need to show them at the airport, girl. That's not a problem."

"How many days will this take?"

"I don't have a clue. What difference does it make?"

She looked at me over one shoulder. "How could I pack intelligently if I do not know how long we will be gone?"

"I can pack my own—" I started to say. Her depth-charge eyes stopped me cold, and I realized what she was really saying.

"Do you like it?" Gem asked me on Monday.

I looked at the inch-and-a-half color photo she was holding in her palm. Gem, staring straight ahead, the barest hint of a smile on her face. "It's okay," I told her. "Not exactly a glamour shot."

"But it looks like me, does it not?"

"Sure."

"Good," she said. And disappeared.

"Chantha Askew?"

"Of course," she said, holding the passport with her picture and that name open so I could see it clearly. "Chantha is a good Cambodian name. And Askew, that is yours. Or the one on your passport, yes?"

"Yeah. But—"

"You don't want to drive to Albuquerque," she said. "Or you wouldn't have asked me about flights, much less to book one. There is some risk in flying. It's not as . . . anonymous. You have not ever used your own passport before, have you?"

"No," I told her, wondering even as I spoke how she could know that.

"And you have no fear of the people who constructed it for you revealing—?"

"No!" I cut her off sharp. "Not a chance."

"All right," she said, so softly that I realized I must have shown something in my face. Wolfe sell me out? She'd die first. And I'd rather *be* dead than to ever know about it if she did.

Gem was quiet for a minute. Then she gently pushed at me until I sat down, and followed me down until she was in my lap.

"They don't have your name, the one on your passport," she said softly, not having to spell out who "they" were. "And they don't have your face, either. They don't know who you are. Or where you are. You are hunting *them;* not they, you. But that doesn't mean they don't *know* you. . . ."

"What are you trying to say?"

"They wanted to kill you because they knew you. We do not know why. Assassins kill when they are paid. But those who hire assassins, it is always for one of two reasons: it is either what you did, or what you are. What you described, it was too intricate for simple revenge. Too expensive. And it has become very, very complicated. So it must be that whoever wants you dead also fears you."

"Look, Gem, all this . . . logic of yours is fine, but—"

"Indulge me, please. Assume they know you. Or know *about* you, anyway. They do not know where you are. Or even if you are alive. But one thing I am certain they would not expect—that you would be married."

"Huh?"

"Oh, I do not mean you *could* not marry. Have you ever—?"

"No."

"Yes. All right. What I meant was, you would not be . . . traveling as a married man. With a wife, see?"

"So you're coming along as cover?"

"I am coming along because I am your woman."

"You keep saying that."

"That?"

"That you're my woman."

"I am."

"My 'woman' . . . What does that mean in Cambodian, my boss?"

"Don't be silly!" She giggled. "I am very obedient."

"So long as—?"

"So long as the orders are sensible," she said, climbing off my lap.

Gem sat quietly next to me in the back seat of Flacco's Impala on the way back up to Portland. Maybe being a married woman required more decorum.

"I am going to build one for myself, very soon," Gordo said to me. I figured Flacco had heard this a few hundred times.

"Which way are you looking to go?"

"Like this one," he said, patting the Impala's padded dash. "But not no Chevy, that's for sure."

"Because . . . ?"

"I need my ride to be . . . I don't know, man . . . like no other one on the road. But I want to stay with the factory look," he said, with a nod in Flacco's direction. "That's what's happening now."

"Me, I like the fifties better than the sixties for that," I told him.

"Fifties? I don't know, man. The sixties, the shapes were . . . wilder, you know?"

"Maybe. Maybe *too* wild. If I was doing it, I'd want something people'd have to look twice at just to figure out what it was."

"Hey, *hombre*," Flacco threw in, "there's no way to do that when they made *millions* of each model then. What you mean? Something like a '55 Crown Vic? Or a '57 Fury? They're cool, all right, but you could pick one out at a hundred yards if you leave them looking near-stock."

"You're right. But the one I was thinking of, it'd slip right by, you did it right."

"So which one, man?" Gordo wanted to know.

"Picture this," I told them. "A '56 Packard Caribbean. The hardtop, not the convertible. Strip all the chrome, even that fat wide strip down the sides. Then you slam it all around—not put it in the weeds, just a nice drop. Give the top a subtle chop . . . maybe only a couple of inches. I see it with some old-style mag wheels, like American Racing used to put out. Paint it about twenty coats of the deepest, darkest purple-black—you know, that Chromallusion stuff that changes color depending on how you look at it."

"I never seen one of those," Gordo said.

"I did," Flacco said. "It had those giant taillights, right? Cathedrals?"

"That's the one."

"The man's nailed it, *compadre*," Flacco told his partner. "That would be the biggest, bossest, most evil-looking ride on the whole coast. And those suckers had some *serious* cubes. *Mucho* room for anything you wanted to do with the rubber, too."

"Problem is finding one," I reminded him.

"Oh, they'll be out there," Flacco assured me. "This part of the country, people *keep* their old cars. There's always Arizona, too—we got plenty people down there could keep a lookout for us. And you should have seen *this* one when I first got it. Just a rusted-out shell."

"You went frame-off?"

"*Sí!*" he said, proudly. "Me and my man, here, we got about a million hours in it. Gordo's the mechanic, I'm the bodyman."

"Be harder for the Packard," I said. "They make all kinds of NOS parts for Chevys, but . . ."

"Be more work, is all," Gordo said, reaching over to high-five Flacco.

"It sounds very beautiful," Gem said, her chest puffed out a bit, proud of me for some reason.

It was still dark when they dropped us off in front of the Delta terminal at PDX. The first-class line was empty. Check-in was nothing at all—the clerk glanced at my passport photo so quick I could have been Dennis Rodman for all he knew.

The first-class thing was all about keeping our options as open as possible. We were only taking carry-ons, and they cut you a bit more slack with the size of the bags up in the front of the plane. You get out faster, too, and that can count for something when you have to change planes. But most important was that we wouldn't have any company right next to us—I could take the window seat and just lie in the shadow until it was time to make our move.

The corridor leading to the gates at PDX was like an indoor mall. Upscale shops, some brand-name, some "crafts," even a fancy bookstore—Powell's—a real one, not the usual magazine stand with a couple of paperback racks.

Gem failed to surprise me by suggesting that we had plenty of time to get something to eat. A bakery-and-coffee-shop was open, with little café-style tables standing outside. Inside, music was coming over the speakers. Kathy Young's version of "A Thousand Stars." The sound system must have been real sophisticated, because someone had the bass track isolated . . . and cranked up so high you could barely make out the lyrics. I know it's hip to say the Rivileers' version is the real thing, and Kathy's was just a white-bread cover. But I think the girl really brings it, her own way.

I got a hot chocolate and a croissant. Gem got a tray-full of stuff. We sat outside all by ourselves, listening to the music. The Spaniels' version of "Goodnite Sweetheart, Goodnite." The Paradons doing "Diamonds and Pearls." The Coasters on "Young Blood."

"What do you call that?" Gem asked me, head cocked in the direction of the music. "Rock and roll?"

"No. It's doo-wop. From the fifties, mostly. Where the voices were the instruments—a *capella*. The kind of stuff that sounds the same in the subway as it does in the studio. If you ever heard the Cardinals, or the Jacks, or the Passions, or—"

"And today it does not?" she interrupted.

"Today it's all sixty-four-track, electronic-mixmaster stuff. The engineers are as important as the musicians. Except for the true-blues stuff."

"What is that?"

We had time, so I told her about Son Seals. And Magic Judy Henske. And Paul Butterfield. Gem was so obviously listening, *really* listening, that I would have gone on for a much longer time . . . but she finally tapped her watch and raised her eyebrows.

The metal implants in my skull didn't set off the detectors like I'd thought they might—I wore one of those Medi-Guard ID bracelets, just in case I had to explain. I'd left the never-fired twin to the piece I'd put Dmitri down with at Gem's, and made her leave her baby Derringer there, too, so I figured we were golden when our bags went through the conveyor without attracting any attention. But as we turned to enter the corridor to the gate, someone called out, "Sir!"

It was a guy in some kind of uniform. He motioned me over. "Sir, do you mind if we check your luggage?"

"Go ahead," I told him.

But instead of opening my bag, he put it on a small, flat platform, then ran a wand over the outside. "Supersensitive," he said. "It can detect the most microscopic traces."

"Of what?" I asked him. "Cocaine?"

"No, sir," he said, a thin smile on his face. "This tests for the presence of explosives."

"That's nice. So why did you decide to check *my* bag?"

"Well, sir, this was just a random check, you understand."

"I understand you didn't *randomly* check anybody else."

"Honey, sssshhh. The officer is just doing his job," Gem said, tugging at my sleeve as if she thought I was going to lose my temper.

"All finished," the ATF cop announced. "Thank you for your cooperation, sir."

As we walked away, I put my arm around Gem's waist. She moved slightly closer to me. I dropped my hand to her bottom and gave it a hard pinch.

"Oh!" she said. Then: "What was *that* for?"

"Overacting," I told her.

"Pooh!" is all I got in response. But she didn't move away.

When you fly first-class, they let you board first, right along with the people with infants and the ones who need assistance walking. Not for me. You take your seat first, everybody passing through to the back entertains themselves by checking you out.

And they always have plenty of time to do that, because some certified hemorrhoid is guaranteed to stop by the first overhead, where they keep the magazines, and root through them one by one, taking his own sweet time before grabbing a whole fucking handful he can hoard for himself.

By the time we boarded, the overhead racks were crammed full. Gem said something to the flight attendant, and he opened a closet near the kitchen and placed our stuff inside. I climbed in first. Gem brought me a blanket and a pillow, then settled herself in.

The porthole next to me was dimpled with raindrops by the time we were cleared for takeoff, but it didn't delay things.

Our flight attendant was a man in his forties, maybe, with carefully combed brown hair and a tight smile. He made the mistake of asking Gem if he could get her anything before takeoff. Me, I closed my eyes and tried to keep images of Pansy from opening inside my window.

When Gem finished her dozen sacks of peanuts and four bottles of water, she carefully spread a blanket over my lap. Then she slipped her hand under it.

We only had about a half-hour to catch our connecting flight, but Gem decided that was enough to make me buy her a frozen-yogurt cone topped with hot fudge.

It was just after eleven-thirty in the morning when we touched down in Albuquerque. I felt the tension go out of my body as soon as we got inside the terminal—you miss a meet with Lune, you might never get another.

I wanted to go outside to the parking lot right away, see if the tiger-striped car was where the message said it would be. But I knew better, so I just let Gem pull me through the airport until she found a place that sold a pair of boots she just had to have. That killed more than an hour. The search for just the right restaurant took some time off the clock, too. And by the time we'd finished there, we only had about twenty minutes to contact.

We walked past the taxi stand and headed for the parking lot. I held a scrap of cardboard in my hand and kept glancing down at it. Anyone watching would assume I'd written down the location where we'd left our car on the back of the claim ticket.

I led Gem straight to the top floor, figuring whoever left the contact car in place would have picked the least desirable spot, so it would attract less attention if it had to stay there for a while. We stepped off the elevator and started a brisk circuit, as if we knew where we were going. It didn't take more than a couple of minutes to find what we wanted: a generic GM boxcar sedan covered in orange primer and black tiger-pattern stripes.

"Wait," was all the message Mama had given me. When we walked up closer, the GM turned out to be an eighties-era Buick. An empty one. And it looked like it had been that way for a while. I glanced at my watch: 1:51. I patted my pocket for the cigarettes that weren't there. Pulled Gem close to me so whoever showed wouldn't think she was a spectator. Breathed slow and shallow through my nose.

A once-red Land Rover, one of the old ones, came to a stop perpendicular to the tiger-striped Buick, blocking us in. The windows were too deeply tinted to see inside. The back door closest to us opened slightly. I pulled it toward us, gently. The back seat was empty. I got in first, Gem right behind. The driver didn't turn around. All I could see was that he was wearing an Australian Akruba hat. And next to him, on the passenger seat, was a mammoth pit bull, a brindle with white markings. The dog turned and regarded us with the flat, confident stare of someone who knows, no matter what you're holding, he's packing something a lot heavier.

The Land Rover pulled off. Gem opened her mouth, but I put two fingers across her lips before any sound came out. I knew what the problem was . . . just not how the driver was going to handle it.

We exited at the gate, turned left, and proceeded at a leisurely pace through the city. From where I was sitting, the only gauges I could see were navigational. I spotted a small-screen GPS unit, as well as a large mechanical compass and altimeter—whoever put that rig together was a heavy believer in backups. We were driving east on a complicated highway system. After a while, we got off and curled back so that we were going north. And climbing. When the altimeter got past six thousand feet, the driver suddenly pulled over and stopped.

Nothing happened for a minute or two. Then he dismounted. I waited for him to come around and open up the back doors, but all he did was let the monster pit bull out, leaving that door wide open. Through the window, I could see him step back a few yards, but the dog didn't move, holding its ground. The driver took off his hat, tossed it aside, then made a "come toward me" gesture with his hand. I knew better than to exit from the door out of the driver's vision, so I reached across Gem, opened her door, and guided her out, with me right behind.

"Close enough," the driver said, as soon as both of us were on the ground. I could see he was an Indian—heavy cheekbones, dark eyes, thick black hair combed straight back and worn close to his skull, a calm interior stillness radiating off him. His skin had a faint coppery tone, but the shade was too light for his features—I figured him for a mixed-blood.

It was close enough for me to see the heavy semi-auto that materialized in his right hand, too. He held it way high up on the butt, against the curved grip-safety, just short of where the web of skin between the thumb and trigger finger would catch the slide. The barrel was pointed at the empty ground between us, as if he were just showing the pistol to me, not threatening me with it.

I zoomed in on his hand. His thumb was held extended and absolutely parallel to the slide. On the other side of the pistol, his trigger finger was positioned the same way, parallel to the slide, from the knuckle to the first joint. A hardcore pro. And holding all the cards.

But then he moved the pistol just enough so that I could see the tip of his finger curled down, inside the trigger guard. That last part hit me like an aftershock—*inside* the trigger guard. The Indian was standing quiet, his face stony. But he was over-amped. Pre-visualizing, ready to shoot.

I moved my hands away from my body. Slowly, sending out gentle waves.

The Indian nodded as if he understood my gesture. "Tell the woman to get your bags and bring them out," he said. His voice was more twangy than I'd expected, New Orleans in there somewhere. Exaggerated maybe by his nose—looked like he'd broken it one time and they hadn't done a great job in the ER.

"Do it," I told Gem, not taking my eyes off the Indian.

He said something to the dog in a language I didn't understand. It jumped back onto the front seat as easy as a beagle climbing a curb. When Gem came back out with our bags, the dog was right behind her.

"Put them over there," the Indian told her, gesturing with his free hand toward a clearing to his right.

Gem did it. The pit bull trotted alongside her like they were going to the park to play Frisbee.

"Go back with him," the Indian told her, moving so he was between us and the bags. Then he moved a few steps closer, held my eyes: "There was only supposed to be one person."

"It was a one-way communication," I told him. "There wasn't any way for me to say I was bringing my—"

"Who are you?" he asked, as if it was a test.

"Burke."

"Why are you here?"

"To see Lune."

"Can you prove who you are?"

"I don't know. It depends on what would be proof to you."

The Indian nodded as if that made perfect sense. "We are in the Sandia Mountains," he said. "About a mile and a half up. Sound carries in the thin air. But nobody pays attention. Another mile or so straight up that road, it's snowing. I have to be satisfied with who you are or we all drive up there and I come back alone, understand?"

"Yeah, I understand. What I don't understand is what you want me to do about it. He wouldn't recognize my face. I was—"

"Shot, it looks like," he interrupted.

"Right. You want to take my fingerprints? Would that do it?"

"No. I have to ask you a question."

But he didn't ask one. Just stood there, as if waiting for the question to come to him. When I heard the cell phone trill in his breast pocket, I realized that maybe it would.

"We're here," he answered.

He listened for a second, then said: "He is not alone."

More silence, then: "No."

He listened for another minute, closed the phone, and slipped it back into his pocket.

"What was the name of your problem?" he asked me.

The name of my problem? If I knew that, I wouldn't need to . . . And then I snapped on it. He didn't mean now, he meant *then*. Back when Lune and I were . . . "Hunsaker," I told him. "Eugene Hunsaker."

The Indian nodded his head slightly. And put the pistol back inside his coat. "I still have to go through your bags," he said. "I can't watch you and do that at the same time. But Indeh will. Just stay in one spot, and he won't bother you."

The pit moved a few steps toward us, but he stayed as relaxed as he'd been all along, the hair on the back of his neck nice and flat.

"Help yourself," I said.

The Indian did a thorough job. Took out every single item and laid it on the ground, then checked the bags for seams and compartments before he went through the contents.

"Okay," he finally said. "I'll let you repack your own stuff—I wouldn't want to mess it up."

When Gem and I were done, we all piled back in the Land Rover. The Indian turned it around and headed down the mountain.

he Land Rover's compass told me we were heading north, and the highway signs said we were on I-25. The Sandia Mountains remained a looming presence on our right, but to the left was a vast open space, mostly flat except for some scattered mesas . . . and another mountain range off in the far distance. The Indian saw me looking in that direction. "The San Mateos," he said.

As the Land Rover rolled past a landscape of sand and low scrub growth, we were buffeted by gusts of wind that vanished as suddenly as they appeared . . . then came again.

"That's the biggest pit I've ever seen," I said to the Indian, trying to engage him. "What is he, a bandog?"

"Indeh is not a pit bull," he said, pride deep in his voice. "He is a purebred Perro de Presa Canario."

"I never heard of—"

"They were originally bred in the Canary Islands, so some call them Canary dogs," the Indian said, his tone reverent, as if reciting a tribal legend. "They were a cross between an indigenous breed, which is now extinct, and the English mastiff."

"What were they bred *for*?"

"For fighting," he replied, contempt now ruling his voice. "And once dog-fighting was banned on the islands, it took some very dedicated people to save and preserve the breed."

"He's a real beauty," I said. "How much does he weigh?"

"Right about one ten, depending on the season."

"Why did you name him Indeh?" Gem asked, speaking for the first time, pronouncing the word exactly as the Indian had, accent on the second syllable. "Was it to honor your ancestors?"

The Indian half-turned in his seat to look at Gem. He nodded slowly. "You have a gift," he told her. "His name is for my people. The Chiricahua Apache. Do you know of them?"

"I am ashamed to say I do not," Gem answered, her head slightly bowed.

"They were the greatest guerrilla fighters America ever produced," I said, quietly. "Battled the entire U.S. military to a draw for a dozen years. Cochise and Geronimo were Chiricahua Apaches."

"You know our history?" the Indian asked me.

"Just tiny bits and pieces. Enough for my deepest respect."

"You know this from reading?"

"I did time with a guy, Hiram. He was the one who told me."

"He was Chiricahua?"

"Chickasaw."

"Uh!" is all the Indian said. He held my eyes for a split second before he reached across the seat and scratched his Canary dog behind the ears.

The way I used to with Pansy. I . . .

Gem gently elbowed me in the ribs. I opened my eyes and looked into hers. She shook her head slightly . . . to tell me the Indian hadn't noticed where I'd gone—but she had. I bit down hard on my lower lip and looked out the window, concentrating on what was *outside* me, like I was supposed to.

We were just pulling off the Interstate, toward a little town called Bernalillo. The Indian threw a quick left and crossed back over the Interstate, and then we were rolling along Highway 44, heading northwest according to the dash compass. For a while, there was nothing but open desert. A hideous tumor of a subdivision—from the look of it, already metastasizing—appeared on the left. Farther along, the desert on the other side of the highway turned spectacular, stretching to high mesas ranging in color from light brown to almost yellow. As we moved along, we got so close I could see their individual layers of rock.

Less than a half-hour later, we passed a pueblo. It wasn't anything they'd photograph for *National Geographic*—just a collection of poor-ugly little houses and guys in pickups eye-fucking anyone passing by.

Next we turned onto Highway 4, which turned out to be a little road that was mostly curves, dotted with a few scattered trees and even fewer houses.

Then another pueblo. This one had bigger houses, most of them actual adobe. But it was still a rez-type setup with a lot of junker cars scattered around like refuse on dirt roads. There was a wall of rock on the right, sheer and unbroken, going up maybe a hundred feet in some places. It was such a bright red I thought it must be a trick of the afternoon sun.

Down the road a piece, I saw the signs for Jemez Springs. After we passed through the town, the road started to get steep. The Indian nodded his head in the direction of a church. There was a row of rooms behind it, like some motel out of the fifties, but very neat and well maintained. "Servants of the Paraclete," he said.

I'd never been near the place, but I'd heard about it for years. A safehouse for pedophile priests, where they could hole up for a while . . . and then go back into a new parish, all "cured." The church doesn't call them child molesters, or baby-rapers, or anything so terribly stigmatizing. No, predatory priests were "ephebophiles," part of the church's PR campaign to "dimensionalize" its own degenerates.

They know exactly how to play it. First you make up some "syndrome" or "disorder" that covers the crime. Then you give it some fancy-sounding name, and count on the whores and fools to spread the word. You don't have to prove anything, just repeat it often enough, preferably through a good media machine. Doesn't matter if the entire scientific community sneers at it. What counts is that it gives defense attorneys an argument for a "non-incarcerative alternative." And black-robed collaborators all the excuse they need.

I could see why they wouldn't have a sign out front. But I didn't know if the Indian was offering to educate me, or trying another test to see if I was who I claimed to be. So I just said: "Oh yeah. The recycling center."

He grunted an acknowledgment. Or maybe it was an agreement.

We kept climbing. The altimeter read six thousand, and jumped up another fifteen hundred in the next few miles along a paved two-laner. A faint smell of something like *very* rotten eggs wafted up as we came alongside a fast-moving river. The side of the road was pocked with little hot springs. When we slowed way down, you could hear the earth gurgling not far below the surface.

The Land Rover negotiated the curves slowly until we passed a huge rock formation that looked like the bow of an old battleship, cut into a V, the prow vertical. We kept on climbing until we reached a fork in the road. The Indian went left, and we started climbing again.

The higher we climbed, the higher the pines grew—some of them were redwood-size giants. The road made one big looping turn, and then we were moving due west. I spotted a few occupied-looking houses, way back among the trees. And the shell of one that looked like it had been abandoned during the Civil War.

As we kept climbing, we left the pavement behind again. After we passed eight thousand, we came to a good-sized lake, maybe a half-mile across, the water very blue. Here the shoulder of the road was about the same height as the Land Rover. The Indian kept it moving, but very slowly.

We passed the lake, and then the road got worse. The skyscraper pines spiked up between enormous rock formations—sheer walls of stone that went up higher than I could crane my neck to see.

The air felt almost supernaturally clean, but it felt thin in my chest, too. I knew only the sun was keeping the temperature from getting dangerous . . . and we were going in and out of shade as we drove.

For the next few miles, we saw houses again, spaced real far apart. The terrain was nothing but dirt with occasional low grass. We rolled past a place called Seven Springs. And a sign that read THIS ROAD IS NOT MAINTAINED IN THE WINTER MONTHS, followed immediately by a drop from a bumpy, potholed dirt road to just plain dirt, with ruts wherever the water cared to run. We were at eighty-five hundred feet. And still climbing.

"We're in the national forest now," the Indian said. If that meant we were trespassing, it didn't seem to concern him much.

There were no more houses. Sometimes on the right, but mostly on the left, there was either dirt or rock going very nearly straight up where the road had been cut into the side of a hill. Whenever the rise was on the left, we were plunged into deep shadow. Huge trees met overhead, almost like the jungle canopies I remembered from Biafra. Except now the only chill in the air was from the altitude.

The road was so deeply rutted that, sometimes, the Indian had to work up speed and just bounce over them. Other times, when the ruts were running in the same direction we were traveling, he slowed to a crawl and drove the narrow little spaces between them, carefully placing all four tires. I wouldn't have tried with anything less than the Land Rover's ground clearance. Huge pines stood sentinel on either side of the road, which had clearly been cut right out of mountain rock, twisty and steep. It was all as familiar to me as Mars.

Finally, we came to what looked liked a little spur, just a place where the road swung out and widened a bit. But the Indian slowed even more, and soon there was no road at all . . . just a clearing. And that's where he brought the Land Rover to a halt.

"Are we—?" Gem started to ask. I made a hand gesture for her to be quiet. It was the Indian's call; no point pretending otherwise.

He climbed out, walked around the front of the Land Rover as he had before, and released his dog. At his signal, we got out, too.

"It's about three klicks," he said to me, the vaguest trace of a question in his voice.

"Let's go, then," I said, shouldering my duffel and picking up Gem's little suitcase in my right hand.

The Indian went back to the Land Rover and took out a scoped rifle from somewhere. He slipped the sling on and started off without another word.

The walk felt like a fucking treadmill—a greasy one. All slippery low grass and dirt. Gem kept up with me easily, but gave up trying to take her bag from me after a few attempts.

We finally came to a Y-shaped intersection, and the Indian called a halt. I flopped down gratefully, ignoring a look from Gem.

The Indian took a strip of what looked like beef jerky out of his coat and made a soft whistling sound. The dog trotted over to him and sat expectantly. The Indian tossed the strip and the beast caught it easily, then walked off a short distance, tail wagging. He found a spot that suited him, lay down, held the strip between his paws, and went to work on it.

The Indian pulled a single cigarette out of his breast pocket and lit it. It was unfiltered, with a dark-yellow wrapper; leaf or paper, I wasn't close enough to tell.

A hawk soared overhead.

The Indian finished his smoke, carefully pinched off the glowing tip, then shredded the tiny bit that remained between the fingernails of one hand, dropping the result into the palm of the other. He held that hand high, opening it as a bolt of breeze came through, scattering the traces.

I rested my head on Gem's thighs. It was out of my hands.

The Indian sat on the ground cross-legged. He unslung his rifle and laid it across his knees. It had a heavy, fluted barrel, and the stock was obviously fiberglass, colored in broad bands of black and gray. Not a camo-pattern, almost a geometric design. I tried to figure out what kind of rifle it could be, but my eyes kept losing its outline. That's when I figured out the black-and-gray banding was no accident.

"That's an unusual-looking piece," I told him, trying for engagement again.

"It wasn't built for looks," he said.

"Remington 700?" I guessed, thinking of Wesley.

"It's a .308 Bedeaux."

"I never heard of—"

"It's custom," he said. "The man whose name's on the barrel, he tunes them. And he's the best in the world at it."

"Minute-of-angle?" I asked him.

The Indian wasn't impressed with my knowledge. Or my standards. "Less," he said. "This one'll ten-inch group at thirteen hundred *meters*." He raised his eyebrows slightly. "You believe that?"

I wondered if he was testing again. Decided it didn't matter. "I wouldn't know," I told him, truthfully. "I never really handled a rifle for serious."

"I thought you worked jungle, once."

I wondered if there was anything Lune *hadn't* told this guy.

"Sure. Jungle, not plains, or mountains. And I was never a sniper, anyway."

"What'd you carry?"

"Over there?"

"Yeah."

"Whatever I could pick up. There was no resupply chain. Time I got on the ground, whatever *anyone* carried over there, it was like a fucking Bic lighter, understand? Runs out of fuel, you throw it away, look for another."

"You work close-up, anyway, don't you?" he said. It wasn't a question. And I guess there *wasn't* anything Lune hadn't told him.

I just nodded.

"I apologize for my lack of politeness," Gem said, suddenly. "You already know my husband's name. I am Gem."

"I am Levi," the Indian replied, nodding his head just short of a bow, as Gem had done. Then, to me: "I didn't know you were married."

"Lune and I haven't been in touch for a while," I said.

A trace of a smile played across the Indian's face. "Lune is always in touch," he said. "That's what he does."

"May I offer you some water?" Gem asked him.

"Do you always carry water in your luggage?" he asked, an undercurrent of approval in his voice.

"Always."

"No, thank you," he said, almost formally. "But if you . . ."

Gem reached over, unzipped her bag, took out a plastic bottle of water, handed it to me. I took a couple of grateful sips, handed it back. She glugged down about half the bottle.

The Indian's eyebrows rose a fraction.

"You should see her eat," I told him.

Then I felt someone behind me.

They entered the clearing in a pincers movement—bracketing Gem and me, standing at an angle so they could watch us and the Indian at the same time. As they came closer, I could see they were both women, dressed exactly alike in padded camo-pattern jumpsuits. They were carrying exactly alike, too: backpack straps over their shoulders . . . and pump-action shotguns in their hands. The resemblance stopped there. The one closest to Gem was tall, slightly plump, and rosy-cheeked, with her cornsilk-blond hair in twin braids. I named her Heidi, in my mind. The other was a dark-complected, raven-haired Latina, a half-foot shorter than her partner.

"All right?" Heidi asked the Indian.

"He is who he is supposed to be."

"And her?" the Latina asked, gesturing at Gem with the barrel of her shotgun.

"Wild card," the Indian said. "*He* trusts her."

"Get up," the Latina told Gem.

I measured the distances with my eyes. The Latina looked quicker, the blonde more solid. I had to get one of them between me and the Indian if—

"Easy!" the Indian warned her off, reading my body language like it was a billboard. "It's not what you think," he said to me, his voice calm. "We weren't expecting her. You know that. Lune trusts you. He doesn't know her. You vouching for her . . . Well, no offense, but any man can be fooled."

"*Especially* a man," the Latina said.

"So what we need to do now is to search . . . Gem," the Indian continued. "I promise you it will be as dignified as possible. And that, if we find weapons, it will not mean anything. But if we find a transmitter. Or a recording device . . ."

"I understand," Gem said, getting slowly to her feet and facing the Latina as if the shotgun was a bureaucratic annoyance.

The Latina turned and started walking off, Gem following. And the blonde following Gem.

It took much longer than I thought it would. I made some no-content conversation with the Indian, forcing myself to not listen for a shotgun's roar.

When they came back, the shotguns were pointed at the ground. The blonde went over to the Indian, unhooked a canteen from her knapsack, and handed it to him. He took a long drink. And then I understood why he had refused Gem's offer earlier.

Each of the women took out a padded jumpsuit similar to the ones they were wearing from their knapsacks. The Latina handed one to Gem, the blonde to me.

"Ready to go?" the Indian asked, once we'd climbed into the suits.

"Yes," I told him.

The blonde picked up my duffel. The Latina took Gem's little suitcase. I didn't say a word.

The Indian waved his hand. The dog jumped to its feet and ran over to him.

Then we all started walking.

After a couple of hours, I was grateful the women were carrying all the gear. When the Indian finally held up his hand for us to stop, we were right next to a fence that was mostly concealed by vegetation. He checked his compass, walked to his right along the fence line, and stopped again. He showed us a gap someone had cut in the fence. If he hadn't shown me, I never would have spotted it.

We followed him through. And started walking again until we came to a sheer-faced rock ledge.

The Indian motioned for us to stay where we were. Then he and the dog moved off until they were out of sight.

The Latina kept checking her watch. Or, at least, looking at some dial she wore on a band around her wrist. I wasn't near enough to see, and didn't plan on closing the gap.

Finally, she nodded at the blonde, who stood up and said: "You'll have to carry your own stuff now. It's not far. And we have to keep our hands free, all right?"

"Sure," I said. But, this time, Gem snatched her little suitcase before I had a chance.

The blonde went first, climbing on what looked like random cuts in the rock. Normally, watching a woman climb stairs is one of life's great treats, but the muffling of her camo-suit and the fading sun's occasional glint off her scattergun killed any of that for me. Gem was behind me, with the Latina bringing up the rear.

As we topped a ridge, I could see down into a cleft in the rocks big enough to hold a large building. And when I looked closer, that's what it was. Like a Quonset hut, a damn big one, painted the same color as the rock formations surrounding it. The only thing that drew my eye was the antennas. There were enough of them to bring cable to a small city. All different heights and thicknesses, with a random assortment of satellite dishes as well.

"He's in there," the blonde said.

We had to stoop to get through the door. Inside was a small, square room, as antiseptic as a decompression chamber. The women racked their shotguns on either side of the doorway, took off their camo-suits, and stood silently, hands clasped behind their backs, like some parody of parade rest.

"Have a seat," the Indian said, pointing to what looked like a transplanted church pew against the far wall. "He's working on something now, but he'll see you soon."

"Would you like some coffee, or something to eat, while you're waiting?" the blonde asked.

"Please!" Gem said, making it clear she was saying yes to all the above.

The Latina glared at the blonde, but she didn't say anything.

The blonde went out of the room, came back in a few minutes with a coffeepot in one hand and a tray of fancy cookies in the other. "Just a second," she said, and went back out again. When she returned, she had coffee cups and saucers, and plates for the cookies. Which was a good thing, since it prevented Gem from simply putting the tray in her lap and going to work on the goodies.

I passed on the coffee, but I had a couple of the cookies. "These are *wonderful!*" Gem told the blonde, her mouth full.

"Aren't they? Juanita makes them."

The Latina rewarded her with a glass-cutter look—apparently, her domestic skills were supposed to be a secret. But before she could acid-tongue a response, the Indian returned.

"You can go in now," he said.

Gem and I both stood up. The Indian shook his head. "Just you, Burke."

The place was a lot bigger than I'd been able to tell from the outside—a labyrinth of rooms opening off other rooms, most of them loaded with equipment: file cabinets, computers, something that looked like a giant periscope. There were people around, too, but they all seemed too busy to look up from what they were doing. I kept my eyes down, not knowing the rules. At the end of one of the long corridors was a pair of swinging doors, like saloons used to have in old Westerns. The Indian pushed through. I was right behind.

A man was seated behind what looked like a triple-size drafting table. He looked up. Studied my face for a second, and . . . connected. Flashing us both back to where we'd started.

nside, it was. Not the orphanage where they'd started me off, not the juvie joints I'd graduated to. This one they called a hospital.

It was different, all right. Everything was softer. The words, I mean. They didn't call the windowless cells "solitary." Even padded the walls for you. And, instead of clubs, the guards carried hypos full of quiet-down juice.

My trip to the crazy house started when I was locked up for thieving. One of the look-the-other-way "counselors" said they had a new program for kids like me. I was too young to be paroled to the streets, and I had no parents, so they had these special foster homes. For kids who'd had "trouble with authority," as he put it, not even bothering to hide the sneer.

And I *was* just a kid then. Foster home—it sounded pretty good to me. At least the "foster" part. I already knew what a "home" was. I'd been in a couple of them. They were the same as the institution, only they didn't have bars on the windows.

Same rules, though: always walk light and be ready to move, fast.

I ran away from the first one they dumped me in. I probably could have stayed out forever except for some lousy luck. I was steering for a hooker, only the john turned out to be a cop. Not an undercover looking to make a bust, just a freak with a taste for pain and a badge to take it on the house. I always hung around outside the ratty hotel room where Sandi took her tricks. If it worked out good, sometimes she gave me a little extra on top of what the johns paid me for "finding" them a girl.

Of course, when Sandi wasn't working, I switched from legit steering to mini-Murphy. I'd bring the johns to another hotel, then tell them I always held the money for my sister—she was nervous about getting robbed up there. I'd give them the room number and a key that wouldn't fit any of the doors . . . and run like hell the second they started climbing the stairs to the top floor.

When I heard Sandi scream that time, I wasn't too worried, at first. She always made noises when she worked. Told me the johns liked that. But in a minute, I knew it was for real. I was old enough to know what it sounds like when someone's doing . . . the things people do to kids. This was the same. I pounded on the door, real hard, yelled, "I'm calling the cops!"

The john ripped open the door. Sandi was lying on her stomach. The back of her was all bloody. The john told me to shut the fuck up, gave me a hard slap to the face. I came up with my knife in my hand. He laughed. But when he saw I knew how to hold it, he backed up a little, being careful. I grabbed an ashtray from the dresser and threw it as hard as I could. It missed him by a mile. But it went where I aimed it—right through the window. It was only on the second floor. I heard the fat pig at the front desk yell something. The john looked like he didn't know what to do.

Time stopped, freezing us all, until we heard footsteps pounding up the stairs.

Cops. In uniform. They took over. One of them pulled me outside the room and cuffed me. He didn't say anything.

I could hear Sandi inside. "That's not him," she said. "He came in after this other guy was . . . doing it to me."

"That's your statement, miss?" one of the uniformed cops asked her.

"Yes," she said. The door swung open and I could see inside. Sandi had a sheet wrapped around her shoulders.

"That little bastard pulled a knife on me," the john said, pointing at me.

"I saw you—" I started to say, but a look from Sandi cut me off.

So they took me back to the institution. And, after a while, they tried me on another foster home.

That's when it happened. That's when they . . . did what they did. To me. Whenever they wanted. It was summer. No school. Nobody ever came around to check on me. I was theirs.

But no matter how bad they hurt me, I never forgot what Wesley had told me the very first time we were locked up together. One night in the dorm, we saw a kid twice our size make a little one suck his cock in the shower. "They all have to sleep sometime," the ice-boy whispered to me.

I knew I couldn't shank them. Even though they were passed-out drunk most nights, there were still three of them. The man and his wife, and their teenage son. If any one of them screamed out while I was doing it, I'd be finished. And even if I pulled it off, got them all done, I'd still be the only suspect.

But I remembered something else Wesley had taught me. And that's all I thought about, from then on.

One of the things they made me do was clean. All the time. Everywhere, especially their foul bathrooms. It took me a while, but I found a place to hide the plastic squeeze bottles of cleanser I emptied—some by using it up, most by just dumping it down the sink.

I never really slept. I was too afraid. Late one night, I got into their garage and filled my plastic bottles from the gas can they kept for their power mower. I hid them again, waiting.

I knew they took pills, but I didn't know where they kept them. The only thing I could find in the bathroom was aspirin, so I started stealing that, a couple of tablets at a time.

They kept hurting me. I knew someday I'd just split into pieces from what they were doing to me.

I couldn't wait any longer. One afternoon, I unscrewed the caps on their bottles of wine and carefully poured in the aspirin I had ground into a fine powder. I did the same with their other booze. I couldn't know which ones they would drink. Or even if what I heard about mixing aspirin and booze would work. But I couldn't run, and there was no place to hide.

If it didn't work, I told myself, no matter what happened, it would be over. What they were . . . doing to me, it would be over. I didn't care about anything else.

When they fell out that night, the woman was on the couch. The man made it to their bedroom. The son slept in the basement—the same basement he used to make me go down into with him. Whenever he wanted.

I did him first, spraying him with a gentle mist of gasoline. Then I crept upstairs for the man. The woman was last. I think I hated her the worst. I don't know why—I was already old enough to know that all that stuff about mothers was a lie.

Then I opened the door to the oven and turned on the gas, full-blast. I went around the house, making sure all the windows were shut. The smell was making me sick. I eased open the back door, used the last of my hoarded gasoline to soak a bundle of rags. I dropped a match on the bundle. As soon as it was blazing, I threw it as far inside the house as I could.

And I ran.

I was just a kid, but I'd been schooled. No matter how many times they asked me, I told them the same story. I was out when it happened. Prowling the streets, looking for something to steal. When I finally got back to that wood-frame foster home, it was real late. I was going to sneak in, like I had plenty of times before. That's when I saw the flames and the fire trucks and all the rest.

One of the cops hit me on top of my head with the flat of his hand. He kept asking me questions, then hitting me every time I answered. It made me so dizzy that I threw up. On him. He picked me up and flung me into the wall, cursing. A couple of other cops pulled him off. They told me to get in the bathroom and clean myself off.

When I came out, there was a woman there. A pretty woman, I thought, with reddish-brown hair and a nice smile. She asked me the same questions as the cops. I gave her the same answers.

They put me in a cell.

In court, all I remember is the judge yelling at one of the men in suits. They used a lot of words I didn't understand, but I remember hearing "evaluation" a lot.

That's how I ended up in the crazy house.

wasn't afraid of the people who asked the questions. All their questions were stupid. Did I like to play with matches? Did I like to watch fires? One even asked me if I wanted to be a fireman when I grew up.

The big-cheese doctor there, he got mad when I asked him if I could have a cigarette. He thought I was fucking with him. Maybe that's why he was the boss—he was smarter than the others.

One of them—a social worker, I think, but all I knew was that she was "staff"—asked me if the people in that foster home had . . . done anything to me. I told them they were mean. I said they hit me and made me work all the time and only gave me the crappiest food. And I told her they were drunk all the time, especially at night. She nodded when I said that, like I'd just confirmed something they already knew.

I knew if I said it had been a nice place they'd know I was lying. But I never told anyone what those people really did. Then they'd know a lot more. Not about those people. About me.

They had all kinds of kids in there. Just like the institution. They were all State kids, too. Or poor ones. If you had people, and if your people had money, they said there were "private facilities" you could go to.

Some of the kids cried all the time. One kid played with himself. Right in front of everyone. His cock was bloody from him constantly pulling at it. Some of them talked to themselves . . . or to somebody I couldn't see. Some just stayed wherever staff put them. On the floor, in a chair, in bed—it didn't matter to them.

I knew the kids to watch out for. The ones with all the best clothes. The ones with the best bunks. Stuff like that. I knew how they got those things. And I knew I didn't have anything worth taking. Except for . . .

So the first thing I did was find something to make myself a shank with. Soon as I did, I let one of the kids with all the good stuff see it. Just like the institution. And, just like the institution, I had to stick one of them just so they'd know I wasn't bluffing.

Nobody called the cops. What could you do to a crazy kid, anyway? That's how I found out about the padded rooms.

When Lune came in, I knew he was going to do his time bad. He was the prettiest boy I'd ever seen in my life. He looked like a little doll. And one of the kids with all the stuff wanted to play with him. Eugene Hunsaker was his name. I guess Lune never forgot it, either.

It was none of my business when Hunsaker's crew grabbed Lune over in a corner of the ward. But when Lune broke free and ran, he headed straight to my bunk. Hunsaker and one of his boys were right behind him. Taking their time. Laughing, knowing nobody was going to come in and stop them. A few extra screams in that place wouldn't raise an eyebrow, much less a guard.

I don't know what happened. Maybe Hunsaker's rape-partner looked a little like the son in that foster home. My circuits just snapped.

All I had was the thick end of the antenna I'd snapped off a portable radio, with the open part ragged and sharp. I stabbed Hunsaker's partner in the arm with it. He shrieked like it had been an icepick to the balls, and that was it for him.

I yelled "Fight!" to Lune. He turned around like a robot following orders. He did his best, but you could see he'd never fought before. Hunsaker was pounding his beautiful face into a pulpy mess, giggling.

I nailed the scumbag in the back of his neck with my antenna, driving hard. But Hunsaker was a lot tougher than his partner. He just dropped to one knee, grabbed my arm, and flipped me over his shoulder.

Hunsaker was on top of me, trying for my throat. Lune dove down on him, flailing away—all he did was add to the weight. I kept trying for Hunsaker's eyes, but he'd been there before and blocked me easily. It was all going hazy when I heard the whistle, and I knew the guys with the hypos were on the way.

Hunsaker and his partner wouldn't tell what happened. They knew I wouldn't talk, either—we'd all come up in the same places.

But Lune told them that it was his antenna, and that he stuck both of them because they were all part of "it." He kept demanding to see his parents. One of the orderlies laughed when he said that. If he could have seen what was in Lune's eyes then, he never would have.

Lune told me that his real parents had been stolen, and he had to find them. There was some kind of plot—I couldn't follow everything he said—and the people who *said* they were his parents were part of it. He was a very logical kid. Parents wouldn't hurt their own children, right? So anyone who did that, they couldn't be the kid's *real* parents, understand?

I did understand. But I didn't know how to tell him what I knew. Being crazy was his only treasure, his one protection. I was his friend, and I wouldn't steal from him.

Instead, I schooled him. There were some groups they made us go to. Sometimes we had to make things out of clay and crap. And we always had to be taking those tests. But, most of the time, they left us alone. I told him he couldn't be telling people about his real parents—they wouldn't understand.

"And they're probably in on it, too," he said, nodding.

Lune was always seeing patterns in things. He figured out that the big-cheese doctor was getting it on with one of the women who worked there. Not that Lune actually saw them, or anything. He just put it together. He tried to explain to me how he did it; but, even when he broke it down, it still seemed like magic.

One time after Lune told me, I was alone with the big cheese. I asked him for another cigarette. I could see his face get red. I told him I thought sometimes people did things other people wouldn't understand if they knew about them. He gave me a weird look. I knew Lune had nailed it then, so I told the big cheese sometimes people did things with *other* people. Everybody had secrets. I liked to smoke cigarettes. Couldn't that just be a secret between him and me? I mean, I'd never tell if I knew one of *his* secrets.

The big cheese's face turned dark and ugly, like he was being strangled. I thought maybe he was going to step on that button under his desk and get some people in there to fuck me up. I didn't move.

But when he pushed his pack of Marlboros across the desk toward me, I knew Lune was smarter than all the people who were keeping him locked up.

Lune kept charts. Of everything. You couldn't make any sense out of them if you saw them, but he said that was the point.

Other kids started hanging around with us. For protection, I thought, at first. That's the way we always did it Inside. Four little guys can stop a gorilla, if they're willing enough. But it wasn't me; it wasn't for protection. It was to get close to Lune. No matter what any of the kids told him—even the *real* crazy ones— Lune had an answer. An explanation that made sense. To them, anyway. He always said it was all patterns; you just had to figure out what they meant.

I think he even scared the doctors after a while. That's when I knew we had to go.

"There's a way out of here," I whispered to him one night. "It's all in the patterns, right?"

"Yes! It's always in the patterns. But if I left, how would my real parents—?"

"They're never going to let your real parents know you're here," I told him, urgently. "You've got to get out. And get *away*. Far fucking *far* away, understand?"

"What would I do?"

"I don't know; I'm not smart like you. But I know you have to get older before you have any power. We're just kids. Nobody's going to do anything we want."

"Where would I get power?"

"Money," I told him, with the smugness of a baby thug's world-view. "That's the one thing that will always make people do what you want."

"I could get money. . . ."

"Sure you could, man. You're smart enough to get all *kinds* of money. But not in here."

"Would you come with me?"

"I'll go *out* of here with you. We'll break together. But we can't *stay* together, Lune."

"Why?"

"Because I'm going to jail again," I told him, no smugness in my words then, but no less certainty. "I know how to get along locked up, Lune. But you don't. And they wouldn't let us be together in there, anyway."

"I could—"

"No, you couldn't," I cut in, heading him off. "You could *never* be safe Inside, Lune. But out there, in the World, you could make it. You'd figure it out, for sure."

"I still don't under—"

"Listen to me!" I hissed at him. "If you stay *here*, if you fucking *keep* talking about your real parents, they're gonna shoot you up with so many of their fucking 'meds' you'll end up like Harry."

Harry was a diaper-wearing vegetable who'd once been dangerous . . . to the guards.

"That would fit their pattern," Lune said, finally coming around.

"You're not a criminal, brother," I told him. "And you're big-time smart. You'll find a way to be out there, *stay* out there, make some money. *Then* you'll be able to look for your real parents."

"What are you going to—?"

"I'm going to steal," I told him, pridefully. To be a good thief was my highest ambition back then. So I could buy what I wanted more than anything on earth—to be safe. "And they're going to catch me sooner or later and put me back Inside. I have to wait until I'm big enough to steal *good*. Then I'll have money, too, see?"

"Sure!"

That same night, Lune started looking for a seam in the fabric.

He found one so fast I didn't trust it at first. I thought he'd look for a ventilation duct we could crawl through or something like that. But Lune told me to keep an eye on a kid named Swift. Not let anyone see I was doing it, but watch him *close*. I already knew how to do that.

Swift wasn't one of the tough kids, and he wasn't mobbed up. But he had a nice bunk in a good section of the dorm, and he always had comic books and candy bars. Even a portable radio— in fact, that was where I'd gotten my antenna.

I couldn't figure out why Hunsaker's clique hadn't made a move on him, especially when it came time to draw commissary, but they never did. For sure, Swift wasn't scoring off his parents; he never had any visitors. There were things you could do to get stuff in there, but he didn't have enough horsepower to rough it off, and I never caught him creeping anybody's stash, either.

It didn't add up. I started sleeping most of the day, like the meds were really doing me in. Of course, I tongue-palmed the fucking things whenever they gave them to me, and I stayed quiet enough not to court the hypo again. So I was awake at night. All night.

In the dark, I slitted my eyes and watched, trusting Lune and his patterns.

I was watching real late one night—I didn't have a watch, and there was no clock in the dorm—when Swift sat up. He looked around, real careful. I figured, okay, *now* he was going to make his move; now I'd see where he scored all his stuff from.

He got up like he was going to the bathroom, a big white place with hard tile and no door. He walked right past it, straight to the dorm door. The one they locked every night.

He pulled down on the handle, very slow and careful. And the door opened! I couldn't believe it. I *knew* that they locked that door every night. And that the late-shift guard would walk by the giant wire-meshed window that gave him a good view of the whole dorm every couple of hours or so. But Swift pulled the door closed behind him and he was gone.

In another minute, so was I, my bare feet soundless on the filthy linoleum as I stalked him down to a long, dark hall where the floor switched to carpet. I knew where *that* hall led—right to the part of the building where the big shots had their offices. I figured I knew what he was up to then. I'd always wished *I* could get in there one night and do a number on all that nice furniture and paintings and plants and trophies and . . . all of it.

But everything changed when I ghosted around a corner and saw Mr. Cormil. We had to call all the guards "mister" or "sir." Cormil was the guy who was supposed to be cruising by the big window, looking at all the crazy fish in the concrete aquarium. But he wasn't doing that. He was doing Swift.

He held Swift's hand like he was his father. They walked along until Cormil opened one of the offices with a key from the big ring he wore on his belt. They went inside. Cormil left the door open, probably so he could hear if anyone was coming.

But he never heard *me* coming. They don't call it reform *school* for nothing.

It didn't look like rape. Not to me. Not to a kid my age. Not to a State-raised kid who'd *seen* rape. It looked like . . . like Swift on his knees, sucking Cormil off while the guard leaned forward and stroked the kid's hair. And then it looked like Cormil pulling his cock out and helping Swift stand up. And bend over. He smeared some greasy stuff on his cock and fucked Swift in the ass. But slow and gentle, talking to him like a lover all the while.

It wasn't anything like I knew rape to be. There was no gun. No knife. No fist. No threats.

It took a lot of years before I understood what I had seen that night.

As soon as we were alone the next morning, I told Lune. He just nodded—you could see his mind was somewhere else.

"How'd you know?" I badgered him.

"I didn't," he said. "But I knew there was a pattern. Swift had things. He had to get them from somewhere. He was . . . special. How come? I didn't know. But I knew, if you watched him close enough, we'd find out."

"You're a dangerous motherfucker," I told him.

Lune and I didn't speak the same language. He didn't get that I was showing him high respect. "I just want to find my real parents," he said, sadly.

After that, the only hard part about busting out was waiting for Swift to visit Cormil again. And keeping Lune from screwing things up. He didn't know how to move quiet. And he was so nervous, I thought they'd hear his raspy breathing as we slipped past the room where Cormil and Swift were doing what they did.

But once we made it past them, it was easy. We dropped down flat on the carpet in the hall until they were finished. As soon as they walked back down the corridor together, we made our move. I loided the door to the big cheese's office—it was nothing but a doorknob lock, no deadbolt—and we went inside.

I picked that room because I'd been in there before. That's how I knew there was no deadbolt. And what was right outside the window. A parking lot. A parking lot *outside* the walls around the hospital where they kept us.

I opened the window, moving real slow against it squeaking, but it didn't make a sound. The office was right on the first floor, and we dropped down easy. Then I pulled the window back closed.

The parking lot was almost empty—just a few scattered cars, and not a Cadillac in the bunch. The big shots wouldn't be showing up for hours.

I didn't know how to hotwire a car then. And even if I had known, it would have been a dumb risk.

I had nine dollars in singles. Lune didn't have anything. I didn't know where we were, but I could see it was out in the country someplace.

We could have tried hitchhiking, but it was too close to the nuthouse. And if a cop cruised by . . .

So we walked, following the road but staying in the darkness of the shoulder. I was looking for a place where we could hole up before it got daylight when Lune spotted a diner a few hundred yards ahead.

I told him to let me do the talking if we had to go inside. First I checked the parking lot. Most of the cars had New York plates. Some of the big trucks had a whole bunch of them, from different states. I couldn't figure out why that would be, but I knew they *locked* the backs of those semis.

I tried door handles, one after another. If I hadn't believed God hated me personally, I probably would have prayed. A big new Ford station wagon called to me. The back door opened. "Come on!" I whispered to Lune. We climbed inside. There was some stuff there, but it wasn't crowded. "He could spot us here. We got to get all the way in the back," I said to Lune, putting my hand over his mouth when he opened it to ask a question.

In the space behind the rear seat, there was nothing but a pair of suitcases. "All right," I told Lune. "We're going to just lie down here. If the guy comes out and gets in the front seat and drives away, we go wherever *he's* going, got it? But if he opens up this back part, Lune—brother, listen now—we got to *run*, all right?

Just fucking *blast* outa here before the guy knows what's happening. See the woods over there? Right across from us? All right, that's where we head for. I don't think he'll even chase us. Maybe figure it was a joke or something."

"I can't—"

"Lune, you *have* to! Look, if he opens up this part, I'll try and kick him or something. Give you a little time to get going. Remember how you fought when Hunsaker . . . ? Remember that? It's like that now, too. We *got* to do it, or we're fucked."

He didn't say anything, but he was breathing real hard. And real loud.

"Okay?" I asked him.

He just nodded.

I don't know how much time passed before we heard the front door open. Lune squeezed my hand tight. We felt the weight of the driver as he plopped into his seat, even back where we were. Then we heard the blessed sound of the engine rumbling into life.

When the station wagon pulled out onto the highway, Lune let go of my hand.

It was just coming daylight when the driver slowed down. I couldn't tell if he was getting gas or what, so I snuck a quick look up. It was another diner. We heard the front door open, then slam shut.

When we climbed out of the back of that station wagon, we saw that the diner the guy had stopped at was in the Bronx.

"We're okay now," I promised Lune.

L une stayed with me for almost three weeks. I knew better than to go back to where they'd grabbed me before. I knew some other things, too. Like places where kids our age could make some money. But shining shoes was out—if you took a corner, you had to be able to hold it, and Lune wouldn't be able to help. If I'd been bigger, or even if Lune had been better at violence, we might have tried to rip off one of the Times Square chickenhawks.

But there were plenty of other ways.

Lucky for us, it was summer. Lots of kids on the streets. The cops wouldn't give us a second look once we got some fresh clothes. *That* I knew how to do. Not shoplifting. That was for the artists. All I knew was snatch-and-run.

I wouldn't let Lune come with me when I hit the stores. It wasn't just to protect him—I knew he'd screw it up.

Once we had clothing, we hit the strolls, looking for working girls who'd pay me a little for steering, like I'd done for Sandi. But as soon as they saw Lune, they couldn't stop fussing over him. They all wanted to pat him, or give him a kiss, or cuddle him . . . that kind of stuff. If I heard "dollface" or "angelpuss" one more time, I was going to puke. But at least they never bothered *me* with any of that sappy stuff. And some of them gave us money, too.

People were a lot more careless back then. Stealing was easy. The hard part was finding places to sleep. I knew kids from reform school, but I didn't know their last names, or their addresses or anything—just where they'd be hanging out if they *were* out.

There were gangs all over the City back then. Small ones, mostly, with four-block squares of turf, although there were a few that could call out a hundred guys for bloody battles that only the newspapers called "rumbles." I knew I could work into a gang as a Junior—I had all the credentials. But I also knew Lune wouldn't be able to handle the initiation, so we steered clear of them.

Finally, I found Wesley. Or maybe he found me. He knew places down by the docks that were perfect for hiding out. Wesley couldn't figure out what I was doing with Lune, but he let him come along. That was Wesley then. If you were with him, anyone with *you* was with him, too.

Years later, after he'd made his mark so deep the whisper-stream trembled every time he went on the stalk, people said he'd been born a killing machine. They didn't know Wesley when he had a heart. A heart of napalm, ready to explode into flame for anyone who would love him.

Lune was one of the softest, gentlest people I'd ever known. And Wesley became an assassin so deadly that even his own death didn't stop his name from invoking terror. But when they were kids with me, they had the same heart.

Late one night, I told them about the fire. Wesley said I could have made sure if I had done them all first. I said I'd thought of that, but I'd seen kids stabbed and not die from it—even turn on the kid holding the shank and fuck him up. And I knew he had, too; we'd watched it together.

"That was in there," the ice-boy said. "It's different out here."

"How come?" I asked him, puzzled.

The next day, we went into a pawnshop. Wesley bought a pearl-handled straight razor for two dollars.

And that night, he showed me how good it worked.

We had a little more than three hundred and fifty dollars put aside—a lot of money, back then. It was time for Lune to go. I thought he'd kick about it, want to stay with me and Wesley. But he kept telling us that he couldn't find his parents hiding out—he had to go looking for them. Lune figured his parents couldn't be from New York. The way he reasoned it out was, the place where we'd been locked up—the nuthouse—*that* was in

New York. So his real parents, if *they* were from New York, they would have found him.

He asked us about our parents, once. We just told him we didn't have any. When Lune asked us if we wanted to try and find them, Wesley gave him a look that would have scared a scorpion.

Lune was smarter than me and Wesley put together, I think. But he had a special kind of mind. And he wasn't raised where we were. So it was our job to spring him.

Once we figured out that they put Lune in that nuthouse because they really thought he *was* crazy, we knew they wouldn't spend a lot of time looking for him. He had to be a throwaway kid of some kind, like us, even though Lune always said he had a family. A real family that loved him.

We knew he could never get out of the City on his own. Even if the cops *weren't* looking for him, a kid traveling alone would get questions asked. And once they heard Lune's answers, he'd be right back Inside.

We knew places where you could jump freights, but I didn't think Lune could handle that. And Wesley said, even if he could, the older guys riding the rails would eat him alive. That was after he had tried to show Lune how to use the razor. Lune wouldn't even touch it.

We found the answer where kids like us always found their answers. Wesley was even better than me at being invisible, but I was better at talking to people. *Way* better—Wesley didn't like talking, and he didn't like people.

The hooker's name was Vonda. All we knew about her was that she got ten bucks for half-and-half, and that she had a pair of dreams. One was to go to Hollywood and be discovered. The other was to get away from her pimp—a gorilla who snatched her right off the stroll every night and made her turn over the take. He'd already shown her what would happen if she ever held out on him. With a coat-hanger whip and the glowing tip of his cigarette. She was too scared to ever run on her own.

Wesley and I figured she and Lune were a natural pair.

"He'll never let me go," she told us, standing under an over-hang to get some shelter from the rain, but still scanning the street for a customer. "And I don't ever have more than a couple of bucks at a time of my own, anyway."

"We can get you two hundred and fifty," I said.

"I guess maybe you could, you little hustler," she said, giving me a grin. "But he'd come after me. No matter where I went. I know he would. He's got contacts all over the country." There was a twisted mixture of pride and terror in her voice.

"When he picks you up after work, where do you go?"

"Home."

"With him?"

"Sure," she said, shrugging at the silly question.

"Is he a heavy sleeper?"

"Like a fucking log. But it would only give me a few hours' head start, and—"

"You'd have a lot more time than that," I promised her. "But the deal is, remember, you have to take Lune with you. All the way to Hollywood. And you have to *keep* him with you—just a place to sleep and some food—until he's ready to go out on his own."

"Like I was his mother, right?"

"Yeah, like that."

"I . . . It wouldn't work. What's to stop Trey from—?"

Then Wesley spoke. From the shadows, his natural home. He was a kid then, maybe twelve years old, I never knew for sure. But his voice was already ice-edged. "After he goes to sleep, just go downstairs and unlock the door," he said.

I didn't think Vonda had been taking us seriously until right that moment. She looked into the shadows where Wesley stood. And the gleam she saw wasn't coming from his eyes.

"When do I get the money?" she asked me.

esley was right about the razor. The first cut did it. The pimp made some spastic movements, trying to hold his throat together with his hands . . . but not a sound came out of his mouth.

We'd made Lune wait downstairs, telling him to keep the hundred bucks we'd given him a secret, no matter what, until he made his break in California. We told him it wouldn't be long—Vonda would be going back to hooking the second she got low on dough.

After we all made it downstairs, we walked for a few blocks. I gave Vonda the money. Then she hailed a cab, and I didn't see Lune again for more than twenty years.

he cops never found me or Wesley. We both hooked up with a gang, and ended up busted a few weeks later. We gave them phony names, but it didn't matter—when nobody came to claim us at Juvie, they put us back Inside. At least it wasn't the nuthouse.

I never got a letter from Lune while I was Inside. Not for the juvenile beefs, not for the felonies that turned me into a two-time loser later. And during the times I was out, he never called me on the phone, either.

But he always knew where I was, somehow. One of the hacks would come by my cell, tell me someone had sent me a money order. They never actually gave you the money, they just put it on the books for you so you could draw against it for stuff they sold in there—like miners who could only shop at the company store.

The money orders were always from Vonda-something—the last names were always different. And they were always for the maximum amount the institution allowed. I always wrote to the return address, but the mail always came back. So I knew that it had to be Lune. And that he'd learned some tricks.

I had my own wires, too. I'd catch something about Lune every once in a while. Not by name. But there'd be something in the whisper-stream about an organization that did "forecasting." You gave them the known facts, and they'd work out "scenarios" on a "probabilities scale" for you. Something a team of entrepreneurs could use, if they were thinking of opening a new restaurant. Or an armored car on its way to the bank.

When I finally saw him again, he was in Cleveland, a whole crew working with him. I couldn't tell exactly *what* they were working on, but it all had something to do with "patterns." They were like a gang of crazed journalists, gathering facts at random, checking and rechecking and cross-checking them until Lune pronounced them "authentic." Then they got to be pieces on this giant chessboard in Lune's head.

And when it was all done, he could predict white's next move as easy as black's. But all he did was watch; he never played.

The people who followed him weren't his partners. I mean, maybe they were, financially or something. But they were all looking for answers. And they believed that if they learned Lune's patterning methods they could find what they needed.

It wasn't that Lune could deconstruct assassinations of major public figures, tell you who did them, and why. Anyone can have a theory. But Lune told his people that the murders were going down *before* they happened. He could explain why Albert DeSalvo *wasn't* the Boston Strangler. And why Xerox was going to be a dominator when it was still a two-dollar stock.

I never asked Lune what had happened in all the years we hadn't been in touch. I didn't *have* to ask him if he ever found his parents—he greeted me by telling me he was still looking. Getting closer all the time. But I'd been right about one thing: whatever problems Lune still had, money wasn't one of them.

He didn't ask me what I'd been up to. Never even mentioned Wesley's name. I'd come all the way to that waterfront warehouse because I was looking for a roll of 8mm film. And the man who had it.

Lune treated it like a training exercise. He brought his whole crew in there. Told me to tell them everything I knew. Then he kind of vaguely pointed at the others, and they started to ask me questions. In a few minutes, I realized I knew a lot more than I thought I had. They were like a pack of starved rats, rooting through concrete to get to grain stored on the other side of the wall. Grain they *knew* was there. They sliced and diced my narrative, culling "authenticated" facts from the rest of what I told them. And then they started on "patterning," using index cards and pushpins on a whole wall covered in cork.

When that was done, they all split. "Fieldwork," Lune explained. I guess some of it was done on the phone, but I know some of them took off, too. And didn't come back for a few days.

It took almost two weeks. When Lune assembled them all again, they told me there was a "high-eighties probability" that the man I was looking for would be in a rooming house in Youngstown, Ohio. Lune told me I could move the probability into the high nineties if I wanted one of his crew to make a little trip . . . carrying the photo I'd brought with me.

Youngstown is maybe an hour and a half, two hours from Cleveland. I told Lune I'd go look for myself. If it didn't work out, I'd come back.

Lune told me his operation was mobile: they could be gone tomorrow. But he gave me a bunch of ways to get in touch.

The man with the film was right where they said he'd be. And he never saw me coming.

ow it was a lifetime later. And there was Lune. The beautiful boy had turned into a man so handsome he looked unreal. Me, I'd gone in the other direction.

"It's me," I greeted him.

"I know," he answered. "What's wrong?"

was in the middle of talking with Lune, heads close together like when we were kids in the crazy house. The Latina stalked into the room. She had a large photograph in her hand—color, so sharply etched it looked like it was composed of a zillion tiny crystals. Me. Holding my institutional number across my chest as the prison photographer logged me in the last time.

"This is the mug shot, hyper-enhanced, of the man you call Burke," she told Lune, as if I wasn't in the room. "It is absolutely authenticated. And he is recorded as 'Deceased/Homicide/Perp Unknown' on both local and FBI databanks."

"This is Burke," Lune said to her, gently.

"That is not how we have been trained," the Latina fired back, hands on her hips.

Lune made a sound like a soft sigh. Then he nodded at the Latina. She turned and walked away, swinging her hips in triumph.

Lune gave me a "What can you do?" gesture. His matinee-idol looks may have mesmerized women, but didn't change them.

The Latina came back with some sort of scanner. Big surprise—I already had my right hand extended, ready to be printed.

"You don't need to roll the prints," she told me, tartly. "Just rest your hand there. And hold it *still*."

I went back to explaining what I needed from Lune. Maybe ten minutes later, the Latina walked in again.

"It's him," is all she said. Then she spun on her heel and walked out.

That night, they showed me where Gem and I could sleep. It wasn't as fancy as the hotel, more like a studio apartment, but so clean it looked like we were the first occupants, ever.

Heidi told us that they all ate together but, seeing as we were guests, it would be better if they just brought the evening meal in to us. She looked apologetic while she explained, but I told her I understood. I'd known Lune a real long time, and it made perfect sense to me. But I did ask her if we could have a triple portion.

"Are you very hungry?" she asked, a concerned tone in her voice.

I just nodded my head in Gem's direction. Her blush was a sweet-pretty thing to see.

L ong, slow days after that. Every time I gave any of the people running around the place a piece of information, they had to do their check and cross-check routine before they could add it to the "pay-out matrix," whatever that was.

There wasn't much point spending the waiting time catching up on things with Lune. Nothing had changed for him. He was still working the patterns. And making a living at it while he kept looking for his real parents.

As for me, Lune seemed to know everything I'd been doing since we parted that last time in Cleveland. It was spooky. Not that I had any secrets from him—except for the one his insane mind would never acknowledge that we shared—but . . .

Lune filled the time by explaining some of the patterns he'd been tracking. My old partner wasn't interested in cults, conspiracies, or politics. He didn't care whether Bigfoot was real or Nessie was in the Loch. He didn't believe the truth was out there . . . not in one single place. Patterning was his religion, and he'd stayed true to it all these years, gathering disciples as he moved closer to the Answer.

I told him that Gem had reached out to a bunch of websites, trying to send a message. That pushed one of his switches:

"The Internet? You think there's no pattern *there*? That's what *they* think—they're so sure it's all unregulated anarchy. But every single keystroke is recorded, somewhere. Their sex lives, their financial records, their circle of contacts. It's the ultimate wiretap."

"Sure, but there must be gazillions of data-bits out there. Who could possibly go through it all and—?"

"You construct a screening device," Lune said, patiently. "It only looks for certain words, or phrases, or even numbers. Then you tighten the mesh with combinations, until only what you want to track comes through. It's not so difficult. All it takes is resources."

"So the government—?"

"There is no 'government,' Burke. There are only institutions. Agencies. The permanent ones."

Lune tapped a few keys, pointed an immaculate fingernail at his computer screen. "You know what that is?" he asked me, as what looked like a string of auction bids popped into focus.

"A bunch of dope dealers talking in code?"

"No. It's the IRS."

"Huh? I don't get it."

"It's a *pattern*," he said, spinning on his chair to face me. "You know all this talk about America's 'underground cash economy'?"

"It's not just talk."

"*Exactly!* It's authenticated fact. And that's where the *real* money is. Not in cocaine cartels or topless clubs; it's in flea markets, garage sales, all the 'hobbyist' stuff that's being trafficked back and forth every second."

"Flea markets? How much could—?"

"You have to watch the patterns," he said, reciting his mantra. He turned back to the screen, beckoning me to look over his shoulder. "Look! Here's one, right there on the screen. He's selling a signed copy of a first-edition book by . . . Martha Grimes. See it?"

"Sure. The highest bidder is . . . forty-five bucks so far, right?"

"Right. And what *this* guy—I mean the seller, okay?—what *he* did was, he bought maybe twenty copies of that book when it was remaindered. You know, you've seen the tables where they sell them in bookstores, haven't you?"

"Yeah," I said, knowing that everybody pays, and that the currency I needed to pay Lune's tolls was patience.

"First, you have to understand that *all* books get remaindered. It doesn't matter if they sell a million copies, there's *always* some left over. Well, the publisher isn't going to throw them away, so they sell them, in bulk, very cheaply. A book you spent twenty-five dollars on when it was new, a couple of years later, you'll see it for a dollar ninety-eight."

"Yeah . . . ?"

"Now the guy has all these books, so he waits until this Martha Grimes is doing a book-signing someplace. Then he ambushes her, gets her to sign as many copies as he can get away with. Some writers will just do it, some will limit the number of copies. But this . . . merchant, his story is always what a huge fan he is and how he's going to give the books away to all his friends as Christmas gifts or for their birthdays or something. See?"

"I . . . guess so. But . . ."

"Look at the *pattern*, Burke. Come on. This guy buys a book for, say, less than two dollars. He gets it signed. Then he sells it for forty-five dollars on this Internet auction site. Do you think, for one single solitary *second*, that he declares that profit as income?"

"Of course not."

"Good. Now multiply by . . . oh, ten million transactions per year."

"Are you serious?"

Not a brilliant question to ask Lune. "Come closer," he said, pulling back from the screen so I could do it. "Take a look as I scroll through for you. See how every single seller and every single buyer has to provide information just to participate? Their e-mail, a credit card, a street address . . . a *ton* of authentic data. What you see here is the clearest, cleanest audit trail that any IRS agent could ever dream of."

"Damn!"

"Sure. All they have to do is *watch*. That is, if they didn't set up the site themselves—there's so many of them, now."

"What a sting that would be. Jesus."

"Net people aren't the only ones. But they're certainly the easiest. You know those scams where they tell you you've just 'won' something? If you use the mail, the return will be very low. But on the Net . . . My goodness, Burke, even the best *browsers* are free. You can get a free e-mail address from too many places to count. And never mind all those free downloads! Do you think those outfits that give away all this 'free' Net stuff aren't turning around and *selling* your address to all kinds of people compiling their own sucker lists?"

"Something for nothing, huh?"

"Some 'nothing.' Every time you use that 'free' stuff, you're making a perfect record. Of yourself. Every place you go, every site you check out, everything you buy on-line. Think about it."

I *did* think about it. How Lune had tapped into that bizarre borderland where the Möbius strip crosses over itself. The one sure nexus between the hyper-right and the ultra-left: fear of government intrusion into their lives. That strange place where people who want to smoke marijuana in peace make common cause with the people who want to carry concealed automatic weapons. They share one great, unifying fear. It's called Registration.

"Christ! I'm glad I don't have one," I told him.

"One what?"

"Computer."

"You don't have a computer?"

"Nope."

Those big liquid-topaz eyes that had charmed hookers a million years ago filled with pity. I could read his thoughts like they were printed on his forehead: "And people think *I'm* crazy!"

In bed that night, Gem reached for me. It was no good. I kept seeing that Indian, scratching his dog behind its ears, talking to it in a language only the two of them understood. He'd want his partner to die in battle, too. I knew that. But I didn't have centuries of tribal tradition to comfort me. I knew Pansy wasn't in some fucking Happy Hunting Ground.

"You are so big," Gem whispered from between my legs.

"You are one sweet bitch." I chuckled.

She came up on her elbows. "Are you laughing at me?"

"No, little girl. I was being . . . grateful to you, I guess. Some women, all they live for is to chop a man's *cojones*. If not off, at least down to size. You, all you can think about is building me up."

"So you are saying I am lying?" she asked, crawling closer to my face.

"Not lying, honey. Let's say . . . exaggerating. And it's very—"

She interrupted me with a slap to the right side of my face. My blind side. I never saw it coming—maybe because it was the last damn thing I expected. It wasn't a hard slap, but it got my attention. Her eyes were flaming. "I do not lie!" she whispered, harsh in the darkness. "You are not fully . . . engorged, are you?"

"Hell, no. Every time that window—"

"Yes! But even *partially*, you are . . . It is obvious that when you . . . when you are completely yourself, you would be huge."

"Gem . . ."

"But you think that will never be again, don't you?"

I took a deep breath. Let it out. Tried to think about it. Couldn't. "Yeah," is all I said.

"So what?" she countered.

"Huh?"

"It would not matter."

"But if—"

"You are a fool, Burke. Give me your hand."

I did it, not even trying to guess this woman anymore. She guided it between her legs.

"You see?" she said. "I am . . . embarrassed at how wet you make me. This never happened to me before. Look," she said softly, "even here . . . ," pulling my hand down. The insides of her thighs were slick with estro-juice.

"That's just because—"

"I will not listen to any of your stupid man's explanations. You do not understand, even when I show you the truth."

"Gem . . . Look, I wasn't . . ."

"Last night, after you fell asleep, I put your thumb in my mouth. I love to do that with you—I don't know why. I thought it would help me sleep, like a child's pacifier. But do you know what happened?"

"What?"

"I had an orgasm. So deep I can *still* feel it."

"Great. So even if my cock flops, so long as my goddamn thumb holds out—"

I was ready for her slap this time, but I didn't move to block it. It was a lot harder than the first. Then she jumped up, grabbed one of my sweatshirts, pulled it over her head, and walked out the door.

It was very late when she came back inside. I was half asleep, but snapped awake as soon as I heard the door. She pulled off the sweatshirt and climbed into bed next to me.

"I apologize," she said.

"You didn't do anything wrong."

"I did not *say* anything wrong. But I should not have slapped you."

"It's all right."

"No, it is not. Would you slap me?"

"No."

"I do not mean, would you slap me of your own volition? I understand you would not. That is not you. But . . . would you slap me if I asked you to?"

"Gem . . ."

"Would you? Please? It would make me feel better."

I reached toward her face. She was unflinching, eyes wide. I tangled my left hand in her hair, pulled her across me, and smacked her bottom a couple of times. Harder than she had slapped me.

When I let go of her hair, she stayed where she was.

"Gem. If I—"

"Feel me," she said, softly.

I fell asleep with Gem lying across me. And woke up to her mouth on my cock. Full. She pulled away, held my cock in her fist, said, "See, stupid man!," and climbed on top of me.

I nstead of a gigantic corkboard, Lune now used some sort of projection system—whatever one of his crew typed into the notebook computers they all had on their laps showed up on a broad expanse of pristine white wall. Lune connected to the individual words with some kind of electronic pointer—changing their color and moving them around to construct his patterns.

Every day, more facts passed their "authentication" test. And the list grew:

Russian mafia

Dmitri

Sergei-Sophia-Petya {Pyotr?}

Chicago (Winnetka) → **Portland (Lake Oswego)**

Skinheads (youth)

Ruhr
Timmons } **teamed**

crystal meth

"What's *that* all about?" I asked Lune, pointing to a spot on the wall where **Nazi Lowriders** was displayed in green.

"Supposedly another hate group," the Latina answered for him. "But they operate as roving gangs—the Aryans call them 'street soldiers.' They're not into turf at all. They're younger than most white-supremacist crews, and they tend to focus on blacks, rather than Jews, for as-yet-unknown reasons."

"So Inside . . . ?"

"Yes. They often ally themselves with Chicanos against the blacks," she finished for me.

"So how do they connect to . . . ?"

"They may not," Heidi put in. "But, even though they wear the kill-tattoos—they use lightning bolts instead of spiderwebs—and do the whole Hitler thing, their *raison d'être* is drug-dealing. And crystal meth is their product. So, when you look at Ruhr and Timmons . . ."

"It's time to plug in the personals," Lune announced.

Nobody said anything. But they were all looking at me.

"It's up to you," Lune said.

"Take your best shot," I told them all.

It took the better part of four full days, and Lune's crew weren't nine-to-fivers—every time I looked around, there was still another one I didn't know. Working. The new wall they created finally got filled. With my life.

I'd never have thought there was that much to it. And, when they put it all down, I could see there really wasn't.

Father unknown. Orphaned-by-abandonment when my teenage mother gave a phony name and then checked out of the hospital ward without me. The whole trail from there. Always dropping, never climbing. Tighter and tighter levels of custody as I aged. Both my long prison jolts—the hijackings and the shootings—and all the short stays in jail. The madness in Biafra. All my scams, hustles, and cons. Kiddie porn that never got delivered. Crates of guns that did.

I went all the way with them, leaving nothing out except for when I'd been with Lune—that part had to be his call.

All the way *down*, trampolining off the Zero itself. Even the kid I'd killed by accident in a gunfight in that basement in the South Bronx. The basement where they were making the kind of movies where the star dies at the end. But that truth had never erased the guilt I'd carried ever since. Other killings—ones I still felt good about. Belle's daughter-raping father. Strega's Uncle Julio. Mortay, the karate-freak who wanted a death-match with Max—and got ambushed by me instead. All the things I'd done with Wesley.

I kept going through the swamp of my life, dredging up memories with every name. So many dead. So many gone. It was like a thirtieth high-school reunion, where everyone looks around to see who's going to show up this time. Or not.

I wasn't proud of what they put up there. But I wasn't ashamed of it, either. When you make a Child of the Secret, sometimes he comes back "home" for a visit.

Lune flicked his pointer. One word popped up on the wall, in bright blue letters: **Pedophile(s)**.

"It's the single common thread," Lune said to all of them. "Burke makes his . . . living in a variety of ways, all of which could motivate enemies to the sort of assassination that was attempted on him. But the *resources* necessary to orchestrate such an attempt . . . No, it has to be someone who believes Burke is pursuing *him*."

"Or her," the Latina added.

"Yes," Lune said. "Certainly. Our own research indicates that Burke's reputation is . . . mixed. Some see him as a mercenary. Others as a hired killer. There are even those who believe him to be some sort of private investigator. But most know him professionally as a contraband-dealer. The one unifying thread on which we can rely is . . . Aydah?"

Aydah, a tall, slender black woman, got to her feet to speak. "In New York," she said, in a faint French accent, "when it comes to pedophiles, Mr. Burke is considered a homicidal maniac. An irrational, dangerous individual who is blamed—or, depending on the source, credited—with virtually every type of violence against them—assaults, murders, arsons, explosions."

"Personality as perceived?" a guy from the far corner asked. He was white, medium-height, slim build—a good-looking kid with very close-cropped hair.

"Single most distinguishing characteristic is pathological vengefulness," she answered him.

"Thank you, Aydah," Lune said formally.

"But the operation it*self*," an Asian kid with cold eyes offered, ". . . the way it was coordinated, the assassins were certainly professionals. So it isn't just a question of money, then. Whoever *hired* them had to know where to *find* them."

"That's right, Minh," Heidi said, "and you can't just find a contract killer in the *Soldier of Fortune* want ads anymore."

"Maybe the connect is to Timmons and Ruhr," Aydah said.

"That doesn't authenticate," the Latina argued. "Those white supremacists aren't even good at killing, never mind gunfighting. It smells more like the government."

"Oh, *they're* real experts, all right," Aydah shot back.

Lune held up his hand for silence.

"Burke, it's your time now," he said. "You have to sit down and start making out a list. It doesn't matter how long it is, but it has to be as complete as you can possibly make it."

"A list of . . ."

"Pedophiles who might want revenge for something you did. Or who might have had reason to believe you were hunting them."

"That could be any—"

"You're safe here," Lune said. "Take all the time you need."

I knew better than to do that kind of work without a break. Your body gets tired, it moves slower. But when your mind gets tired, it turns on you.

There was a heavyweight-championship fight on the giant-screen TV they had in one of the common rooms. Not many were watching: the white kid with the close-cropped haircut, the Asian they had called Minh, the Indian, the Latina, and a couple of others.

"Clint," the white kid said to me, holding out his hand for me to shake. "This is my partner, Minh."

I shook both their hands—they were the first ones I'd met there who offered them.

The fight was pitiful. One boxer spent most of each round leaning against the ropes like a wino using a wall to prop himself up. The other guy slapped at him as if he were trying to keep flies off a corpse.

"If I hit a guy like that on the street in front of a dozen witnesses, I wouldn't even get arrested," I said.

Clint laughed, offered me a high-five.

The Indian nodded a silent agreement.

The Latina glared at me.

Since neither of the boxers dropped dead of a heart attack, the decision went to the judges. I didn't wait around for it.

I kept working on my list, following Lune's parameters: they had to be either wanting revenge, or fearing it.

The first category was much longer than the second. The people I would have wanted to hurt the most—the ones who had hurt me so much when I was little—I didn't know most of their names, much less where to find them. They wouldn't even know I was alive.

Anyway, *they* would know what the dumb-fuck government doesn't. Most of us, damn near *all* of us, we don't turn on the ones who hurt us. No, we turn on ourselves, mostly. Or on you.

And then you say we were born bad.

You and Hitler. Yeah, you don't like the comparison? Then, while we're doing time for what was done *to* us, don't fucking tell us, "It's all in the genes," okay?

Just thinking about it made the back of my neck burn. A guy goes to work and spends the day kissing the boss's ass. So he goes home and kicks his wife's. Makes him feel like a man. We know what he is. A lowlife coward. But a kid who finally can't take it anymore and kills the people—you call them "parents"—who've been torturing him forever, *he's* the one you send to prison.

I love it when some punk prosecutor tells a jury the kid didn't have to *kill* his father. The father who'd been sodomizing him since he was six. Why didn't the kid just, like, assault him, or something? I'll tell you why. Because we all know. We know what happens if we *don't* kill them. As soon as they recover, they'll make us pray we had.

When babies are born to beasts, when the government pats the beasts on the head and lets them keep feeding, when the kids know they'll never get away because their baby brother or sister will be next . . . Oh, there's a lot of things kids can do. To *themselves*. That's okay. But if they ever dare to do it to the beasts, they're penitentiary-bound.

I was there for patterns. So I could see the truth. And maybe the whole process was getting to me. I was starting to see a pattern myself. People hurt their kids. And the government doesn't do anything to protect the kids. Soon, one of the kids figures it out—he can't go through life without backup, and he's not getting it from where other kids do. Next thing, he's in some juvenile institution. Learning to be everything they said he was when they put him in there.

Meanwhile, there's all these people who would give *anything* to have a kid of their own. And they can't get one. If the government just *moved* on humans who hurt their kids, took them away, handed them over to people who wanted to be real parents, they could shut down a lot of the prisons.

But that would put too many people out of work.

I stopped it right there. Drove it out of my mind. Concentrated, focusing *down* to tiny points until I was . . . somewhere else.

And a lot of the names Lune wanted from me were right in there, too. Waiting for me.

I asked Lune if Gem and I could go outside one morning. "Go with Levi," is all he said.

The Indian took us out through a different door from the one he'd used that first time. We were on a jagged expanse of rock that seemed to go on forever, but I could see trees in the distance. The air was thin—and so pure it was almost sweet inside my lungs.

"How long have you been with—?" Gem started to ask the Indian, before a look from me cut her off.

"Lune is a sensei, not a guru," he answered, guessing where she was going. "The answers to every question a man can have are in what most of the world believes to be a series of random, unconnected events. To see the pattern in the randomness is to unlock the mystery . . . whatever the mystery is.

"Lune knows how to do that. Better than anyone who has come before him. If he wanted to lead a cult, he could. If he wanted to make a billion dollars, he could do that, too. But he is a seeker, just as we are. The greedy ones—the ones who learn of Lune's work and want to profit from it—they never get past our screens."

"Do people find their answers here?" I asked him.

"Some do."

"And when they do—?"

"Ah. I understand. Yes, some leave then. But some return."

"Why would they do that?"

"Because a person of honor must honor his debts."

I didn't ask him if he was talking about himself.

"Do you know why Lune is helping Burke?" Gem said.

"Yes. Lune said they were brothers when they were very small. And that Burke was the first person who understood his gift. And his need."

"So you know he's—?"

"Searching for his real parents? Yes," the Indian said, his face flat, but pain for his soul-wounded sensei clear in his eyes.

I kept working on my list. Gem wanted to help, but I told her I just didn't see how she could.

"Tell me your life," she said. "I will listen. Maybe I will hear something of value to you."

So I started from the beginning. Again.

Occasionally, I would walk past their patterning wall. And see things on it that made no sense to me—I couldn't imagine any connection.

Cayman Islands

          New Utopia

   Liberian registry

             Dominica

Nauru

But I wasn't a sensei, or even a student, so I just went back to doing what I knew how to do.

They had a pool table there. I spent some time teaching Gem. Played cards with Clint, Minh, and Heidi—she was murderous at poker, with that farm-girl face covering up a statistician's mind. The Indian and I talked about his people. I learned a lot more than Hiram had ever told me. About a warrior named Juh, who Levi said actually did some of the things credited to Geronimo.

"No one knows what 'Juh' means," he said. "It may be a nonsense name, or just a sound he made to refer to himself. But in historical accounts of several of the most famous and most tactically accomplished raids, survivors remember seeing the warriors looking toward a large, dark man who was signaling with his hands. Juh had a bad stutter and couldn't really speak, so he used a complicated set of hand signals. He and Geronimo were childhood playmates and lifelong friends. And, if the stories are true, Geronimo may have been more vicious but it was Juh who never failed to find an enemy, even when it took years."

I got along with—and learned something from—every one of them except the Latina. I asked Gem if she knew why that woman wouldn't come anywhere near me.

"Yes," is all she said.

It was late at night when I found Lune. He was alone at his computer, his angel's face bathed in blue light from the screen.

"I'm done," I told him.

He didn't look away from the screen. "Are you sure, Burke?"

"Yeah. Yeah, I am. I've been going over and over it. Again and again. I must have told poor Gem my whole lousy life story a dozen times. If there's anyone not on this list, I don't know it."

His head swiveled suddenly. "Sometimes . . ." he began, his voice soft, "people don't remember things that—"

"It's not like that for me, Lune," I said, quickly, cutting him off before he went someplace he'd never return from. "I remember every one of them. Right to this day. You know what? You're right—the stuff some people repress, it's all right on the surface for me. And if I *could* find any of them . . ."

"Yes," he said. "I've been working, too. Now we're going to have to take what you've got and see where the pattern is."

"Is there any way I can help?"

"Not yet," he said, taking the thick looseleaf book I'd been working in from my hand and turning back to the computer screen.

"I could stay here," Gem said that night.

"What?"

"I could stay here," she repeated, calmly. "Minh is searching for the same pattern I am. Only I did not know there could *be* a pattern to the killing fields. It all seemed so . . ."

"Random?"

"Yes. Random. But now I am not certain."

"Are you going to?"

"What?"

"Stay here."

"Oh no."

"Why not, girl?"

"Because you are not," she said. Then she pulled my thumb into her mouth.

A nother few days went by. I'm not sure how many. Even though I'd turned in my list to Lune, I kept going over it in my head, thinking maybe there *was* something I wasn't facing. But it was no good—my tank had been drained.

I was lying back on the couch when someone knocked on the door. Gem walked over and opened it. The Latina was standing there.

"It's time," is all she said.

T hey were all there in the patterning room, waiting on me. The screen was empty except for one word:

Darcadia

I took a seat, Gem next to me. "What does it mean?" I asked Lune.

But it was Clint who answered: "It's a corruption of 'Arcadia,' a mountainous region of the central Peloponnesus of ancient Greece, represented as a paradise in Greek and Roman bucolic poetry and in the literature of the Renaissance. It was a plateau, bounded by mountain ranges and itself divided by individual mountains. For a number of geographical reasons, it was cut off from the coast on all sides—like an island on land, if you can picture that. So it survived a number of invasions but, eventually, it accepted a forced alliance with Sparta, and fought with the Spartans during the Peloponnesian War. It finally fell into decline during Roman times."

"I don't see how—"

"The key is Sparta," Minh said. "For a number of white-supremacist organizations, the Spartans represent the ultimate warriors."

"I'd've thought it would be the Vikings," I said. "The ones who call themselves 'racialists' are always hooking to some religion, and you hear 'Odinism' down there a lot."

"Oh, but the Vikings in the *modern* era are not as acceptable to Nazi mythology," Aydah said.

"Why is that?" Gem asked.

"Because they fought against the Nazis in World War II. Norway was invaded and occupied, but it always maintained an active resistance, even with Quisling in charge. And *that* ultimate collaborator was executed for treason as soon as the country was liberated. Finland never surrendered at all. And everyone knows what the Danes did to protect Jews. Sweden was allegedly 'neutral,' but it actually served as a training ground for Norwegian resistance fighters. And what Raoul Wallenberg did would be enough by itself to make the Nazis hate his whole country. They probably feel betrayed because Scandinavians *look* so perfectly Aryan," Aydah finished, bitterly. "That probably hurts the most."

"There's another reason for Sparta to be their Promised Land," Minh said quietly.

We all turned to look at him.

"The Spartans are also revered by so-called boy-lovers. And the concept that a warrior is entitled to whatever he is capable of *taking*—that, too, is considered 'Spartan.' As is a high tolerance for pain and hardship . . . and superiority in battle."

"I still don't see the—" I stopped myself before I could say the word that flashed on *my* screen: "pattern." Maybe I'd been there too long already.

Lune flicked his pointer, and words popped up on the wall. He talked as he pointed and clicked, like the spoken bridge in doo-wop I'd tried to tell Gem about.

"Thematic with hate groups," he said, as everything from **Nation of Islam** to **Aryan Nations** popped up on the wall, "is this concept of a 'homeland.' While the more floridly disturbed of them actually believe a portion of the United States will be set aside for them—"

"Like Casino Indians," Levi put in, bitterness blood-deep in his voice.

"—the more serious and committed ones understand they would have to go outside American borders to have their 'paradise,'" Lune continued, as if the Indian hadn't spoken. "There is ample precedent for such belief. There was that aborted white-supremacist coup on the Caribbean island of Dominica about twenty years ago. And the tiny Pacific island country of Nauru has converted itself into a major offshore-banking operation." He looked over at Heidi.

"That's authenticated," the farm girl said. "They are, in effect, selling foreigners the means to cloak transactions. Although there is probably no *actual* foreign money on the island, hundreds of *billions* of dollars pass through it every year. Interpol believes it to be the largest money-laundering vehicle in the world today. The Republic of Nauru—all eight square miles of it—provides even stricter secrecy than such legendary havens as Switzerland and the Cayman Islands."

"All right," I said. "Maybe I'm dense, but . . . ."

"The overwhelming majority of that laundered money comes from Russian organized crime," Heidi said.

I shut up. And paid attention.

Lune took over again. "Ever since the failed coup on Dominica, there have been numerous schemes, mostly but not exclusively promoted on the Internet, to purchase 'citizenship' in various 'republics.' The promoters purport to be creating these in the Pacific by purchasing and developing unclaimed . . . or even mostly submerged . . . islands," he said. "Each project targets certain types. Mostly right-wingers who want freedom from any government intrusion into their lives—taxes, gun control, education. And there are the supremacists who want to live exclusively among their own while they arm themselves for Armageddon.

But there are other groups seeking 'paradise,' too. A place where they can behave as they wish without fear of consequences."

"Freaks," I said, getting it now.

"Pedophiles, polygamists, incest-breeders, child-pornography manufacturers . . . yes," Lune said, nothing in his voice but the patterns.

"Where does this all tie in?" I asked him.

"Darcadia," he said. "A Pacific island with enough land mass to accommodate a small nation. It is undeveloped. Completely raw. It has a natural freshwater supply, but no infrastructure at all. Estimated cost to fully develop so that it could sustain, say, twenty thousand people . . . ?"

"Somewhere around ten billion," Heidi answered. "A prospectus of sorts has been floating around for almost two years now. The shares are in blocks of a hundred thousand, but 'citizenships' go for ten thousand."

"What's a—?"

"A 'citizenship,'" Heidi continued, "buys you the right to bank there, be free from personal income taxes . . . and a passport."

"All right, so someone's building a degenerate's heaven on some island. I'll probably die of old age before it ever really happens."

"I don't think so," Lune said. "The pattern is complete. Because we know the name of the person at the top of the Darcadia pyramid."

He tapped his keys. The wall cleared. And then a single name popped up in red letters.

I looked at the name. Nothing. I stared at the red letters, reaching for the connection, dropping deeper and deeper into myself, the way I used to do with the red dot I had painted on my mirror years ago. Deliberately dissociating, going somewhere else . . . where the answers always were.

 never thought of him by a name. Never thought of him as a person. He was always the Mentor to me. More than fifteen years ago, when I first met him. A little boy had been raped by a maggot in a clown suit. Someone had taken a Polaroid of it—and the child believed his soul had been captured. A witch named Strega hired me to get it back. I went down one tunnel after another, looking. And ended up in a junkyard bunker in the South Bronx.

"Mole," I said, "I've got a picture I need to find. The way it was taken, Polaroid camera and all, it had to be for sale. If it goes in a magazine, then it's in the stream of commerce and there's nothing I can do about it."

He looked up, listening the way he always does—silently.

"But I don't think that's the deal," I told him. "I think it was taken for a collector—a private thing. If they put it in a magazine, someone could see it. Cause a lot of problems. I need some freak who gets off looking at this stuff. You understand? Someone who's got shoeboxes full of pictures like that."

The Mole nodded, not arguing with my logic. So far.

"So I need to talk to a collector," I went on. "A serious, hardcore pedophile. Someone with the money to buy things like this. This is a no-consent picture, understand? The freaks might trade copies back and forth, but this one would be too risky for general commerce."

"I don't know anyone like that."

"Mole," I said, keeping my voice level, "you have friends. Associates, anyway. People I did some work for a couple of times. When we first met." No point mentioning names—they were all part of some wet-work group.

The Mole turned so he was facing me. "So?"

I was fast-talking now, knowing the door wouldn't stay open long.

"So they have to keep files on freaks like that. Blackmail, whatever. They have to know what's going down on the international scene—know who the players are. I know they don't do law-enforcement or vice-squad stuff, but information . . . that's something all the services want. Anything to give them a leg up . . . a handle."

We made our deal. It took a while to set up, and I had to let the Mole come with me, but it finally went down.

A limestone-front townhouse just off Fifth Avenue, three stories high, level with the rest of the buildings on the block. Maybe thirty-five feet wide. A seven-figure piece of property in that neighborhood, easy. Four steps took us to a teak door, set behind a wrought-iron grating. The Mole's stubby finger found the mother-of-pearl button, pushed it once.

We didn't have long to wait. The teak door opened. A man was standing there, waiting. You don't need a peep-hole when you have a couple of hundred pounds of iron between you and whoever's at the door. I couldn't see into the dark interior. The man at the door was tall and slender, both hands in the pockets of what looked like a smoking jacket.

"Yes?" he asked.

"Moishe Nineteen," the Mole said.

"Please step back," said the man. He had a semi-British accent, as if he'd been born here but gone to prep school over there or something.

The Mole and I stepped back so the iron grate could swing out.

We walked past the man inside, waited while he bolted the grate shut and closed the door. We were in a rectangular room, much longer than it was wide. The floor was highly polished dark wood, setting off overstuffed Victorian furniture, upholstered in a blue-and-white floral pattern. Only one light burned off to the side, flickering like it was gas instead of electricity.

"May I take your coats?" the man said, opening a closet just past the entranceway.

I shook my head "No." The Mole wasn't wearing anything over his jumpsuit.

"Please . . ." the man said, languidly waving his hand to say we should go up the stairs before him. I went first, the Mole right behind me. We were breaking all the rules for this human.

"To your right," I heard him say. I turned into a big room that looked smaller because it was so stuffed with things. A huge desk dominated the space, standing on thick carved claws at each corner. An Oriental rug covered most of the floor—it had a royal-blue background with a red-and-white design running from the center and blending into the borders. A fireplace was against one wall, birch logs crackling in a marble cage. The windows were covered with heavy velvet drapes the same royal blue as the rug. Everything was out of the past—except for a glowing amber video terminal on a butcher-block table parallel to the desk.

"Please sit anywhere," the man said, waving one arm to display the options as he seated himself behind the big desk. I took a heavy armchair upholstered in dark tufted leather. A large flat glass ashtray was on a bronze metal stand next to the chair. The Mole sat on the floor, blocking the door with his bulk, putting his satchel on the ground. He looked from the man to where I was sitting, making it clear that we had an agreement and he expected me to honor it. Then he pulled out a sheaf of papers and started to study some of his calculations—taking himself somewhere else.

"Now, then," said the man, folding his hands in front of him on the desk. "May I offer you some refreshment? Coffee? Some excellent sherry?"

I shook my head. The Mole never looked up.

"A beer perhaps?"

"No," I told him. I'd made a deal not to do anything to him, not even to threaten him, but I didn't have to pretend I was his pal.

The man reached for a cut-glass decanter on his desk. Something that looked like a silver leaf dangled from just *below the neck of the bottle, attached by a silver chain. He poured himself a wineglass of dark liquid from the bottle, held the glass up to the light from the fireplace, took a small sip. If he was any calmer he would have fallen asleep.*

It was hard to make out his features in the dim light. I could see he was very thin, balding on top, with thick dark hair around the sides of his head. Heavy eyebrows jutted from his skull, hooding his eyes. The face was wide at the top, narrowing down to a small chin—a triangular shape. His lips were thin. His fingers were long and tapered, with a faint sheen of clear polish on the nails.

"Now," he said, taking a sip from his glass, "how may I help you, Mr. . . ."

"I'm looking for a picture," I told him, ignoring the request for my name. "A picture of a kid."

"And you think I have this picture?" he asked, his heavy eyebrows lifting.

I shrugged. I should be so lucky. "No. But I hope you can tell me about that kind of thing in general. Give me an idea where to look."

"I see. Tell me about this picture."

"A picture of a kid. Little chubby blond-haired boy. About six years old."

The man sat behind his desk, patiently waiting, making it clear I hadn't told him enough.

"A sex picture," I said.

"Um . . ." he mumbled. "Not such an unusual picture. Little boys in love do things like that."

Something burned inside my chest. I felt the Mole's eyes on me, got it under control, stuck a cigarette in my mouth, my teeth almost meeting in the filter. "Who would have a picture like that?" I asked him.

"Oh, just about anyone. It all depends on why the picture was taken."

"Why?"

The man made a tent of his fingers, his semi-Brit

accent making him sound like a teacher. "If the picture was taken by his mentor, then it wouldn't be circulated commercially, you understand?"

"His mentor?"

"A mentor, yes. One who teaches you, guides you through life. Helps you with problems . . . that sort of thing."

I looked at him, picturing a little dot of cancer inside his chest, keeping my hands still. I raised my own eyebrows as a question.

"Men who love boys are very special," the man answered, his voice reverent. "As are the boys who love them. It is a most unique and perfect relationship. And very little understood by society."

"Could you explain?" I said, my voice flat.

"When a boy has a sexual preference for men, he is at grave risk. The world will not understand him. Many doors will be closed to him. It is the task of a dedicated mentor to bring the tiny bud to full flower. To help nourish the growth of the boy into manhood."

"By taking pictures of the kid having sex?"

"Do not be so quick to judge, my friend. A true mentor would not take such a photograph for commercial purposes, as I said before. Such pictures preserve a unique and beautiful moment. Children grow up," he said, his voice laced with regret for the inevitable, "they lose their youth. Would not a loving parent take pictures of his child, to look upon in later years?"

I didn't answer him—I didn't know what loving parents did. The State raised me. And the State takes a lot of pictures—they're called mug shots.

"It is capturing a moment in time," the man said. "A way of keeping perfection with you always, even when the person is gone."

"You mean people . . . people like you . . . just want to keep the pictures? Not sell them or anything."

"People like me . . ." the man mused. "Do you know anything about 'people like me'?"

"No," I said. The deal was I couldn't hurt him—nobody said I had to tell him the truth.

"I am a pedophile," the man said. The same way an immigrant would one day say he was a citizen—pride and wonder at being so privileged blending in his voice. "My sexual orientation is toward children . . . toward young boys, specifically."

I watched him, waiting for the rest.

"I am not a 'child molester,' I am not a pervert. What I do is technically against your laws . . . as those laws now stand. But my relationship with my boys is pure and sweet. I love boys who love me. Is anything wrong with that?"

I had no answer for him, so I lit another cigarette.

"Perhaps you think it's simple," he said, his thin mouth twisted in contempt for my lack of understanding. "I love boys—therefore, you assume I am a homosexual, don't you?"

"No, I don't," I assured him. The truth, that time. Homosexuals were grown men who had sex with other grown men. Some of them were stand-up guys, some of them were scumbags. Like the rest of us. This freak wasn't like the rest of us.

He watched my face, looking for a clue. "You believe my orientation to be so unusual? Let me say this to you: some of the highest-placed men in this city share it. Indeed, were it not for my knowledge of such things—of powerful men with powerful drive-forces in their lives—I would not have the protection of you people," he said, nodding his head in the Mole's direction.

The Mole looked straight at him, expressionless.

"Any boy I love . . . any boy who returns that love . . . benefits in ways you cannot begin to understand. He grows to youth and then to manhood under my wing, if you will. He is educated, both intellectually and spiritually. Prepared for the world at large. To such a boy, I am a life-changing force, do you understand?"

"Yes," I said. Thinking I finally knew what to call Mr. Cormil after all these years. A "mentor."

"And I would . . . I have taken pictures of my boys. It gives us both pleasure in later years to look at this icon to our love, as it once was. A boy is a boy for such a short time," he said, sadness in his voice.

"And you wouldn't sell these pictures?"

"Certainly not! I have no need of money, but that is not the point. It would cheapen the love. Almost immeasurably so. It would be a violation of the relationship—something I would never do."

"So nobody would ever see your pictures?" I asked him.

"Nobody outside my circle," he replied. "On some rare occasion, I might exchange pictures of my boys with others . . . like myself. But never for money."

"You mean you'd trade pictures? Like baseball cards?"

The man's eyes hooded again. "You have a crude way of putting things, sir. I know you do not mean to be offensive. . . ."

I nodded my head in hasty agreement. I didn't want him to stop talking. The Mole's head was buried in his papers, but I could feel him telling me to watch my step.

"My boys enjoy knowing they give me pleasure. And it gives me pleasure to show their love for me to other men who believe as I do." He took another sip of his drink. "To be sure, there may be an element of egotism in exchanging photographs with others. I am proud of my . . . achievements. But—and I am sure you understand—one must be very discreet at all times."

I gave him another nod of agreement. I sure as hell understood that part.

"There are those who produce pictures of children for purely commercial purposes," he continued. "Not those who share my . . . life-style, if you will. But no true boy-lover would buy such pictures. They are so impersonal, so tasteless. One knows nothing of the boy in such a picture. Not his name, his age, his little hobbies. . . . Commercial photographs are so . . . anonymous. Sex is only a component of love. One brick in a foundation. Do you understand this?"

"I understand," I told him. It was true that Satan could quote Scripture, as the Prof was always saying. "Would a person ever destroy his pictures . . . like if he was afraid there was a search warrant coming down or something?"

"A true boy-lover would never do that, no matter what. I can assure you that if the police were battering down my door at this very instant, I would not throw my memories into that fireplace."

"But the pictures are evidence. . . ."

"Yes. Evidence of love."

"People get convicted with evidence of love," I told him.

A smile played around his lips. "Prison is something we face all the time. A true believer in our way of life accepts this. Simply because something is against the law does not mean it is morally wrong."

"It's worth going to prison for?" I asked him.

"It is worth anything and everything," he said, rapt in the purity of his love.

"The people who . . . exchange . . . pictures of boys. You'd know how to get in touch with them?"

"We have a network," the man said. "A limited one, of course. You see the computer?" he asked, tilting his head toward the screen.

I nodded.

"The device next to it, with the telephone? It's called a modem. It's really quite complicated," the man said, "*but we have something called an electronic bulletin board. You dial up the network, punch in the codes, and we can talk to each other without revealing our identities. And photographs can be transmitted the same way.*"

I gave him a blank look.

"*As I said, it's really quite complicated,*" he said smugly.

I could feel the Mole's sneer clear across the room.

"*Could you show me?*" I asked.

"*Very well.*" He sighed. He got up from behind the desk, bringing his wineglass with him, and seated himself before the computer. He took the phone off the hook and placed it facedown into a plastic bed. He punched some numbers into a keypad and waited impatiently, tapping his long fingers on the console. When the screen cleared, he rapidly tapped something on the keyboard—his password, I guessed. "*Greetings from Santa*" came up on the screen in response, black letters against a white background now.

"*Santa is one of us,*" the man said, by way of explanation. He typed in: "*Have you any new presents for us?*" The man hit another key and his message disappeared.

In another minute, the screen blinked and a message from Santa came up.

"*Seven bags full,*" said the screen.

"*His new boy is seven years old,*" said the man. "*Are you following this?*"

"*Yes,*" I told him. Santa Claus.

The man went back to the screen. "*This is Tutor. Do you think it's too early in the year to think about exchanging gifts?*"

"*Not gifts of love,*" came back the answer.

The man looked over his shoulder at me. I nodded again. Clear enough.

He pushed a button and the screen cleared once more. He returned to his seat behind the desk, glanced at the Mole, then back to me. "*Anything else?*" he asked.

"If the boy's picture, the one I want, was taken for sale, not by a boy-lover—I couldn't find it?"

"The original? Not in a million years," the man said. "The commercial producers will sell to anybody. Besides, those pictures are not true originals, you see? They make hundreds and hundreds of copies. The only way to find an original is if it was in a private collection."

"Say I didn't give a damn if the picture was an original, okay? If I showed you a picture of the boy, would you ask around, see if you could find the picture I'm looking for?"

"No," he said. "I would never betray the trust of my friends." He looked at the Mole for reassurance. The Mole looked back, giving nothing away.

"And you don't deal with any of the commercial outlets?"

"Certainly not," he sniffed.

This freak couldn't help me. "I understand," I said, getting up to leave.

The man looked at me levelly. "You may show yourselves out."

The Mole lumbered to his feet, standing in the doorway to make sure I went out first.

"One more thing," the man said to me. "I sincerely hope you learned something here. I hope you learned some tolerance for our reality. Some respect for our love. I trust we can find some basis for agreement."

I didn't move, willing my hands not to clench into fists.

"I am a believer," the man said, "and I am ready to die for my beliefs."

There's our basis for agreement, I thought, and turned my back to follow the Mole down the stairs.

It all came back, in thick blocks of memory, exploding silently, like mortar rounds hitting near you when your ears are already so clogged with fear-blood that you're deaf. And when I replayed the tapes in my head, I understood why it *had* to be him. Because I'd gone back to see him years later. Not to kill him, to try and play him into doing something. And he'd gone for the bait.

"You!" he said, a whisper-hiss of surprise.

"Can I talk with you?"

"We've already talked."

"I need your help."

"Surely you know better than that."

"If you'll hear me out . . . it's something you'll want to do. And I have something to trade."

"You're alone?"

"Yes."

He touched one finger to the tip of his nose, deciding. Then a twisting gesture with his other hand. I heard a heavy deadbolt slide back, tugged gently on the wrought iron, and the gate came toward me. I stepped inside.

"After you," he said, gesturing toward the staircase.

The room hadn't changed. Old-money heavy, thick, and dark. Only the computer marred the antique atmosphere—a different one from last time, with a much bigger screen that blinked into darkness as I glanced at it, defying my stare.

"Notice anything new?" he asked, pointing to the chair I'd used last time.

I sat down and eye-swept the room, playing the game. In one corner, a rectangular fish tank, much longer than it was high. I got up to look closer, feeling him behind me. The fish were all some shade of red or orange, with wide white stripes outlined in black.

"This is different," I said. "What are they?"

"Clowns. The family name is Pomacentridae. They come in many varieties. The dark orange ones are perculas," pointing at a fat little fish near the top. "And we have tomatoes, maroons, even some flame clowns—my favorites."

The flames had red heads with a white band just behind the eyes—the bodies were jet black. They stayed toward the bottom of the tank.

"Saltwater fish?" I asked him.

"Oh yes. Quite delicate, actually."

"They're beautiful. Are they rare?"

"More unusual than they are rare. Clowns get along wonderfully with other fish. That is, they never interact—they stay with their own kind, even in a tank."

"They don't fight for territory?"

"No, they don't fight at all. Occasionally, a small spat among themselves, but never with another species."

I watched the aquarium. Each tribe of clowns stayed in its own section, not swimming so much as hovering. I saw his reflection in the glass fade as he went over to a leather armchair and sat down. I took the chair he'd first indicated, faced him.

He regarded me with mild interest, well within himself, safe where he was.

"You said you had something . . . ?"

"Yeah. The last time we talked, when you told me your . . . philosophy. About kids."

"I remember," he said stiffly. "Nothing has changed."

"I know. I listened. You told me you loved little boys then. I came because I need to see how deep that love goes."

"Which means . . . ?"

"What you do, what others like you do, it's all about love, right?"

He nodded, wary.

"You don't force kids. Don't hurt them . . . anything like that."

"As I told you. What is wrong with our behavior—all that is wrong with our behavior—is that it is against some antiquated laws. We are hounded, persecuted. Some of us have been imprisoned, ruined by the witch-hunters. Yet

we have always been here and we always will be. But you didn't come here to engage in philosophical discourse."

"No. Just to get things straight."

He got to his feet, turned his back on me. Tapped some keys rapidly on the computer, too fast for me to follow. He hit a final key with a concert pianist's flourish. The machine beeped.

He got up, went back to his easy chair.

"You've been logged in. Physical description, time of arrival, your code name, everything. It's all been transmitted. And the modem is still open."

"I didn't come here to do anything to you."

"I'm sure."

"Listen to me," *I said, leaning forward, keeping my voice low.* "Can we not be stupid? I said I didn't come here to do anything to you, and I meant it. But don't fool yourself—the Israelis aren't your pals. I don't know what you did for them, what you do for them . . . and I don't care. But all they are is a barrier. A deterrent, like a minefield. Somebody wastes you, they aren't going to get even. Understand what I'm saying?"

"Yes, quite well. You are saying, if I don't give you information you want, you will kill me."

"That's cute. You got enough for your tape recorder now? I'm not threatening you. Not with anything. I'm just trying to tell you something. And you should listen. Listen good. Maybe you don't want this on tape."

He steepled his long fingers, regarding me over the top of the spire. I counted to twenty in my head before he moved a muscle. He got to his feet languidly, tapped the computer keys again. Then he sat down, waiting.

"This is the truth, okay?" *I told him.* "You don't have friends in high places. Not true friends. What you are is an asset, something of value. Everybody protects what they value. You know that good as anyone. Let's say you have this valuable painting. Somebody steals it, you try and buy it back. But if there's a fire, and it gets burned to *ashes, all you can do is collect on the insurance. The Israelis can only protect you from the federales. They got no reach with the locals. What I have for you, it's another barrier. Another layer of protection. Something you can't get from your other friends."*

He raised his eyebrows, didn't say a word.

I reached in my pocket, handed him an orange piece of pasteboard, about the size of a business card. He turned it over, held it up: GET OUT OF JAIL FREE.

"Is this your idea of a joke?"

"It's not a joke. You got a lawyer, right? Probably got a few of them. Have your lawyer go over to City-Wide, speak to Wolfe—you know who she is?"

"Yes."

"See if I'm telling the truth, then."

"I would get . . . ?"

"Immunity. Kiddie porn's the only way you're ever going down, right? The only real risk you take. You're not going to get stung by Customs. And you don't deal with strangers. So the only way it could ever happen is somebody drops a dime to save their own ass, and City-Wide does the search."

"There is nothing here."

I pitched my voice low, let him hear how deep the commitment really was: "You're looking at the big picture, pal. And that's a mistake. What you should be looking at is the frame, see?"

He took a breath. Small, cold eyes on mine. "You couldn't deliver," he said quietly. "We know about Wolfe. People have . . . talked to her before. She's not amenable to . . . whatever you propose."

"Have your lawyer talk to her again. Do it first, before you do anything for me, okay? I'll tell you what I want, tell you right now, in this room. Just listen—I guarantee you it won't be against you or your people. Give me a couple of days, have your lawyer go see her, all right? Nothing's changed, you don't have to do a thing. You decide, okay?"

*He steepled his fingers again. I counted in my head.
"Tell me what you want," he said.*

*I lit a smoke, centering. I'd only get one shot. "We
both know how it works, you and me. Child molesters . . ."*

*His thin lips parted. I held up my hand in a "Stop!"
gesture, going on before he could speak. "I'm not talking
about your people now. There are people who molest children, right? I'm talking about rape. Sodomy. Hard, stick-
it sex. It happens. Don't go weak on me, now. I know what
you do—I know what you told me. I could play it back for
you, word for word. The kids you're involved with, it's
love, right? There's always true consent—you wouldn't do
a thing without it. I remember what you said. You're a
mentor, not a rapist. Listen good. I'm separating you now.
Those people who say child sexual abuse is a myth—we
know better, you and me. I'm not saying you do it—I'm
saying it gets done. People do it, right?"*

"Savages do it."

*"Right. Fathers rape their daughters, that's no fan-
tasy. Humans torture kids, make films of it, it's not a
myth."*

"And you think we're all the same, you think—"

*"No," I said, eyes open and clear, calling on a child-
hood of treachery for the effortless lying that they made
second nature to me before I was eight. "What you do,
people could argue about it, but I know you love children.
Maybe I don't agree with it, but I'm not a cop. It's not my
job. It's the baby-rapers who make your life hell, isn't that
true? You love children. You'd be as angry about torturing
them as anybody else would. Even if the laws changed,
even if they eliminated the age thing, made it so a kid
could consent to sex, then they'd be like adults, right? And
rape is rape."*

"Society calls it rape when—"

*"I'm not talking about statutory rape, here. Listen
close. Stand up to it now. I'm talking about black-glove,
hand-over-the-mouth, knifepoint rape. Blood, not Vase-*

line. Pain. Screaming, life-scarring pain. A little boy
ripped open, maybe one of your little boys . . . you like
that picture?"

"Stop it! *Stop it, you—*"

*I dragged deep on my cigarette, staying inside.
"That's what I want to do—stop it. That's what you've got
to do. Help me."*

"I . . ."

"You know. You know it happens. They did it to my
client. A little boy. They split him open like a ripe melon.
He's a basket case. And they videotaped it. A group. An
organized group. Satanists, they call themselves, but we
know what that's about, don't we?"

"I don't deal with . . ." His voice faded away, sweat
streaking his high forehead, tendons cabling his hands,
veins like wires along his throat.

"I know you don't," I finished for him. "You wouldn't
do anything like that. Or your people. I know." I spooled
velvet over him, a cop telling a rapist he understands. . . .
Those dirty cunts, displaying themselves, wiggling like a
bitch in heat, fucking *begging* for it, right? Men like us, we
understand each other. "But freaks like that, they have to
be stopped. They bring heat, and heat brings light, you
know what I'm saying? You know what I do. But it's been
years, and I've never made trouble for you, right? So help
me now."

"How could I—?"

"The computer. They raped that little boy to make a
commercial product. Not like your icons—not to remember a boy as he was—pictures to sell. The kid was a product, and they need a market. They'll be on the board
somewhere. You could find them. Your friends could find
them. That's all I want."

"And . . ."

"And, one day, if you should happen to slip yourself,
Wolfe will make sure you don't fall."

He searched the pockets of his robe. Found a black

silk handkerchief, patted his face dry, deciding. I waited, watching the dice tumble across the green felt in my mind.

Finally, he looked up. "Tell me what you have so far."

"Leave him alone!" Gem's voice. From somewhere outside . . . me.

I shook my head. It wouldn't clear. My eyes wouldn't open, or I'd gone blind. But then my mind started to clear, and I realized my body would catch up—I'd been down there before. I concentrated on staying quiet, letting the air in my lungs bring me to the surface.

They were all standing around me in a loose semicircle. Only Lune hadn't moved.

I took deep breaths through my nose, coming the rest of the way back.

Everyone watching could see it happening. Maybe they knew what they were seeing, maybe not. Maybe some of them had been there, too.

They all breathed in rhythm with me, helping.

I felt Gem's hand against my cheek, her little thumb against the bullet hole, rubbing it in tiny circles.

My screen cleared. I knew where I was. Why I was there.

And where I'd been.

I turned to Lune. "You broke me out, brother," I told him.

His eyes looked wet. Or maybe my own were still cloudy from the trip.

I told them the whole story, exactly as it had just flashed back to me. How the freak had stumbled into the trap I'd set and found out his "immunity" was as real as his "love" for little boys. I knew he went down, heard it was a pretty significant jolt.

"He fits either side of the pattern," Lune said. "He might want vengeance for what you did to him. Or he might believe you would be coming after him, anyway, once you connected him to Darcadia."

"Or both," the Latina said.

"Or both," Lune acknowledged. "He knows you are dangerous in ways your 'reputation' does not indicate. And he knows you have resources within law enforcement. This Wolfe . . . the prosecutor who—"

"She's gone," I told him. "Off the job. Fired for not kissing political ass. Wolfe wouldn't be a problem to him."

"The way you describe her, she sounds like a fierce woman," Heidi said. "What does she do now?"

"She runs a private network. Mostly info-trafficking."

Clint and Minh exchanged looks, but it was Levi who put it into words: "And she still has deep law-enforcement contacts, yes?"

"She does," I admitted.

"And if she came across this Darcadia thing, she'd know who to take it to, right?" Clint asked.

"Yeah," I said, seeing the tiles drop into the mosaic.

"This man knows you have a . . . relationship with Wolfe, as well," Lune said. It wasn't a question.

I just nodded.

"And he must have *considerable* resources. Indicated by several authenticated factors in addition to his financing of the assassination attempt. But the Darcadia project has already taken in . . . ?" he asked, turning to Heidi.

"No less than twenty million. Double that would not be beyond probability," the math girl answered.

"I got it," I told them all.

And I did. It was a familiar song. I'd learned it as a tortured baby, and heard it the rest of my life.

What it always comes down to.

Them or me.

Just before we were ready to pull out the next morning, I went to see Lune. He was in the command center, working at his charts.

"Lune, will you do something for me?"

"I would do anything for you," he said. "If it wasn't for—"

"If it wasn't for *you*, I'd be a walking target, stumbling around in the dark until they finally took me out," I cut him off. "I know what to do now. That isn't the favor."

"Just tell me."

"Tell *me*, Lune. Tell me about your real parents."

"Why?" he asked, topaz eyes bright with something I'd never understand.

"Because, as soon as this is over, I'm going to try and find them for you, brother."

And for the next couple of hours, I listened while the beautiful crazy man with the desperado's searching heart told me all about his parents, who never were.

We went out the same way we'd come in. Not the same route, but with Heidi and the Latina pack-muling, while Levi led the way, his sniper's eyes checking the path. Indeh trotted alongside, happy to be out working again.

Even though it was pretty much downhill, it was a good thing we had help lugging out our stuff. Lune's crew had put together reams of material about Darcadia and the man behind it, and I was going to need it to get my work done.

They walked with us all the way to where Levi had stashed the Land Rover. The Latina gave Gem a deep hug while Heidi shook hands with me and said, "Good luck, Burke." Then she turned to hug Gem herself. The Latina turned her back and started walking away.

Levi drove us down through the mountains, his Canary dog on

the front seat next to him. He didn't say a word until we got into Albuquerque.

"Lune gave you a way to reach us," he said. It wasn't a question.

"He did," I acknowledged.

"There are always two tasks. One is to find the path; the other is to walk the path. Yes?"

"Yes."

"There is no rule about walking the path alone," he said.

"I won't be," I promised him.

"I would walk it with you, if you wish."

I was too stunned at the Indian's dealing himself in to say anything. Gem didn't have that problem. "We would be honored," she said.

On the trip back, I stayed inside myself, thinking through that last exchange. Gem didn't press me, letting me have my silence. Finally, on the last leg of the flight into PDX, I told her where we stood: "What you said to the Indian . . . There's no more 'we' in this, little girl. Understand?"

"It is not your choice," she said, her lips drawn tight.

"You know what I have to do now?"

"Yes. I am not stupid."

"I have to go back to New York," I said, ignoring her tart answer. "To my family. I need a plan. This is a bad guy. With bad people backing him up. When it's over, I'll—"

"I will come to New York with you," she announced, like it was something she planned to serve for dinner.

"You don't understand, Gem. I got no place to go *to* there. I'm supposed to be dead. I don't know who's looking . . . or even if anyone is. But I have to stay *very* low. You'd just be in the way."

"I will not. I have places I could stay there myself."

"No."

"No? You are my husband, not my master. I *am* going to New York. I will give you a phone number where you can find me there. I will be close, if you need me."

"Gem . . ."

"In the meantime, it is better if we travel together. As I said before, that is not what people would expect of you."

Two weeks later, I watched Wolfe's tango-dancer legs flash in the sunlight as she climbed out of her battered old Audi. Her Rottweiler stayed in the car. I was glad of that, and not just because I was afraid of the beast. Seeing people with their dogs . . .

"I heard you were dead," she said, sarcastically.

"Sure. Are you telling me nobody's buying?"

"Oh, I think they are. Word is you got blown away by some drug dealers you'd ripped off a long time ago. Remember that?"

Remember it? I'd done time for it when the wheels came off. And I'd done it the right way, too. Alone.

I didn't bother to answer her.

"So what do you want?" she asked, gray eyes glacial.

I told her everything. Well, not everything. Nothing about Lune. Or how I got the information. But all the facts.

"So this dirtbag has graduated to international, is that what you're telling me?" she finally asked.

"What I'm telling you is that he tried to take me out. Spent a lot of money doing it. If it's revenge for what we did to him years ago, you could be on his list, too."

"Fine. Now he's on mine," is all I got out of her.

"You never heard of this Darcadia thing before?"

"Sure. It's no real secret, especially with the kind of money they've been raking in. But I didn't know this freak was the big player."

"Aren't the *federales* interested?"

"Maybe IRS. Or the money-laundering guys. Might even be a

candidate for RICO-fraud, I don't know. But it's not lighting up anybody's screen, I can tell you that."

"Good."

"I don't under— Oh. It's like that, huh?"

"I've got no choice."

"You had choices *once*," Wolfe said. Then she turned and walked away.

The building directory was all in Chinese. I followed Max up the stairs. On the second floor, he made a gesture like pulling a tooth, telling me the office we wanted belonged to a dentist. The mute Mongol turned the handle of the office door and stepped inside. It was almost two in the morning, but a young Chinese woman in a white dental smock bowed to Max in greeting as if he were an expected patient. She didn't acknowledge my presence. Max made a series of quick hand signals. The dentist led us into an operatory, then left the room. Max went over to what looked like a closet. It turned out to be an opening to a flight of stairs, leading down. I followed him again, and we ended up in an alley.

We walked for a couple of blocks, then Max rapped on a door the exact color—New York dirt—of the building it led into. The door opened. A Chinese man with a small meat-cleaver in his right hand stood there. He bowed to Max and stepped aside. I followed, still invisible.

This time, the exit was from the basement. But not into an alley, into a tunnel. It had obviously been there a long time, probably built by coolie labor for one of the Tongs, back when Chinatown was another country and tourists weren't welcome.

When a branch of the tunnel finally took us into the cellar of Mama's restaurant, I wasn't surprised.

It took me a while to tell the story. When I was finished, the Prof spoke first. "Ain't but one way for us to play, Schoolboy."

The "us" came out of him so natural that I had to bite my lip to keep my face flat. Almost dying had really fucked up my internal controls.

"If we could find where he is . . ." the Mole offered.

"Not a prayer, Mayor," the Prof chopped him off. "Motherfucker's not putting him*self* on the spot. We want a date, we got to have the bait."

"And he will have plenty of firepower behind him, Father," Clarence added. "That team that tried to kill Burke . . ."

"Soldiers," Mama said. "Very expensive."

"What are you saying, Mama?" I asked her.

"All about money. This . . . place you talk about."

"Sure, but . . ."

"Money is bait," she finished for me. "Money bring him to you."

"But he's *got* all the—"

"No, he doesn't, honey," Michelle put in. "Mama's right. If he did, why would he still be raising all this cash? You said the operation's still going on, right? Still soliciting in the right places."

"Sure!" the Prof backed her up. "Motherfucker had his whole rack stacked, he'd just jet off the set."

"Okay, so he's still collecting cash. How does that—?"

"Investor," Mama said. "Big investor."

I thought it through, taking my time. And kept coming up against the same flaw.

"No way this guy's going to go face to face without knowing who he's dealing with," I told them. "I'd need an X-ray-proof ID, back-legend and all."

"Didn't your girl build you one of those before, youngblood?" the Prof asked.

"Wolfe won't . . . won't work with me anymore."

"I can do it," Michelle piped up.

Nobody said anything, waiting.

"I know just the man," she said. "An old man. Lives in Key West. A real recluse. A *rich* recluse. Never goes out. I think he needs oxygen just to get around."

"How's that going to—?"

"Baby, let me *tell* it, all right? He's an *old* man, if you understand what I'm telling you. He spends his money on anything that might give him back what he's lost. Powdered rhino horn, tiger testicles—you know. Plus, he's a real fascist. Anyone checks him out, they'll see he's been giving money to those save-the-race freakshows for years."

"Yeah, fine. But this Darcadia—why bother? He's already *got* his paradise right here, all that money."

"No, sweetheart. There's one thing he's heard that's *guaranteed* to give him back what he wants. Little girls. Fresh ones, understand? But he's scared to death of trusting any kiddie pimp. Plus, he's afraid to fly, so he only travels by boat. His *own* boat."

"So maybe he'd want to buy a piece—"

"—a *big* piece."

"—a big piece, okay, of this operation so he could have what he wanted . . . hell, be a *king* down there. Christ."

"It sounds very perfect," the Mole said.

"What are you saying?" Michelle challenged.

"That it is not true. It sounds as if you took Burke's specifications and built a person to fit them."

"Just *some* of it is built," Michelle said, not resenting the Mole's insight.

"How much?" I asked, already tired from the weight.

"The part about little girls. He's not into that at all."

"How do you know?"

"Because I know what he *is* into, you idiot."

I risked a glance at the Mole. He was calm as a snake on a hot rock. A venomous snake.

"What makes you think he'd go along with me taking over his identity?" I asked Michelle. Quickly, before she could go into details.

"Like I said, I know what he wants."

"But we don't have—"

"Sure. We have," Mama said, radiating calm. "In special clinic, yes?"

She'd snapped to it way before I had. "What special—?"

"And it would take considerable time to complete all the testing necessary," the Mole said, soberly.

"Mole," I said, "we wouldn't *really* be—"

Patches of red showed in the Mole's subterranean complexion as his eyes flicked rapidly behind his Coke-bottle lenses. "I know," he said. As close to sarcasm as he gets.

Mama knew an outlaw doctor based just outside of Galveston. The guy only did plastic surgery. And he didn't keep records. All it took was cash for him to close down his clinic for a month.

Eight days later, Michelle called from Key West to say, smugly, that the old man was ready to travel. I asked her what kind of boat he had.

"It's me," I said, when I heard Gem's voice on the phone.

"I knew you would call."

"Are you as certain of the phone you're speaking from?"

"Oh! No, perhaps not."

"Can you find the corner of Ninth Avenue and Seventeenth Street?"

"Yes."

"You have your red coat with you?"

"Yes. It is precious to me."

"Be sure to wear it. A black man with a West Indian accent will meet you."

"When shall I leave?"

"Now."

watched from my back booth as Gem entered Mama's restaurant with Clarence. Mama was at her register, but didn't look up as Gem walked back toward me. Clarence went out the way he'd come in.

As soon as Gem was seated, Mama walked over, snapping her fingers for the mandatory tureen of hot-and-sour soup. One of the gunmen who pretend they're waiters when some tourist mistakes Mama's for a restaurant brought it over.

Mama took the lid off the tureen, looked a question at me.

I nodded a "Yes" at her, and she put a small bowl before Gem and filled it, making it clear I could serve my own damn self. She regarded Gem thoughtfully, doing an ethnic read. Then she tried a greeting in Tagalog, but Gem smiled and shook her head, replying in Cambodian. Now it was Mama's turn to shake her head. She tried French, and Gem answered right back.

Mama bowed slightly and sat down next to me, bumping me over to the wall so she could sit directly across from Gem.

"You both speak English," I said to her. "What's with all this—?"

Mama cut me off with a look. Gem giggled.

And they went back to speaking French.

I was well into my third bowl of soup when they decided to let me in on the conversation.

"So? You Burke's wife?" Mama asked in English.

"Yes," Gem answered her.

"You understand, Burke my son. Not marry for . . . final unless I say."

"I understand," Gem said, solemnly.

"Your mother . . . ?"

"The Khmer."

"Ah. Sorry. So many . . ."

"Yes."

"After this . . . thing all finish," Mama promised Gem. At least, it sounded like some kind of promise. I couldn't figure out what it meant, but I wasn't dumb enough to ask.

After Mama went back to whatever she had been doing, I read Gem the specs on the old man's boat I'd written down from my conversation with Michelle.

"It's a ninety-two-foot Cheoy Lee cockpit motor yacht," I told her. "Whatever the hell *that* is."

"I am sure they could handle it, but I will call to be certain."

Then I told her the rest of it. Gem didn't say a word, didn't interrupt me once. When I was finished, she said, "There is another way I could help, I think."

Mama came back over to my booth as if she'd been listening in on a wiretap and knew we were done talking.

"Eat now, yes?"

An hour later, Gem was still shoveling it away.

Mama passed by the booth, saw the carnage, and chuckled approvingly.

The boat should have at least a four-person crew," Gem told me the next day.

"At least?"

"It is an oceangoing vessel," she said, as if reciting a lesson. "So it must be manned around the clock. It is a *very* big boat, probably cost in excess of three million dollars. You have never been at sea?"

"Me? The only boat ride I've ever been on in my life was the Staten Island Ferry."

"Ah, well. It does not matter. You will not be posing as a sailor. And if you appear . . . ill at the time of your meeting, it will be in character. But we *will* need one more person."

"One more? You said four, right?"

"Oh, I will be going, too," she said.

"I need a driver, Sonny," I told the kid. Only he wasn't a kid anymore.

"I heard you were—"

"Now you know better."

"Oh man, this is great! I—"

"In or out, kid?"

"Can I use my own ride?"

"Which is?"

"A Viper GTS. But it's got—"

"No. We need something with plenty of room. Got to carry some people, long distance."

"Can we use your—?"

"No. That's gone."

"Damn! That was one sweet—"

"The job is a delivery. You bring some people somewhere, you pick someone up when you get there, you drive them all someplace else. Then you come back on your own."

"Why would you need me for that?"

"You thought I was . . . what? Remember?"

"Yeah. Sorry. Okay. You need fast or smooth?"

"Smooth. And roomy. *Lots* of room."

"My buddy has a Ford Excursion. We use it to tow mine to the races. Big enough?"

"Plenty. With clean papers all the way through, son. You're going to be crossing a lot of state lines."

"Just tell me where to meet you."

"Sonnyboy!" the Prof greeted him with a hug, then stepped back to look him over. "The wheelman's a real man now!"

The kid whose mother had named him Randy blushed.

We loaded the truck in the back alley behind Mama's. The guy she brought over to do the heavy lifting was so big he should have given off a beeping sound when he backed up.

"It's about fifteen hundred miles," I told Sonny.

"This one's got the V-10 in it. I can make fifteen hundred miles in—"

"You can make it in about thirty hours, kid. *No tickets*, understand? Max might be able to stop a rhino, but he drives like one, too. So you'll have to break up the run. Just grab a motel anywhere along the—"

"I am an excellent driver," Gem announced.

"You ever drive anything this big?" I asked her, pointing at the red Excursion's huge bulk.

"Bigger," she said. "And over much worse roads than we will be traveling."

Sonny and I exchanged shrugs. When I didn't argue with her, he decided he wouldn't, either.

When the Excursion pulled out, it carried a silent Mongolian who could take a life with either hand; a pasty-faced, pudgy guy with thick glasses and a satchel full of stuff they don't allow on airplanes; and a cargo hold full of equipment. And Gem.

Right behind them was a dark-blue BMW 7 riding caravan, Clarence and the Prof inside. And me.

I jumped off in D.C., grabbed a flight to Tampa. Met Michelle at the airport. She had a man-and-wife rental at the Hyatt Regency, where we spent the night going over it, again.

The next morning, we took off for Key West.

When the rest of the crew arrived—a couple of hours ahead of schedule—we went over it one more time. I finally thought we were all finished, but Michelle had one more thing.

"That nurse's outfit does look cute on you, but are you sure you can handle the needle?" she asked Gem. "The Mole will get the dosages perfect, but you've got to slip it in like you've been doing it for years."

"Shall I show you?" Gem asked, reaching for the syringe.

It took hours to get the old man into the back of the Excursion. Not to load him, to convince him. Michelle had greased the skids, all right, but the man was old . . . not dumb.

I was the businessman, in my alpaca suit. Michelle was the working girl who was going to get a cut of the profits—that part actually calmed the old man down, as we expected. Max was the bodyguard, Gem the nurse.

The Mole's role was mad scientist. Fortunately, that wasn't much of a stretch. By the time he got done explaining how individual cells could be extracted from first-trimester aborted fetuses, tested for a unique DNA combo-string with a producer-multiplier effect on testosterone, and, once isolated, IV-dripped into a man kept in a quasi-comatose state—"The body must be regulated in all respects during the transfer. Any sudden acceleration of heartbeat, for example, would negate the bonding process. We are not *adding* to blood. We are making *new* blood, which will then self-replenish. The goal is a compound, not a mixture"—he had me wanting to try it myself.

"I apologize for what may seem an excessive need for secrecy," I told the old man. "But this work is illegal on too many levels to describe."

"You mean the FDA?" he asked, slyly.

I knew where he was going. I gave Michelle the high-sign and she ushered the Mole out of the room, chattering away about whether injected collagen really collapsed after only a few months. The old man's sulfur eyes followed the whole thing. As soon as the room was empty, I moved my chair closer to him, lowered my voice:

"That's not the problem," I said. "Well, certainly, FDA approval would take, perhaps, *decades* in America. And that would be only if there was a drug company willing to spend the lobbying money. But doing it in Switzerland, or any country that allows revolutionary medical procedures, just wouldn't work. In order for the procedure to be effective, we need to screen more than just the fetuses."

"I don't understand."

I glanced over my shoulder, as if to assure myself that the Mole wasn't within earshot. "Dr. Klexter is a brilliant scientist. But he's a Jew. . . ."

The old man's eyes reflected the truth of what Michelle had told us about him, but he didn't say a word.

"And you know how those people are," I continued. "Fantastic minds. But they're not of our race. An intelligent man uses them, but never takes them fully into his confidence. The truth is, sir, that we've run the doctor's calculations ourselves. And the *most* effective method is with *late*-term fetuses . . . if you follow what I'm saying."

"I believe I do," is all he said.

"And the early-aborted fetuses which theoretically *could* be available for scientific purposes are not screened as *you* would want, either."

"As *I* would . . . ?"

"What the doctor was describing—and, look, I don't pretend to be a scientist, but our consortium has invested so much money in this that I've had to learn some things—is a permanent alteration of your blood. This isn't some 'injection' that you get periodically, or some pill you take. It changes your chemistry, the way your blood works. That's what he meant by a compound, not a mixture. The new blood, those little drops you get day by day until you're done, will be indivisible. It will be *your* blood. Do you follow me, sir?"

"Yes. And I would only want Aryan—"

"*Pure* Aryan," I interrupted him. "And we are in a position to guarantee it. And from *very* late-term fetuses. Do we understand each other now?"

His face was calm—maybe the oxygen mask had that effect—but now his eyes were luciferous. "Perfectly," he finally said.

The Excursion's cavernous back area was filled with the old man's special chair, his oxygen tanks, and his new private nurse, Gem. The back windows were deeply tinted. Randy drove, Max on the front seat next to him. The Prof and Clarence would pick them up somewhere out of town, and ride cover for them all the way, the Mole in the back seat of the BMW.

We figured it for approximately the same distance that the Manhattan–to–Key West run had been. Then we factored in some extra time to attend to the old man. He wouldn't like staying in anonymous rattrap motels along the way; but he'd bought into the whole total-secrecy thing, so he'd go along quietly enough.

And if not, between Max and Gem, he'd *stay* quiet.

His yacht was already on the water, heading for the South Texas coast. "Just in case," I had explained it to him. "Nobody wants any exposure here. If your boat's on the water, *you're* on the water, should there be any . . . interest in your whereabouts. We have people who can move the boat back out to sea while you're at the clinic. And we'll just keep it there until you're ready to return."

"My own crew is on permanent—"

"But they don't need to know your business, do they, sir? Wouldn't it be a better plan to simply tell them you're having work done to the boat where it's being taken, give them a month off, and have them stay no more than a few hours' drive from where it's tied up? No matter how long they've been with you . . . well, you know what the tabloids are paying for information today."

"I do," he said, grimly. "The bloodsucking Jews."

Michelle and I flew ahead to Houston, where we picked up another rental and headed down to Galveston. The hand-over of the clinic went nice and smooth. The doc who owned it didn't *want* to know anything—just when he could come back.

The Excursion pulled in about an hour before we expected it. But we'd timed it for three in the morning, so we unloaded the old man in darkness, as planned.

"Thanks, kid," I told Randy. "We'll take it from here."

"Burke, you know I'd do—"

"You just did," I said.

"No," he said. "Let me finish, okay? I don't know what you're up to, and it's none of my business, okay? But if you need to leave here *quick*, I'm your man, and you know it. Besides, who's going to truck the old guy back to Key West? What's it going to be, a week or two? Let me hang out with the Prof and Clarence, catch up on old times. Please?"

"My man's hip, and he's got the chips. I say, let him play," the Prof ruled.

The old man had a good night's sleep, thanks to one of the Mole's potions.

And in the morning, we all went to work.

First we explained to the old man that we'd have to run a lot of tests. Sure, we had his complete medical records—he'd had a copy in his safe—but this wasn't exactly a routine medical procedure. The clinic had all kinds of incoming communications. Big-screen TV, radio that could pick up anything on the airwaves, a T-1 line to the Internet. But we only used cell phones, outgoing. We explained that the clinic was off the charts. And any land-line call could be traced. We wanted him to be able to do any business he needed to do, so he was free to use one of the cellulars, but if he had a fax or an e-mail or even a FedEx that needed to go out, he'd have to give it to us, and we'd see it was sent from another location.

He just nodded. Hard to tell if it was from understanding or the drugs.

The Mole showed me how the cellulars would patch through a microphone into the harmonizer. I'd learned my lesson from Max's daughter, and I wasn't going to have this whole thing die if the target had voice-recognition software.

The T-1 found it in a few seconds. Darcadia had its own website, very slick and professionally done. But the phone and fax numbers were offshore. And there wasn't even so much as a PO box for a physical location.

On the surface, it looked not only legitimate, but . . . possible. Why *shouldn't* an island in the Pacific form its own country? Darcadia was nothing but an intersection of coordinates on a map, the very tip of a long archipelago, several hundred miles from its nearest neighbor. And it was unoccupied, so there wouldn't be any indigenous people to dislodge. It could be purchased outright from the country it was . . . theoretically . . . part of. And a sovereign government could make its own laws.

The language of the website's prospectus was veiled, but so thinly that even a third-generation inbred could figure it out. *Strict* control of immigration. *Specific* citizenship requirements. Complete freedom of religion "within the obvious constraints." No gun control. No taxes—all revenues to be generated from "pre-screened tourism." Abortion was against the law in Darcadia, which had a no-extradition policy for "citizen warriors charged with acts of revolution against New World Order nations." Restrictions on "acts of personal or intrafamilial conduct" would not be tolerated. And on and on.

It sounded as if everything was in place. Although it was called "the Republic of Darcadia," the site said the new country was "a confederation, not a democracy." It had a chancellor, and a

Cabinet consisting of various "ministers," all of whom were named. I didn't recognize any of them, and their affiliations weren't listed. But a few hours on the Internet connected some of them with the kind of groups I expected, covering the White Night spectrum. No pedophiles, though; they weren't going *that* naked. Not yet.

Then it got down to the money.

"Citizenships" were going for ten grand. For that, you got a passport, "business banking" privileges, and a whole list of "exemptions" while on sovereign Darcadia soil. You could visit your new homeland at will, since citizens, unlike tourists, would be exempt from visa requirements. A "homestead" would set you back a hundred thousand, which bought you a five-acre plot and the right to build on it "free of the sort of building codes and restrictions under which many have suffered in other jurisdictions."

Voting was limited to owners of *developed* property, and various configurations were offered, including "self-contained" electrical and sewage systems, pending development of a country-wide grid. In something lifted right out of H. L. Hunt's *Alpaca*, Darcadia would not hobble itself with a "one man, one vote" system. Votes were allocated on a "unit" basis, the units being reflections of property ownership.

The crown jewel was an "ambassadorship," a fully loaded package which included—what else?—diplomatic immunity in the ambassador's posted country. That package was a cool million.

As soon as the old man wanted a message sent out—to an on-line broker—we captured his e-mail, and I was ready to roll. Using the "investment information" button of their website, I clicked into a blank screen and typed:

I am considering an investment of a magnitude considerably
beyond an ambassadorship, provided the benefits are com-
mensurate. I have the resources to relocate immediately
should your bona fides prove adequate. Please feel free to
conduct whatever investigation of my standing in the various
communities of concern to which you refer thematically. I
await your response.

W. Allen Preston

We kept the old man in a twilight stupor while we waited on
the answer. He seemed fine with it, almost blissed out.
Maybe because that big TV had a VCR and DVD with about a
thousand movies to choose from—anything from black-and-white
gangster flicks from the thirties to porn foul enough to gross
out Larry Flynt. Or maybe the Mole had recombinated some
anti-anxiety drugs into a cocktail that would make a heroin high
look mild.

It was four days before the old man's e-mail popped open with
the message I'd been waiting for.

Sir:
Because your proposal is intriguing on several grounds, not
the least of which is the potential for you to contribute in ways
well beyond financial to the growth and development of Darcadia, it was referred to my personal attention. However, as
we are certain you will understand and support, certain pre-
cautions are necessary. Cyber-communication is immune to
neither impostoring nor government surveillance. Please indicate your current whereabouts so that the negotiations
toward a personal meeting may commence.

Garrison König, Chancellor,
Republic of Darcadia

"Very cute," Gem said, looking over my shoulder.

"What do you mean?"

"König. Do you know what it means in German?"

"Nope."

"King."

"How fucking subtle," I told her, already at work typing out my response.

To: Garrison König, Chancellor of Darcadia
Current location is southeast coast of Texas. My yacht, whose name should be known to you if your research is adequate, is being modified for a protracted cruise. We will depart as soon as all is in readiness, and I will be at sea for approximately 4–6 weeks. However, the ship is fully equipped with all communication devices, and whatever method you choose to make contact can be accommodated.

W. Allen Preston

I held it for six hours, then let it fly. This time, he fired right back. He had a big fish on the line, and he didn't want it running before the hook was set. Deep. His message got right to it:

Please call the number below. Monday, April 3 @ 20:10 CST.
Principals *only*, both ends.

As soon as I saw that the number started with 011, I knew I'd be calling offshore. And probably from there to a relay. But that was okay—the freakish fisherman had hooked an orca.

"Monday is three days from now. Are you not anxious?" Gem asked.

Max tapped her shoulder to get her attention, made a "Nothing you can do about it" gesture.

She nodded. "Flacco and Gordo are in Brownsville now. They can be here in a day's drive."

"That's close enough. Let them stay where they are for now. I don't know how this is going to play out. We've got the ship's papers from the old man. I think all they'll have to do is get the damn boat out into the Gulf and let it hang out there for a while, anyway."

Max pointed at Gem. Then at me. Clasped his huge, horn-ridged hands together and brought them to his heart, and then turned his face into a question.

"Yes," Gem said, nodding her head for emphasis. She'd already figured out Max could read lips. "He was asking if I am your wife," she said to me.

"No, he wasn't. He was just asking if we are in love," I told her.

Max shook his head "No!" Then he pointed at Gem, and nodded "Yes." Telling me she'd gotten his question right.

I made a "Why not ask *me*?" gesture.

"Michelle never asked *me*," the Mole contributed.

I shut up.

The old man was holding up fine. Apparently watching porno flicks under the influence of the Mole's mixtures was a new experience, even for a guy who had enough money to buy pieces of a whole country.

The Prof and Clarence kept a low profile. Their part was fire-power, and it wouldn't come into play unless we had visitors.

So far, all quiet.

Monday night, 8:08 p.m. I punched the long string of numbers he'd given me into the cellular, giving myself a two-minute margin for the international connections to go through.

The Mole nodded to tell me the harmonizer was working perfectly. Gem knelt at my feet, her cheek against my thigh. Max was in another room of the clinic, watching the old man. The Prof and Clarence were outside, checking the grounds.

Showtime.

The phone was answered on the third ring. By a crisp-sounding young woman who spoke unaccented English. Aryan English.

"Chancellor of Darcadia's office. How may I direct your call?"

"To Chancellor König himself, please. This is W. Allen Preston. I understand he is expecting my call."

"Yes, sir. Please hold while I connect you."

The connection took a lot longer than it would to push a button. No surprises yet.

"This is Chancellor König," a voice said. Not one that I recognized. I brushed the dark fluttering wings of panic off my mind, staying focused. Would I really know his voice after all these years, anyway? And with the bridged-through connections . . . ?

"Chancellor, this is Allen Preston, calling as agreed. I am honored to speak with you."

"The honor is mine, I assure you," he said. "So I trust you will forgive my bluntness, sir. Before we get to specifics, to the entire authentication process"—a window opened in my mind: *Authentication. Lune's own word. What if?* I slammed that window shut, focusing hard on him saying, ". . . we would need to know the size of your contemplated . . . investment."

"I am prepared to invest twenty-five million dollars," I told him, my tone conveying that, while I respected such an amount, I wasn't in awe of it.

"You do understand that, given the fledgling nature of Darcadia as an international entity, we cannot, at present, accept—"

"The investment would be liquid," I cut him off, trying for an old man's imperious timbre. A *rich* old man's. "The twenty-five million would be in American dollars only as a point of reference. It could be delivered in any currency you select, via wire transfer."

"Yes, I see we understand each other. And you would expect . . . what, precisely, for your investment?"

"The opportunity—no, the *guarantee*—to live as I choose, *exactly* as I choose, without fear of government intrusion. *Any* government's."

"Surely that sum of money could buy you those same—"

"Forgive an old man's abruptness," I cut him off again. "But all such options have been explored, thoroughly. And rejected on two grounds: First, I wish to be a *participant* in government, not a mere guest. This is because I will not tolerate being an extortion victim for various 'taxes' of an ever-escalating variety. Second, the most accommodating governments are inherently unstable, and I cannot risk a change in power placing me at risk, especially as I will not use air transport of any kind."

"I understand. And on Darcadia—"

"I assume the third consideration is not necessary to mention, despite its being inherent in my requirements."

"I am sure not," he said, smoothly, refusing to take offense at my constant interruptions. "Waterfront property is available, with sufficient dockage constructible to accommodate ships of any size. But I believe ambiguity is a potential source of dissatisfaction between associates and, thus, should be eliminated. So, as to your other specifications, if you will enlighten me . . ."

"Certainly, sir. Those 'accommodating' governments of which I spoke are run by mud people. I will not spend my final years in a country controlled by animals. You describe Darcadia, if I have read your prospectus correctly, as a country which would be openly racialist in its orientation."

"Darcadia is a sovereign area. As such, it is free to—"

"Are you deliberately evading my question?" I snapped at him.

"Mr. Preston, my apologies if you took that to be my intent. Let me match your bluntness with my own. Non-Aryans will not be permitted on Darcadian soil."

"Ah, that is unfortunate," I said, setting my own hook.

"Sir?"

"I have certain . . . servants, if you will, who are not Aryans. They are my . . . preference. Am I communicating sufficiently?"

"You are," he said, returning serve effortlessly. "My apologies. I should have explained that the prohibition is against citizenship *and* tourism. But Darcadians who enjoy a certain . . . status would be free to operate their private estates entirely at their own discretion. Is that satisfactory?"

"It . . . sounds so," I said, centering myself for the bluff that the whole thing hinged on. "But I would need to see who I would be dealing with as *well* as the specifics of the deal. After all, what I would be investing in is, to some extent, intangible . . . at least for the present. But what I would be delivering is *quite* tangible. So, if you can come to my estate on Key West, at your convenience of course, we could finalize—"

"My regrets," he said. "This would be, frankly, impossible. News of Darcadia has attracted considerable government interest. And I *am*, at least on paper, an American citizen. Neither I nor my Cabinet can subject ourselves to the jurisdiction of—"

"Yes, yes," I cut him off, impatience dominating my voice. "All right. *You* pick our meeting place, then. But let me caution you: I will *not* fly. I simply don't trust airplanes. So, if it is a considerable distance, be prepared to wait until I can make the journey by ship."

"You are being more than reasonable, sir. Could I ask you to call back in twenty-four hours? I will have an answer for you then. A satisfactory answer, you have my word on that."

"Twenty-four hours from right now? Or at eight-ten my time tomorrow night?"

"You are a very precise man." He chuckled appreciatively. "Let us say eight-ten once more. Agreed?"

"Agreed," I said. And hung up on him.

"Call them in," I told Gem.

The next night, I went through the same routine, including the "receptionist," and got him on the line. As soon as he started talking, I had to shut him down.

"Look," I told him, allowing the impatience of the character I was playing to come through clearly, "just because I own a yacht doesn't make me a damn sailor. You're going to have to go slow; I need to write this all down."

"Certainly," he said, calmly. "Remember, we are meeting on your terms. That is, a place you can reach by boat. Your captain will know the Oregon coast . . . ?"

I felt a bone-deep chill. How could he . . . ? I rotated my head, slow and soft, like Max had shown me. Then reversed the direction. When I had control of my voice, I said: "What are you asking? Can he *find* the damn coast, or is he *familiar* with it?"

"The former, sir."

"Then of course!"

"All right. Please set sail for the coastline on the California-Oregon border. Once you are in that area, I will provide your captain with precise instructions."

"I'm not pulling in to any—"

"No, sir. We will meet at sea. Fair enough?"

"I'll be traveling a long way—"

"I understand that, sir."

"—with a lot of money. I trust I won't be disappointed."

"You will not, I promise you. Until then."

"**B**y the time we get there, it will be right around the first of May," Flacco said. "Even out where he wants to meet, the sea'll be sweet and calm. Like glass, especially at first light. Anyway, as calm as it ever gets off Oregon; that is one *bad* coastline, *hombre*."

"That's more than three weeks," I said. "It'll take that long?"

"I'm giving us a little margin, just in case of weather, but that's about right. We looked his ship over, and she's like new. Perfect. We can carry about thirty-five hundred gallons, cruise around twenty-two knots, and we're working with a range of maybe four thousand miles. So figure Galveston to Progreso to Panama, maybe a week. Then we go through the Canal to Cabo San Lucas. . . ."

I gave him a "What?" look.

"That is the tip of Baja, *hombre*. Me and Gordito, we know it well, don't we, *compadre*?"

Gordo just smiled.

"Our next leg is into Dago, then up to San Francisco. Got to allow, oh, two weeks max for that one. Finally, we lay in once we get near the Oregon border. From there, we can hit any spot he picks in two, three hours max."

"I thought the Panama Canal was only for commercial ships."

"No way. You pay the freight, they let you ride. We lock it from port to port—Cristobal going in, and we exit at Balboa. Whole trip takes maybe nine, ten hours; nothing to it."

"How much is the toll?"

"Depends on the size of the ship. The one we got, under five grand, my best guess."

"And you just drive up and pay the toll, like going over a bridge?"

"No," Gordo answered. "It is not like that at all, my friend." He used his fingers to tick off requirements he'd obviously memorized. "We have to radio prior to arrival—ninety-six, seventy-two, forty-eight, and twenty-four hours in front. We make contact on VHF Channel 12, then they find us a working channel to finish up. Then everyone on board needs ID; it's called a Landing Card. You get those when you hit the first pier. *After* you pay them."

"Damn."

"Oh, there's more," he went on. "They'll want a Quarantine Declaration and one for any cargo, too. A crew-and-passenger list. Lots of stuff. And they can inspect you at *any* time. So we also need an International Tonnage Certificate with all its calculation sheets attached, Lines Plans for the Offset Tables, *mucho* paper, man. I don't know if all that's on board. It *should* be—that beauty's an oceangoer, no question. But they'll do all the measuring and stuff right there if we want. So long as we—"

"—pay for it," I finished for him.

"You got it. And when it comes to paper, Gem . . ."

She nodded. "We have all gone through the Canal before," she said. "It is no problem."

It took a half-dozen relays, but Levi was on the line in under eight hours.

"You still want to walk that path with me?" I asked him.

"Yes."

"Ever been on a boat?"

"I was a Marine," he said, as if that answered the question.

I gave him the meet-point in Galveston. "Bring your tools," I told him. "There's something we're going to need to fix."

"Can you make one, Mole?"

"It would depend on whether the contact point is organic or inorganic."

"Huh?"

"Wood is organic. Metal or plastic is inorganic."

"Ah. I don't know."

"I would have to make two, then. The simple one is a penetrator. The other would require either a magnet or suction of some sort. How long would it have to remain in place?"

"An hour?"

"Exposed to the elements?"

"*Hell*, yes. Probably get blasted with salt water all the time."

"The miniaturization is very simple. But given your limited options for a propellant, and the need for accuracy, both devices would have to be the same external configuration."

"I guess so."

"My man can do it," Michelle said, confidence radiating off her gorgeous face.

The Mole blushed. But he didn't deny it.

"I'll need at least three of each of them," I told him.

"Okay," I said to everyone, "here's how we've got to work it. Flacco and Gordo will be handling the ship. Levi will ride along with us. With me, Gem, and Max, that's six."

"Plus the two props," Gem added.

"I'm not so crazy about that part," I told her.

"You said yourself, they would be perfect cover for your persona," she replied.

"But I'm only going to need the cover for—"

"An extra tenth?" she said, lassoing me with my own words about raglan sleeves.

"Okay. That part's true. But there's no guarantee that—"

"There is a risk. They *all* know that; the children, too. But for what you are paying, you will be changing their lives—*giving* them a life, and their families as well."

Gem wasn't wrong about the payments. This whole crazy thing was emptying my stash so deep I'd be into my case money by the time it was over.

"Right," I told her, surrendering. "That's a pretty good load for that boat, I think. Michelle, you stay here and keep the old man calm. Mole, you know what to do if he gets twitchy. Prof, you and Clarence and Randy stay here, too. Everybody hangs until you get the word. Things work out like we plan, Randy motors the old man back to Key West, where he can try out his recovered virility. If it doesn't, cut your losses."

The Prof nodded agreement. The others may not have caught what I meant, but our years together Inside had given us a different level of communication. If they had to get out of there fast, the old man wouldn't be coming along on the ride.

"This thing looks like a prop for a sci-fi movie," Levi said a few days later, the Mole's creation cradled in his arms. "What's this little canister thing?" he asked, touching what would be the clip if the thing were a real firearm.

"A pressure regulator," the Mole told him. "This is a modified air rifle."

"Okay, I get it. Hell, they use these things in the Olympics now. Supposed to be unreal for accuracy."

"It should deliver the . . . projectile between five and seven hundred yards perfectly," the Mole assured him.

"That's no distance," Levi said. "What am I supposed to hit with it?"

"We don't know yet," I told him.

Whatever the Mole cooked up for me worked better than I'd even hoped for. The boat made me a little sick—okay, maybe a *lot* sick—but I got over it pretty quick. There wasn't any harm in me going on deck—the old man they'd be watching for wouldn't do that, but I didn't look anything like him. Still, I stayed below all through the Canal just in case.

One day Gem came into the stateroom where I spent most of my time. "I am going to give you a manicure," she announced.

"What the hell for?"

"Because a rich old man would not have hands like yours. I cannot do much about the . . ."

She let her voice trail away. My hands are like my life: some of the breaks hadn't healed straight. And the scars spoke for themselves, if you knew how to read them.

"It doesn't matter," I told her. "Once he—"

"It is part of your role," she said, solemnly. "Another tenth. Besides, you know how much I love your thumb in my mouth. It would be nicer if it was manicured, perhaps?"

"Sure," I said, letting it go.

"If you wish, I can easily teach one of the children to do it, too. That would be right in character."

"No!"

"Burke, what is so wrong? It would just be part of the—"

"I said no. That's the fucking end of it."

Gem got to her feet, a thoughtful look on her face. Then she turned away from me, sticking her thumbs in the waistband of her shorts. She pulled them down and bent over in one smooth movement.

I smacked her bottom half-heartedly. "More," she said. I did it again, a couple of times, the cracks loud in the closed space.

She straightened up, adjusted her shorts. Turned around and knelt next to me as she had been before. "I have been punished now, yes?"

"Sure."

"It is not enough?"

"It's plenty, Gem. It's not your fault. There's some things I just can't—"

"It *was* my fault. I know you. I never should have suggested what I did. I apologize. Do you accept?"

"Yes, baby girl. Just forget it, okay?"

"I have been punished, so my debt is paid. I will forget it. But . . . now may I give you that manicure, please?"

The next evening, Levi sat down next to me. "It'll work," he said, confidently. "I wasn't sure at first. But I've been practicing. Every time there's no other ship in sight, I toss one of the flotation devices overboard, wait till we've got some distance. If I can hit something that small at a hundred yards, what you're talking about, I can handle it three, four times that distance, no problem."

"And you can't beat it for silence."

"That's for sure. Even over water, you can't hear a thing."

"We'll probably never get to use it, you understand?"

"I understand. But if I have to go with the other option, you could double that distance and it'd be no big deal."

We made even better time than Flacco had estimated. When he pulled in for the last refueling, I called the Chancellor.

"Please write this down very carefully," he said, his voice more cocksure and commanding than it had been when he thought the old man was a long distance away. "Starting from the mouth of the Chetco River, from Red Buoy No. 2, proceed on a course of 238.5 true. This will take you out to 124 degrees, 31 minutes west; 41 degrees, 51 minutes north. Repeat: course is 238.5 true, heading to 124 degrees, 31 minutes west; 41 degrees, 51 minutes north. Please note, that point is slightly more than twelve-point-five nautical miles from the United States coast. If you would please read that back to me . . ."

I did that, except for the twelve-mile-limit part.

"Precisely," he said. "Please tell your pilot that Red Buoy No. 2 has a flashing red light with a four-second interval. It also has a bell."

"I've got it."

"And the last buoy out, 'CR,' which marks the start of the Chetco Channel, is red-and-white-striped. This one flashes white in morse code the letter 'A.' And it is equipped with a whistle, not a bell. Are you still with me?"

"Yes," I told him. And repeated what I'd written down, word for word, to prove it.

"Tomorrow morning at oh-seven-hundred."

"I'll be there."

"If fog proves a problem, we will radio—"

"Fine."

"Very well, sir. I look forward to meeting you."

"**W**hat's he mean, 'pilot'?" I asked Flacco. "Guys who drive ships're captains, right?"

"Right. When you drive, you're the captain. But the guys who take the boats—the big ones, I mean, like the liners—the guy who brings it in or out of port, they call him the pilot. That was me, through the Canal. Got to have a pilot's license to work those locks."

"And you understand what all this stuff means?" I asked, showing him the directions I'd written down.

"Sure," he said. "Just means he wants us to stay with the gyro compass. See where he says *true* north? That's different from *magnetic* north. Could be ten, maybe even twenty-five degrees of difference."

"And the true one is the more accurate?"

"That's right," Levi answered. Flacco and Gordo turned to look at him. "That's working off the GPS, so it'll be right on the nose, every time. You just dial in latitude and longitude, and it'll tell you how to steer, stay right on course. But ships have to carry both. Even if we lost electrical power, the magnetic compass would always work."

The Mexicans nodded approval. "That's the truth, man," Gordo said. "You ever drive?"

"No," Levi said. "I was just on board a lot while I was in the Corps. But I'm a good listener."

He was a good watcher, too. It was just getting light as Levi stood at the rail, a pair of binoculars to his eyes. "Christ," he said, softly, "that's a fucking Zhuk."

"A what?" I asked him.

"A coastal-patrol craft. The Russians started making them thirty years ago. For export only—who'd try and patrol the *Russian* coast?"

"Where'd they find buyers? Something like that must cost a few million bucks, right?"

"Maybe once. Now one, one and a half max. The mobs in charge over there have been selling off the military surplus for a long time now. Hell, you could probably pick one up for half what I said, if you knew where to look. Nicaragua was a big buyer."

Russian surplus, I thought to myself. Another piece falling into place. "So it's nothing like . . . this one?"

Levi made a snorting sound. "*That* one's packing enough horsepower to fly a good-sized plane. Probably has a crew of fifteen, twenty men. She can make thirty knots and cover over a thousand miles if they go to half-throttle. And that's if it's nothing but refurbished stock. If they replaced the original diesels with General Motors or Volvo Penta jobs, it'd be a lot stronger."

"So it's *much* faster than——"

"That's the least of our problems," he said. "You look close, you can see the fixed machine guns. Those they *had* to have replaced. We're probably looking at .50-calibers. Enough to turn this barge into shredded wood."

"How could they just run around with stuff like that? They've had to dock it somewhere."

"Each gun's on a tripod," Levi explained. "They could just remove the guns and stow them below when they have to enter a port."

"How are they going to get him on board?" I asked, watching the gray metal gunboat slice through the water toward us.

"When they get close enough, they'll cut their engines. So will we. After that, we can just orbit—you know, make minor position adjustments—so we'll be close enough to make the transfer. But I don't think they'll come alongside, not with the firepower they're packing. It'd be like coming down to handgun distance when you're holding a rifle—makes it harder to use it right.

"Besides, it's real calm now and . . . There! See how their wake is disappearing? Their engines are off now. Go down and tell Flacco to cut ours, too."

By the time I'd gotten belowdecks, Flacco had already cut our power. And when I got back up top, Levi handed me the glasses, said: "What did I tell you? Here comes their Zodiac."

"That little rubber thing?"

"It's not rubber, it's . . . never mind. There's four men on board, three of them openly packing. I've got to get into position. And you better get out of sight, quick!"

When only one man came down the steps, I knew the others were still waiting in that Zodiac. If they'd tried to board, any of them Levi didn't pick off would have met Max in the shadows where he waited. And our boat would be flying as fast as it could.

I'd expected a military uniform of some kind, but the man Gem ushered into the stateroom was dressed in a dark-blue suit over a white shirt and wine-red tie. Very presidential.

Gem ordered the two stick-thin Cambodian girls in matching schoolgirl outfits out of the room in a harsh, commanding tone. Then she escorted him over to where I was sitting in the wheelchair, the oxygen mask in place over my nose and mouth.

He shook my extended hand, then took a seat in the deep white leather armchair right across from me.

"May I offer you coffee? Or tea?" Gem asked him, bowing at the waist like a stewardess. Or a geisha.

"No, thank you," he answered, politely.

"Then perhaps—?"

"Nothing," he said, dismissing her. He turned his full attention to me: "So, Mr. Preston, we finally meet."

"It is my honor, sir."

"*I* am honored that a man of your stature would consider becoming one of us."

"If we can come to agreement," I wheezed through the mask, "it can be done today, as I promised. Surely you have a means of confirming a currency transfer on board your vessel?"

"Certainly."

"I have people standing by," I told him. "A transfer could be completed in minutes."

"Very well. Then let me take this opportunity to answer whatever questions and concerns you have."

I pulled the oxygen mask off my face and stared at him, making sure. Dead sure. It was him, no question. The only change was that his remaining hair was cut very short.

He regarded me calmly, not a flicker of recognition showing in his own eyes. But when I asked, "Why did you try to have me killed?," my voice penetrated right to his core.

"You're—" he gasped.

"Right. You remember me now, don't you? I've got a new face, but I'm the same man you met with in that fancy townhouse of yours."

"Burke," he said. Just a statement of fact. If he was frightened, it didn't show.

"Yeah. And now maybe you'd like to—"

"I don't know why you went through this incredibly complicated ruse," he said, unruffled, the semi-British accent I'd remembered now completely erased from his voice. "But I'm sure you understand that you can't do anything to me without fatal consequences to yourself. And to everyone on board this vessel. My ship—"

"Yeah. The Zhuk. I know. We're outgunned. I didn't bring you here to kill you. It's all about some answers."

"Answers?"

"Yeah. Answers. To the question I just asked you."

His answer was to laugh.

I waited, as calm inside as the sea around us, gentle waves lapping at my insides. But not touching them.

"Here's your 'answer,'" he said, still chuckling. "And it's not the one you think."

I said nothing, waiting.

"I realized I had you to thank for my prison sentence—you and that cunt Wolfe—before I ever started doing it. But I am a professional. I wouldn't spend a fortune on petty revenge."

"A professional pedophile."

"Yes," he said, chuckling again. "That's the problem. *Your* problem."

"I don't get it."

"You want to know the truth? Here it is. You called me a professional pedophile. That's only half right. I am a professional. A true professional. And you, you're a rank, incompetent amateur. The reason for the assassination—which I now see failed—is not because of what I do, but because of your delusions about it."

"It's your story. Tell it."

"Oh, I'll be happy to. And when I'm done, I'll be able to tell something else. I'll be able to tell if you truly understand."

"Why is that important?"

"You'll see. The man you met in that townhouse was a fiction. The Israelis knew it, but, apparently, they didn't see fit to share their knowledge with you. I was playing a part. A role. Espionage can't make much use of certain . . . information as it once could. At least not in America or many European countries. Homosexuality, a mistress—even the most bizarre sexual preferences—those are not good blackmail tools anymore. At least, not reliable ones. But pedophilia . . . ah, *that* one is an ironclad guarantee."

"You're telling me you didn't deal in kiddie porn?"

"Of *course* I did. *I* was that horrible 'commercial element' I described to you," he said, switching back to the slightly effeminate, semi-British voice he'd used when I'd first met him. "The market for such product may not be broad, but, I assure you, it is astoundingly deep. And the profit margins are truly incredible . . . virtually infinite.

"Look," he said, his voice shifting again, letting me feel the steel beneath the froth, "use your fucking head, all right? If I was a child molester, when City-Wide popped me, how long do you think it would have taken me to rat out every single person I'd ever dealt with?"

"About thirty seconds."

"Yes. And that's the way you figured it, didn't you? Only problem is, you never bothered to check. I didn't drop dime-fucking-one, pal," he said, hard-voiced. "And the people I *didn't* rat out, well, they were very grateful. How much time do you think I *actually* did?"

"Six to eighteen, with the judge's recommendation that you do the max."

"Ah, so you at least followed the proceedings *that* far. What happened after that was an appeal—"

"You pleaded out. What kind of bullshit appeal could you put up?"

"Oh, that the guilty plea was coerced by use of improperly obtained evidence, what else?" he said, switching voice again, showing off his chameleon moves. "And, of course, there was a sealed brief submitted by the State Department in support of my application. I understand it was quite persuasive. Bottom line? I did a little less than a two-year bit."

"Beautiful. And now you're setting up a paradise for freaks, not because you're one yourself, but for the money?"

"You mean Darcadia? I'm surprised at you, Mr. Burke. You have a reputation for utter insanity when it comes to child abusers, I grant you. But, in some circles, you are also known as a very clever confidence man. And not above playing some roles yourself when there's enough money in it."

"What are you saying? That you and me, we're the same?" I asked, pushing a little button on the side of the oxygen mask I was still holding in my lap.

"Oh, but we *are*, Mr. Burke. We're both predators. And we both prey on the same victims, albeit in different ways. There *is* no Darcadia. And there never will be. Of all the congenital defectives ever birthed on this godforsaken earth, those pathetic little wannabe Nazis have to be the most extreme example. Who else would believe such a fairy tale? And pedophiles? Perhaps even easier to gull. Ah, how they *dream* of such a place! And I am making their dreams come true."

"Nazis and child molesters on the same little island?"

"Please! Spare me your incompetent attempts at political analysis. Hitler marched Jews into the ovens because . . . why? They were *defectives*. As were Gypsies, homosexuals . . . a long list. But you never saw pedophiles on that list, did you?

"Extremists don't fit themselves along a continuum, Mr. Burke. They don't form lines; they form a circle. And the 'sexual liberation' frauds who include children among their 'causes' eventually met the Nazis who think incest preserves the race.

Pedophiles don't have politics," he said, contemptuously. "They only have . . . preferences. This is *business*, pure and simple."

He took a long, deep refueling breath and went on: "Any businessman understands it's not enough to know your product; you also have to know your market. And I have been *successfully* marketing information to pedophiles for years. There are states where sex with a child under eleven can get you twenty-five years in prison . . . unless it's your *own* child. Then, if the DA can be persuaded to charge 'incest' instead of 'sexual assault of a child,' the offender can *expect* probation. Do you know which states have the loosest requirements for running a day-care center? Which organizations don't do background checks for those who volunteer to work with kids? Which jurisdictions make it easiest to get a foster child? Which won't prosecute polygamy?"

I didn't answer him. Truth is, I didn't know the answers.

"I didn't think so," he said, after a pause. "But I do. And do you know how to package a pedophile for probation? Or for early release if sentenced? Do you know how to teach these sickening men how to avoid mouthing their cognitive distortions when they're interviewed?"

"Cognitive distortions?" I asked, stalling—I needed time to deal with the info-overload.

"The classic example," he answered, "goes something like this. People are primarily motivated by desire for pleasure. Children are people. Children seek pleasure. Sex is pleasure. Children seek what they want by communicating their desires. That is why so many children are deliberately seductive—they are seeking pleasure, for them*selves*."

"And people *buy* that crap?"

"Law enforcement doesn't. Just the treatment centers that make a living from it. *My* task is to make sure the . . . client doesn't *repeat* any of it, regardless of his personal belief system."

"So you sell them the keys?"

"Certainly. And each client subset is different. With the incest offenders, we have to eliminate their expressions of a profound sense of 'entitlement' to their own children. Learning to feign remorse is critical to their survival, once apprehended."

"Christ!"

"Of course, the worst are the 'true believers.' You're familiar with their rhetoric, I'm sure." His voice switched to a singsong parody of a memorized litany: "'Those children who *later* claim to have been harmed by a loving sexual experience with a caring adult are not victims of sex, they are victims of *programming*, playing the victim role as dictated by self-interested therapists, and exploited by greedy lawyers. The media never report that there are numerous studies which show that the child participants themselves, interviewed later as adults, did not consider their earlier experiences to be harmful in any way at all. The only "perversion" going on is the perversion of love.'"

"Nice."

"Be honest, if only with yourself. I sell these people images—pictures and videotapes. And if they are later *caught* with such product, I sell them information on how to minimize the consequences. And, of course, if their status warrants, I sell their names to certain foreign governments *before* there are any consequences. In short, I prey upon them. Are your own operations any different?"

"I promise them kiddie porn, sure. But I never deliver."

"And so you are better than I, somehow? Morally superior? I don't *produce* the pornography, I procure it. Do you think the people from whom I obtain the product would go out of business if I stopped buying? Parents sell their children all the time. All over the world."

"What's all this got to do with Nazis?"

"Are you really this dense? If you want to preserve the bloodlines, you do what the royals always did. Keep it in the family. It's called inbreeding. Or, if you prefer, incest.

"Anyway, the whole 'Nazi' concept is nothing more than a marketing tool. It isn't about politics, it's about packaging. A skillful profiteer always tailors his product to the market. Does the phrase '*National* Socialism' register with you? Hitler was all about *German* dominance. Do you think he would have welcomed Greeks or Poles or Italians as 'Aryan'? They might have been at the end of the line for the ovens, but, rest assured, they would certainly be *on* that line.

"Modern merchants understand that young people are where the money is. So, instead of limiting their pitch to the genetically correct, they simply change the definitions. Today, any kid who could conceivably call himself 'white' can qualify . . . even a good number of Hispanics."

He was right. And tapping a deep vein, too. Even when I was a kid, the dark-skinned Puerto Rican kids they brought into the lockup would only speak Spanish, making certain the cops didn't take them for blacks.

"Am I really telling you anything you don't know, Burke?" he went on, completely composed. "How many crates of nonexistent weapons have *you* sold to these imbeciles? I'm selling them a nonexistent Valhalla-on-earth where they can practice whatever perversion suits their disorders. Only I operate on a grander scale than you could ever have conceptualized."

"Then why have me killed?"

"Because, until this very moment, you didn't know one single word of what I just told you. No, you thought I was some sort of super-pedophile. And you wanted to kill *me*, didn't you?"

"Yeah," I admitted, way past gaming now.

"I acknowledge that the scheme you hatched—that phony 'immunity' I was fool enough to purchase—was a clever one, although I suspect the woman was the real instigator."

"You never went after her, though."

"Why should I? She's a stupid policewoman in her heart. She did her job. I went to prison. She's done with her work. Besides, I know what happened to her. What good's a prosecutor without a jurisdiction? She's out of business, permanently. But you . . . in a way, you represented the last impediment to me acquiring enough money to disappear and live, literally, as a king. With you alive, I'd be looking over my shoulder for the rest of my life."

"How long—?"

"Was I planning this? I hatched the final plans for Darcadia in my prison cell. They took my freedom, but not my resources— my government friends saw to that, too. I thought it would be a perfect irony for you to be murdered by one of the children who appear to mean so much to you."

"That kid . . . he was one of—?"

"He *became* one of them. His parents sold him. . . . Well, more accurately, I should say his mother sold him. She wanted her child to grow up as a warrior for his race. Despite the money she garnered from the transaction, I believe she was quite sincere in her Nietzschean politics. In fact," he said, somewhere between a laugh and a sneer, "she plans to join us on Darcadia someday. The boy's father was not a factor. A weak, ineffectual man. He told himself his child was going to some sort of military school. But he knew.

"In any event, the child was sold, for a considerable sum, I may add, to what I call a 'fusion' group—one that merges its pedophilia with whatever ideology seems to permit or promote it. Nazis seem to make ideal candidates. Although I assume that pedophiles without the correct racial credentials find some other ways to band together," he said, contempt heavy in his voice.

"In this case, the buyer was an assembly of warrior pedophiles who desire to emulate the Spartans in all ways important to *them*. The child was 'kidnapped,' as you know. By the time he was a teenager, his indoctrination was complete. And, I was told, his skills were excellent. That plan should have worked."

"It did. He put a few rounds in me. They just didn't do the job."

"I see. In any event, it was I who arranged the sale. And, in so doing, discovered this 'fusion' principle. I investigated further, and learned that there are many such groups. That, in turn, eventually gave birth to Darcadia. And," he said calmly, "to the reason to have you taken out."

I let the silence sit there, building. Then I said, "You don't need me dead anymore," so still inside myself I wouldn't have bounced a polygraph needle.

"Because . . . ?"

"Because more fucking power to you, pal. This whole Darcadia thing is nothing but a whale-scale scam, right?"

"What else *would* it be?"

"I get it. I get it *now*, anyway. Besides, you want to hear something funny? I wasn't ever after you. I didn't know where you were, and I didn't care. I thought you were doing a long jolt, and that you'd get protection from the Israelis again once you got out. I'd done all I wanted to do when I Pearl Harbored you with that immunity thing. I wasn't going to risk Mossad on my ass just for the fun of blowing you away."

"So we were both mistaken, it seems."

"Yeah. I *did* think you were a baby-raper. But if I went around killing every one of *those* . . ."

"Point taken. But I assumed you had some personal stake, after going to all that trouble just to get me into a brief prison sentence."

"Personal? I hate them *all*. And that's no secret, right? Look, what's the point? It looks like we both have to gamble here. You've got a crew of halfass Nazis who think you're the next Führer waiting on you in that boat. They're ready to blow us all into dust if you don't come back. Sure. But I still get to decide *if* you come back. You go back there and give the order to total us, they'll do it. So, if I think that's what you *are* going to do, we might as well just sit here and wait for it . . . together. No way I'm going to let you snuff us all and live to laugh about it."

"And if I give you my word—?"

"You know what?" I said, leaning forward. "I'd take it. What's in it for me to blow the whistle on you? The freaks aren't going to pay me—even if they believed me, and fat fucking chance of *that*. Besides, if the feds knew what you were *really* up to, they'd probably pay *you* to keep tabs on your own suckers.

"And the way you play things, I know you've got your back covered. I'm sure you've got a few of them in on it with you. I mean, even some of the Nazis themselves know it's a scam, too, right?"

"Obviously. In fact, two of them are on my ship right now. They have been very helpful," he said, voice heavy with contempt for his stooges. "There were three of them originally, but one didn't survive that little encounter with you. The dog was a surprise."

"So there's nothing I could do to screw up your play," I told him, my voice calm even as my mind screamed to Pansy that I'd finally found the puppets who killed her. "And I couldn't find you again even if I wanted to. You go back to stealing from them your way, and I'll go back to mine. Besides, even with those machine guns, you can't kill us so easy as you think."

"I don't understand that last part."

"You can't board us from that Zodiac—you'd be mowed down like wheat. And if you get back to your ship and tell your storm troopers to blast away at long range, it's going to take a while. You're not packing anything that could make a whole boat just go boom! But *we* are . . ." I said softly, letting the bluff float gently in the air between us.

"There's going to be wreckage in the water," I promised him. "Maybe even survivors. And the second anyone starts shooting, a full description of your boat goes out to the Coast Guard, together with our GPS. The message'll say that we were attacked by terrorists on a 'training mission.' How many fucking Zhuks are floating around out here? Sure, I know, we're out past the twelve-mile limit. You trust the feds enough to think they're going to turn back at the border? Especially with no one watching . . . ?"

His face was all the answer I needed.

"You know what?" I told him. "It might make *you* feel good to kill me, but it wouldn't do a thing for anyone else on your boat. All it could do is get them Life-Without or a needle in the arm. And no matter what you say about them, they can't be *that* fucking stupid. Go out on deck. Signal them to pick you up, get in your boat, and go your own way. I promise you, we'll never see each other again."

I didn't offer to shake hands—that would've been too much. He sat back in his chair. I could see him thinking it over. And I let *him* see I was doing the same math.

"I don't trust you," he finally said. "Not personally. But I do trust you to be a lot smarter than the dimwits I've been using.

Exposing Darcadia wouldn't do a thing for you. In fact, I expect you'll make some little forays of your own, trying to poach on my territory."

"The flock's big enough for us both to fleece."

"Oh, the flock is enormous, no question. But if you're proposing any sort of partnership . . ."

I held up both hands in a "No way!" gesture, but he went right on talking: ". . . forget it. I believe I *have* convinced you that I'm no more a pedophile than you are. But I maintain my belief that you are a disturbed, dangerous individual. And I wouldn't want you within a thousand miles of anyplace where such people gathered in groups."

"Well, like you said . . . be pretty hard to bomb an island that doesn't exist."

"You caused me to go to prison. I took that as the cost of doing business. You seem healthy enough, although your face—"

"—is part of *my* cost of doing business," I told him, meaning it. "Besides, we each hold the other's hole card."

"What do you mean?"

"I know the truth about Darcadia, sure. But *you* know I'm not dead."

"Ah. Well put, then. Besides, I believe it is just about time for me to, as they say, move on. Most of the juice has been squeezed out of the lemon. Only the prospect of one last giant financial repast tempted me this time."

He got to his feet. I stayed where I was.

"May we never meet again," he said.

"We won't," I told him. "I swear it."

He turned his back on me. Held that pose for an extra second. Then climbed the stairs to where his Zodiac was waiting.

ax appeared in the stateroom, signaled to me that the Zodiac was on its way back to its home.

I made the sign of a man shooting a rifle. Max nodded and left. Levi was down in the stateroom a minute later.

"You nail it?" I asked him.

"Right to the mast," he assured me. "I'd never used an air rifle at a distance like that, but it was a big target—sticks way up there, nice and thick. And with three shots, prone, off a bipod rest, it was a sure thing. Gordo locked on to the frequency, said he could hear the whole thing as it was being transmitted to their ship. If I hadn't gotten it full-confirm, I would have gone back to Plan A."

I'd *hoped* the freak would say enough to hang himself, but I hadn't guessed within a hundred miles of his real game. Once that started to come out, I'd signaled for Levi to try and attach the transmitter.

Plan A was a lot more straightforward. Gem had taken the honored visitor's slicker from him and stowed it away before bringing him to me. She would have returned it to him marked with a dye that would fluoresce its entire back under the scope Levi would be using on his beloved custom Bedeaux.

But the flying transmitter had found its mark. The collection of life-takers waiting for the Chancellor of Darcadia to return to his ship had been passing the time listening to our whole conversation. And they'd know Ruhr and Timmons were the ones closest to the man who'd been screwing them all along.

Some movies, you don't wait around for the ending.

"Tell Flacco to open her up," I said to Gem.

We found a berth somewhere along the coast that Flacco and Gordo knew about. I paid them what Gem told me to. They were going to sail the old man's boat back to its home, with Max aboard.

An old station wagon came by the motel and picked up the little girls. Gem dealt with it.

Levi vanished without saying goodbye . . . and I wouldn't have offered him money, anyway.

I phoned the clinic. Randy and Michelle would haul the old man back to Key West. She'd make the Mole come along, too.

The Prof and Clarence would cover their route. They'd all be in place before the boat got back.

And then they'd all head back home.

"I must return to my house," Gem told me. "There are things I need to attend to; things that I have neglected."

"Okay."

"And you will come with me."

"Gem . . ."

She just stared at me, unblinking.

It wasn't a good time for me to go back home. And I couldn't operate where Gem lived. But Portland was close by. And that town looked ripe for the kind of work I do.

As far as New York was concerned, I was dead. So, for now, I figured I might as well be dead and gone.

And once I learned Portland better, there were a couple of Russians in Lake Oswego I wanted to visit some night.

So I could tell them how their son turned out.

An excerpt from

PAIN MANAGEMENT

by Andrew Vachss

available in hardcover from

Alfred A. Knopf, Inc.

The light was gone by the time we got back to Portland. Ann had changed in a gas-station restroom, so when she popped out of the Subaru she looked ready for work. I was slouched in the passenger seat, making it look like she was working unleashed, no pimp. We couldn't be sure what information the knifeman had given his boss. We couldn't even be sure he'd given any information at all. There hadn't been anything in the papers, but that didn't necessarily mean he'd even survived. So we stayed with the script.

Ann took a few tentative steps on the cheap spike heels, wiggling her bottom like she was practicing her moves. She headed for the same patch in the vacant lot where it had all started. I settled in to wait.

When it happened, I almost didn't pick him up. A black kid, looked maybe nineteen, smooth brown-skin face, neatly trimmed natural. He was wearing a way-oversize black-and-white flannel shirt with sleeves so long they covered his hands, moving in a bouncy, prancing strut, covering ground like he owned it. Typical gangsta-boy moves, about as menacing as Martha Stewart.

But I was working, so I hit the switch and the window slid down in sync with the kid rolling up on Ann's left side. That's when I saw the chrome muzzle protruding from the tip of his right sleeve. He was maybe fifteen feet away and closing when he brought the gun up in the trigger-boy's Hollywood flat-sided grip.

By then, my left forearm was along the windowsill, with the Beretta resting on top. I had three into him before Ann heard the sound of the shots.

"Get in here!" I yelled at her.

She ran toward the car, stumbled to her knees, got up quickly, snatching one of the spike heels off the ground, and half-hopped her way around to the driver's side. I was already next to the kid's body, relieved despite myself to see the faint light from down the block reflect on the flashy chrome semi-auto in his hand—it was the real thing, all right.

I knew, from the standard mumbo-jumbo every shooter gets when he can't afford anything better than Legal Aid, that "self-defense" also includes "defense of others." But if I shot the kid again once he was down, I couldn't ever use that one in court. I balanced it in my head for split seconds. The people who'd ambushed me back in New York hadn't made sure of their kill, and paid heavy for it later. But I couldn't see a sign he could make it even if someone around there *had* 911'ed the action. He spasmed once. Then he crossed over.

I was back inside in a flash, and Ann had us gone from the scene in less than that.

Her hands were steady on the wheel as she slid the Subaru around corners, not giving the impression of great speed, but really covering ground. My hands were trembling a little, so I left them in my pockets.

"What happened?" she asked.

"That was the other one."

"He was going to——?"

"Kill you? Yeah. That's what the fucking gun was for."

"B.B., take it easy, okay? I'm all right. He didn't——"

"This piece—the one I used—it has to go. Quick. We get stopped with it in the car, I'm done."

"But you were just protecting me!" she said, as if reading my mind back when I stood over the kid's body.

"That's a law-school thing. Maybe even a courtroom thing. But with my record, even if I eventually walked, I'd be no-bailed for months, maybe years. And by then, people would know who I am."

"Who you *really* are, you mean."

"That's right. Now, just go where I tell you."

"¿**Q**ué pasa?" Gordo asked me, as if walking into the garage at one in the morning was the most normal thing in the world.

"I need to borrow some tools."

"What for, man? You ain't no mechanic. Just bring whatever you got in here and we'll——"

"It's not a car. And it doesn't need fixing; it needs destroying. Better you don't see what it is, okay?"

He gave me a long look. "This . . . thing, it's, like, metal, right?"

"Sure."

"Not another . . . ?"

"No."

"¿*Cuánto?*"

"Just the one," I told him.

"I know this guy," he said. "He's got his own junkyard. Works a car-crusher there."

"It has to be now, Gordo."

"*Sí.* Just go and get it, *compadre*. Take me ten, fifteen minutes. Take you hours. I do it perfect. You do it, maybe not so good. Just go and get it."

The unrecognizable pile of metallic filings and shavings and chips made a gentle rattling sound when Gordo shook the clear plastic box that held them. "Like a maraca, huh?" He laughed.

I pointed to Gordo and Flacco, separately. Bowed slightly. Said, *"Obligado."* And walked out of the garage.

Ann was still in the front seat of her Subaru, but now she was dressed casual, in a pale-blue pullover and jeans.

"Where to?" she asked me.

"You've got all kinds of medical stuff, right?"

"Sure."

"Got sulfuric acid?" I asked.

In the shadows of one of the bridges, just before a steel-gray dawn broke, I poured all that was left of the pistol out of a big glass jar into the Columbia River. We'd kept the news on the radio, but either the kid's body was still in that vacant lot, or he hadn't been important enough to crack the airwaves.

I went back to the apartment Ann used as a hideout. She said she wanted a shower. I wanted about four of them, but I told her to go first.

The next thing I remembered was waking up. It was late afternoon. I'd never had that shower, but I was stripped, laying across the bed, a soft, warm blanket across my back.

Ann.

ALSO BY ANDREW VACHSS

"Vachss is in the first rank of American crime writers."
—*The Plain Dealer*

BORN BAD

Born Bad is a wickedly funny collection of forty-five stories that distill dread down to its essence, plunging readers into the hell that lurks just outside their bedroom windows.
Crime Fiction/0-679-75336-2

DOWN IN THE ZERO

The haunted and hell-ridden private eye Burke, a man inured to every evil except the kind that preys on children, is investigating suicides among the teenagers of a wealthy Connecticut suburb, and, along the way, discovers a sinister connection.
Crime Fiction/0-679-76066-0

STREGA

The implacable Burke has a new client, a woman who calls herself "Strega" (Italian for erotic witch)—and a new assignment that leads him into the deepest oceans of the twisted city.
Crime Fiction/0-679-76409-7

ALSO AVAILABLE:

Blossom, 0-679-77261-8
Blue Belle, 0-679-76168-3
Footsteps of the Hawk, 0-679-76663-4
Everybody Pays, 0-375-70743-3
False Allegations, 0-679-77293-6
Flood, 0-679-78129-3
Hard Candy, 0-679-76169-1
Sacrifice, 0-679-76410-0
Safe House, 0-375-40084-2
Shella, 0-679-75681-7

VINTAGE CRIME/BLACK LIZARD
Available at your local bookstore, or call toll-free to order:
1-800-793-2665 (credit cards only).